THE MAN WHO LOVES TIRAMISU

URSULA FISCHER

◆ FriesenPress

Suite 300 - 990 Fort St
Victoria, BC, Canada, V8V 3K2
www.friesenpress.com

Copyright © 2015 by Ursula Fischer
First Edition — 2015

All rights reserved.

No part of this publication may be reproduced in any form, or by any means, electronic or mechanical, including photocopying, recording, or any information browsing, storage, or retrieval system, without permission in writing from FriesenPress.

ISBN
978-1-4602-7398-2 (Hardcover)
978-1-4602-7399-9 (Paperback)
978-1-4602-7400-2 (eBook)

1. Fiction, Romance, Contemporary

Distributed to the trade by The Ingram Book Company

TABLE OF CONTENTS

Prologue
1

I: Love gave life within
3

II: Patience is a tree whose root is bitter, but its fruit is very sweet.
21

III: Love me little, love me long
65

IV: The morning hour has gold in its mouth
175

I'd like to dedicate this book to my sunshine girl, Julia. Julia is my "adopted granddaughter." I love her from the bottom of my heart, and in four years I hope she becomes my personal medical doctor. I'm invited to her wedding already.

I'd also like to dedicate this book to Jaishree.

Also, I'd like to dedicate this to my beautiful granddaughter, Nicole. She was the one who made it possible to write this book.

FOREWORD

I MET URSULA FISCHER FOR THE FIRST time last year. From that first day, I knew that the passion in her would take her on beautiful journeys and would help many people along the way.

From the time she was a little girl born in Germany, she has suffered many hardships throughout her life- one of those being her loss of eyesight as an adult. Yet, she has more courage and drive to accomplish things than many people I know with 20/20 vision. Each day that I spend with her I am reminded of the importance of living a full life. Although she has faced many difficulties, there isn't a day that goes by where she doesn't laugh or make me laugh. She is persistent and determined, and is without a doubt one of the most positive- minded people I know. She is passionate about everything she does, whether it be writing a book, playing an instrument, or being your friend.

The Man who Loves Tiramisu is a book that truly reflects her personality and is thus a tale of courage, persistence and love. The making of the book itself, is also a tale of persistence.

A few weeks after we met, Ursula mentioned she had always wanted to write a book. I offered to help, as she cannot type due to her eyesight. For the next couple of weeks, she created a series of 32 cassette tapes filled with Josh and Tashi's story. She recorded the countless hours of romance onto the tapes, and then I listened to them and typed out her story. It was a long process, but in the end we achieved our goal- Ursula had overcome the challenge vision loss brought to her, and had written a book front to back. Not only has she written a book, she wrote a beautiful book. It reminds me to be thankful for situations in my life that bring me joy, and to learn from situations that bring me pain.

I hope that you too will learn from this, while simultaneously enjoying Ursula's unique and riotous sense of humour. I promise you, you will never be able to eat a slice of tiramisu without thinking of her ever again.

Julia "Sunshine" Kostka

Ursula Fischer and Julia Kostka, 2015

Some of the story comes from the author's own experience, while all the rest is fiction. If any characters or figures resemble actual persons or figures, this is completely coincidental.

PROLOGUE

ON JANUARY 26, 1975, KAUAI HAD SUCCUMBED to winter weather. It was pouring and windy, and rather than hearing the soft waves of the ocean, Jack Montgomery heard the whistling wind as it tried to enter the room of the hospital and blow away everything it touched. He tried to focus on that, rather than his wife's yelling as she was giving birth to their first child. He put one hand under hers and let her squeeze it as hard as she could, while the other he clenched into a fist. He hated seeing her in pain. He kept it like that while the nurses and doctor helped his wife to push their daughter into this world. At four o'clock in the morning, he felt her squeeze him harder, and just when he thought she would break his hand, her grip slackened. He looked to see where the baby was.

Instead, he saw the nurses and doctors scrambling. They were taking out tools and seemed concerned.

"What's going on?" Jack asked.

"Your wife has a hemorrhage and we need to operate to get the baby out. There's a chance they might not make it," the doctor said quickly.

Jack froze, unable to let go of her hand.

"Sir, you need to leave. We have to operate," a nurse said.

But Jack's legs wouldn't let him walk. They stayed planted on the ground. He didn't remember much of what happened next, but remembered that he was pushed out by someone, who then shut the door. He stayed in front of the door until his legs gave out, and then he sat down on the hospital floor beside the room where his wife was.

The next part was even more of a blur. He doesn't know who told him, or how he ended up sitting on a chair with a tissue in his hand, but he remembers the words,

"I'm sorry, sir. Mona didn't make it, but your baby girl survived."

Jack loved his wife more than he thought was possible. At that moment, nothing else in the world mattered except for the fact that he would never see her again. He sat in the chair holding his tissue for a long time. He didn't know how long, but he sat there until he didn't feel the stabbing in his chest, until he only felt numb.

He couldn't bear to look at his daughter that morning, the baby girl his wife wanted to name Natasha. To any other parent, she would have been the perfect baby — healthy, beautiful and full of potential. To Jack, though, Natasha was the reason he would never see his wife again. Jack stayed numb for the next five years. He lived and provided, but he couldn't love. His daughter Natasha, who became known as Tashi, was raised by the nurses who came to their house.

He knew he should try to be a good father, because that is what his wife would have wanted. But after so many years of being numb, he no longer remembered how to love and care. He began to try as she started growing up, but it was too late. Tashi grew from a girl to a teenager and into a young woman. She was raised by the nurses, those around her and the peaceful nature of Hawaii. The relationship she had with her father was forever wounded.

1: LOVE GAVE LIFE WITHIN

CHAPTER 1

BY THE EDGE OF THE OCEAN DOWN in the beautiful island of Kauai, below her father's property, she's standing on the sand, wearing a beautiful white bikini with a sarong wrapped around her waist. Over her deep blue eyes she's wearing Sun Ray shades. On top of her long dark hair she's wearing a sun hat, which she has taken off, shaking her hair out as the wind blows through it, making it blow all over the place. She stands calmly watching the waves of the ocean roll against the sand, letting the sun kiss her already sun-kissed skin. She begins to walk towards the other properties further down the beach to where her friends live.

As she turns around she sees a big German shepherd running towards her and thinks to herself,

Oh, my gosh. I really hope this dog is a friendly dog! I don't want to be bitten by a dog. Why is this dog down here?

Beyond the dog she sees a man calling out something to the dog, which she can't hear over the sound of the waves. The dog continues to come closer to her, not responding to the man who is calling to him. She just stands frozen in the sand as the dog comes right up to her with his tongue hanging out, breathing heavily. He sits in front of her and wiggles his tail.

"Oh, aren't you a good boy?" she says. "I hope so, and that you don't decide you want to take a piece out of me! You look pretty friendly but I better be cautious in case that cute face is deceiving. What's your name, big guy?"

The dog just looks up at her and wags his tail from side to side.

Behind him the man approaches and she can hear him say, "Hero! Hero! Come back!"

But Hero takes just one glance behind him and turns back to Tashi. Tashi looks up and sees the man is pretty close to her already. She looks through her shades at him and sees that he is also wearing sunglasses, and that he is absolutely breathtaking. He is tall with dark hair and his mouth is perfectly shaped and slightly open, as he is breathing hard from chasing the dog. He is wearing khaki pants rolled up over his knees, his bare feet covered by the sand, and his torso is bare as his shirt is unbuttoned and blowing in the wind.

"I'm so sorry. Did my dog scare you?" he asks Tashi.

"I was a bit startled, but his tail-wagging seems harmless." She smiles to reassure him.

"I'm sorry, I don't know what came over him. He normally listens very well and has never run off like this. It was almost as if he knew you. It didn't matter that I called his name, he just wouldn't stop," the man says.

They both look at Hero, who sits there expectantly, looking proud of himself.

"Do you mind if I give him a pat?" Tashi asks.

"Not at all, I think he'd like that."

Tashi bends down and to give Hero's head a scratch and he relaxes into her hand.

"My name is Josh, by the way."

Tashi looks up at the gorgeous guy.

"Nice to meet you, Josh. I'm Tashi."

"Nice to meet you, too. And I think Hero is also enjoying your company." They both look down at Hero who is still getting scratched and patted by Tashi. "So do you live around here or are you on vacation?"

"I live right down there." Tashi points to a big home facing the water, right at the edge of a small cliff, with stairs leading down to the sand.

"Wow, that's beautiful." Josh looks in amazement.

"Yes, I love it here. I couldn't imagine living anywhere else."

"It's a beautiful place," Josh agrees. "What is it you do for a living on this island?"

She says, "I'm an artist, I paint. My father is a famous artist. His name is Jack Montgomery. Maybe you've heard of him?"

"No, I can't recall," he says." I've never really looked into Hawaiian art."

Tashi smiles and says, "To me, Hawaiian art is the best because of the colours. It's so bright and you can't help smiling when you look at it. For instance, the colour of Kauai is purple, which represents the spirituality of the island, which I love. We really have a lot of nice things going on on this island."

"Yeah, I can tell. I love it here so far," Josh agrees.

Tashi says to Josh, "So do you have a house along here? I don't think I've seen you here before."

"Friends of my father have a house along here. They are in Europe for the summer and they said I could stay here for a little vacation if I wanted, so I took advantage of the offer," he explaine. "I'm glad I did because since I came here I have fallen in love with this island.

She asks him, "How long will you be here?"

"About three weeks."

"That's not very long, but long enough to get to get to know the island and its people. And then you can go to Hanalei. It's a little town where there are a lot of artists. There is a famous beach there, and I go there once or twice a week. I love watching the little kids do body surfing. They're talented, but you need to be a really good swimmer and always watch the waves. You never want to turn your back to the ocean because the waves are so big," Tashi explains.

"Yes, even here I notice the waves." He glances at the ocean where the waves rolled onto the golden sand.

"We also have a canyon here. It's so nice — have you been there yet?"

"No, I just got here, and I'm still intrigued with the beach and the long runs I can take Hero on."

7

"Oh," she says, "you definitely have to go to the canyon sometime before you leave." She stops to think. "And you have to take a sunset cruise and see the native island!"

He could tell that she was very excited about these ideas, so he nods and promises to see everything.

"It's sweet of you to tell me all this," he says.

She smiles, and for a moment they just look at each other, neither of them moving.

"Would you like to walk with Hero and me along the beach towards my place?" Josh asked. "I'd like to hear more about this island."

"Sure," she says. "Why not?"

So she steps beside him and the dog follows beside her, and they walk quite a distance. They talk the whole while about the island and what Josh has seen so far. Finally they reach the guest place he is staying at and he says, "How about a nice cool drink while you're here?"

"That would be lovely."

"Go make yourself comfy by the pool while I go get something. What would you like?"

She says, "Iced tea would be great."

Tashi walks around the large living room and looks out the big window facing the water. She watches the waves roll onto the sand.

Josh brings her a drink and they sit down together.

"I think I'll leave Hero here. He's a good dog. It looks like he fell in love with you instantly." He takes a breath and looks at her, continuing, "And I think I'll have trouble not falling in love with you, because you are honestly the most beautiful woman I have ever seen. When I look at you, I love you almost already."

"Oh," she says, taken aback by his forwardness and unsure if he's telling the truth.

"I mean it. You're so intriguing. You have beautiful, beautiful blue eyes and a mouth that can be kissed all the time."

She smiles. "Your mouth looks pretty kissable too."

"Really?" he asks.

She nods. "Yes."

He takes a sip of his drink and then says, "Tell me a little bit about your life."

"Well, what's there to tell? I work in my studio, I paint and I love every minute of it. I explore the island by myself and with my friends. I also play the piano."

"Wow," he says.

"But I don't play the piano to entertain, I play it for myself," she explains.

"Well, that's great, because I love to listen. Actually, there's a piano in here. Would you like to play?"

"Not right now. If you don't mind, I would love to get to know you first." She looks at Josh. "Tell me a bit about yourself."

"There's not much to tell about me either. I haven't had a holiday in a while, so my parents said, 'Josh, why don't you go over to Kauai and take a few weeks off from work because you work too hard?' And here I am!"

"Where do you work?"

"My dad has a law firm in Vancouver, Canada, and I'm one of the partners," he explains.

"Wow," Tashi says in awe. "That's impressive." She takes a sip of her drink and then continues, "So can I be your tour guide while you're here?"

"I would love that." Josh smiles.

Tashi asks, "Do you mind taking your sunglasses off?"

He nods and takes them off. She studies his eyes. He has long eyelashes and green eyes that look at her piercingly as she studies him.

"Why are you looking at me like that?" Josh asks.

"You are an unusual man. You have the most intriguing eyes I have ever seen. They change colour as I look at them," Tashi answers.

"Yeah, I change my colour all the time, like a lizard."

She laughs. "Well, as an artist, I would call you a beautiful man."

"No, no, no. Don't call a man beautiful. You call a man handsome," Josh says.

"Why not? I see it as I see it."

"Can I say the same for you?"

"If you want to," Tashi replies shyly.

"Yes I want to. When I saw you standing there on the beach without moving a muscle as my dog ran, and you didn't scream or anything, I thought, my, what a beautiful woman, flawless body, long legs, beautiful sun-kissed skin and long dark hair flying in the air from the wind, and your sarong was flying in the wind to the back, and I could see the bottom of your bikini. I kept thinking to myself, what a beautiful woman. She could be a model, a movie star." Josh continues to look at her.

She smiles and laughs. "No, not me, I couldn't be either."

"Why not?"

She shrugs her shoulders. "Well, I wouldn't want to be either of those."

He smiles and nods understandingly. They sit in silence just staring at each other.

Finally Tashi says, "So what do you have planned for tomorrow? Would you like to go sightseeing with me?"

"That would be wonderful. I could not have a better tour guide than you. You were born here, right?"

Tashi nods.

"Alright, let's do that then." Josh pauses for a second. "What about tonight? Can I take you out for dinner? I'd love to get to know you more."

A smile starts on Tashi's face. "Alright, but only if I get to choose the restaurant."

"Okay," Josh says, "I'd like that. What about Hero, can he come too?"

"I think he'll have to stay home alone for a bit, if that's okay."

"That can definitely be arranged."

Tashi looks at her watch. "Well, we don't have to go until about six, want to go for a swim in the meantime?"

Josh agrees and leaves to go change. Tashi takes the sarong off her waist and sits at the edge of the pool. When he returns, she jumps in and starts splashing him.

"Oh, you're playing this kind of game! Getting me all wet before I get in!"

He tries to catch her but has a really difficult time because she swims like a dolphin. The way she swims, she's more under the water than above it, and every time he looks, she is gone again.

All of a sudden Tashi comes up right beside him and gives him a push and is gone again.

He finally catches her, and grabs her in his arms against the side of the pool. For a second she loses her breath because they are so close together. Finally he moves in closer and gently kisses her on the lips. When he pulls away, she leans in again and they get lost in each other.

Finally Josh pulls away and asks,

"Tashi, how old are you?"

She looks at him knowingly and answers, "Seventeen."

He smiles and leans in to kiss her again. Tashi is the first one to pull away this time, and she says, "I should probably get going. I have some things to do at home before we go out for dinner."

"If you have to." Josh pulls her up out of the pool and dries her off with a towel. "So what time should I pick you up?"

"How about five-thirty?" Tashi suggests.

Josh nods in agreement. "Would you like me to drive you home?"

"No, thanks, I think I'll run back along the beach." She smiles and gives him a quick peck, and then runs off down the stairs towards her house.

Josh stood frozen staring at her. *I think I just fell in love with her,*" he said to himself. Then he shook his head. *Josh, what's wrong with you? You just met her... But Hero, you fell in love with her too, didn't you?* He looked down at his dog, who wagged his tail as if to say, "Of course I did, and clearly so did you."

Tashi went to her studio and back to her painting. She was working on a specific painting for a customer, but she didn't do too much because her thoughts were consumed by Josh.

I have never seen a man like this before, he is so sexy and I love everything about him, his eyes, his lips his hair... Her thought were interrupted by her father when he came into the studio,

"Where have you been?"

"I was just out for a walk" she answered, her voice confident.

"Okay. Are we having dinner together or are you going out somewhere?"

"Oh, I'm going out with a friend, what about you, Dad?"

"I have something in the fridge for supper. See you later, then. I've got to go out right now, but I'll be back later." He left and closed the door behind him.

Tashi looked at her painting and thought, *I can't even paint now, I'm so wound up inside, I think I need to sit down outside by the pool and find myself, because I'm all mixed up and shaking.*

So she walked back out, sat by the pool and lay back on the lounge chair, dreaming about Josh. She dozed off for a bit, and when she woke up, he noticed it was four. She got up and went to take a shower. On the way to her ensuite bath, she walked by the piano and ran her fingers over it, but continued to walk up the stairs. She went to her bedroom and into her beautiful ensuite, where everything was covered in ceramic tile, with light from the window reflecting off of it. Everything was colour-coordinated in deep coral.

She took a quick shower and then stepped into her walk-in closet to decide what to wear. She found a cute little yellow dress with a flared skirt that clung to her small waist, with tiny little straps and a sweetheart neckline pointing to her cleavage. It looked great with her dark hair, blue eyes and tanned skin. She picked out a little silver chain with a tiny locket with her mom's picture in it, and a pair of small silver earrings. She blow-dried her hair and put a little bit of lipstick on. She looked in the mirror, satisfied, and said to herself, "Well, girl, this is the way you are, and either he likes it or he doesn't."

She picked out some sandals and put them on and got downstairs just as she heard him pulling up. She hurried outside to meet him in his Jeep. As she ran the wind blew her hair from one side to the other. Her dress was also blowing around and it made her feel really sexy.

Josh got out of the car and opened the door for her.

He said, "You look absolutely stunning."

"Thanks." She smiled.

"You look beautiful and you look like a cute girl in that dress."

"Cute girl?" she said. "I thought I was a woman?!"

"Well, you're half and half..." He smiled and gave her a kiss. "Okay, fine, you're a woman."

"That sounds better," she said.

As she hopped into the car, she noticed that he was wearing cargo shorts that fit perfectly, and a light cotton shirt rolled up at the sleeves that showed off his big muscular arms. She admired him, and eventually her eyes were drawn to his lips.

"Why do I have this feeling that you want another kiss?" He smiled coyly and gave her another long kiss.

"I can't get enough of your lips," she said as she pulled away.

"Oh, you beautiful woman, you're the one who is gorgeous. I can't get enough of you! You are honestly the most perfect girl I have ever laid eyes on."

She laughed and said, "Woman, remember?"

"Right!" He closed her door, walked around to the driver's side and hopped in.

"Okay, are you starving?" he asked. "Because I know I am!"

"Yeah, I am too. I hope you like the food!" She directed him to a Thai restaurant called Mema, and they park, behind the restaurant. There were already some couples inside but a small table was reserved for them because Tashi knew the owner.

After they sit down, the owner came up to them.

"Tashi! How are the paintings coming along?"

"They are great, thanks, Kai."

"Good, I'm glad." He looked at Josh and pointed to the wall, "this is Tashi's work here."

Josh admired the art hanging there. "Wow, you painted these? You are very talented."

The owner of the restaurant introduced himself to Josh, and then left the two alone to look at the menus.

"Josh, do you know what to order?" Tashi asked.

He said, "At home I do, but here I might not. The Thai food might be different here."

"Do you mind if I order for us?"

Josh nodded and Tashi continued, "Are you sure? Do you like it spicy?"

"I sure do," Josh answered.

Kai came back and Tashi ordered a few items. Then she added, "Make it hot, but not too hot."

"But what about Josh?" said Kai. "Does he know how hot you like your food?"

"Well, he doesn't, but he will find out!" Tashi laughed.

"That's okay, I can handle it!" Josh insisted.

"Alright. If you say so." Kai smiled and walked back to the kitchen.

They took sips of lemonade and looked into each other's eyes.

"How crazy is it that your dog is the one who brought us to together?" Tashi recalled. "If it wasn't for Hero, I would've never met you!"

"Yeah, Hero is a good dog. He knows a good thing when he sees it!"

Kai came back and put the first dish down in the centre of the table. Josh spooned some food onto both their plates and then he took his first bite as Tashi watched him carefully.

"Holy!" He gasped, grabbed his lemonade and gulped it down.

"Didn't I tell you?!" Tashi said.

Kai smiled as he watched them. "This fellow asked for it. He doesn't know Tashi the way we know her yet. He is a brave guy, though." He left to make their other dishes, making sure to ease up on the spice.

Sweat poured out of Josh while Tashi sat there as cool as a cucumber, eating her meal and enjoying herself.

"Look, if it's too hot, don't sweat it, I'll order you something with less spice," Tashi offered.

"Well, if I want to get married to you, I have to get used to these spices!"

"Oh, we're getting married?! I didn't know that!"

"I like to think so."

"Alright then, I guess you'd better stick to the hot food!"

About an hour later, they were finished eating.

"I need to get some fresh air, I am sweating and that's not ideal for a first date." Josh paid the bill and they thanked Kai and walked outside.

"Well, we have the ocean right across the street, so you can go take a swim before you go home," Tashi joked.

"If you keep making fun of me, I'm going to have to throw you in the ocean!" Josh teased.

"Well, I am sorry about the spicy food, but you did say you liked it hot."

"I know, it's my own fault, but now I'll be more careful with what I say and do with you, because you're unpredictable." Josh grabbed her hand and they walked to his car. He drove them back to his place so that they could go for a walk along the beach, but first he wanted to take a shower.

"Do you mind?" he asked.

"Not at all" said Tashi. After he went upstairs, she walked over to his piano and began to play. She got so carried away that she didn't hear Josh come down and take a seat behind her. He poured some wine for the two of them, continuing to listen as she played.

All of a sudden he said out loud, "My God, this is a wonderful woman."

She turned around and saw him behind her. "How long have you been there?" she asked.

"Oh, just a couple of hours," Josh joked.

Tashi laughed. "Right."

"Let's go sit outside. It's so nice out there. Would you like some wine?"

She said, "Just one glass? How about a couple of bottles?"

"I don't think you could handle that," said Josh.

"Never underestimate a woman!"

"Well, let's start with one. "

They sat down and he put his arm around her. They clinked their glasses together. One sip led to two, which led to three, which led to kissing. It started getting really hot.

"I know you just had a shower, but if we keep this up, we'll both need a shower," Tashi joked.

"That would be alright with me," Josh said and continued kissing her.

They got entangled again but then she pulled away and said, "Well, I think we should stop right here before we go any further."

He nodded.

"I better go home, and I think it's good if I go now because otherwise I will ravish you," Tashi teased.

"You'll what?"

"I will ravish you!"

"No woman has ever said that to me." Josh was smiling.

"I told you I was unpredictable."

"So if you say you would ravish me, is that promise?"

"If you want it to be," Tashi answered.

"Can you stay?" Josh grabbed hold of her hand.

"Sure I could, but not tonight, not yet. We have three weeks to get to know each other, so I'll let you know when I want to ravish you." Tashi got up and started putting her sandals on.

"Okay," he replied. "I'll drive you home, then."

He drove her into her driveway and stopped the car.

Before she got out, Tashi said, "Thank you for this wonderful day and your wonderful dog for bringing us together. I love your gorgeous lips and I love everything about you so far."

"I feel the same about you, Tashi. But I think it's time for you to go inside the house, before I make you ravish me!"

She agreed and gave him a quick peck on the cheek.

"Wait, when do I see you next?" he called.

"I'll let you know tomorrow! Bye, Josh!"

"Goodnight, Tashi."

And she was gone.

He sat in his car for a bit and then drove back to his house, thinking. *Wow, what a wonderful three weeks this will be. I never counted on something so beautiful. I have to get this woman to myself. I have always wanted someone like her. I can't believe I met her two days after I landed. No wonder they call this the spiritual island.*

He sat outside by the pool and thought about her until his thoughts turned to dreams.

The next day, Tashi walks to Josh's place along the beach. He is already up, by the stairs looking down. She comes up the stairs towards him, looking perfect in her shorts, halter top and sunglasses.

Hero runs towards her and she bends down and pets him. He is so happy to see her. He sits down beside her.

"You are a good boy, aren't you? How could anyone not love a good boy like you?" Tashi pats him.

"What about the owner of the dog?" Josh smiles.

She gets up and put her arms around his neck, "Whether you like it or not, I love you, Josh."

"Honestly, I've fallen head over heels in love with you too, Tashi. I can't imagine thinking of any other woman except you. Can I seal our engagement with a kiss?"

"Are we engaged already?"

"Of course! We love each other." He bends down and gives her a really hot kiss.

"I think it's time for you and me to go up to the house. I have something to show you. Would you like to see it?"

"Uh-oh…" Tashi smiles. "Sure, I'd love to."

So they walk over to the side of the pool and he says, "Look at the ocean and how beautiful it looks."

"That's what you wanted to show me?"

"What were you thinking?" he asks.

"You really are tricky," she says to him.

"I know what you want me to show you. I'd like to, but I'm scared."

"Why are you scared?" she says. "You don't have to be scared, I'm not."

"Okay." So he pulls her into his arms and gives her a long hot, searing kiss.

She puts her hands in his hair and runs her fingers through it.

He says, "Don't tear my hair out my head!"

"No, no, I'll just play with it."

They keep kissing until he says,

"Okay, now I'll show you something."

They go inside the house together.

"Just wait here, I'll be right back." Josh comes out with a small box in his hands.

Tashi opens it up and there is a beautiful white-gold locket with his picture inside.

"Wow," she exclaims. "I love that you put your picture inside."

"I wanted you to have it because I want you to wear me around your heart."

"Did you have this made in Vancouver, knowing that you'd meet someone here?" Tashi asks skeptically.

"No! I went to the jewelry store this morning and bought it!"

"Wow, you're a fast one."

On the back of the locket it says,

To Tashi with all my love, your Josh, forever.

"Oh, this is beautiful." Tears well up inside her eyes.

"Why are you crying?" he asks.

"Because it's so nice." She walks into his arms.

"This is the way I feel about you," he says, "and I can't help it, and I want you to know."

"I can't either, she says. "I feel the same."

At home that night, Tashi decides to go for a swim. From the pool she looks out at the ocean in front of her, and the big waves rolling in one by one. The sun is setting as she watches. The sun sets pretty quickly; it looks almost as if it sinks into the ocean. Right before it disappears, she sees a sliver of green, and then it is gone. While she is watching, she thinks about Josh and a future with him. She thinks about walking down the aisle together with him, having many beautiful kids together and being happy together forever. She hopes this will happen soon.

11: Patience is a tree whose root is bitter, but its fruit is very sweet.

Chapter 2

FIVE YEARS LATER.

Natasha Montgomery was sitting in the lawyer's office in Vancouver, waiting to be called in. She was sipping on a cappuccino the receptionist had given her.

A woman came running out of the hallway from the back, then stopped at the reception desk and yelled at the girl behind it,

"You make damn sure that he gets home by six tonight because he needs to be on time for the dinner party!"

Natasha looked at her and saw a medium-height brunette who would have been a beautiful woman if she wasn't wearing so much makeup and if she didn't look so angry. The woman stormed down the hallway and disappeared.

About five minutes later, the receptionist — a cute little woman with blonde ringlets — called Natasha.

"You can go and see him. His door is just at the end of the hall on the right."

Natasha walked down the hallway and gingerly knocked on the door.

"Come in," said a voice from inside.

She walked in and he looked up from his desk.

"Tashi!" Sitting in front of her was Josh, looking absolutely stunned. "Is that you? Wow. Tashi."

He got up and walked to her, grinning and holding out his arms. She slowly walked towards him and then put her full weight into his embrace. "What happened to you? I thought I'd never see you again," he whispered into the top of her head.

"Nothing. I mean everything. "

She stayed silent and let him embrace her for a long moment. Finally she spoke again. "My dad," she said, "shipped me off to Europe, and I had to stay there for two years after you left. I went through hell for a long time. It was very painful, and it still is. One day I will tell you, but not right now. I can't right now." She left the story unfinished, resting in his arms.

They continued to stand in silence until he said, "Why can't you tell me now? I would love to know what happened."

"Don't push me, Josh. I will tell you when the right time comes around, and that's not now. Stop pushing me."

He nodded slowly and then he said, "Tashi. I didn't know it was you. I thought maybe, but didn't let myself think about it too much." He let a smile roll across his lips. "But I should've known. There's a big resemblance between Tashi Monty and Natasha Montgomery."

"That's my artist name," she explained. "I thought you knew."

He shook his head slightly. "I didn't, but I'm so happy it was you who walked through my door."

They finally let go of each other.

"So, you're here to adopt a little girl?" he asked.

She nodded. "Kate was one of my closest friends, and I promised her that I would take care of her little girl in case anything ever happened."

Josh looked at her with sad eyes. "Oh, Tashi, you are such a good person. If only I had known that you would come back into my life, I wouldn't have gotten married."

"Wait a minute, Josh. I figured you didn't want anything to do with me anymore. I thought you had your fling, some nice sex on the beach and then you had enough of me," Tashi said.

"You weren't just a fling. I wrote to your dad after I left Kauai, asking where you were after I never heard back from you. He never replied back to me, though. I went back to Kauai, Tashi. I needed to see you again, or at least know that you were okay. Your dad wouldn't let me onto his property, though. I asked around, but no one knew where you had gone. They were all as confused as I was. So I flew home, I didn't know what else to do.

"Soon after that, my parents introduced me to Joanne, and pushed me to marry her."

"So that was more important than searching for me?" asked Tashi. "You had more power to look for me, Josh. You're a lawyer. Did you love her? Did you? Because you said you loved me. Does she work here? Because I saw a crazy lady running down the hall screaming that you shouldn't be late for dinner. If that is her, I'm disappointed in you, Josh."

"I knew all along that my family was pushing for us to get married for business. They wanted to join our firm with her family's. Joanne seemed nice enough at the time. She wasn't anything close to you, and I never loved her, but she was good to me. When we got married, everything changed. I will never love her, Tashi. You are the only woman I have ever and will ever love."

"Are you sure, Josh?" Tears started flowing down her face. "I don't know if I can ever trust you again."

Josh walked over to Tashi and knelt down in front of her. He tried to put his arms around her but she resisted.

"I'm so sorry, I didn't mean for this to happen. I had no other choice, Tashi. I didn't know what else to do. I only love you, and that's the way it will be. Can you please try to forgive me? If you do, I want to try to make it work."

"Well, you're a married man now, what do you think we should be doing?" Tashi asked. "She has you, not me. Where do we go from here?"

"I'm going to do everything in my power to get a divorce from Joanne. I can maybe talk to my dad and try to convince him to open up a new firm in Honolulu. I can visit you, I want this to work, Tashi."

After a while, Tashi said, "I'm okay with that."

So Josh stood up and took her in his arms. He gave her a kiss on the lips and the next thing she knew, they were clinging to each other, having a real hot kiss, neither one of them wanting to let go.

But then she pushed him back and said,

"We can't do this. You are married, and I came here to adopt my little girl. So let's do business, get this over with. Maybe we can meet up sometime while I'm here in Vancouver and have a serious talk."

CHAPTER 3

NATASHA WENT BACK TO HER PENTHOUSE ON the 52nd floor of West Robson Street. The sight of Josh had just about knocked her over. She was still so much in love with him. At twenty-eight, Josh was as handsome as ever. She just couldn't forget the sight of his green eyes — the most beautiful eyes she'd ever seen on a man. His mouth, she wanted to kiss all the time. His body was so muscular and his skin was tanned, reminding her of the nights they spent together in Kauai.

She continued to daydream as she rode up the elevator and stepped into her apartment. She dropped her purse on the floor and walked into the living room. It was a very bright room with windows all around so she could see the mountains and the ocean surrounding Vancouver. It used to belong to her dad, but she inherited it when he passed away, and kept it as a second home in Canada, while she continued to live in Kauai.

She needed a stiff drink to relax from everything that had just happened. She got herself a brandy. She needed something to steady her nerves, because that experience had really unnerved her. She sat down and closed her eyes, thinking about Josh. She wished she could have him forever. But now he was married, and she assumed the woman she saw today was his wife. She felt sorry for him.

She decided that if he wanted to see her again, she would see him. *Why not? Life is too short to think otherwise.*

She drank her brandy and sat down to study Leilani's adoption papers. She couldn't wait to see the little girl. She had been very close with Leilani's mother, Kate, and cared deeply for her. After Leilani was born she had immediately agreed to being her godmother, and to being her guardian in case anything ever happened. Unfortunately, something awful did happen, leaving poor little Leilani an orphan at the age of five. Kate and her husband, Nick, went skiing one day, and on the way driving home they got into an argument. Kate grabbed Nick's arm and he lost control of his driving, and their car rolled down over the edge of the cliff, taking their lives.

So now, Tashi was waiting to adopt Leilani and be her new mother. In three days' time she would be her new mother officially, and then they would fly back to Hawaii.

How strange life is, she thought. Something tragic has allowed for good things to take place. Like the fact that she would be a mother, and that she was reunited with Josh. As she thought, she walked through her apartment. In her bedroom was a four-poster bed and to the right were sliding doors that led to a private roof garden. The sun was shining into her room, illuminating the beautiful sea greens and blues of her walls. She then walked into the room that would be Leilani's from now on. It had a small bed, and toys placed carefully around the room on various shelves and in cupboards. Pictures hung on the walls, on the pink wallpaper, and a large window faced the ocean.

She looked into the nurses' room, a guest bedroom that she rarely used. She had changed the bedding on the queen-sized bed and added extra pillows and blankets to make the room feel extra cozy. She had also purchased a comfortable big chair and situated it next to a small table and reading lamp. This room also had a beautiful view and sliding doors that went out onto the rooftop as well. She chose this one for the nurse because it had a beautiful ensuite as well as a nice walk-in closet.

She walked through the rest of the penthouse. Her father had been a very wealthy man, so it was a beautiful, large place, with three other guest bedrooms, a studio, a library and a gym. She finally went back to her ensuite and, deciding that she would take a relaxing bubble bath, started to run the water and then stepped into the tub filled with bubbles, and thought about how lucky she is.

She was thankful for everything she had inherited; she knew she was a very lucky woman in that respect. What she did not have luck in, though, was love. She had always believed Josh would be the one for her, but after their time together in Hawaii, nothing went their way.

She was still daydreaming when all of a sudden the intercom buzzed. She quickly grabbed a towel and hopped out of the tub.

"Tashi, can I come up and see you?" It was Josh.

Her heart skipped a few beats until finally she answered,

"Yes, of course!" She buzzed him in, knowing that the elevators always took a couple of minutes. She quickly ran back to the bathroom and let the water out of the tub, then went into her closet and put on a simple but flattering dress, and then brushed out her hair. Just as she was putting on a necklace, he knocked on the door.

She opened it to see him standing at the door, looking as handsome as ever, holding a beautiful bouquet of flowers and a bottle of champagne.

"Oh, what are we celebrating?" She let him in.

"We're celebrating that we have found each other again. This time, though, I'm never ever letting you go. I will have you, if you let me. Is that okay with you?" he asked.

"Of course that's okay with me. I wouldn't want it any other way."

Chapter 4

JOSH PUT THE BOTTLE OF CHAMPAGNE DOWN and began to open it.

"I was just taking a bath when you buzzed in, do you mind if I just take a couple of minutes?" Tashi asked.

"Go right ahead, I'll open this up and enjoy the beautiful view you have here."

So she went back to her bedroom and changed out of the plain dress into a sarong that hugged her in the perfect places. She also slipped on black lace panties and her favourite matching black lace bra. She put some earrings on, sprayed a bit of perfume on and then made her way back to the living room, where Josh waited.

"Oh, my God, are you ever beautiful. Tashi, you are honestly the most beautiful woman I have ever seen."

"Oh, come on, you've seen lots of beautiful women —"

He cut her off.

"Don't argue with me Tashi. You have always been the most beautiful woman for me, ever since I met you that first day on the beach." He handed her a glass of champagne and they sat down on her couch.

Tashi took a sip and felt Josh staring at her.

"What?" she asked.

"I'm sorry, I just can't take my eyes off of you." He put his glass down and took her into his arms and gave her a passionate kiss. The kiss got deeper and deeper and they clung to each other. She could feel his hardness through her sarong.

She kept kissing him and then she said,

"Wow, I need some air. I'm getting so hot."

"Baby, so am I," Josh agreed. They each took a sip of champagne. And then he said, "Tashi, I can't stay very long. I have a dinner engagement tonight and I need to show up. But if you don't mind, I'd love to come see you again tomorrow."

She nodded and laid her head on his shoulders. She could smell him and he smelled so delicious. He kissed her and all of sudden they were entangled together again.

"If we don't stop this I will need to take that sarong off of you. I just wish I had more time tonight. Tashi, Tashi, what are you doing to me?" He smiled and kissed her again.

"The same thing you're doing to me, Josh."

"I don't know where this will end up," he said.

"I don't either. But I do know that I want you, Josh, and there never has been and never will be a man like you for me."

"Oh, Tashi, you are the woman for me too. I wish things had turned out differently. You're so beautiful, and your heart is made of gold. I can see it by the fact that you're adopting Leilani. My wife would never do something like that."

He looked deep into her eyes. "I have one more thing that I need to tell you. Out of this loveless marriage came a beautiful little boy. His name is Damian, he is five years old, and I love him from the bottom of my heart. He's all I have, besides you. I love you the same way, maybe even more. Unfortunately his mother doesn't love him. I do everything in my power to make him happy. I love him more than I can explain to you," he said to Tashi, "but I love you even more."

She put her arms around his neck. "Josh," she said, "I'm happy for you that you have your little son. I will love him as if he were my own little boy. But I love you even more."

Josh kissed her and said, "Just looking at you and being near you makes me feel better about everything. I hope that one day we can truly be together." He gave her another kiss on the lips and the pressure increased. They kept kissing and finally he said, "I want to stay, more than anything, but I should really go."

Tashi nodded understandingly. Then they both got up, he gave her a big hug and she walked with him to the elevator.

Josh said, "I'll call you about tomorrow."

"Okay, have fun tonight!"

"I'll do my best, sweetheart," he said, and the elevator doors closed.

The next morning, it was raining when Tashi woke up. She wasn't surprised because it normally rains in Vancouver, although she did miss the heat of Kauai. She ate breakfast and then decided to go for a walk, since it wasn't raining too hard. She put on her coat and went outside. She walked by English Bay and took in the scent of the ocean, and the view of all the green luscious trees by the water. She then walked all the way down to Robson and by the shops. She stepped into a few of them, just looking around for nothing in particular, when all of a sudden she saw Josh's wife. She was standing in one of the stores arguing with the salesperson over what looked like a silk shirt.

Tashi quickly turned around and left the store, everything that Josh had told her about his life flooding into her head. She didn't stop walking until she reached her apartment. She got into her elevator and rode up to the 52nd floor, stepped into her apartment and closed the door behind her.

She decided to work out in her gym to get her mind off things.

After she'd showered, she put on some jeans and a white T-shirt. She put on a bit of makeup and as she was finishing, the phone rang.

"Hey, babe." It was Josh's deep, manly voice. "How are you doing?"

"I'm good, I'm happy to hear from you. I just freshened up after getting all wet from the rain outside. How are you doing?"

"I'm good, I was just wondering what you're doing for lunch?" he asked.

"Actually I was planning on making a stir fry. Would you like to join me?" she asked.

"Oh, yes, my favourite! I'd love to."

"Great, how's twelve?"

"Sounds perfect. I'll see you soon."

He hung up and her heart started to race. She began making the stir fry, cutting vegetables and frying some shrimp together in a sauce.

Soon enough, it was twelve and Josh was at the door. He brought over some wine this time. He gave her a deep kiss on the lips, and then they went into the dining room. He got out some wineglasses and began pouring for them. Tashi brought out the stir fry and they toasted each other and began eating.

"Wow, this is delicious!" Josh said.

"Thanks, it's one of my favourite dishes." Tashi took a small bite. "Although I'm not that hungry." She looked up at Josh. "I'm more hungry for you."

"Baby, I feel the same. But, we should eat first, especially you. You look like you could put on a couple more pounds."

"Thanks, Josh." She smiled to herself and tried to keep eating even though all she could think about were his lips.

Tashi ate all she could and then pushed her plate to the side. "Would you like dessert?" she asked him.

"Nope, only you," he said. "How about you go into the living room with your wine, and I'll clear everything up here."

After cleaning up, he walked over to her, bringing the wine bottle with him. He sat next to her and took her in his arms and gave her a deep kiss.

"I have something for you," Josh said, and pulled out a little box from inside his jacket.

"What is this, Josh?"

"Open it up and you'll see."

So she opened it up and she saw a beautiful white-gold heart that had an inscription on the back:

With all my love, to Tashi.

Forever, your Josh.

"Wow this is beautiful." Tears began to sting her eyes. "It's just like the one you gave me when we first met."

"Open it," Josh said.

She opened the locket and inside was a picture of him when he was twenty-two, the age he was when they met. Tashi couldn't hold back her tears any longer.

"Why are you crying?"

"I'm just so happy you're in my life again. I'm happy, Josh."

"Me too, sweetheart." He kissed the tears off her face and then kissed her lips. "I hope we can stay together," he said. "If you let me, I would love to always see you, Tashi."

"I would love that too," she said.

They continued kissing for a while until finally Josh said,

"I'm sorry, Tashi, but I have to get back to work. But if you're free tomorrow evening, I'd love to spend some more hours with you."

"What did you have in mind?" she asked.

"Maybe we could have dinner together, and I could take the afternoon off and spend more time with you," he suggested.

"I love that idea," said Tashi.

So again Josh left, leaving Tashi with kissed lips and a heart full of love, happiness and sadness, all at the same time.

CHAPTER 5

THE NEXT DAY PASSED SLOWLY, AS TASHI anticipated everything. She filled her day by going out for a long walk and exercising, and then catching up on some reading. Finally she decided to take a nice long bath, with extra bubbles and with a glass of wine next to her. She thought about Josh arriving that night, and was curious to see what their night would be like. She was also anticipating finally meeting her new daughter, Leilani. When she thought about her, she felt so excited but also sad at the same time. Sometimes thinking of Leilani made her think of the girl she lost five years before.

As in most love stories, she and Josh had made love together in Hawaii when they met. It was beautiful and it was perfect, but it also made a child. Tashi's father couldn't bear the thought of his daughter becoming a mother at the age of seventeen. That was when he sent her away to Europe, so that no one would find out. She gave birth to a baby girl, who was taken away from her and sent to an orphanage. Then, after two years, Tashi was brought back home and expected to return to her ordinary life. Eventually she did, but not a day passed that she didn't wonder about her daughter or what she was doing. Two years ago, her father passed away. While she felt sad, she also felt a sense of freedom. He had always controlled her life, and now she finally felt she could do what she wanted.

Adopting Leilani would never have been an option before, while he was still alive. Tashi was so thankful that she got to take care of this little girl and give her everything she was unable to give her biological daughter.

Josh didn't know about their daughter, of course. He had left before she knew she was pregnant, and then they hadn't been able to contact each other again until now. She wanted to tell him, but she knew now was not the time. He had a lot going on, and she didn't want to stress him out. She promised herself she would tell him soon, because she knew that she owed him that.

Tashi got out of the tub, dried herself off and put on a robe. She then went to her piano and let her fingers take her away into a beautiful melody. She thought about Kate, Leilani's biological mother, and the sadness in her life.

Tashi met Kate while she was in Switzerland after being sent away by her father. She attended school there for her last two years of high school. Kate was a beautiful girl from the island of Kos, in Greece. They were in the same class and instantly became friends. While they were in their senior year, Kate fell in love with Nick, an older, domineering man. As love goes, Kate didn't realize how overpowering he was until it was too late. He controlled everything she did, and made her depend on him. He was a composer and director, and she was a pianist. They travelled the world together, and for some moments, they were happy. But then she became pregnant, and Nick had never wanted kids. She gave birth to two baby girls, and Nick insisted that one of them be taken away and sent to live somewhere else. He sent one girl to Greece, to live with his parents. They never went to see her, and she was never taken to see them.

Kate was always sad, but was also so happy with the one daughter she did have. She did everything she could to give her the best life possible. One day, Kate sat down and wrote a letter to Tashi explaining everything. She also wrote that, if Tashi agreed, she would be the legal guardian for Leilani if anything happened to them. Unfortunately, something did happen. When they were driving back from skiing in the mountains, they got in a terrible fight. He threw in her face that she had twins, and she grabbed him by the arm in anger. He lost control, and the car rolled down into a ravine, killing them both.

Her reflections brought Tashi back to the present moment. As tears rolled down her cheeks, she played on and imagined the future she would give Leilani. She would teach her how to play the piano, how to swim in the Hawaiian waters and how to follow her dreams.

She played and played until her fingers began to ache, until there were no more tears. She went to her room and took a quick nap, trying to shake off all the thoughts that were running through her head.

Finally when she awoke, the evening had rolled around. She began to get ready for the night that awaited her by cleaning up around the house.

When the phone rang, it was Josh.

"Hey, baby, I took the whole evening off. I can even stay the night if you want me to. What do you think?"

"What a stupid question. Of course, I want you to stay!" She started getting excited.

"Alright, I'll be there in half an hour!"

She got ready and picked out a nice outfit. She put on a beautiful sea green sarong, with a champagne bra and panties underneath. She put some makeup on, and brushed out her long hair. Then she put on the necklace she had received the day before, and admired how it hung perfectly around her neck.

The buzzer sounded, and she let him in.

Josh had a huge smile on his face, and was holding a large bouquet of flowers and a box of chocolates.

"Oh, what's with all the flowers?"

"They're for my sweetheart!" he said as he stepped inside and gave her a kiss. She put the flowers in water and placed them on her dining-room table. He came up from behind and put his arms around her gently. He kissed her on the neck and then moved to her shoulders. Then he turned her around and kissed her on the lips, and they begin kissing deeply, barely breathing.

Josh stopped for a second. "Wait. I have to catch a breath of air! I'm just so weak in my legs I can't even begin to tell you."

"I feel the same way," Tashi admitted.

Josh picked Tashi up and she let out a little scream of delight. He carried her with one arm, and with the other he grabbed his full bottle of wine. He carried her all the way down the hall, finding her bedroom with ease. He set her down on the bed, and the wine on the bedside table. He looked at her and she looked at him.

"You know you are the love of my life, and I will always love you. And if you let me, I will do everything so that we can be together," Josh promised.

"Yes, Josh. I can wait, because there won't be any other man for me except you," Tashi said.

He took her into his arms and kissed her passionately. He stroked her hair and felt her skin until his hand reached the opening to her sarong. He untied it easily, letting it fall open so that he could see her champagne lace bra and underwear.

"Baby, you look so delicious, I could just eat you."

"Why don't you?" Tashi asked.

"Are you daring me?" Josh smiled.

"I am."

"Don't be surprised if there's nothing left!" He pulled the cup of her bra down and kissed around her breast. She was all excited and moaning. Then his hand wandered down her navel, his lips following, and he kissed her there. She moved restlessly.

He opened up her bra and let it fall to the floor. He suckled her breast and she moaned and groaned. Then he swiftly took off her panties and let his hand feel her.

"What about you?" she said with difficulty between breaths.

He took off his overcoat and she undid the buttons of his shirt. His smooth chest was bare and she could smell the musky scent of him as she ran her lips over his chest. She took off his grey pants and his briefs all at once. When they hopped up onto the bed together, his manhood was already erect. He took her in his arms and they kissed for a while. He started kissing her breast and his hand wandered down in between her thighs again.

Now she was really excited and wet.

"What are you waiting for?" Tashi asked.

He got on top of her and they made love passionately for a long time. After they finished, they lay arm in arm, side by side, and looked at each other. She admired him and he admired her. They couldn't get enough of each other.

Finally after a few minutes she asked, "Are you hungry?"

"Not for food, just for you," he said and kissed her. First softly and then harder, and soon enough he was on top of her again, and then inside of her. They started their lovemaking all over again. They couldn't get enough of each other.

They lay side by side again, exhausted but blissfully happy.

"We either eat or go into the tub," Tashi finally decided.

"Why don't we get a bite to eat and then go into the tub?" Josh suggested.

She put on her little housecoat, made out of black silk. She tied it around her waist and gave a black one to him, also in silk but made for a man. She had bought it once when she was in Thailand and it had never been worn.

"Here, this will be yours every time you see me," she said.

They went to raid the fridge. They had a light supper and went into the living room and listened to some music while they sat around talking, remembering the days they had spent together in Hawaii. Finally they were done eating and Tashi said,

"I think it's time for a bath."

Together they went down the hall into the bedroom and past the bed into the ensuite. There was a large jacuzzi tub with candles all around it in the middle of the bathroom.

"Wow, we can almost swim in there!" Josh exclaimed.

He went to go get them a drink, and she lit the candles. He came back with two glasses of wine. They stepped into the bath and took their first sips.

"Who gets washed first?" he asked as he picked up the bar of soap and started lathering it.

She started to giggle. "It looks like I don't have a choice."

She moved closer to him and sat in his lap.

"Hey, what are you sitting on? You're sitting on the wrong part!" He grimaced but laughed at the same time.

"Oh, I'm sorry! Did I hurt you?" She also giggled.

"Just a little."

She got up and straightened out, repositioning herself. He continued to lather her everywhere. He started with her shoulders and her arms and her back, and then he got to the front and he was just playing around with her breasts.

"Is that washing?"

"It's part of the process," he answered.

He then pulled her up and washed her buttocks and her tummy and down her legs and finally he got to the most important part. He threw the loofa down into the tub and instead used his soapy fingers and touched her everywhere, gently massaging. Then he kissed her and they sat back down in the water.

"Your turn," she said and picked up the loofa. She started washing him and got him to stand up again and began to scrub his buttocks. He quickly put his hands over it to shield himself from her.

"Are you trying to take the skin off my butt?" he asked.

"I guess you're a little sensitive! We'll have to desensitize you." She laughed.

"I can't go home with a red butt on me!" he reminded her. So she continued to wash him, this time moving to the front.

"Don't be afraid of it; it doesn't bite!" he joked.

She gave it a kiss and then moved her lips to his tummy, kissing him all the way up.

"If you keep that up, I'll have to throw you into the bathtub and make love to you right here and now," he said.

"Well, what's keeping you from that?"

He pulled her down on top of him. They had another love session going, but this time the water was getting splashed all around. He picked her up and stepped out of the tub, drying her off first, and then himself. Back into the bedroom, they both lay down on the bed.

"Would you like to have a massage?" he asked her.

"Maybe. Where are you thinking?" she asked slyly.

"That's my problem, not yours!" He flipped her onto her tummy and massaged her back and buttocks and then kissed her down her spine.

"Time to flip over!"

He started with her shoulders and arms. When he came to her breasts, he massaged oil into them gently and kissed them. He then moved his hands down to her tummy and did the same there.

She moved all over the place while he was touching her.

"Why can't you keep still?" he asked.

"It's pretty hard to keep still with this kind of massage!"

"That's the way it should be."

Finally he got down to her legs and feet and toes. He started kissing her legs and toes, working his way all the way back up her long legs

"There's a long way to go to where I want to get!"

Tashi was just about out of her mind when he got to her triangle. She clung to the sheets and moaned loudly.

"Please, Josh, please."

She didn't have to finish her sentence, as he knew what she wanted. He slipped into her and they performed their ritual, all steamy and hot, and had the most terrific climax. They lay side by side and kissed each other, holding each other in their arms.

Josh sat up and gave her the glass of wine, barely touched, on the bedside table.

"Would you like another?" he asked as they finished their drinks.

"I think I need one. I'm so thirsty!"

"I am too after all that." He kissed the top of her forehead.

When he left to pour another glass of wine, she got up and looked in the mirror at herself.

"It looks like I've been put through the wringer!" Her cheeks were flushed, all nice and rosy. Her whole body was glowing with his fingerprints on her, but it felt so damn good. This was the best thing that had happened to her in a long, long time.

He came back and put the wine glasses down on the table. He bent over and kissed her on the neck.

"I love your body. I love your skin; you have the most beautiful skin. You are the most beautiful woman I have ever seen, and I will love you forever and ever, Tashi, for my whole life! Please always come to me when I need you, because I can't be without you anymore. Will you do this for me?" Josh asked her. "I know it won't be easy when we're apart, but we must try to make this work. When we have free time, we can visit each other and take advantage of it."

Tashi looked into his eyes for a while and then finally said, "Yes, Josh, I will be there when you need me. Always, I promise you. No matter what. You can't keep me away. The same goes for you. You must come to visit me in Hawaii because I need to see you and be with you."

He brushed the hair off her face, kissed her and said,

"Of course I will. I have to try to change my schedule around. Maybe I can get a business going in Honolulu and then move there! That would make everything a lot easier. I have to talk to my father and other firm partners, and see what we can do. The more I think about it, the more I realize that it will probably be good for our firm."

"But you will have to take your wife with you, won't you?" Tashi asked.

"Yes, I know, she won't like that. She loves it here. She has all her friends and all her circles and tennis clubs. That's why she has no time for me or her son."

Tashi nodded compassionately, understanding the complicated situation he was in. They held each other for a while and finally Tashi said,

"So would you like some dessert? I have a tiramisu cake in the fridge, and I can make some coffee. Would you like that?"

"Yeah, we'll get our strength back and then we can do some more exercise." Josh held her tightly and pressed his lips against hers.

Together they headed towards the kitchen, hand in hand.

"Can I help?" Josh asked.

"I'll bring the plates out for the cake and some cups, and the coffee will be done in no time " Tashi answered. "Can you just slice the cake and put it on plates, please? And we can sit wherever you want."

"Okay, I will find us a spot."

She got the coffee going while he sliced the cake and disappeared down the hall with it. She finished making the coffee and then looked for Josh.

"Where are you?" She walked down with her coffee and there he was in the bedroom with the cake on the side table. He had lit two candles beside the bed as well.

He walked over to her. "Would you mind putting the coffee down?" he asked her.

Tashi noticed music was playing in the background as well.

He took her in his arms and started dancing with her slowly, holding her very tightly while she clung to him. She could smell that familiar scent of his, the same one she remembered from Hawaii, when they first met. They got lost in the music.

Then he kissed her, slowly, and whispered into her ear,

"Alright, young lady, I think it's time to have dessert." He pulled her to sit on the edge of the bed and asked, "Can I feed you?"

"If you think I need to be fed!"

"I think so." He knelt in front of her while she sat on the bed in her open kimono. He started to feed her some tiramisu and she really enjoyed that. He picked up another piece with his fork.

"Okay, open up!" He held it up to her lips, but the piece was so big that some fell off and trickled between her breasts and down between her legs.

She giggled as she licked her lips.

"Uh-oh! We're having a real disaster now!" He gently started licking the cake off her body, first between her breasts and then moving down between her legs.

"Oh, my God, this man is eating me alive!" Tashi couldn't help but giggle while he was licking her.

He looked up and smiled. "I told you I would!"

He traced his lips up her body, planting kisses and licking her in places as he moved up. Finally he gave her a big kiss on the lips.

"Do you mind if I have my coffee now?" Tashi asked.

"Not at all!" He passed it to her.

"Sit down and eat your cake with me," Tashi ordered.

"Okay, are you sure you don't want me to finish feeding you?" Josh asked slyly.

"Oh, I'm sure," Tashi insisted.

He sat down on the bed and picked up his cake. By the time he was done, she hadn't even started.

"What are you being so slow for?" he teased her.

"I enjoy my dessert. And don't just shove it down my throat!"

"Oh, trust me, I enjoyed my cake too." He winked at her. He came over to her and took the plate out of her hand, and put some more cake in her mouth.

"Okay, you have to eat it now! If not I'll smear it all over your body and eat it off!" He teased.

"You wouldn't," Tashi said.

"Oh, yes I would!"

"I dare you!" she insisted.

"If you say so!" He took her kimono off completely this time, and smeared the cake all over her body. He ate it all off, licking her everywhere. She got so excited she almost finished.

"Wow, I've never had this happen!" she said.

"I hope not!"

They were lying side by side. She turned over to him and said, "Now it's my turn to explore you."

"Did I give you permission?" he asked.

"No, but I don't think I need it."

He smiled as she climbed on top of him, her legs straddling him.

She started exploring him by kissing his nipples and then making her way all over his chest and down to his navel.

"What are you doing to me, Tashi?" Josh asked, taking a deep breath.

"The same thing you did to me." Tashi smiled knowingly, and continued to kiss him slowly all over his body.

She ran her lips over his chest and then she went to the bottom of the bed and started kissing his toes and his legs. She then moved to the inside of the thigh, ignoring what was between his legs. She went down the other leg and came up again.

It was obvious he hardly had control over himself either, just as she had felt earlier.

"Are you trying to kill me?" he asked.

"Kill you? No I'm kissing you!" Tashi responded.

"You're driving me crazy, woman!"

He swooped her up and flipped her onto her back.

"You didn't let me finish!" Tashi protested.

"Next time." He didn't play around; he slipped into her and they made passionate love and not just once or twice, but quite a few times until they had to stop because they were both so tired.

In the meantime, it had gotten late. They fell asleep in each other's arms, feeling exhausted but very pleased.

Josh awoke up during the night and she wasn't there beside him. He looked for her. She was standing in the living room looking out over Vancouver, a large moon in the background. He came up behind her and kissed her on the neck and she turned around into his arms.

He saw she had been crying.

"Baby, why are you crying?" he asked.

"Josh, I love you so much. I don't know if I can bear to be without you. I don't know how I'll manage."

"Baby. I don't know what I can do, but please hang on. I need you in my life. I will make sure that we will be with each other as soon as possible, I promise you that. You know how much I love you and I always will. I know it's hard, but this will have to be enough for us now. Somehow we were brought back together, and we should be thankful for that. You will have your baby now..."

"I am, I am thankful!" Tashi interrupted. "I just want you so badly and I will miss you so much. I miss you already."

"I'm still here, Tashi. I will always be with you."

"No, Josh, in a few days I'll be home while you'll still be here."

"I told you about my plan. If that works we will see each other all the time. Promise me you will give us a try?" he begged.

She nodded with tears in her eyes.

They shared a deep passionate kiss and walked back to the bedroom together. He held her close as she fell asleep in his arms.

Tashi woke up in the morning to no Josh, but a note on the bedside table.

Sorry baby, I couldn't wake you but I had to be in the office at nine. I had an appointment this morning and I couldn't change it. Please forgive me. I would've loved to have breakfast with you. Have a good rest. You need it after all that exercise! Thanks again, sweetheart. I hope we can repeat this again soon. I'll give you a call today when I can. Love you, take care, always yours, Josh.

She read this and the tears came back.

Okay, she thought to herself, *I have to accept this now the way we said we would. And I have to prepare myself for little Leilani. I need to put this mess aside and put all of my thinking and feeling into this little girl, so it won't be so hard when I leave here in a couple of days. I have to survive for her.*

CHAPTER 6

THE NEXT MORNING, TASHI WOKE UP WITH a better attitude. Josh had called her the night before and calmed her nerves and sent over flowers.

She jumped out of bed. Not only was she feeling more relaxed about her relationship with Josh, but also she was so excited because today was the day she would meet little Leilani. Tashi checked everything over for the hundredth time. The playroom was ready, she had meals for Leilani, and beds set up for her and the nurse. She was sitting down, not sure what to do next when the phone rang.

It was Josh.

"Hey, it's me. I have Leilani here. She and the nurse got dropped off here instead of your home. I can take them over to your place and make sure they get there in one piece. Is that okay?" he asked.

"Sounds great."

"See you soon."

Tashi couldn't believe it! She had only ten or fifteen minutes before they would arrive! She checked herself out and put on some lipstick. She was wearing her tight dark jeans and a white T-shirt that looked really good on her. Her locket was hanging over her T-shirt, and on her wrist she wore a simple silver bracelet. She felt ready, but she made her way to the kitchen and put the coffee on. She needed to keep herself occupied because she was nervous, but excited, to see everyone. She decided she wouldn't serve the rest of the tiramisu because she would probably burst out laughing. Instead she brought out some cookies and put them on the kitchen island. She was getting so nervous that she couldn't even sit down. When the buzzer sounded she jumped up and answered it.

"Hi, can you let us in?" Josh asked.

"Yes, sir!" She buzzed them in and waited for the elevator to come up. She held the door of her apartment open and watched as a nurse came out of the elevator along with Leilani. The cute little five-year-old girl was walking cautiously, holding onto the nurse's hand. She had dark, dark hair and dark eyes with long lashes and a round little face. She was wearing a white dress and purple shoes, and was holding a teddy bear in one hand. She was a beautiful child.

"Hi, Leilani, how are you?" Tashi asked.

Leilani put her finger in her mouth and looked up at her.

The nurse bent down at said to Leilani, "Leilani, this is your mommy. Don't you want to say hi?"

"No-o-o-o, not mommy," Leilani answered. She continued looking at Tashi.

"This is your new mommy. She's been waiting for you for a long time!"

Leilani just looked at Tashi without speaking.

"Well, come on in!" Tashi welcomed them all, including Josh, who was standing behind the nurse and Leilani, looking amazing as usual.

The nurse introduced herself. "Hi, my name is Anne. Do you mind if I use your restroom?"

"Of course! It's down the hall on the left. That will be your room."

The nurse disappeared down the hall and Josh gave Tashi a quick kiss. Only little Leilani saw.

"Josh, what are you doing?" she whispered.

"I was just saying hello to the lady of the house. This is the custom in Canada, don't you know that?" he joked.

She laughed. "Maybe we have the same custom in Hawaii. Who knows?"

Tashi looked down at Leilani. "Leilani, can I take your hand and show you something?" she asked.

The girl nodded.

She walked her down to the new playroom and opened the doors. "Look what mommy got for you." In the playroom were a few dolls, some stuffed animals and other toys. "Would you like to play?" Leilani smiled and nodded.

Tashi sat down with her and picked up some toys as well. Josh stood in the doorway watching with awe. Tashi was great with Leilani already. Although it would take the little girl a few days to get used to everything, he was sure Tashi would be a great mother and that Leilani would open up to her soon enough. The nurse came back and found them in the playroom.

"Oh, can I play too?" the nurse asked. Leilani nodded and soon she was playing with both the nurse and Tashi. Even Josh came and sat down with the stuffed animals for a little.

Finally Tashi asked,

"Would anyone like something to eat or drink?" Leilani was too consumed with the toys so she didn't answer, but the nurse asked for a coffee and Josh said he would like some too.

"Here, I'll come help you make and carry everything," he offered. So he and Tashi made their way to the kitchen together while Leilani and the nurse stayed in the playroom.

As soon as they were out of sight, Josh grabbed Tashi and gave her a passionate kiss on the lips.

"Josh, if you don't stop this, I'll take you to bed right now!" she teased.

"That doesn't sound too bad." He continued to kiss her.

Finally she pulled away. "Let's get everything ready." So together they poured some coffee and juice for Leilani.

"Do you have any appointments or meetings today?" Tashi asked.

"Yes, I have to back in an hour," he said. "But I'll stay here until then if that's okay?"

"Of course." Tashi brought the drinks to the nurse and Leilani and told them she was going to quickly go over some paperwork with Josh.

She sat down beside him the living room and signed the last couple of official papers. "So I guess you know we're going back to Hawaii tomorrow," she finally said.

"Yeah, I know." He sighed.

He grabbed hold of her hand. "I wish we could have had one more night together, Tashi. Actually, I wish we could spend every night together for the rest of our lives. I will truly do everything I can to bring us together again in Hawaii."

Tashi nodded. She was trying to have a positive attitude, so she fantasized with him about how nice it would be if he moved to Hawaii. They talked about where they would go and what they would do. They were laughing together when the nurse came out of the playroom.

"She's so involved with her toys, she doesn't even know I'm there!" she explained.

"I'm happy she's taking it so easy so far," Tashi confessed.

"The places she stayed at before weren't the best places for her, so I'm not surprised. This is very good for her to have a new home and to have you as a mom. She is a lucky girl. I can see it already."

"Thank you, Anne. I'm trying. I will do my best to be a good mom to her. She deserves that. I owe it to her, and to Kate. She didn't have a good life herself."

"You're a good person," Anne said.

"So tell me, what are your plans?" Tashi asked Anne. "Will you stay with me in Hawaii?"

"Well, I thought I would come with you to Hawaii and see if I like the heat. And once Leilani becomes comfortable, I will decide from there."

"Of course, that's totally okay and is your choice. I would love to have you stay," Tashi said.

"So what time do we leave?" Anne asked.

"Nine o'clock in the morning."

"Alright well, I think I will have an early night tonight and get Leilani ready for bed early too so that we're well rested for the flight tomorrow. If you don't mind, could I just get organized in my room and Leilani's too?"

"Go ahead! I'll join you soon! If you need anything, please let me know."

Anne got up and said goodbye to Josh. "Thanks for bringing me over here."

"You're welcome. Enjoy your stay in Hawaii."

Then the two were alone again and all they could do was stare at each other and look into each other's eyes. Tashi took her hand and placed it on his face. She ran her finger over his lips, pulled the lower one down and suckled on it.

"Tashi" is all he managed to say. "Baby, you're driving me crazy again."

"You're driving me crazy. I'm getting hot under my collar."

Josh looked at her as if to notice she doesn't have a collar.

"'I know I don't have a collar, but you know what I mean." She kissed him again. "So will we stay in contact while I'm in Hawaii?"

"I will call you as much as I can. I need to hear you voice and know that you are okay. Otherwise I will worry about you. You know that, don't you?"

"Yes, I know, and I have to know too. I hope you won't have any problems with your wife."

"Don't worry, she won't know. And anyways, she's been cheating on me ever since we've been married, so my office is taboo for her. Now it's my turn."

"So I guess this is it? I won't see you tonight?" she asked.

"I will come by if I can, but I'm not sure. If not, I will say goodbye to you now because I have an important appointment soon."

She stood and he pulled her into his arms. They walked to the foyer where they stepped around the corner. He held onto her and they shared a deep kiss and clung to each other and said all the sweetest words to each other.

"Okay, you need to go," said Tashi. "I have to understand that and, if you can't come by tonight, I will understand."

"Alright, I will call you," he said and kissed her one more time. He moved away and she watched as he stepped into the elevator. The doors closed and he was gone.

CHAPTER 7

TASHI'S EYES BEGAN TO WATER AS SHE wondered when she would see Josh again. She went into the living room, looked out the window and tried to compose herself. She needed to focus on Leilani. She put the dishes away and then walked down the hall to see Leilani and Anne.

"Are either of you hungry?" Tashi asked.

"I'm alright," the nurse said, "but Leilani, you should eat."

"Leilani, what would you like to eat?" Tashi asked her.

"Pudding!" The little girl had a big smile on her face.

"What about some fruit? I have bananas and apples and some strawberries. Do you like any of those?"

"Yes, Mommy," the little girl replied.

"Okay, how about you come with me to the kitchen and I'll get you some," Tashi said. She took Leilani's hand and led her to the kitchen.

"Here, sweetie, you can sit on this stool and I'll get everything out for you." Leilani hopped up onto the stool by the kitchen counter. Tashi pulled out a placemat she had bought especially for Leilani with all the Disney princesses on it. She put it in front of Leilani and then got fruit out and cut it up for her. Leilani was happily naming all the characters on the placemat. Tashi gave the girl some fruit, and then pulled out some chocolate pudding.

"Would you like Mommy to feed you?"

"No, I can do it myself!" said Leilani. She picked up the spoon and happily dug in to the pudding.

Anne came out from down the hall and said,

"Actually, Tashi, do you mind if I have a sandwich?"

"No, not at all! I want you to feel like this is your home, so go ahead and help yourself to anything in the fridge! I'll get out the bread for you," Tashi insisted.

"Thank you," said Anne. "So what will you do with all this leftover food when we leave for Hawaii?"

"Well, I have a lady who comes by to clean the house every once in a while, so she will probably take it home." Tashi explained.

"Oh, that's great!" Anne began to eat her sandwich.

"Would you like some wine?" Tashi asked.

"Sure!" Anne said.

So Tashi poured her a glass and then left the bottle out.

"Help yourself to more if you like!"

"Oh, no, I have to keep my brains together for tomorrow!" Anne said jokingly.

Tashi laughed. "Yes, I know what you mean!"

The two of them had one glass of wine, while Leilani ate some fruit.

"I'm full, Mommy!"

"That's okay, honey. Would you like something to drink?" Tashi asked.

"Yes, please!"

"Oh, you say please! You are so polite, Leilani." Tashi smiled and got her some juice.

Anne put away her plate and then said to Leilani, "Okay sweetie, let's get you ready for bed! When you're all ready, your mommy will give you a goodnight kiss! And tomorrow we will take a big plane to Hawaii! You'll love Hawaii. It'll be warm and there's water, and you'll get to see some big fish!"

"Yes!" said Leilani.

Anne offered to help clean up, but Tashi insisted that she would do it while the two of them got ready for bed.

Anne got Leilani dressed for bed in her pajamas and helped her brush her teeth and brush her hair.

"Should I get your mommy?"

"Yes, please!"

So Anne called Tashi, and Tashi came into Leilani's room. She tucked the girl into bed, and brushed the hair out of her face.

"Mommy really loves you, little girl. I will show you so many nice things in Hawaii. I am so happy you will be staying with me now. I love you. Goodnight."

"Goodnight, Mommy!" Leilani answered.

Tashi gave her a kiss on her forehead. She turned the light off and closed the door, leaving it slightly open.

Tashi packed everything that she needed for Hawaii, and then got the coffee maker ready for the morning. She then took a shower and put on her silk nightgown. She picked out a pair of jeans and a nice coral blouse to wear on the plane. It would go perfectly with her hair and her eyes. On top of the blouse she placed the locket from Josh and her watch. She then picked out a pair of shoes with the heel a little lower than usual, keeping in mind that she now had a little girl to take care of and run around with!

She combed out her hair and looked in the mirror. Although she felt sad about not seeing Josh for a while, she was filled with joy from the love they had shared the past couple of days, and from the reality that Leilani was with her now. She finally got into bed and pulled out her book. She had read only a couple of pages when her phone started to ring.

It was Josh.

"Hi, sweetheart, it's me. I'm downstairs."

"You are? How did you swing that?" she asked, surprised.

"Never mind that. Just let me see you."

"Alright!" She buzzed him in and a few minutes later he was standing outside her door. He wore a dark Armani suit with a bright white shirt underneath and a silk tie. She just couldn't stop looking at him because he looked so perfect. He came over to her and put his arms around her and gave her a passionate kiss.

"How did you manage to come here?" she asked.

"I took my chance on this one, but I needed to spend another few hours with you," he said. "So, do you have some wine ready?"

"As a matter of fact, I do!" Tashi brought out the bottle she and Anne had been drinking earlier. They got two wine glasses and then headed down the hall to her bedroom. Josh poured wine for each of them.

"I see you already have your nightie on. Do you usually wear a nightie?" he asked.

"No, I don't, but I'm not sure if I will have to get up to comfort Leilani tonight so I decided to wear it," she explained.

Josh kissed her and soon enough he was taking off his clothes. He pulled her onto the bed.

"You have a devilish look about you tonight," Tashi whispered to him.

"I like being devilish when I'm around you," he said.

Tashi had worked her way under the covers.

Josh slowly pulled the covers back. "We don't need any covers, do we?" he asked. He began by kissing her on the lips and then took her nightie off. He suckled on her breast and eventually worked his way all over her body. Then they were kissing passionately and clinging to each other. They just couldn't get enough of one another.

For the next couple of hours they made beautiful love together. They then lay side by side in Tashi's bed for a while, just holding on to each other.

Finally Josh said, "I'm sorry, but I should get going. If you don't mind, I should take a shower to get your perfume off of me."

"I completely understand."

He took a shower and got dressed. Tashi got up and walked him to the elevator. They kissed each other passionately one last time.

Tashi said, "Okay, this is it, Josh. You have to let go."

"I know, baby. It's just so hard to say goodbye to you. But I will do everything in my power to meet you in Hawaii soon."

"I know. That would be amazing."

"I will call you the day after tomorrow so that you have time to settle in, and then we can have a nice long chat," he said.

"Okay, sweetheart." She kissed him one last time and shoved him in the elevator, because she knew he had to go. The doors closed and he was gone.

She went back to her bedroom and took her robe off. She hopped into bed and quickly fell asleep, exhausted from the eventful past few hours.

Chapter 8

THE NEXT DAY WAS A BRIGHT SUNNY day. That was a change for Vancouver, as normally it was raining. Tashi woke up at eight o'clock, and Leilani was already in the kitchen. She was eating scrambled eggs and a piece of toast, and drinking a glass of milk, all of which Anne had prepared for her.

Tashi walked over to her and give her a kiss on the forehead, "Good morning, Leilani. Did you sleep okay?"

"Yes, Mommy!" the little girl said happily.

"Can I get you some scrambled eggs as well, and some coffee?" Anne asked Tashi.

"Yes, that would be lovely," Tashi said. "While you do that, do you mind if I take a shower?"

"Not at all!" said Anne.

So Tashi hopped into the shower, quickly washing her hair and her body, and then dried off and got dressed. She put on her favourite pair of jeans, the nice blouse she had laid out, the locket from Josh and a pair of dainty earrings. She checked her purse to make sure that she had all the papers she needed for everyone, which she did.

She walked into the kitchen just as Anne was putting the scrambled eggs onto a plate for her. "Thank you, Anne, this smells delicious."

She took a couple of bites and then looked over at Leilani.

"So, honey, did you dream of anything last night?"

"Pooh Bear!" the little girl said excitedly.

"Oh, really? Was Winnie the Pooh nice?" asked Tashi.

"Yes, he talked to me and we held hands and danced together!" explained Leilani.

"Oh, that's lovely. Did you talk to him too?"

"Yes! I told him I was going to Hawaii with my mommy. I told him I will see lots of big fishies!"

"Yes, that's true. You will also learn how to swim there, because Mommy has a big pool so that you can learn."

"Yay! Can I go play now?" Leilani asked.

"Of course you can."

The little girl bounced down the hall to the big playroom.

Anne turned and said to Tashi, "She's a beautiful girl and she's well behaved! She really deserves this life, Tashi. I'm so happy for her."

"I will give her all the love I have," said Tashi.

"I'm going to go put the last few things together. Can you let me know when we have to leave?"

"Yes, of course," said Tashi. "Thank you so much for this wonderful breakfast."

While Tashi was finishing her breakfast

she thought about Josh. He was probably in his office right now. Would she dare call him? No, she had already said goodbye, so she had to move on for now. She had better not. *But I would really love to talk to him. Should I call? No, maybe not. That would be a bad idea.* She decided she needed to leave it alone for now.

Just as she was thinking this, the phone rang.

"Good morning, babe. How are you feeling today?" Josh's sexy voice asked.

"I'm feeling great. How about you?"

"I'm very good too. But deep down," he confessed, "I'm so sad knowing that you're leaving."

"I know, me too, but let's not start that up again! It's a beautiful day, and the sun is shining in Vancouver."

"Yes, you're right. Well, I just wanted to call and wish you a good flight. I will call you tomorrow, but in the meantime take good care of yourself and your little girl. I love you."

"I love you too, Josh. Thank you and take care." She hung up the phone. She felt so much better now that she had talked to him again.

She cleaned up quickly, and checked and then rechecked that she had everything. *Just like all women have to check everything twice,* she thought. She brought her suitcase out to the living room to get ready for when the limo arrived to take them to the airport. Then she helped Anne do the same, and finally Leilani. Leilani continued playing while they waited.

"Is there a toy that you'd like to take on the plane with you?" Tashi asked her.

"Yes, I love to!"

"What would you like to take, sweetheart?"

"Winnie the Pooh!"

"Okay, you can take him onto the plane. We have to get going now, though, sweetie. It's time to go to the airport." Tashi took Leilani's hand, and Leilani hung on to her Winnie the Pooh stuffed animal.

The buzzer sounded, it was the limo driver. Tashi let him come upstairs, and he helped them with their bags. They went down the elevator and into the limo, making their way towards Hawaii and Leilani's new home.

Chapter 9

AFTER THEY TOUCHED DOWN AT KAUAI AIRPORT, they walked outside into the heat. Waiting for them was Tashi's housekeeper, Lilly-Ann, and her husband, John.

"Hello, Leilani, we are so happy to have you here in Hawaii with us!" Lilly-Ann said to the little girl.

Leilani stared at them and waved.

"Leilani, this is Lilly-Ann, and this is her husband, John. You will really like them. They will help you whenever you need help with anything," Tashi explained. "But you will also have to listen when they tell you there is something you can't do. Will you promise me that?"

"Yes, Mommy," Leilani answered.

Tashi introduced Anne, and then all of them loaded into John's car. They were a little squished with all their luggage. They drove past beautiful scenery, making their way to Princeville in Kauai. They drove along the highway and could see beautiful beaches, white golden sand and sparkling blue water. There were big waves coming in, and they could see surfers taking advantage of them.

"Look, Mommy, water!" Leilani pointed out.

"Yes, I know. You will see lots of water from now on," Tashi explained. "But you will always have to be careful around it!" she warned.

They eventually arrived in Princeville and drove into her estate. They pulled up right by the front door and made their way out of the car. Tashi invited them inside, while John got their bags.

"I have a light lunch ready for you." Lilly-Ann said. "You must be exhausted and hungry! I'll bring it outside on the patio so you can enjoy the warm weather of Kauai. I'm sure you missed it while it was raining in Vancouver!"

"Oh, thank you, Lilly-Ann. You're the best."

"I will quickly show Anne and Leilani their rooms first, though, and then I'll meet you outside," Lilly-Ann said. She took the two of them down the hall.

John came in with all their luggage.

"Thank you, John. I'm so glad to be back here," Tashi said. "I love Vancouver, but I always miss this place when I'm away from it."

"Yes, I don't blame you," replied John, "We do live in a wonderful area of the world."

Tashi walked around her home slowly. After her dad passed away, she had it remodeled. The kitchen was filled with stainless-steel appliances and a large kitchen island. The floor was made from slate, brought all the way from Italy.

"While you were away I cleaned up the pool, Tashi. So everything is ready for you and your little girl if you want to go swimming," John said.

"Thank you," said Tashi. "I really appreciate that."

"Let me know if you need anything else," he said. "I'm going to put the car away and let you relax here."

"Okay, thank you, John."

"Don't thank me, it's my job," he said.

"I know. I still appreciate all that you and Lilly-Ann do, though."

John left and Tashi walked through her living room. Nothing had changed since she was away. She had a grand piano in the corner and a palm tree at the side. There was a nice couch and two chairs on one side and two chairs on the other, with a coffee table between them. The couch was multi-coloured, and sat on a white carpet, which covered a dark oak wood floor. The chairs were a cream colour, and she put beautiful bright pillows on them in orange and blue to match the couch. The walls were also off white, like most walls in Hawaii.

On the opposite side of the wall she had a nice bar with all the glassware for drinks you could think of. There were French doors that led outside to the patio, where you could see the pool.

Tashi decided to get herself a drink and wait until Leilani came back out. She sat and looked at the paintings hanging in her living room, which she had painted herself.

She has a painting of her mom, whom she never met, so this painting was done from a photo. On the opposite wall, she has a painting of the waves of Hawaii. The blue against the white walls of her living room gave the space a nice ambience.

She then went down to her studio, walked up to the wall and stood right in front of her painting of Josh, when she was seventeen and he was twenty-two.

She looked at it and said to herself,

I really see the man in him now, the passion in his eyes and face. I need to repaint him as he is now. This will be the next painting I will work on, and I hope that I will be able to show him the finished product someday soon.

III: LOVE ME LITTLE, LOVE ME LONG

CHAPTER 10

FIFTEEN YEARS LATER LEILANI GREW UP TO be a beautiful girl and was twenty years old now. Her fifteen years with Tashi had been wonderful. Both of them grew to love each other so easily, and they were the perfect mother and daughter. Leilani always knew that Tashi was not her real mother, as she remembered the crash in which her parents had died. Although she often wondered about her biological mother, and missed her, she loved Tashi wholeheartedly. Tashi loved Leilani just as much, and did everything in her power to make sure that she was always happy.

So when Leilani turned sixteen, she asked Tashi if she could attend school in Vienna. Tashi agreed. The school was world renowned for language education, and that was what Leilani was interested in. She was a very smart and trustworthy girl, so although Tashi knew she would miss her, she agreed anyway. Now Leilani was studying music and language — she was fluent in four languages. So far she has learned German, Greek, Spanish and Russian, and next she is hoping to learn Japanese. She talked to Tashi on the phone each week.

Tashi was so impressed by her daughter's ability to pick up these languages so easily.

"Wow, Leilani, how do you learn so quickly?"

"Honestly, Mom, I love it, and that's why I can learn all these languages. My days are so busy, though. I barely even have time to see my best girlfriend. I met her here at the school. Her name is Anita, and she and I have become very good friends. She's from Germany. Actually, I was going to ask you something." Leilani paused.

"Yes?" Tashi asked.

"Would you mind if, for my next holiday, I go to Germany with her instead of coming home?" Leilani asked.

"Well, I will miss you a lot. But, if that's what you want…"

"Please?" Leilani asked.

"Alright, sure. Maybe I'll fly over to Europe after, and I can spend time with you there?" Tashi suggested. "Just for a couple weeks or so. We can go someplace to have fun together! Like Greece!"

"Oh, that would be great! Thanks, Mom! I would absolutely love that. I'll let you know the dates and then we can figure our trip out."

"That would be great," Tashi said. "I miss you so much and I can't wait to see you!" T

"I miss you and love you too. But I have to get going, Mom. I have quite a bit to study for tomorrow." Leilani said.

"I love you too, honey. I understand. Take care of yourself!" Tashi hung up. She thought about her beautiful daughter and just how pretty she had grown up to be. She had long brown hair and beautiful dark eyes, and nice long eyelashes. Her figure was amazing; she was quite tall and she could be a model if she wanted to. She didn't, though: she would rather study and learn than strut her body.

Tashi went back to her studio and looked around. She looked at the new portrait of Josh she had on the wall.

"Josh, I'm so thankful for my daughter, but I wonder where our other little girl is. Is she smart too? Does she have green eyes like her dad? Is she happy? I always wonder about her. Maybe one day I will search for her and find her." She continued to study him and said, "You are the most beautiful man, and I'm so thankful I have you in my life."

She then looked at a painting of Leilani that she had done recently. She would hang that in the living room. She also had a number of paintings of Hawaii that she would sell, because they were going like crazy! The tourists loved them. So she picked a few to take into town, and occupied herself there for a couple of hours.

After returning home, she had a swim in the pool, as she does every day. It was a beautiful pool, all fenced in with chairs and umbrellas all around. To an outsider, it appears that Tashi has everything, but she was still missing Josh. She hadn't got him yet. He was still living with his terrible wife. His son had grown up to be a man, and was now twenty years old. He was at Harvard, studying to be a lawyer just like his father.

On the positive side, Josh had opened up a firm in Honolulu and he came down about four times a month. So Tashi did have time with him each week. When Leilani was still living at home, Tashi and Josh had to be cautious about their relationship. Josh was "Uncle Josh" to little Leilani, and uncles don't go to bed with mommies!

Today, as usual each week, Josh would give Tashi a call, as he would be arriving in Honolulu the day after tomorrow.

He finally called at around eight o'clock in the evening.

"Hey, babe, how are you doing?"

"Oh, I was worried about you! I didn't want to call your firm, but normally you call earlier," Tashi said.

"I'm sorry. I had quite an ordeal with Joanne. I told her I wanted a divorce, Tashi. I finally had the courage, because now that Damian is in college, I feel like it won't hurt him as much as when he was a little boy."

"Wow. Are you sure about that?" Tashi asked.

"Yes. I am so sure. I have been sure since the day I saw you again. I've had enough and I'm ready to start my new life with you," Josh admitted.

"I'm glad to hear that, Josh. I'm sorry you have to go through a divorce but I cannot wait to be with you," said Tashi.

"I can't either. But Tashi, I have a few things to do at the office since I just arrived, so I will call you again tomorrow and plan a time to come see you."

"Okay, I understand."

"Have a great sleep, love," he said.

After hanging up, Josh rose out of his office chair and walked to the window overlooking Honolulu. He looked down to the ocean and the busy street below him. The view wasn't the same as the one in Kauai, but he had to put the office where the money was. And anyways, he couldn't really complain. He got to visit Hawaii each week, and that also means he got to stay close to Tashi, the love of his life.

He had just begun the divorce process, which would bring him one step closer to her. Joanne was giving him a lot of trouble, of course. She wanted to own more than she deserved. But once that was all sorted out, he would be a free man, and he could move to Hawaii for good.

He turned around, went back to his desk and began working again. He worked hard, trying to finish everything before he went to see Tashi.

Chapter 11

TASHI IS SO EXCITED TO SEE JOSH. Although she gets to see him most weeks, she never loses the butterflies in her stomach before he comes over. She is so happy to hear that he is finally getting a divorce, and that they will finally be able to be together. She will also tell him the news that she is going to Europe to see Leilani, and maybe he will be able to go with her too. They would have a wonderful holiday in Greece together! She is so excited that she reaches her hand over to the phone to give him a call back and let him know the good news, but then decides against it, realizing that he needs his space, and time to finish his work.

Instead, Tashi decides to take out a good book. She picks up the book *Monsoon* by Wilbur Smith, and goes out to the patio. She puts her feet up and opens up his book. She loves his style of writing, and the way it took you into another world. Sure, it was gruesome, but isn't life gruesome sometimes?

She got into the story and forgot about everything else going on in her life.

Some time later, Lilly-Ann asked Tashi, "Would you like some dinner? You can have it outside on the patio if you like."

"No, that's okay, I'll come inside. Lilly-Ann, why don't you join me?" Tashi asked.

"Oh, no, I'm going to eat with John."

"I won't eat all of this, though! Why don't you take some home with you?" Tashi suggested.

"Are you sure?"

"Of course, I'm sure. Do you think I'm a horse?"

"Okay, thanks. I really appreciate it."

"No problem. You can take it now and I'll finish cleaning up the kitchen," Tashi said, "and I'll see you tomorrow morning."

"Great. Have a good night, Tashi."

"You too!"

Lilly-Ann headed off back home and Tashi began eating the dinner Lilly-Ann made for her. She also looked through the kitchen. She wanted to be very sure that she had a tiramisu cake when Josh came over. The last time they had it together was one of the most romantic nights she'd ever had!

After she finished her dinner she poured herself a glass of wine and went back out to sit on the patio.

As the sun was going down she watched as it sank into the ocean. She watched the sun's routine every night that she spent in Kauai, because it was just so beautiful. She loved Kauai for this reason.

She poured herself another glass of wine and then sat down in front of the grand piano. She played her favourite song, one that reminded her of Leilani. Leilani also learned how to play the piano, and always loved playing this song.

As Tashi played, she thought of her daughter and how lucky she was to have such a talented and wonderful child. She played until her fingers were sore, and then she hopped into bed and dozed off into la la land.

The next day was a beautiful day again. They had a bit of rain fall overnight, which was good. It refreshed the air, and she could feel the stinging salt in her nose as she stepped outside to look at the ocean.

Tashi decided that today would be the day that she went to visit her best friend, Donna, down in Hanalei. They would have lunch together, as they hadn't seen each other for a little while.

So Tashi washed up, got dressed in shorts and a halter top and slipped flip flops on her feet. She drove to Hanalei in the BMW with the roof down and parked near the wooden sidewalk, right next to all the little stores. She walked into one of them, a boutique. Donna was working but Tashi ran over anyways and gave her a hug.

"Hey, Donna. I know you're still working but as soon as you're ready, let me know! Maybe today we'll go to the "Dolphin" for lunch?"

"Sure, that sounds great! Let me just finish up here."

Tashi looked around the boutique while Donna finished up with a customer and gave some duties to the other girl working at the store.

Once Donna was done, the two of them walked over to the "Dolphin", which was just a block away.

They found a perfect place to sit and talk a bit before they both ordered their usual, the mahi-mahi fish. It came with a salad that had the best dressing — to die for! They enjoyed their meals and had a glass of wine together as well.

"Donna, what are you doing tonight? Would you like to come over and we can have some more wine at my place? You can even stay over so that you don't have to drive home," Tashi offered.

"Thanks, Tashi but I can't tonight. I have a date."

"A date! With who? Tell me everything."

"There's a new man in town that I met the other day."

"Is he a hunk?"

"He is and actually, you know him."

"I do? Who is it?"

"Christopher." Donna smiled as she said his name.

"Josh's business partner?"

"Yeah!"

"Wow! That's exciting! How did this happen?"

"Well, remember that one day when we went shopping in Honolulu but you had to stop by Josh's office? While you were talking to Josh, Christopher came by and we started talking. He asked for my number then," Donna explained. "He texted me yesterday and asked me out."

"Wow, good for you girl! That's great to hear. So what are you two up to tonight?"

"We're going for dinner in the evening and then we will see where the night takes us."

"Well, enjoy, my dear, enjoy. I'm happy for you," Tashi said, excited for her friend. They finished their last sips of wine and then walked back together to Donna's store.

"So what are you doing tonight, then, Tashi?" Donna asked.

"Josh called and is in Hawaii. He will probably come by tomorrow, but maybe he'll come by tonight instead if he finishes all his work."

"Oh, that explains it," Donna said.

"Explains what?"

"I can see that you're all nerves!" She laughed.

"I am not!" Tashi joked, but inside she felt the nervousness that she gets before he visits.

"Well, you enjoy too, my dear. I'll talk to you another time."

"Thanks, good luck tonight!" Tashi hopped into her car and drove home slowly, taking the scenic route by the water and the golf course.

She saw John outside gardening. The garden looked amazing, and so did her magnificent pool overlooking the ocean. Even though the waves were not too big, she decided to go to the pool anyways rather than the ocean. She is always a little skeptical of the ocean, and doesn't always trust it.

First though, she took a little rest on the patio. The heat made her fall asleep as usual.

She wakes up when she feels someone kissing her on the lips.

She is a little startled but then hears Josh's voice.

"It's just me, my honey bear."

"Honey bear, again?"

"I know you're not a bear." He laughs. "But the way you just looked at me made you look a little like a bear."

"Well, I was just a little shocked that someone in the house kissed me on the lips!"

"Yes, I know," Josh says with a laugh. "I wanted to surprise you! Do you want me to come back instead after I call?" he jokes.

"For heaven's sake, Josh, I was only kidding." She leans in and kisses him again. She then takes his hand and gets up, saying, "Come in. I want to show you something."

She walks with him to the studio and shows him the painting she has done of him.

"Wow, you made another painting of me!"

"Do you like it?" she asks.

"I love it, Tashi. You made me look pretty good!"

"I really tried to make it realistic! I got every wrinkle on your face."

"Thanks Tashi." Josh laughs.

"You know, you were twenty-two when we met the first time." She points to the first painting. "And you were twenty-seven the next time, and by then you already had that deep passion in your eyes." She points to the next painting. "Man, oh man, that's when you were eating me alive! I still have those fingerprints on my body. "

"You want some more?" Josh walks over to her.

"Later." She points to the last painting. "And now we have this painting, when you are forty-two years old. You have a few wrinkles in your face but it makes you look strong. I can really the see the love you have for your son, Damian, in this one. You are such a loving man, Josh. I love you so much. Please always stay with me."

"I will, Tashi," he says and kisses her. "Especially now that the divorce is finally going through, I know that I will be with you forever. I think Joanne has found someone else. I'm happy for her."

"Yes, that's all the better for us," Tashi says.

"I'll be a free man, and we can celebrate…" Josh says, "…with tiramisu cake."

Tashi laughs. "I would love that." She gives him a quick peck. "How is Damian doing with all of this?"

"He's doing alright. He's twenty now, and as you know doesn't live at home but on campus at Harvard, so I think that makes everything easier for him. He's really focused on his studies in law, which is good. To be honest, Tashi, I think he is a little relieved. Joanne was never a great mother to him," says Josh.

"Yes, I thought that from everything you have told me " Tashi says. "I'm glad he's taking it well."

"Yes. And Tashi, I am so relieved to have moved on from her, and found you again. I want to marry you. I want to officially be with you forever."

This is not the first time that Josh has said this, but it makes Tashi excited every time. "I would love that. Now that you are almost divorced, we can actually start planning for it."

"That's right. We can think about being together for the rest of our lives." He gives her a soft kiss. "Now how about a nice cool drink?" he says. "I'll bring us out two cold beers."

"I'd like that," Tashi says.

Josh brings out two cold beers, and they sit on the patio. Josh puts his arm around Tashi and Tashi rests her head on his shoulder.

"So Tashi," Josh begins. "Would you like to continue living in this house? Or do you think that we should get a new house for ourselves? Maybe we can even move to Honolulu."

"Actually, I would love that. I've been thinking about that as well. If we get a new place together, maybe we can give our house to Leilani," Tashi says, "and Damian, depending on where he would like to live."

"That's a great idea," says Josh.

"And actually, while we are on the topic of our kids, I talked to Leilani and I was thinking that maybe we could go visit her. She has a girlfriend from Germany, and they want to travel together in Europe over the summer. I suggested that I could meet them in someplace fun, like maybe Greece. I've been to Greece before and it was actually beautiful," Tashi explains. "I would love for you to join me." T

"You know what? If we get married, I'd like to take you on a honeymoon, just the two of us. So maybe we can let the girls travel for a bit on their own, and then we can meet them in Greece for a little bit. How does that sound?"

"That sounds perfect!" Tashi says. "I will talk to Leilani and discuss when we should go."

"That would be great," says Josh. He takes her hand. "And now, Tashi, I'd like to take you in the bedroom and show you something."

"Oh, I know what you're going to show me," she says.

"No, no. Where is your head? That's not what I meant."

"What a disappointment!"

"You'll get to see that afterwards!" he says. Together they walk down the hall. Josh leads her into the bedroom and asks her to take seat on the edge of the bed and close her eyes.

"Now, no peeking!" he says.

She can hear him take something out of his pocket, and then she feels something being slipped onto her finger.

"Now, you can open your eyes."

She opens her eyes and looks down at her finger. She is wearing a stunning ring, with diamonds and blue sapphire. "You are so amazing, Josh. What could this be for?" she asks with a smile on her face.

"This is my official engagement to you, my sweetheart," Josh explains.

"This is so beautiful! I can't believe this!"

"Will you accept me for your future husband?"

"Can you give me a few months to think about it?" Tashi jokes.

"Oh, brother. She tells me every day how much she loves me, but now that I have a ring she can't say yes!"

"Well, okay then, if you're that upset, I'll say yes."

"You're such a tease, Tashi. I was going to put you over my knee and spank your bare bottom."

"Really? Is that a promise?" she asks.

"A promise? I can do it right now if you want."

"No, thank you, maybe later. I still have my fingerprints on your body from last time."

"Alright, I'll be gentle with you. Do you have any cake in the house?" he says.

"Well, actually I think I do," she says. "Should I get you some?"

"I'd love some, I'm starving." He grins.

"Alright."

Tashi goes to the kitchen to slice him a piece of cake. She places it on a plate and then thinks to herself, *Should I put a fork on there, or not? Maybe not.* She goes to the linen closet, and takes out a cotton facecloth. She wets it and places it under her arm. Then she scoops up a bottle of wine, and carries everything back to the bedroom.

Josh is sitting on the bed, only in his kimono. She places everything down on the side table.

"Just one piece of cake?" he asks.

"Just one."

"You don't want any?"

"No, I'm alright," she says. "I'll pour us some wine, though." She pours them each a glass of wine and hands his to him. She sits down on the edge of the bed beside him, and they clink glasses. "To us!" she says. They take a sip, and then press their mouths together, tasting each other.

"Don't get too carried away," she says. "You still have to eat your cake." She passes him the cake. "How about you take off that kimono?"

"What for?"

"You must be too warm in it," she explains.

He takes it off, and then looks at her expectantly. She picks up the plate, and then takes the slice of cake and rubs it all over his body. She puts a piece into his mouth.

"Hey, what do you think you're doing?!" he asks.

"The same thing you did to me years ago!" She laughs. "I didn't bring a fork on purpose, because who needs a fork when you can eat it off my fingers?"

She then begins eating the cake off his body. She licks him everywhere, starting from his neck and working downwards. After she is all done, she wipes him down with a facecloth, and he squirms. "Aha! Now you know what that feels like." She kisses him quickly, and then puts the facecloth away in the bathroom.

When she returns, he pulls her into his arms and takes her clothes off. Then he pulls her into the shower and they have fantastic sex together. When they're finished, they shut off the water and dry each other off.

"That was the best engagement party ever," he says.

She agrees. "We could've taped that. We would've made millions."

"Oh, yes, we would, but that was only for our eyes."

"I'm not ready to go to sleep yet," she says. "Would you like to go for a swim in the pool?"

"Let's do that."

They put their kimonos on and walk out to the pool with the wine. They sit with their feet dipped into the water and their hands entwined together. They talk about everything and drink the rest of the wine under the light of the moon and the stars.

They swim together in the pool, with no clothes on. Josh sits under the fountain, and Tashi circles around him, swimming. When he doesn't see her, she swims up to him and puts her hand in between his legs, making him jump.

"I think there's a snapping turtle in the pool," he jokes.

"There just might be," she says and kisses him again. They get carried away, and so he picks her up, carries her into the bedroom and they make passionate love again.

Chapter 12

A FEW WEEKS LATER, JOSH'S DIVORCE PAPERS are all finalized. Josh and Tashi are planning their wedding, which will take place in Waikiki. They have decided to have a small wedding, with only their closest friends.

Unfortunately, their kids aren't able to attend, since both are in the middle of their semesters at school, but they plan to celebrate with them after. Josh's parents also cannot attend, but call the morning of the wedding to give them their best wishes. Josh invites his best friend, Christopher, to be the best man, while Tashi's best friend, Donna, is the maid of honour. They have a civil wedding on the beach on a warm summer day. Tashi wears a beautiful long, Hawaiian dress that she bought from Donna's boutique, and a lei around her neck. Josh wears white pants and a nice blue-green Hawaiian shirt; he also wears a lei around his neck.

After the wedding ceremony, they have a celebratory dinner with Donna and Christopher.

After dinner together and sharing a bottle of wine, Donna says,

"I should get going. I am going away tomorrow and I told my sister I would come visit her before I left."

"Do you mind if I come with you?" Christopher asks. "I could drop you off on the way home."

"That sounds wonderful." Donna says. They head out together, leaving Josh and Tashi at the table by themselves.

Josh and Tashi order another bottle of wine and then spend the night in Honolulu.

CHAPTER 13

THE NEXT DAY, JOSH AND TASHI DECIDED to book a trip to Vancouver, to visit Josh's parents. They decided to stay in Tashi's penthouse while they are there.

"I will arrange the flights for Mr. and Mrs. Steel," Josh said.

"Oh, my! That sounds so good!'

"From now on, I have my little wife to myself, and she had better listen to me! I will be stricter from now on. No more tiramisu cake for you, my girl!"

"Why not?!" she asked.

"Well, do you want to keep your figure?"

She laughed. "I will keep it. I always do physical activity after I have cake."

"You're right." He laughed. "Okay, well I am going to go to my office and book the flight. Do you mind if we leave tomorrow?" he asked.

"Not at all!" she said.

Josh went down to his office while Tashi went to her studio. She worked for a while on a painting she did of Leilani. She is all grown up now, and is a gorgeous girl.

Tashi got a serious look in her face, thinking to herself,

If I could only find out where our daughter is. I need to tell Josh soon. I can't keep it in any longer.

She sat down in front of her easel and began work on a new painting.

After some time, Tashi was exhausted. *I'll go see what Josh is doing.* She went into his office and walked up behind him, putting her arms around him, and gave him a kiss on the cheek.

"Hello, sweetheart. How is my beautiful bride today?" Josh said.

"She is on top of the world. How is my beautiful husband?"

"You always call me beautiful. You don't call a man beautiful," he said.

"Well then, I'll call you my handsome devil."

"You can call me handsome, but I'm not really a devil."

"Yeah, except when you get carried away with cake!"

He laughed. "Okay, let's go start packing."

The next day, they flew out and arrived in Vancouver around noon. They headed up to the penthouse and unpacked and had a nice long shower together. After they were done, they dried each other off and got dressed. Tashi put on a nice short-sleeved top with a sweetheart neckline with her locket from Josh, a pair of jeans and a cute little jacket.

They took the elevator down to the parked garage and get into the car that Tashi kept in Vancouver. It is a little Porsche... — very little, almost too small for Josh to squeeze into.

They drove over to West Vancouver to visit his parents' home. It was a smaller home, but Josh's dad built it himself. Josh pulled into the driveway and eases his long body out of the car, and opens the door for Tashi.

Josh's mom already had the door open, and then both of his parents came running towards them and gave them hugs at the same time.

"Hi, Ted. Hi, Rosa," Tashi said, giving them both kisses on the cheek.

"Oh, Tashi, you can call us Mom and Dad now. Congratulations, you two!"

They went inside. It was a beautiful home, almost antique, with wooden floors and terra cotta walls and off-white furniture. Tashi looked around. Her paintings were on the walls. There was one of Josh, which Rosa had requested, and also one of Damian and Leilani.

"Tashi, I want a picture of you up here also. You are part of the family now," Rosa said.

"Well, if I have time I will definitely do it. Your son just keeps me so busy! He always sends me to the store to buy tiramisu. It's unbelievable how much we eat."

"He asked you to buy what?"

Josh gave Tashi a look to stop talking, and Tashi burst out laughing.

"Yeah he want's tiramisu a-a-l-l-l-l the time," Tashi said.

"Why does he always want to eat tiramisu?" Rosa asked.

"Oh, there's a story behind this cake, Rosa, you would not understand," said Tashi.

"Why not?"

"Well," Tashi said, "if I tell you that story…no, I'd better not. You're too young for this."

"What do you mean, I'm too young for this?" Rosa asked.

"Well, ask Josh. He will tell you."

Josh said, "Oh, Mom, when she doesn't get her cake, she gets angry and goes into the kitchen and bangs pots around."

"You what?! Why do you do that, Tashi?"

"Just ask Josh."

Josh gave Tashi the evil eye. "Mom, you won't understand. You're too young. Dad understands, but not you."

Rosa turned around to look at Ted, and he said, "Leave me out of this. I don't know what's going on. Besides, Rosa, I think you're too young for this story that they're telling."

Rosa wouldn't leave it alone, though. Tashi started laughing and had to leave the room because she couldn't stop, Josh following her.

"What's going on with those two? Why are they laughing?" Rosa asked. "I don't get it!"

"Just leave them, they are being silly."

"Okay, but I'll have to check her pots when I go to their house," Rosa said.

Finally, Josh and Tashi stopped laughing, and came back out and behaved themselves.

They sat down and all had coffee together.

"What are your plans now? Are you going to stay in Honolulu in the firm? Or will you come to work in Vancouver? What's your plan, Josh?" Josh's dad asked.

"Dad, I really don't know. Tashi and I have not decided yet. We were thinking of giving Leilani the house that Tashi owns, and then we were going to decide where to live. Either in Canada, or maybe in Waikiki, we really don't know yet. Right now we just got married, and we have heavenly bliss."

"There's one other question I wanted to ask you two. Have you ever thought of having a child of your own?" Josh's mom asked.

Tashi's face turned quite pale and she looked down at her coffee cup. Josh looked at her, and wasn't sure what to think of the shock on her face.

"Are you okay Tashi?" he asked.

"Yes, sorry, I'm just exhausted from the flight."

"Okay, we'll get you to sleep soon."

Josh said, "I've thought about it a lot, but I didn't want to put pressure on Tashi." He looked at her. "I figured that if you wanted a child you would let me know."

"Well," Tashi began. "That is true. You know, Josh, all these years I could have become pregnant. I didn't, though, and I think that's a sign. I never took any precautions, and you knew that, but nothing happened. But you never know, it could still happen."

"That would be so lovely, having another little grandchild to spoil! And it would be a beautiful child," Rosa said.

"Well, don't get your hopes up yet, Mom."

"I know. So, will you two be staying for dinner?"

"Unfortunately not tonight," Josh said. "Tashi looks quite tired. But we'll stay a bit longer."

"Okay, well how about you go down to your dad's office and you can talk about the firm, while Tashi and I cut up some dessert?" Rosa said.

"Go talk in his office? What for?" Josh asked.

Rosa smiled. "Just do as you're told."

"Oh, jeez, now I have two women bossing me around! They're ganging up on us, Dad. Let's go."

"Well, now you know what it feels like! Your mom is always on my case," Ted said.

"And you let her boss you around?"

"It's what a man has to do for a home-cooked meal." The two of them walked down into the office.

Rosa and Tashi stood in the kitchen together and began cutting up some cakes. "So do you have any plans that you haven't talked to Josh about?" Rosa asked.

"No, I don't, Mom. I think we need to sit down and really talk about it. I think we will go on a honeymoon to Greece, and while we are there we will see Leilani. I'd also like to visit Damian, too, so we'll see. Maybe we'll do a cruise. I'm not sure." Tashi paused. "You have no idea how good he is to me. He is the best man I could ask for."

"I can't describe pleased I am that you got married to him. I liked you the moment I met you. I wish he met you before he met Joanne."

"Well, actually, he did," Tashi said. "He met me when I was seventeen and he was twenty-two. But he had to go back home, and he wrote to my dad, but my dad didn't answer him. I went away, and he couldn't find me, so he married Joanne. He wanted to please you."

"Oh, dear. I wish I would've known that. I'm sorry, Tashi."

"It's okay. No one ever told you. And anyways, now we are together and happy."

The two men came back down the hall. "Are you finished talking, you girls?" said Josh. "Are we allowed to come out?"

"Alright, you can come back." Rosa said. She placed the cake on the coffee table for all of them to enjoy as they continued their conversation.

CHAPTER 14

JOSH'S PARENTS INVITED HIM AND TASHI OVER for a small get together so they could give the two their blessings after the wedding.

"I'll make your favourite dinner — pot roast," Josh's mom said to the two of them.

"Sounds great," Josh said

"You are both so sweet," Tashi said. She gave Rosa a kiss and then walked over to Ted, put her arms around his waist and gave him a kiss too.

"Oh, Tashi, we are so happy you are in our family," said Ted.

Tashi's eyes started watering.

"Oh, now look what you did, Dad, you made her cry," Josh said.

Ted chuckled. "Well, the tears had to come sometime!"

"Okay, so we are all set for dinner on Saturday then?" Rosa asked.

"Yes, who all is coming?"

"You'll see!" she said.

"Well, I think we should head out," said Tashi. "We should have an early night tonight, since we have a lot to do tomorrow."

"Alright, well, thanks for coming by! I wish you could stay longer," Rosa said. They all hugged and kissed each other again.

Josh and Tashi walked out of the house and Josh squished into the front seat of Tashi's little car.

"Hey, Josh! Don't you think you should get a new car?" Josh's dad asked.

"Probably!" he said, and drove off.

"So," Josh began, "What do you say we go for a drive around Stanley Park, watch the ocean and then go get a drink?"

"I thought we were going to go home!"

"Well, so did my parents, but it's still pretty early, and I'd like to spend more time with you," Josh said.

"Oh, you little fibber!" said Tashi. "But yes, let's do that. I like that plan."

They drove to Stanley Park. It was a nice night, so they could see the stars out, shining above the ocean. It was quiet, other than a few cars.

"It is such a romantic evening," Josh said. "Would you like to go for a walk?'

"I would, although it looks like it's a little chilly," Tashi said, and they both looked up to watch the trees moving in the wind.

"You're right, we might freeze. How about we continue driving around the seawall then, so we can enjoy the view from the warm car?"

"That sounds perfect," Tashi said.

Josh drove along the seawall, past the totem poles and the cruise ships. The water reflected the moon and created a serene atmosphere.

After some moments of silence, Tashi said, "So, maybe we should listen to your dad."

"What do you mean?" Josh asked.

"Well, maybe it would be a good idea to buy a new car."

"Actually, I think it might be."

"Maybe we can go look tomorrow?" Tashi said.

"Okay."

They continued driving, and both of them stayed unnaturally silent for the rest of the drive, especially Tashi, who looked out the window for most of the ride. Finally they arrived home, and Josh offered Tashi a glass of wine.

"I don't know, Josh, I think I'll pass today."

"What's going on?" he asked her as he put her face in his hands.

"Something is on my mind but I just…don't know how to say it," she said.

"Well, I'd like to know whatever it is that bothers you, because it also bothers me. I think we should share our problems with each other when we have them."

"I know, Josh. I've been carrying this problem for a long time, so it'll just take a while to get out."

"Okay, well, how about I get changed into something more comfortable, and you too, and then we can sit down. I'll get some wine, and I'll wait, until you feel comfortable enough to talk," Josh suggested.

So they got changed- she put on a pale yellow sweat suit but still left on her lacy bra and underwear because she knows Josh like to take those off. He puts on a sweat suit then they went to sit on the couch. She sat in his lap and places her head on his chest.

After some time, she began, "I should've told you this before we got married, Josh."

"Well, you're telling me now and that's all that matters."

"You might be angry with me, really angry with me. You may have not even married me if I told you earlier."

"Oh, don't be ridiculous," he said. "I know you, and I love you."

"I'm scared to tell you, Josh. Look at me."

So he looked at her with his green eyes. "I promise," he said, "I will not be angry with you."

"Okay." She took a breath. "You know, the first time you were in Kuawai when you met me? We fell in love, deeply, deeply in love. I was seventeen, and told myself that if I couldn't have you, I will not be with any other man.

"When you left to go home, I found out two months later that I was pregnant. We made beautiful love when you were there, but I had no idea that we also made a child. I didn't know what to do, and I didn't know how to contact you. I hoped and hoped you would come back, but in that time, you didn't. So I told my dad. He was furious. He was already mad because he blamed me for killing my mother, and then he said I was a disgrace since I was pregnant and unmarried at the age of seventeen.

"He sent me to a home for unwed mothers in Austria, and told me that after I birthed my child, I would never see it again. He didn't tell anyone, so as not to make me a bigger disgrace." Tashi said this with disgust, and tears started flowing down her face.

"When the baby was born, I didn't even get to see her. All I know is that it was a little girl. I stayed at the home for a few more weeks. I ended up finishing school there, and stayed in Europe for two more years.

"That's when I became a good artist, because of my teacher. He was very critical, but that made me a better painter. I didn't realize it then, but I did later on. He had to do that to help me. That was also when I met my best friend Kate. She went to the school with me. We went to Kefalas together, and it was so much fun, because that's where Kate is from. After that, I finally went home.

"Living with my dad was dreadful. I put all my energy into painting, but all I could think about was our daughter.

"I don't know where she is, Josh." She looked at him to see how he was taking her news. "I don't know if she is happy, and I don't know if her life is good. But I pray to God every day that it is.

"That's why I was so, so happy to see you in your office that day. Not only was I in love with you still, but I had a child with you." She let the tears fall down her face.

"Oh, baby, if only I knew." Josh looked away and clenched his fist. "I'm so sorry, Tashi. I tried finding you, but now I wish I tried harder. Maybe we could've fixed this, and had our daughter with us all these years."

"It's not your fault, Josh," Tashi said.

"Will you forgive me?" he asked. "For not finding you and, also, for not using protection that night."

"Of course I do. I could've said something too," Tashi said. "We were young, and didn't have a care in the world at that moment. All we were thinking about is each other's bodies."

"Thank you." He paused. "So you have absolutely no idea where she is?"

"No, I don't even know her name. I never looked into it. I was scared to find her without you. That's why I so easily adopted Leilani. I decided I would make it up to our daughter by giving Leilani a good life."

"I understand. Well, I have connections, and I could start looking for her if you want."

"Of course I do! Would you really do that, Josh?"

"Of course. I want to meet her too. But in the meantime, let's hope that she is with really nice parents, and that she is happy."

"In that case, will she want to see us?"

"She will," Josh insisted. "We will make her understand what happened." He kissed Tashi on the lips, a nice, slow passionate kiss. Then he wiped her tears from her face with his hand, and kissed the spots where they were. "Baby, you have no idea how much I love you. All the sacrifices you made because of me. It's unbelievable." He kissed her again. "So, does anyone else know about this?"

"Yes, my best friend, Donna. I had to tell somebody. I had no mom to talk to, and I just needed to tell her. The two of us share everything." Tashi responded.

"I'm happy you had somebody to share it with." Josh said. He kissed her again and held her in his arms and then finally he asked, "Tashi? Do you want another baby?"

"Well, you are forty-four, and I am thirty-nine. I don't think we should. We have Leilani and Damian. If we find our daughter, then we will have three kids," she said.

"I agree," he said. "Thank you for telling me all this. I can't believe you carried this burden on your shoulders on your own for so long."

"I just didn't have the courage to tell you before. But now that we're married, we're an open book. We can't keep secrets from one another."

"That's my baby," he said, and kissed her again, and then pulled her in closer. "This is going to be a wonderful marriage. I will start the search tomorrow."

"So," he changed the subject, "let's talk about something happier in the meantime. What kind of car should we get?"

"Well, my little husband…" Tashi said.

"Little husband? I thought I was your big husband." He winked at her.

"Okay, my tall, dark, handsome, irresistible, BIG husband, I think I'll leave that decision up to you. You have to fit behind the steering wheel, so it's your decision. I think I will keep the little car still, so the new one will be yours."

He kissed her. "Tashi, you are amazing. Especially for a woman who had a baby at the age of seventeen. You have flawless skin, a perfect body and not a wrinkle in sight."

She threw her leg across his lap so that she was straddling him. He slowly took off the pale yellow sweat suit that she was wearing, so she was just in her underwear and bra.

"You're just as beautiful as you were when I first met you. You have so much passion in your eyes," he said.

"Well that passion is only for you," she said.

"I know, and you better keep it only for me."

"I'll do my best."

"Do your best?" he asked.

"I was only teasing, you silly old man."

"I'm no silly old man!"

"Yes, you are, you're *my* silly old man." She took off her bra and threw it at him, and then ran down the hallway.

He walked into the bedroom and heard the water running in the shower.

"I found you!" he said. He quickly stripped down and hopped into the shower with her. Soon they were having passionate sex, so absorbed in each other that nothing else in that moment seemed to matter.

"Wow," Josh said, "this is exhausting! We told my parents we would go home and rest, but this is not resting."

"Well, your parents don't need to know everything," Tashi said.

"You're right. Okay, off to bed with you!"

Tashi went out to the kitchen to turn all the lights off and to grab two bottles of water. Then they hopped into bed, cuddled up like spoons and fell asleep.

Chapter 15

TASHI AWOKE THE NEXT MORNING BECAUSE SOMEONE was kissing her around her neck and ears.

"Is it time to get up already? I'm still so tired!" she said.

"Wakey, wakey! I made us some coffee," he said.

Tashi eventually rolled out of bed and followed Josh to the kitchen, where there was coffee and scrambled eggs waiting for her. Just as she sat down, the phone rang.

"Who could that be?" Josh asked.

"Well, let's see." Tashi answered the phone, "Hello?"

"Hi, Mom!"

"Oh, Leilani! How are you, sweetie?"

"I'm good! I just wanted to call and congratulate you on your wedding."

"Oh, thank you, honey!"

"I can't wait to see you and Uncle Josh when you come visit me in Greece!"

"Well, Uncle Josh, is now Dad Josh…"

"Oh, right, what an old dad."

"Nuh-uh, *young* dad."

"Alright, well, how exciting! I'm looking forward to seeing you both. I'll call you later."

"Okay, I love you!"

"I love you too." Leilani hung up.

"What a sweetheart," Tashi said to herself.

They ate breakfast together and then Josh said, "So, I haven't bought you a wedding gift yet, and I want to get you something very special. Do you have any idea what that would be?"

"A wedding gift? Josh, I don't need anything. I have you and that's all that matters."

"I would like to get you something else too," he said.

"Well, I also have Leilani, Damian, your parents, I have a house, I have jewelry, what else would I ever need?"

"Just something special from me to you," Josh said.

"Well, you gave me a beautiful locket, isn't that enough? And on top of that, you gave me an engagement ring and a wedding ring."

"Well, I know, but if there was ever anything you desired in life, I want to get it for you."

"Oh, can I have a couple hours to think about it?" she asked.

"Fine, but that's all you get!" he said.

"Okay, so are you going car shopping now?"

"You won't come with me?"

"Well, I think that is a man's job, and I'd like to shop for some clothes."

"Alright, sounds good," he said.

They showered quickly and both got dressed. Tashi, as usual, wore jeans — she really loved them — with a nice dark blue top and a black leather jacket. She put on some pumps and finally some earrings.

Josh drove them to the car dealership.

"Okay, call me if you need me!" Tashi said.

"Okay, I will, sweetie."

She drove off and parked on Robson Street. She walked up and down through the stores, and decided that she should get Josh something special too.

"But what?" she thought out loud. "He has everything too."

She walked into a jewelry store and looked at the rings. She saw a gorgeous ring for a man. It had elegant diamonds in it, it was white gold and was so nice. She asked the jeweler if he had cufflinks to match it.

"I do," he answered.

"Can I see them, please?"

He shows them to her.

"I really like this," she said. "Are you able to engrave something into this ring? Will it take long?"

"I can, and it should only take about half an hour. What would you like engraved?"

"*To my loving husband, Josh, from his loving wife, Tashi, forever and ever.*"

"Not a problem, ma'am. I will see you back here in half an hour."

Tashi left the jewelry store and walked into the store next to it. She was looking at a dress when a lady asked,

"Can I help you?"

"Thanks, but I'm just looking. I know I need a new outfit, but I'm just not sure what yet."

"Well, with your figure, anything will look good on you."

"Oh thanks," Tashi said, blushing.

"Here, I'll choose a few items for you."

Soon enough, Tashi was in the change room and had five or six dresses to try on. One of them stood out to her the most. It was off white, like a champagne colour. The fabric clung to her body as soon as she put it on, and really flattered her figure. She also tried on a beautiful blue-green dress that was so eye-catching when she tried it on. It shimmered in the light as she walked.

"What about this black one also?" the lady suggested.

"No thanks. I know it's sophisticated, but black isn't my colour."

She also pulled out another dress that was slinky and had straps criss-crossing all over the back.

"Oh, this one is gorgeous," Tashi said. "My husband would love this one."

"I hope he's not the jealous type. This dress will attract men like bees to honey."

Tashi tried that one on next.

"Wow, it looked even better than I thought it would! You look stunning!" The sales lady also brought her a pair of heels to try on.

"Holy Moses," said Tashi. "Is that me?"

"It is!"

"I think this is the winner," Tashi said, "and the shoes too."

"Okay, I'll get them ready for you," the lady said.

Tashi paid and then went back to the jewelry store to pick up the engraved gift for Josh.

"Oh, it's gorgeous," she said when the jeweler showed her.

She walked out of the store and called Josh. "How are you doing?"

"I'm good, just driving around."

"So, do you know what car you're getting?"

"Yeah, it's…big."

"Really big?"

"Well, you'll see when I get home."

"Okay. I love you. Bye."

She drove back to her penthouse and went upstairs. She took out her new purchases and admired them.

She then sat down and began to read, and she was so deep into her book that she didn't even notice Josh come in until he kissed her on the cheek.

He dangled a key in front of her.

"What did you get?"

"You'll see it when you go downstairs!" he said.

"Okay, but first, I have something to give the man who stole my heart so many years ago."

"Me?"

"I think it must be you. You have those piercing green eyes that I love so much."

"Well, Tashi, you shouldn't have."

"I'll be right back."

"Okay, I'll pour us some wine."

She went into her room, put on the dress and her new heels, and combed her hair. Then she put her locket on, as well as a nice blue sapphire ring.

She looked at herself in the mirror. *He better not get carried away when he sees me in this dress. Otherwise I'll never give him his present.*

She picked up the boxes for him and called out to him. "Okay, close your eyes, Josh, and open them up when you reach five!"

He started counting, "One...two...three..." He opened his eyes a little too soon, but she was standing there already.

"Oh, my God, Tashi. Is that you? You are so, so beautiful. Is that what you bought today?"

"Yes, for the Saturday night pot-roast dinner."

"Wow, you will make all the other wives jealous! Turn around."

She did a little spin.

"Oh, wow, and an open back! It looks magnificent on you, Tashi. It goes with my beautiful wife."

He looked down at her cleavage and noticed the locket, "Oh, no, you can't wear this with this dress."

"Like what?"

"Well, I'll take a look at your jewelry. I like the locket but it just doesn't go with this dress."

"I know, but it makes me feel good when I have this dress on."

"My goodness, Tashi," he said. He walked over to her and gave her a kiss. She could feel his hardness already.

"Not now," she said and smiled. "I have something to give you first."

She took a sip of wine and so did he.

"I'm getting hot watching you in that dress," he said.

"Well, take your clothes off. You're at home."

"Not yet," he said.

"Okay." She took out one of the boxes and passed it to him.

Josh opened it slowly and took out the beautiful ring. "You bought this for me? This is so nice, Tashi. It's just gorgeous."

"I knew it was meant for you when I saw it. From now on I always want to see it on your finger."

"I will never take it off," he said.

She then passed him the other box. He opened it and out came the cufflinks to match the ring.

"Wow, Tashi, you are such a spoiler. Thank you." He kissed her gently, and then more passionately.

"I — gosh, I love you," he said, "and if you don't get out of that dress, I don't know what I'm going to do."

"Okay, I'll take it off," she said, and then gave him a kiss before she walked down the hall to her room. She took the dress off, then put her jeans and a plain T-shirt back on.

"You put your jeans back on. Does that mean no loving?"

"Oh, we will do that, but not yet," she said as she curled up in his lap.

After cuddling together, they decided to go see the car that Josh had bought. They went down to the parking garage, and Tashi looked around. She saw her little Porsche, but she didn't see any "big" cars, as he described it, except for a Ferrari.

"Josh, where did you park this new car?"

"It's the one right beside yours."

She looked and realized that the nice big Ferrari parked right beside her Porsche was in fact his.

"Wow, are you for real?"

"Yup," he said.

"It's beautiful," she said.

He opened the car door for her, and she hopped in. Everything was fine leather in there and it was absolutely wonderful.

"Since it's supposed to be a beautiful day tomorrow, why don't we zoom up to Whistler and see what this baby feels like?" he suggested.

"That sounds great," she said.

Chapter 16

THE NEXT DAY WAS SATURDAY, SO THAT morning they took off early to go to Whistler. They drove over the Lions Gate Bridge and onto the Sea to Sky Highway. It was a beautiful day and they enjoyed the drive together. They arrived at Whistler Village and walked around through it until they became tired, and decided to drive home in the afternoon.

By the time they got home, it was four in the afternoon and almost time to get ready for the party at Josh's parents' place. Josh went to his office to do a bit of work, while Tashi gave Leilani a call. She told her about the new car Josh had bought.

"Oh, wow!" Leilani said. "Mom, you better not drive it! You would get scratches all over it!"

"What? I'll be fine, honey. It's you who won't be able to drive it."

"Oh, come on, I'll take it for a nice little spin when I come to visit you guys."

"Nuh-uh, that's not happening," Tashi said.

"Oh, come on, Mom, ple-e-ease," Leilani begged.

"You can talk to Josh about it when you get here."

Leilani and Tashi talked some more about Leilani's visit that was coming up, and then Josh, who had returned, spoke with her for a little while too.

After their conversation, Tashi sat down with her head in her hands.

"What's wrong, sweetheart?" Josh asked.

"Oh, nothing, Josh. I just wish our kids could have been here."

"I know. Me too. But we have very smart kids who are busy with school. Leilani will come to visit us soon, and so will Damian. Just try to have fun tonight and enjoy the evening. And anyways," he said, "this means we have the house to ourselves at the end of the night."

"You're right, Josh." She gave him a kiss. "Okay, we should get ready now."

Tashi got dressed in her new dress, and Josh put on a very nice suit. They looked amazing, both because their outfits were perfect, and because they were glowing with the love they had for each other.

They took their new Ferrari to the party. The driveway was full of cars when they pulled up.

"I guess there are more people coming than we thought!"

They walked up to the front door and rang the doorbell. After a few moments the door opened, and Damian was standing on the other side.

"Damian!!" Josh said, "What are you doing here? I just talked to you earlier and you said you were busy with school!"

"Surprise! I made that up so that I could surprise you," he said.

"Oh, Damian, I'm so happy you're here!" Tashi said.

"I'm here too!" said a voice behind Damian. Tashi looked behind him and saw Leilani standing there, grinning.

"Oh, my gosh!" said Tashi. "You two are the best surprise I could ask for!" Both Tashi and Josh hugged their kids.

"Okay, come on in," said Damian.

Tashi and Josh walked in and a bunch of their friends shouted "Surprise!"

"Oh, wow!" they both said, smiling.

"Mom and Dad," said Tashi, "you outdid yourselves!"

"Yeah, and there's no pot roast? I got all dressed up for nothing?" Josh joked.

"No, no pot roast tonight, son. We had to make a bit more than that to feed all these people." Rosa said.

"And I bought this dress for nothing!" Tashi joked.

"Oh you silly girl, this dress is much more suitable for this type of celebration than for a pot roast." Rosa laughed.

They all hugged and kissed and said hello to all of the guests.

"So, Mom, where is the food? We are starving," Josh said.

"It's almost ready!" she said and then turned to Leilani and asked, "Sweetheart, I put the wine outside to keep it cool, do you mind bringing a couple of bottles in?"

And that's when Josh looked outside, and noticed the big tents in the backyard.

"Tashi, look." She looked out and saw the big tents with decorations, a big Congratulations sign and even a dance floor.

"Oh, wow," she said. "This is beautiful."

They went outside and took a look around. While they were out there, they ran into the photographer that Rosa and Ted had ordered, and he took photos of them.

When the photo session was finally over, a band started to play. At that point, dinner was ready, and the bar opened up.

Josh turned to Tashi and said, "Are you happy, sweetie?"

"I couldn't be happier. Are you?"

"Oh, yes."

So they ate and drank happily and talked to all the guests and their kids.

When they were done eating, Damian walked up to Leilani.

"Come on, let's have a dance, let's leave these two old people alone."

"Old people?!" Josh asked.

"Well what do you expect, you old man?" Tashi smirked.

"Not you too!"

She laughed.

"I'll show you an old man when we get home. You'll be begging for forgiveness," he said.

Tashi giggled like a little girl.

"Okay, come on, sweetie, let's dance. If those youngsters can do it, so can we." So he held Tashi by the hand and led her to the dance floor. After the first song, everyone else stepped off the floor and all eyes were on them.

"Let's give them a show," Josh whispered in Tashi's ear. Then he walked over to the band and requested a song.

The band started playing disco, and Tashi and Josh danced like they never had before. The guests laughed, but they all loved it.

After some time, Tashi and Josh stepped off the dance floor to take a break.

Tashi said, "Josh I'm so happy, and so are the kids."

"I think you're right," he replied.

They stood together, holding hands, and watched as everyone danced. Even Grandpa Ted and Grandma Rosa tried to disco.

By the time the evening was over and they had arrived home, it was way past two in the morning. They took a shower together and then jumped into bed.

"Are we going to sleep, or do you have anything else in mind?" Josh asked her.

"I don't know. Let's spoon for a little and see what happens," Tashi said.

After lying in bed like a couple of spoons for about half an hour, Tashi turned around and said, "Wake up!"

He opened his eyes and said, "Is there something wrong?"

"Yes, terribly wrong!"

"What is it?"

"We're finished spooning, let's do something else," she said.

"Oh, boy, this wife of mine is going to drive me into the ground." He sat up and leaned over her. "Let me take a look at you. I think it's time to put my fingerprints on you again."

"Oh, no, it's my turn," she said. "Turn over, and lie down on your tummy."

"Uh-oh," he said, but he listened anyway.

She started giving him a massage, deep into his tissues, all over his back. "If you fall asleep, I will pour cold water all over you."

"Okay! Okay! I won't fall asleep!" he said.

She massaged him for a few minutes, and at that point he started getting really relaxed. She changed her technique to wake him up, and started moving her hands up and down quickly, on either side of his spine.

"Ow!" he said.

"I just want to make sure you're awake!" she said.

"Ooh, I'm awake."

She continued her massage all the way down his back, and then slid her hands off his butt.

"You know, you have the cutest butt ever!" she said.

"Oh, no, you have the cutest butt, my dear," he said.

She started massaging his buttocks, and he really enjoyed it. She started a kneading motion.

"This isn't a loaf of bread you know!" he said.

"I know, but I just want to leave my fingerprints on something!" She bent down, and then bit his butt.

"Hey! Oh, you wicked woman, you deserve a spanking on your butt now." He lifted her up while she squealed, and turned her over onto her stomach.

He started massaging her butt.

"My dear lady, you just came to Dr. Josh, and Dr. Josh says that you are the most wicked woman in the west," Josh said in a deep voice. "but lucky you, you have the cutest butt in the west." Josh said.

She giggled.

He continued to massage her, and then he bent down and started kissing her there. She got very relaxed, until all of a sudden he gave her a slap on one side of her butt.

"Ow! What was that for?!" she asked.

"That, my dear, was for biting me in the butt." He bent down and started kissing her again.

"Oh, you're back to kissing again? Do you feel sorry for me?"

"No, I just enjoy kissing your butt." He then started kissing up and down her legs.

"Do you want me to roll over?" she asked.

"No, I'm going to punish you now," he said.

"For what?"

"I have a few things stored in my memory," he said, and then he started kissing her on her back, and up to her neck and her ears.

She started moaning and moving restlessly.

"Can I please roll over?" she asked.

"No, I'm punishing you, remember?" he said, and continued to kiss her everywhere.

He then flipped her over and looked into her blue eyes with his green eyes. He bent down and kissed her with his tongue in her mouth. Before she knew it, they were having beautiful, beautiful sex.

"My wonderful wife," he said when they were finished. "I can't get enough of you."

"I can't get enough either," she said. "And don't even think about going to sleep, I just got a taste of what I can get."

"What? Oh, jeez, can I call a friend? I need someone to help me out here."

"No you cannot," she said. "You told me you were a young man, so you can survive this! Unless you are the old man the kids keep calling you."

"Oh, jeez," he said. "Okay, give me a few minutes, and a drink, and then we will continue."

"Okay."

He walked to the kitchen, and she went into the bathroom. She looked at herself in the light and turned around

"Oh, wow, that's big," she said when she saw the imprint of his hand. She laughed and went back to the bedroom.

He came back with some water for them and she said, "Look what you've done," and showed him the big imprint on her bottom.

"It looks nice on your cute little butt," he said, and gave her a kiss.

They sat down next to each other and drank their drinks.

"Tashi, life is so fun with you. I look forward to every day I spend with you. It was not like this when I was with my ex-wife; it was dull and depressing. You made me so happy that day you walked into my office. And now we have two beautiful kids, and a third one somewhere out in the world. We will try to find her," he said. "I promise, I will do everything I can to find her."

"I know, Josh. I am so happy in life with you too. You are everything I could ever ask for. The only thing that would make things better is if we find our daughter. I have to be prepared that she may not want to see us, though." She put her arms around his neck and started to cry.

"Sweetheart, don't cry. She may not want to see us, but if we know she is happy, then that will give us peace. Don't worry, it'll be okay," he said, and kissed the top of her head.

"I would've spoiled her Josh. I would've bought her everything she ever wanted. And I still will if we find her. How great would it be for Leilani and Damian to have a sister," she said. "They would all grow up together, and would have beautiful families, and we would have dozens of grandchildren.".

"One day, that will happen," Josh said. "So, are we going to sleep now?"

"You know, Josh, I wanted to continue, but I am just so tired now. Maybe we will continue tomorrow morning," Tashi said.

And at that, they fell asleep.

Chapter 17

THE NEXT DAY THEY WOKE UP QUITE early, as they were having their parents over for brunch. Leilani and Damian were going to visit some of their friends who live in Vancouver, so they wouldn't be joining them.

Tashi prepared some omelettes and French toast, and bowls of fresh fruit for everyone.

Ted and Rosa arrived just after noon, and they all sat down to eat.

"So when are you going to Hawaii?"

"I'm thinking the day after tomorrow."

"Tashi wants to do some cleaning and pack up some clothes to give away. She also wants Leilani to come over today and see what she doesn't need, so that it can be packed up as well," Josh explained.

"That's a good idea," Josh's mom said. "I have to do that pretty soon too. It's too much. Your dad has so many suits, you know, it's really ridiculous."

"Oh, yeah, I wonder why," Josh said. "I think it's because you keep buying them for him."

"Well, if I don't buy them for him, he would go without them. It would not look very good if the lawyer came in without clothes on, now, would it? He has to be dressed really nice."

"Good, Mom. You keep it up. You always take care of everything, Mom. You are so nice."

"Yes, yes, I do."

Josh said, "Mom and Dad, you threw a great party last night. I think I need some coffee to keep me going today. Would anyone else like a cup?"

Everyone agreed to have some coffee, so Josh and his dad went to the kitchen to start making it, while the two women sat in the living room.

Josh's dad said to him, "Son, you look really happy. It's such a nice thing to see."

"I am, Dad."

"Are you going to buy a house or a condo there?"

"No, I think we want to get a bigger estate house, with a bigger property so that we can get a couple of dogs. That's what we are really looking for," Josh explained.

"That sounds really nice."

"And room to have a guest house where people can stay and have their privacy."

"Yeah, like Mom and I?"

"Sure! But you know you can stay in our home."

"Yes, but you bang the pots and pans too much." Josh's dad laughed. "No, we'd better stay in the guest house."

"Okay, then, we'd better build a bigger guest house for you."

Josh and his Dad brought out coffee to the girls.

"Can you just get me some water, Josh?" Tashi asked. ."I'm so full I can't even drink coffee."

Josh said to Tashi, "You forgot to tell my parents what you call the water you drink."

Rosa asked, "Oh, what's that, Josh?"

"The water she drinks is called wine," said Josh with a laugh.

"Oh, is that what water is called in Hawaii?" Ted asked.

"Oh, yeah, we have our wine every night. We like to sit by the pool and drink some wine while watching the sun go down and then hop in for a swim. It is so enjoyable in the evening, to be with a loved one," Tashi explained.

"Oh, I wish I was young again," Rosa said. "Wouldn't that be nice, Ted? We could do what those two are doing."

"We wouldn't have all those wonderful pots," Ted joked.

"Never mind the pots," Josh said to his dad.

"Don't start that pots thing again; otherwise, Tashi will start laughing and she won't be able to stop."

Tashi rolled her eyes at Josh, saying, "Please stop."

Rosa said, "One day I will find out the meaning of these pots. I'll ask around. Maybe Leilani knows."

"I tell you, Mom, she does not know," Josh said.

"Well, somebody has to know. Maybe Lilly-Ann knows, because she cooks a lot and uses pots," she argued. "Anyways, what does Tashi do with those pots?"

"She goes out and kills crocodiles, Mom," Josh joked.

"Oh, jeez, this is getting hilarious," said his dad quietly.

"You never mentioned there were crocodiles by the pool!" Rosa said.

"Yup! That's why I use the pots to kill them," Tashi explained.

"Oh, I give up!" said Rosa. "I know there is something behind all this. I just don't get it."

"Oh, that's good Mom. Don't even try," Josh said.

"I don't think I will stop trying. I'll just ask your dad."

"You can ask" said Ted, "but you won't get it out of me."

"Oh, yes I will, you know I have my secret way of getting things out of you."

"Oh, I wouldn't say that now," said Ted. "The kids are here listening."

"Well, it's my turn to spill the beans," Rosa said.

"Would you two like to go for a walk?" Ted asked.

"No, Dad, I want to stay right here. So, Mom, what is it that you do to get things out of Dad?" Josh asked.

"Well… …o, forget it." She said

"Good choice, Rosa. If you tell them you will be telling the whole world."

Rosa said "You know what, Ted? I think it's time for us to go before I spill the beans."

"Yes, I think so too."

Ted got up and he and Rosa put on their coats. "Thank you for this lovely brunch, you two."

Tashi and Josh got up to kiss his mom and dad and thank them for a beautiful evening the night before again.

"Mom, on the way out, are you sure you don't want to take a look at Tashi's pots?" Josh asked.

His mom laughed. "Oh, get out of here!"

Once they were alone, Tashi said, "That was hilarious! I just about peed my pants."

"Good thing the kids weren't here, because they would have picked up the inside jokes right away. I can't believe mom didn't figure out what it meant."

"Are you going to call Christopher? Because if you do, I'll be in my closet," Tashi said. "If the buzzer ring, that'll probably be the kids, so you'll have to get the door."

"Okay, I'll do that. You can go down and work on your closet," Josh said.

"Give me a kiss first." She wrapped her arms around him and gave him a big kiss, then said, "See you later, my alligator!"

"See you later, my little gecko."

"Oh, I would love to be a little gecko," said Tashi. "I would tickle you all over the place."

"Anyways, little gecko, go do your work."

She took her water bottle with her and went down to her room to select from her closet all the stuff she didn't want to keep anymore.

She packed the clothes and shoes into big plastic bags that she would deliver to the Salvation Army.

She had her suitcase open so she could pack what she wanted to take back to Hawaii.

Next she went to Leilani's closet. All the clothes in there were from when Leilani was fourteen or fifteen years old. So she pulled them out and, knowing that Leilani will never use it again, packed it all up. By the time she was finished, the closet was half empty. She puts it beside the door to remember to donate it.

When she was just about finished, the buzzer went off. Josh came up from his office to let Leilani and Damian come in. They were glowing from spending time outside with their good friends. Damian quickly packed the things he brought, as his flight back to school was leaving in a couple of hours. Leilani was leaving the next day to go back to Europe and be with her girlfriend. They had to take her to the airport very early, and that was why she was staying with them. There comes a point when the kids are all grown up and each goes their separate way.

Damian said, "I think that's the best decision you have ever made, Dad."

"What is that, son?" Josh asked.

"Marrying Tashi. That's the best thing you have done in your whole life," Damian explained.

"Thank you, son. I love hearing that."

"So do I," said Tashi. "So do I."

Damian said, "And you know what, Tashi? You are the best thing for my dad. I have never seen him so happy in my entire life. I am forever grateful that you give my dad so much happiness." He walked over and put his arms around Tashi.

She said, "Damian, you are such a sweet boy, and I am so happy that you are my son now."

Josh came over and put his arms around the two of them, saying, "It is so sweet to watch this."

Damian said, "I have to say goodbye now, Tashi," and he kissed her on the cheek.

"You're a wonderful man," Tashi said to him. "One day you will make a wonderful husband to a beautiful woman too."

"Alright. Bye, Dad." He held out his hand, but instead Josh pulled him into a hug.

"Good luck, son. You are a good student. I know one day you will make a wonderful lawyer."

"Thanks, Dad."

Damian then went to Leilani and gave her a hug too. "Bye, little sis."

He headed out the door and gave them one last wave.

Leilani left to go to her room, so Josh and Tashi were left alone. Josh kissed her and said, "Well sweetie, wasn't that a beautiful day?"

"Every day with you is a beautiful day," Tashi said.

"Aw, thank you. I feel the same about you." His kissed her again. "So I was thinking we catch the red eye to Hawaii tomorrow night. I have some work to do, but I can do that on the computer, so we can fly straight to Kauai.

"Okay," she agreed. "That sounds perfect."

Josh kissed her again, and then their soft kisses become passionate. "We have your daughter in the house," Josh said as he came up for air, "so we need to be careful."

"Yes, we do." As they spoke to each other, they heard Leilani start to play the piano.

"Let's go listen to her," Josh said, and pulled Tashi by the hand to where the piano was. They sat on the couch and cuddled up, watching Leilani.

"She is a talented girl, isn't she?" Tashi asked.

"She is. I don't know how she plays the piano so well, and learned all those languages too." He answered. "And you, my beautiful Tashi, are one of the most talented artists I know."

"Thanks Josh. It took a lot of hard work. Although I hated what happened to our daughter, and the fact that I had to go to Europe. But," she continued, "I really learned how to paint there."

They sat and talked while listening to Leilani play. They dreamed of their future together in Hawaii and they discussed their plans to buy a new home. They decided that they should live together in Kauai, rather than Honolulu. Although Honolulu was big, they liked the serenity of Kauai, and the fact that they fell in love with each other there. Josh would have to work in Honolulu, but only every once in a while, as most of his work could be done on the computer from home.

They then talked about taking a trip to Greece. They drank wine as they discussed their plans for visiting Europe and meeting Leilani there. As they talked, Tashi stroked his face. She took his hair in her hands and played with it because she loved how it was a little too long.

Leilani turned around all of a sudden and asked, "Are you two sleeping?"

"No, no!" Tashi said quickly. "We are talking a little bit, but I still hear your beautiful piano playing." Tashi paused. "Your mother would have been proud."

"I wish I could have heard her play."

"I know, sweetheart."

"I'm glad I am here with you though," Leilani said.

"We are too, sweetheart," Tashi said.

"So what time does your plane leave?" Josh asked.

"At seven."

"Seven?!" Tashi said.

"That's okay, I'll drive you," Josh said.

"And I will come," Tashi said. "Since the plane leaves so early, you should get to bed soon. Would you like something to eat first?"

"No thanks, Mom. I'm not hungry." Leilani got up off the piano bench. "I do need to pack a little more, though."

"Where are you flying to?" Tashi asked.

"To Berlin. And Anita will pick me up there. She has a brand-new car, so that'll be nice."

"Oh, that will be very nice." Josh said.

"And I will make the arrangements for when you two come to Greece," Leilani said. "We won't stay with you, of course. We don't want to stay with newlyweds, but we will find you a nice place." She laughed.

"Okay, well, go get yourself to bed then, sweetheart," Tashi said. "And I'll check on you bright and early tomorrow to make sure you're up."

"Okay, thanks, Mom." She gave both of them a peck on the cheek and then headed to bed.

"Okay, so if we have to get up early, then maybe we should head up to our bedroom too," Josh said.

"Would you like anything before we go to bed? Like maybe some cake?" A smile came across Tashi's lips.

"Let me guess? Tiramisu?"

"Exactly," she said.

"I would love that, but unfortunately we don't have any in the fridge!" Josh laughed. "Next time we'll have to get some."

So the two of them walk to their bedroom, where they prepare for the morning. Tashi takes out a nice blouse and, of course, her beloved jeans, and places them beside the bed.

"Wow, all you have to do is get up and hop in!" Josh says.

"Yes, well, it's going to be an early morning tomorrow," she says.

"I love you, Tashi," Josh says. He slowly walks over to her and puts his arms around her naked body. She puts her arms around his neck, and then they lie down in the bed together.

"I will never let you out of my life again," he murmurs into her ear. "You are so beautiful, and I just want to eat you right up."

"Then go ahead and eat me," she says.

He starts suckling her breasts and traces his tongue around her nipples. He knows that will drive her crazy. He then circles down to her tummy and keeps going lower. He kisses her legs.

"Come back up here, Josh."

"Stop being so impatient." He listens, though, and comes up to her neck, and then nibbles on her earlobes.

All of a sudden Tashi makes him roll over onto his back. He is surprised and doesn't know what to expect. She sits on his manhood and then bends down to kiss him while she moves.

He starts moaning, and then she bites his bottom lip. He really pushes into her and she says, "Oh, my God."

"That's me," he jokes. He speeds it up, and in no time, they are both done.

"That was beautiful," she says. "Just absolutely perfect."

They both wiggle into each other's arms.

Before they fall asleep, Tashi sits up and says, "Oh, my gosh, we need to set alarms! If Leilani's plane leaves at seven, we should get up at four!" So she gets out of bed and sets a few clocks, just in case some of them don't go off.

"That'll be fun to wake up to," Josh says sarcastically.

"It doesn't matter if it's fun. We'd just better wake up!" She sets the last alarm and then crawls back into bed with him.

They fall asleep as soon as they close their eyes.

Chapter 18

THEY WAKE UP TO THE SOUND OF about five alarm clocks going off at once.

"I guess, you were right!" Tashi said as she ran around turning them off. "This is not fun!"

"Well, we are up!" Josh said.

Leilani burst into the room. "What is going on in here? Is there a fire?"

"No," Tashi said, laughing. "Just all my alarms."

Leilani shook her head and laughed. She left to get ready.

Once they were all ready, they met in the kitchen and quickly had breakfast together. They then carried all of Leilani's things down to the Ferrari and hopped in.

Once they arrived at Vancouver International, they shared teary goodbye' with Leilani and made her promise to call when she arrived in Germany.

Tashi and Josh drove home.

"Well, it's just us now," Josh said.

"What are we going to do with our day before we leave for Hawaii?" Tashi asked as they walked in the door.

"Well, it's still pretty early. Why don't we hop back into bed?"

"I like that idea," Tashi said, and they took off their clothes together and went back into their bed.

By the time they woke up, it was noon. They listened to a message from Damian, telling them that he had arrived safely. They packed, went to visit Josh's parents one last time, and before they knew it, it was time to head to the airport again.

After their flight, they came out into the warm Hawaiian morning air. John was there to pick them up, and he drove them to their place.

Lilly-Ann was outside to greet them and she gave them both hugs. "Welcome home," she said, "I'm so happy to have you here."

"We're glad to be back," Tashi said, "But we will be leaving again soon to Greece. We are going there for our honeymoon, and also we will meet Leilani there."

"Oh, that sounds great, you two," Lilly-Ann said. She and John helped the two of them with their things.

Tashi unpacked and got dressed into her sarong. She walked around the house and then out onto the patio. She breathed in the warm Hawaiian air and thought, *How could I ever live anywhere else?* She was finally calm now that she and Josh had decided to buy a place together in Kauai rather than Vancouver or Honolulu.

Josh came up behind her. "I think I just read your mind."

"Did you?"

"You said, 'How could I live anywhere else?'"

She laughed. "I said that out loud, did I?"

"You did, sweetheart."

They got dressed in their bathing suits, and hand in hand they walked out onto the patio to the swimming pool. First they sat on the chairs and looked out at the ocean. Eventually, Tashi hopped into the pool, and shortly after, she dragged Josh into it as well.

She swam underneath the water and circled around him. He wasn't sure where she was, but all of a sudden he felt her grab him where you're not supposed to grab a man.

"Hey!" he said, and chased after her.

They spent the rest of the day like that —swimming and kissing and enjoying the Hawaiian sun together. Finally, it began to get dark.

"Come on, sweetheart, let's hit the hay," said Josh. They took off their clothes and lay next to each other on their big bed.

"Thank God this isn't hay!" Tashi said as they got snuggled up together. "Because I wouldn't be quite as comfy."

And they drifted off into la la land.

CHAPTER 19

THE NEXT FEW DAYS PASSED BY QUICKLY because they were so busy. Josh and Tashi looked for homes in Kauai, but ended up buying a property near Tashi's old place, because none of the houses for sale meet all their needs. Tashi worked on the design of the house, while Josh contacted contractors.

They also began planning their trip to Greece to meet Leilani and her friend Anita. The rest of their time was consumed by work, and a lot of lovemaking.

"Is my honey bear hungry? Because I made lunch for you and it's waiting out in the dining room," Tashi said to Josh one sunny afternoon, while he was working in his office. He joined her in the dining room, and they sat down together to eat.

"Oh, wow, Tashi, this is all delicious," Josh said. "You are the best."

She smiled.

"How are your paintings coming along?" he asked. "Is that what you're doing after this?"

"Yes," she said. "The gallery in Waikiki actually called me and they need some more paintings. I need to get to work, because all my time has been consumed with lovemaking with you." She giggled.

"Oh, my sweetheart, it has been the best lovemaking ever," he said.

After lunch, Tashi went to her studio and began painting. While she painted, she thought about her daughter. She hoped that she could find her one day. She painted and painted until her wrist was sore, and then she went out onto the patio and fell asleep.

"Hello, my beautiful wife." Josh says as he wakes Tashi up with a kiss. "What were you dreaming of?"

Tashi sits up and kisses him, and then lays her head back on his chest. "About different things," she says.

"Like what?" he asks.

"Well, I was dreaming of our daughter. In the dream she was happy, but her eyes kept changing colour. One minute they were blue, and the next they were green."

"One day we will find out what colour they are," Josh promises.

"I hope so," Tashi says. "I just hope she is as happy as our other kids."

"I hope so too" Josh says.

"I just worry too much sometimes," Tashi continues. "I always worry about Leilani and Damian too."

"Oh, sweetheart, there is no need to worry about them. They will be fine."

"You're right," Tashi says. "I bet Damian will be a heartbreaker."

Josh laughs. "It's possible."

"Or he'll be kind and good to his woman, like his father," Tashi says.

"Well, I was good to my woman, but I wasn't always good," he says. "Sneaking off with my lover during my marriage isn't something I am proud of. Although at the time, it was the only way I could be with you, and I needed to be with you."

"I know, but I'm glad you did it at the same time, because I needed you too," Tashi says.

"We will stay together forever, Tashi," Josh says.

"Yes we will." She smiles and kisses him. "I can look at you all the time. Sometimes, like now, you are this gentle man, but then when we're in bed you have this devilish look to you."

"Oh, Tashi, I feel the same about you. You are always full of surprises," he says. "I was studying you while you were sleeping, and I couldn't take my eyes off your flawless, sun-kissed body. You had this dreamy look on your face and it made me want to cuddle up beside you."

"Josh, you are such a romantic," she says as she sits up. "Now how about I do something romantic, and play the piano for you, while you lie on the couch?"

"Oh, I would love that," he says.

Tashi takes his hand and pulls him out to the living room. She sits on the stool, while he sits on the couch, watching her the whole time.

She plays a few songs, all of them very calming love songs. She starts with "Dr. Zhivago," and ends with "When a Man Love a Woman," her favourite song ever since she listened to Bryan Adam's version.

When she is done, Josh says, "Tashi, that was beautiful. You are so talented; you didn't even make one mistake."

"Do you want to come and join me? And play together?" she asks.

"Oh, no, I make one mistake after the other." He laughs.

She walks over to him to sit beside him and kisses his cheek. "What do you say we go for a nice walk through Hanalei?"

"I'd love that," he says.

They get changed. Tashi wears a pair of shorts with a halter top and flip flops, while Josh put on shorts and a T-shirt.

They hop in the car and drive down to Hanalei, and park in front of Donna's store.

There is a couple playing their guitars on the beach. They have been playing for as long as Tashi can remember, and it's absolutely beautiful.

Tashi and Josh continue walking down the beach, eventually taking their shoes off so they can feel the sand between their toes. They walk so far that they reach a place near the new property that they bought. They walk far inland until they reach the property and stand in the middle of where the house should be.

"Just imagine our master bedroom," Tashi says. "It will be the whole top floor and will overlook the ocean."

"It will be so nice, especially the way you design it with all the little trimmings," Josh says.

"It will be so romantic!" says Tashi.

They walk through the property and decide where the pool will be. They also consider building a small house to the side for John and Lilly-Ann.

Once it starts to get dark, they head back home.

"Let's go swimming again," suggests Josh.

"Okay," Tashi agrees, "but only if it's skinny dipping!"

"You know I'll always agree to that," Josh says.

They strip their clothes off and jump into the pool. They sit under the fountain together, feeling each other's slippery bodies glowing under the moonlight. Tashi then takes off, swimming up and down the pool, and Josh swims after her and catches her in his arms.

She gives him a big wet kiss on the lips.

"Hello, my fish." She smiles.

"Oh, I'm a fish again?" he asks.

"Yes, and watch out, because sometimes I'm also a snapping turtle." She smiles.

After some time, when their fingers start getting wrinkly, they step out of the pool and dry each other off. Josh pulls her into the bedroom, and Tashi lies beside him with her head on his chest. They talk of their plans for the house and for visiting Greece, and about the future, until they both doze off to sleep.

Chapter 20

THEY NEXT DAY, LEILANI PHONED FROM AUSTRIA.

"So, did you book Greece yet? Because we are going next week," Leilani said.

"Yes, we will book it today, sweetheart." Tashi said. "Maybe we'll give you some time on your own and we'll come a week after you?"

"Okay, that sounds nice," said Leilani. "I'm really looking forward to it."

"I am too, honey. I can't wait to see you, and your friend."

"Yeah, and if you like her, I was thinking of inviting her back home in the summer once school is finished."

"That sounds great, sweetheart," Tashi said. "Anyways, I'll tell Josh to book it today, and I'll let you know when he does."

"Okay, sounds great. I love you, Mom!"

"I love you more! Be careful!"

"I always am," Leilani said, and she hung up.

Tashi went to find Josh, and they decided to book their vacation for a week.

A few days later, everything was booked. Their flight was booked for the following Sunday, a week and a half away. They also booked a beach house separate from the girls, so that everyone could have their own space. They spent a few days packing and preparing themselves for this big trip, as neither of them had been to Europe for a few years.

The night before they took off, they invited Donna and Christopher over to their place so that they could all catch up.

Donna and Christopher arrived a bit early. Tashi didn't even hear them come in the house, as she was sitting and playing the piano. Donna and Christopher stood behind her and listened for a few minutes until she realized they were there.

"Oh! I'm sorry!" she said. "Sometimes I just get so carried away once I start playing!"

"I didn't know you could play so well," Christopher said. "Can I play with you?"

"Of course," Tashi said. "I didn't even know you could play the piano."

Christopher sat next to her, and together they played a few songs, each one better than the last. Donna and Josh sat on a couch, and Josh brought them some wine. They didn't even talk; they just listened to the music.

Tashi and Christopher played and played, and got so carried away that they didn't notice the time passing. Finally Tashi looked up and said, "Christopher, do you know we've been playing for an hour? What happened to our partners?"

Tashi and Chris looked over at Donna and Josh, and saw them sitting on the couch with two empty wine bottles in front of them. They all laughed.

"Look what they've been doing! They've been drinking while we were making music!"

"Well, they had to have some fun too!" Christopher laughed.

"You might not get lucky with your little lady tonight! She looked like she's falling asleep." Tashi laughed.

"I'm not sleeping! Just dreaming," Donna said, and Chris got up and gave her a kiss.

"Wow, that was beautiful you two!" Josh said.

"Thank you," Christopher said. "I'm all tired out now, though."

"Here, I'll get you some much-needed drinks," Josh said, and went to pour everyone a glass of wine.

They all sat down together on the couches, sipping on their wine.

"So, are you excited for your trip?" Christopher asked.

"We are!" said Josh.

"Although I truly believe there is no place more beautiful in the world than here," said Tashi, "but I am so excited to see Leilani and meet her friend, Anita."

"You will have a great time," said Donna. "And what about your house, how is that coming along?"

"Well, we have all the drawings ready," Tashi explained. "We just need to find a contractor. And then our dreams will come to life."

"So what about your kids? Will they move with you?" Christopher asked.

"Leilani will get this house once she comes home from school, and Damian can also do the same, but I don't know what his plans are after finishing school," Josh said. "We'll let him decide. As long as he doesn't get married before finishing school and finding a job, I will let him make his own decisions."

"He'll be fine," said Tashi. "He is very career driven, don't worry, Josh."

"Well, anyways," Donna said, "I think it's time for us to disappear, because you have a lot of work to do before you go."

"Okay, thank you for stopping by," said Tashi.

"Yes, thank you. I'll leave my number in case anything important comes up," Josh said.

Josh and Tashi walked them out to the car and waved goodbye.

"We sure have beautiful friends, don't we?" said Josh.

"Yes, we do."

"Well, I have some things prepared for Greece. Do you mind checking them?" Josh asked.

"Of course, and you can check mine," Tashi said.

Josh looked at her clothes. "Okay, I approve. What about your underwear, though?"

"I was going to pack them later."

"How about I pack them for you?" he asked.

"Sure!"

He picked out the teeniest, tiniest underwear, and beautiful bras.

"Wow, that's very daring if I have to wear a dress…" Tashi hesitated.

"Well, never mind that. You are doing this for me."

"Okay, if you say so." She smiled. "Just throw it in the suitcase!"

And just like that, they were ready to go on their trip to Greece. They quickly took showers and then headed to bed and fell asleep easily.

Chapter 21

MEANWHILE, ANITA AND LEILANI HAD ARRIVED IN Greece. They arrived there a week before Leilani's parents so they could have some free time on their own.

They had a bungalow in Kefalas, on the island of Kos. The bungalow was so cute — it had a small kitchen, one bedroom and a nice veranda outside. The veranda had walls around it that were the same height as the bungalow, and they were covered in greenery. From the outside the walls were white-washed, and the roof was covered with clay tiles. They had a key to get in and could lock up from the inside to stay safe. It was right on the beach, and the two girls rented a Jeep to drive around the island.

That day, they got ready and hopped into the Jeep as usual.

"Let's get wild before my parents show up," said Leilani.

"Yes, let's! Because we'll have to behave once they show up, won't we?"

"No, no, I'm just kidding. They're not too bad." Leilani smiled.

The girls headed off into town with just their backpacks and a few bottles of water. It was a beautiful, hot day, and they could already feel beads of sweat rolling down their backs. They headed to the harbour to cool off, and take a walk.

While they were walking along the side of the harbour, a few people waved at Leilani. She waved back but was confused. "The people are very friendly here. They keep waving to me."

"Yeah, I wonder why?" Anita said. "They aren't waving to me at all!"

"Strange," Leilani said, but she didn't think much more of it.

They went into a few tourist stores, and Leilani picked up a statue of David. "Oh, wow, isn't he endowed?"

Anita laughed just as the owner of the store came over to them to explain who he was.

"Oh, thank you, but we already know this," Anita said to him in perfect Greek, which she had learned at school. Leilani understood everything too, as she had learned Greek as well.

"Well, of course. Maya would have told you," the store owner said.

"Who? Who's Maya?"

"Maya, who is beside you," he said.

Anita looked beside her at Leilani. "Does he mean you?"

"Well, I don't think so, because that's not my name," Leilani said, puzzled.

He continued. "You told her about David, right?" he asked Leilani.

"No, I didn't."

"Well, it's high time you tell the people of this island some of its history!"

"Okay, well, I guess it's time for us to go," Anita said, perplexed.

"Okay, see you later!" the man said.

They decided to go get a nice cold drink and sit down somewhere, away from that strange man who kept calling Leilani "Maya."

They sat at a little café right on the water.

"Hello, Maya. How have you been?" the waiter said to them.

Leilani went along with it. "I'm good, how about you?"

"I'm good too. I haven't seen you for a while," he said.

"Oh, that's strange." *Are they all nuts here?* Leilani thought to herself.

Anita looked at her, grinning from ear to ear and holding back laughter.

"So, what can I get you? Your usual?" he asked Leilani.

"Sure."

"And your beautiful friend?"

"I'll have the same," Anita said and blushed.

He came back with two of the same drinks. "Let me know if you'd like anything else."

He walked away, and two girls started speaking in English.

"What the heck is going on here?" Leilani asked out loud.

"I have no idea," Anita said. "Who is Maya?"

"I don't know...?"

"Maybe she is a Greek goddess, and they think you look like her," Anita suggested.

"I've never heard of one named Maya, but you never know," said Leilani. "Anyways, let's play along with it."

"Yes, it'll be fun," Anita agreed. "So what are we drinking?'

"Who knows? We can't even ask because it's our 'usual.'"

Anita laughed. A few minutes passed, and while the girls talked, a few people walked by and waved to Leilani.

"This whole town is nuts," Leilani said. "Is this some hidden camera thing?"

"I don't think so," Anita said. "I think it's some identity mix-up."

"But with who?"

"Who knows!"

After having their drinks, they said goodbye to the waiter.

"Goodbye, Maya!" he said. "And goodbye, Maya's beautiful friend."

They left and continued walking by the harbour. As they were walking, they ran into another girl around their age.

"Oh, Maya!" she said. "Where have you been? I'm having a party tonight. You should come!" She looked at Anita. "And who is this?"

"This is Anita," Leilani introduced her. "But sure, a party would be great. Where is the party?"

"At my house."

"Oh," Leilani said. "Where is your house."

The girl laughed. "You're kidding, right?"

"No...can you write down the address for me?"

"Sure." The girl looked at her strangely. She wrote Pia at the top of a piece of paper, and then her address underneath. "Maya, is there something wrong with you? Have you fallen on your head?" she finally asked.

"Well —" Leilani looked at Anita, "— that must be the case. That's why I can't remember anything!" She laughed it off.

"Oh, my," said Pia. "Well, I'm glad you're okay now. I'll see you at the party!" And she walked away.

"This is starting to get creepy," Leilani said.

"It's fine," Anita said. "I'm sure it's just a crazy coincidence."

The rest of the day passed in similar fashion. As they explored the beautiful Greek island, people kept saying hello to Leilani, and she continued to pretend to know them.

"There must be someone who looks like me," Leilani said. She was beginning to get very bothered by the whole situation.

The strangeness continued when the two girls walked by a small restaurant, and a man came running over to them. "Hello, Maya!" he said, and he took Leilani's face in his hands and planted a kiss, right on her lips! Anita just stood there, laughing.

Leilani didn't know what to do, so she just let it happen and enjoyed it. He was a good-looking guy.

"So where have you been?" he asked, concerned.

"Oh, I went away to Germany to visit my friend Anita here," Leilani lied.

"You went to Germany? Why didn't you tell me, of all people?" he asked.

"Well," Leilani continued. "I had an accident and fell on my head, and I didn't know who I was."

"Are you for real?" he asked.

"Yes. I don't remember anyone's name."

"Do you remember my name?" he asked, now looking sad.

"No, I don't."

"But we are engaged! And I am Marco." He looked down, dejected.

"Oh!" Leilani said. "Wow."

"So how long did they keep you in the hospital for? After you hit your head?" he asked.

"For a while. They wanted to make sure there was no severe brain damage. But don't worry, they say I will start to remember everything again slowly."

Leilani and Anita looked down at the ground, and both had to bite their lips to stop themselves from laughing.

"How long have we been engaged then?" she asked.

"Two years, and we are getting married next year," he said, sadly.

"Oh, dear. Did you hear that, Anita? He wants to marry me!" Leilani was biting on her lip really hard now.

"Well, if he says so, then you'd better do it!" Anita said.

"Anyways, we should get going," Leilani said.

"Okay, I'll see you later, honey," he said. "We need to meet up soon and talk about all of this."

"Alright."

Leilani and Anita tried to sidestep him but then he said,

"Hold on, not so fast, we are engaged!" and held his arms out.

So Leilani slowly went up to him and gave him a quick peck on the cheek, and then turned around.

"Bye Marco!"

She turned to Anita. "I do not understand any of this."

"There must be someone on the island who looks and talks like you," Anita said.

"I guess so. I hope we're not getting ourselves into a bad situation here by playing along with it," said Leilani.

"No, don't worry. Right now it's fun," Anita said.

"You're right. We'll play along with it for now."

CHAPTER 22

EVENING ROLLED AROUND, AND SOON ENOUGH IT was time to go to Pia's for the party.

"I have a bad feeling about this party now," Anita said.

"Well, we came to Greece for an adventure, and this is it," Leilani said. "Let's give it a try."

They drove to the address given to them and pulled up to a huge white house. There were lots of cars already there, so the two girls parked. At that point, they both had butterflies in their stomachs. They rang the doorbell and a maid opened the door and invited them in.

"Maya, you're here!' Marco walked over and kissed her. "What can I get you to drink?"

"My usual, please," Leilani said.

"And your friend?"

"She'll take the same."

So Marco left them alone for a second. They walked further into the house and found a huge room with a lot of people already there.

"Maya!" they all said. They all came to greet her, and asked her where she had been for so long. Leilani couldn't get a free moment.

This continued for some time, but by then Leilani and Anita had made some new friends. The music came on, and they all started dancing together. Both girls began to relax a little and have fun.

Around 10:30, the doorbell rang. Leilani and Anita didn't even hear it because the music was so loud. But all of a sudden, some of the people dancing next to Anita and Leilani stopped dancing, and looked up, past Leilani's head. Leilani then turned around, and standing in front of her was a girl who looked absolutely identical to her. The two of them made eye contact, and neither one of them moved.

"Oh. My. God. "Now I understand," Anita said.

"What do we do?" Leilani asked.

"Just keep playing your role, and pretend she's the imposter. All the people in here believe you already," Anita said.

The other girl walked right up to Leilani. "Who are you?"

"Never mind that, who are you?" Leilani answered.

The other girl got frustrated and called Marco over. "Marco, what's going on here?"

He had no idea either. He stood there looking at both of them, dumbfounded. "How would I know? Who are you?" he asked the girl who had just entered the party.

"What do you mean who am I? I'm your fiancée!"

"No, you're not," he said. "She is. This is Maya." He gestured to Leilani.

The real Maya got very upset at this point and yelled out, "Oh, look at that, he doesn't know who his own fiancée is!" She turned to Leilani and said, "You watch out. I am Maya Greggo. I don't know who you are, or what you are doing coming to this party pretending to be me and stealing my fiancée away. You better watch your back, though, because I won't let this happen on my island."

"How can you be Maya Greggo, when that is my name?" Leilani asked.

The real Maya lifted her hand to slap Leilani, but Marco stepped in and grabbed her arm to protect Leilani.

"You are not Maya Greggo! I am!" she yelled at Leilani. "And you —" she turned to Marco "— how could you not know me and defend her!? I will get you back for this, Marco, mark my words."

At that, Maya turned around and stormed out.

Anita sank to the floor and was shaking like a leaf. Leilani was still dumbfounded. "Who was that?" she asked the party.

No one knew.

"Well, let's just try to have a good time," Leilani said. "Marco, let's go dance."

So the girls stayed a while longer and tried to have fun. After about an hour, they were both exhausted and decided to go home to the little bungalow.

Once they got home, the two girls sat down and talked about the day's events.

"Wow, that was one crazy day," said Leilani.

"Yeah. Well, at least we figured out why everyone calls you Maya," Anita said.

"That's true."

"Who do you think she is?" Anita asked.

Leilani thought for a few moments and then said, "I know this will sound crazy, but I am adopted. Maybe I have a twin that I never knew about?"

Anita laughed. "That is a little bit crazy."

"Well, I'd like to get to the bottom of this," Leilani said. "One way or another." Leilani thought for a second. "Please don't say anything to my mom or Josh."

"No, I won't," Anita said. "You know, I'm kind of scared to go out again. That girl sounded really angry, and wanted to get back at you."

"I know," Leilani said. "But do we just stay here for the rest of our vacation?"

"No, we came here to have fun," Leilani said. "We'll go out, have a good time, and we'll be fine."

At that, the two girls fell asleep.

The next day, they stayed near their bungalow where all the tourists were. They played cards and walked along the beach, but didn't venture too far away. However, after dinner, the two girls became restless and decided to go a little farther into town to the cute café, Bar 52.

Niko the owner is excited to see both of them, especially Anita. She introduced herself to him, and they chatted for some time. He even invited her to go dancing that night, and she agreed.

"He's really cute," Anita said after he left.

"Yeah," Leilani hesitated, "but I don't know if we should be going out."

"When do your parents fly in?" Anita asked.

"Well, not for another couple of days, but that's not what I'm worried about," Leilani said.

"Oh, don't worry, Leilani, it'll be fun."

Later that day, the two girls drove to the disco. Both Leilani and Anita had wine before, and a few beers, so they were feeling good and relaxed, and not too worried about anything.

Anita, who had had quite a few more beers than Leilani, was on the dance floor all night. Everyone loved her, until she started breaking out Spanish moves and yelled out, "Spanish music is way better than Greek music!" Leilani had to pull her away so that they didn't get beat up.

"So, are you having fun?" Niko asked.

"Yes," Leilani said, "but I think it's time I get Anita home."

"You know, I can take her home on my motorbike, and my friend could drive you home," Niko offered. "You have probably had a beer too many yourself."

Niko's friend, the other one with the motorbike, walked over. He was a big guy with a beard and a few tattoos.

"Uh, no thanks," Leilani politely declined.

"I could show you the lighthouse," Niko's friend said.

"I've been there today already. I'm okay," she said. "I'll just drive the Jeep, I'll be fine." Leilani looked at Anita. "So are you coming with me? Or with Niko?"

Anita just looked at Leilani, her eyes barely open.

"Okay, I'll make the decision. I'm going to take you home."

Leilani helped Anita into the Jeep and they drove off. Anita sang Spanish songs all the way home.

"Oh, girl, you're going to have a rough hangover tomorrow," Leilani said.

"No, I will eat pita bread!" Anita yelled.

"I don't know if that will help you."

Once they got home, Anita fell asleep right away, and Leilani shortly after.

Chapter 23

THE NEXT MORNING, LEILANI HEARD ANITA GET up and go to the toilet. She had a rough hangover alright. Leilani got up and gave her some water, and placed a wet towel on her head.

"Do you need help?" Leilani asked.

"No, thank you, it's coming out on its own," Anita said in between gags.

"You were pretty drunk last night." Leilani laughed.

"Yeah, I can tell now," Anita said.

"Okay, well, I'll be outside if you need me." Leilani went to sit outside on the veranda. "What an exciting trip this is turning out to be," she said to herself and giggled.

After she had been reading her book for some time, Anita walked out onto the veranda. Her face was pale as ghost, and she slumped into a chair right away.

"Don't talk so loud," she said.

Leilani laughed. "I haven't said anything!"

"Well, whatever noise you made was way too loud for my sensitive ears," Anita said.

Leilani just laughed and then brought Anita some water and two Aspirins. "Here you go, you silly drunk."

"Thanks, my dearest friend," Anita said, and slowly swallowed the pills and washed them down with some water.

"Anita, I'm hungry," Leilani said.

"I'm not."

"I know you're not, but I think I will go next door to the café and have some breakfast," Leilani said.

"Be careful," said Anita. "That Maya girl might be somewhere nearby."

"Oh, I think it'll be fine," Leilani said. "And anyways, I'm too hungry to care right now. I'll go take a shower and then head out. Do you want anything?"

"No, no, no. Don't speak so loud." Anita said, and curled up further into her chair.

"Okay." Leilani laughed.

Leilani got ready and then went next door. She ordered a nice fresh breakfast and although she missed Anita's company, she enjoyed the fresh air. The scent of the water was strong, and there were grapes hanging everywhere around the restaurant. It was so serene and peaceful.

A few moments later, she noticed a nice little sports car driving along the road. Maya was driving it and was looking up and down.

Oh, no, she's looking for me, Leilani said to herself.

Maya didn't see her, as she was hidden in the restaurant, but she stayed there as long as was necessary to make sure it was safe.

She then went back to the bungalow, and took a nap.

When she awoke, Anita was finally up and getting ready to go out.

"Oh, thank God you're up," Anita said. "I'm starving!"

Leilani laughed. "Well, yeah, you didn't eat anything all day! Would you like to go get some food? We can go to Bar 52."

"Sure," Anita said, "I'd like that."

While they drove up to the bar, Leilani told Anita that she had seen Maya looking for her.

"Wow, what a crazy bitch!" Anita said. "I wonder if Niko will know anything about her."

"Actually, that's not a bad idea," Leilani agreed. "We can ask him today."

So they sat down at a table, and Niko came by to serve them.

"How are you feeling today, Anita?" he asked.

"I've been better," she said, slightly embarrassed.

"Oh, don't worry, we've all been there," he said. "What can I get for you girls?"

They ordered their food and two tall waters with lemon.

He came back with the water shortly after.

"Hey, Niko, can we ask you something?" Leilani said.

"Sure."

"Who is Maya Greggo?"

He looked at her with a puzzled look at first, because all this time Leilani had claimed to be her, and then he pulled up a chair and sat down.

"I knew you weren't her," he said. "You're too nice to be her. What's your real name?"

By this point, Leilani trusted Niko, so she introduced herself and told him all the stories of their strange encounters from the past couple of days.

"Yes, I heard something about the party incident," he said. "You girls may have got yourselves in some trouble."

CHAPTER 24

FOR THE NEXT HOUR, NIKO TOLD LEILANI and Anita the true story of Maya Greggo.

"Maya Greggo is a very wealthy girl who has lived on this island for as long as I can remember. She lives with her grandfather on a huge house on top of that hill overlooking the water." He pointed behind him. "Her grandmother passed away a few years ago.

"Her father was a composer and conductor and his wife was a pianist, but they both passed away when she was a very young girl."

Leilani's face turned pale. "Would you mind repeating that?"

"Why?"

"What was her mother's name?"

"Kate."

And suddenly, it clicked. Leilani had been right. She had a twin that she didn't know about, and they happened to be in the same place at the same time.

"Oh, my gosh, those were my parents," said Leilani.

"Oh, my God," said Niko. "Are you sure?"

"I'm adopted," she explained, and that's my mom's name. It all makes sense."

"You mean your mom had twins? She gave you away and kept Maya?" Anita asked.

"No I don't think so," Leilani said. "I lived with my mom and dad until I was five, and then was adopted. Maya was the one who must have been given away before, because I don't recall ever having a sister."

"You're right," Niko said. "Maya was here. She has always lived with her grandparents. Her dad brought her over."

"Holy smokes," said Leilani. "She is my twin sister. I don't know what to do. I think I should phone my mom."

"No, wait until she gets here," Anita said. "You shouldn't worry her yet."

"If I were you, though, I would stay clear of Maya. She's very vindictive," Niko explained. "You don't want to get tangled up with her."

"I can't believe she's my sister. I feel sad that she sounds like such a terrible person."

"I guess we went to the wrong island, Leilani!" Anita said.

Niko said, "When is your mom coming?"

"The day after tomorrow."

"Well, I would wait it out. But just stay safe, and always stick together. You never know what Maya is up to," he warned.

"What have I done?!" Leilani said. "We are in a huge mess!"

"You haven't done anything! It was meant to be, I guess. To finally meet her. But it's too bad it happened in such a bad way." Anita said.

Leilani thought for a little. "I would like to go to my grandfather's house and introduce myself."

"He's a mean old man too!" Niko said.

"Niko, I think I'll take that chance," Leilani said.

"I don't think you should."

"Well, I'm going to," Leilani decided. "Anita, you're coming with me."

"Me?!"

"Well, I need someone to come with me! I can't go on my own. What about you, Niko?" Leilani asked.

"No, I don't think I will join you," he said.

"Why not, are you scared?"

"No, I just don't have any business out there," he said.

"Can I talk you into it?" Leilani asked.

"You can talk Marco into it. He thinks he's your fiancé, after all." Anita laughed.

Niko agreed. "He probably wishes he was engaged to you and not her, because you're way nicer."

"Niko, are you sure we can't entice you to come with us?" Leilani asked.

"I guess I will," he finally said. "I don't want you two to go alone."

"You have no idea how much I appreciate that. Thank you so, so much," Leilani said.

"When would you like to go?"

"Tomorrow?"

"What if the bitch is there?" Anita asked.

"We'll have to face the music when we get there," Leilani said.

"What have you girls gotten me into? I think I need a drink. I need courage for tomorrow," Niko said.

Chapter 25

THE NEXT DAY AT TWO O'CLOCK THEY drove up to the beautiful large house on the hill. It was gleaming white, with almond trees and olive trees all around it. They drove up the driveway and walked to the door. The maid opened the door and looked in shock at Leilani.

"Did you forget your key?" she asked Leilani.

"No, can I come in?"

"Of course, you live here," the maid answered.

"Where is Grandpa?" she asked.

"In the study."

"Where's that?" Leilani asked.

"You should know…"

"Well, what side of the hallway?" Leilani asked.

"Are you trying to be funny?"

"No, I'm serious."

"You go to the left, and it's the second door."

They walk towards the door and a man's voice said "yes" when they knocked on it.

"What's up, Maya? I'm kind of busy," an old man said without looking up.

"Well, Grandpa, I need to talk to you. Can I sit down? This is Anita and Niko."

He finally looked up when Leilani introduced them.

They all sat down across from the desk on a sofa.

"Grandfather, I have something to tell you," she began.

"Well can you make it snappy? I'm looking through my stamp collection and I'm busy."

"Well, it's very important."

"Then start telling me!" he yelled.

She was just about to start when there was big commotion in the hallway and all of a sudden Maya came rushing into the room.

"What the hell are you doing here?" she asked.

"Who are you?" Grandpa Greggo said to Maya.

"I'm your granddaughter," she said.

"No, she's right here." He pointed towards Leilani.

"She's an imposter!" Maya yelled.

"No, I'm not, I am your granddaughter!" Leilani said.

He looked at Leilani and then he looked at Maya. "Which one is?"

Both girls said "I am."

He repeated the question.

Leilani said, "Let me tell you."

"You shut up and get out of this house," Maya interjected.

"Don't tell me to get out!" Leilani said.

Maya stormed out of the room, fuming.

"Okay, you had something to tell me?" Grandpa Greggo said.

"Okay, I am your granddaughter, except I didn't know until yesterday," Leilani said.

"What do you mean?"

She told him her story, starting from her parents and then how she was adopted and came to the island.

"Oh, my God," he said. "I can't believe this. You mean my son, Nick, lied to me?!"

"I guess so," she said. "My mom who adopted me is arriving on Monday, tomorrow."

"I see. Maybe I should meet your mother then," he said.

"I think you should."

"You look exactly like Maya. But I think I like you better," he said.

"Why do you say that?"

"Well, you have more warmth and compassion in your eyes. Maya's face is harsh and she wants everything."

"I've been told that," Leilani said.

"She's also vindictive. You have to be careful with her around."

"Yes, I've been told that too."

"Well, I'll do everything in my power to protect you if I can. You can live in this house if you like," he offered.

"Oh, no, I wouldn't do that and impose. But thank you," Leilani continued, "It's funny I have a sister. I have always wanted one. It's just too bad that she's a plain old bitch!"

"I know, Leilani," Grandpa Greggo said. "Trust me, when I heard I would be taking care of my granddaughter, I was thrilled. If I knew she would be such a challenge to deal with, I'm not sure I would have agreed to become her guardian. Anyways, would you like to see the house?"

"I would love to, but I don't know how Maya will feel about that," Leilani said.

"She has no say when it comes to this house. If you would like a tour, you will get a tour," he said.

"Okay, I'd like that. Can my friends come too?"

"Of course." He took them on a tour of his beautiful house. The gardens were nicely done and looked absolutely perfect. From the top floor you could see the ocean all the way around the house. It was a huge property. Everything was amazing inside too. The ceilings were high, and the walls were all painted beautiful colours. It was a very large house, and Leilani could tell that there was a lot of money involved in making it.

"Can you tell me a little about my father?" she asked.

"He was a very stubborn son. But, he was hard working and very talented, so he often got what he wanted from life. Unfortunately, the money and power got to his head sometimes, and he could be mean. Your mother put up with a lot."

"I'm so sorry to hear that. I heard she was a beautiful woman," Leilani said.

"Yes, she was."

"I have a necklace at home that is from her. I carry it with me always when I go out. That's the only thing I have from my real mom. I love my new mom with all my heart, though. She is so good to me," Leilani explained.

"I can see the happiness in your face. I would like to get to know you better while you're here."

"I would like that too," she said.

They wandered through the gardens some more and then he asked, "Would you like some refreshments?"

"Thank you for the offer, but I'll let you get back to your stamp collection, and I'll see you another time," Leilani .said "This must be a huge shock for you also."

"Yes it is, but so far it has also been a pleasant surprise. Can I give you a hug?"

"Yes of course." She hugged him and kissed him on the cheek. "Grandfather, I like you already."

"I like you too and I'm so glad you came to this island. Be careful, though!"

"Okay, we will see ourselves out. I'll call you when my mom is here and maybe we can get together and you can meet my mom and my dad," Leilani said as they were leaving.

"I'd like that a lot," he said, and he gave her one of his business cards so she would have his phone number.

The three of them got back in the Jeep.

Leilani said, "Wow, what a pleasant surprise. My grandpa is actually very nice! This Maya girl, on the other hand, I just can't believe someone could be so mean."

"I told you so," Niko said.

"She scares me too!" said Anita.

"Would you like to come in and have a drink?" Niko asked them as they pulled up to his bar.

"Sure!" they both said.

The bar wouldn't open until the evening, but Niko let them in anyway. They talked and had a few drinks together, and discussed their plans for the next couple of days.

"I can't wait for my mom to come here tomorrow! She will be so surprised by everything!" Leilani said.

"Until then, don't go anywhere alone!" Niko warned. "Does Maya know where you live?"

"Not yet, but she probably will when she sees my Jeep parked outside our bungalow."

"Oh, boy, maybe we can park it somewhere else. Like behind my place here," Niko suggested.

"You don't mind?" Anita asked.

"Not at all. I only use my motorbike, so there's plenty of room."

After they finished their drinks, Niko drove them home and then he parked the Jeep by the bar. The two girls relaxed that evening and played cards, as they had experienced a lot of adventure the past couple of days.

CHAPTER 26

THE NEXT DAY, LEILANI AND ANITA WENT for breakfast next door, the same place as always.

"Would you like to walk along the beach to the lighthouse?" Anita asked after they were done eating.

"Yes, but let's keep our eyes out for Maya's little sports car," Leilani said.

They walked down to the lighthouse and stood there for a long time. They were enjoying the view, but also people watching, as many buses filled with tourists drive in. There were many elderly ladies who got off the buses. They all wore bathing suits but then they would drop their tops. Leilani was very shocked by this, as no one went topless in Kauai.

"Would you do that?" Leilani asked Anita.

"I do it all the time! It's normal in Germany," Anita explained.

"Is it? I guess it's okay when you do it. At least you don't have sagging boobs," Leilani said and they both laughed.

"Yeah, when I'm older I won't do it anymore," Anita said.

They had a good laugh and slowly walked away.

"Would you ever take your top off?" Anita asked Leilani.

"No, not me," said Leilani.

"I'm sure you have beautiful breasts!" Anita said encouragingly.

"I'm just scared that everyone will look at me like a piece of meat!"

"Don't think that. It's normal here, so everyone is used to it," Anita explained.

"No, it's not me, though. At home when I'm alone I go skinny dipping sometimes, but that's different. I just didn't grow up accepting that this was normal," Leilani explained.

They started walking back to their place.

"Don't fall in love with Josh when he gets here, by the way!" Leilani warned.

"Why would you think I'd fall in love with him?" Anita asked.

"You'll see, every woman does."

"Okay, I won't. But he does have a son, doesn't he?" Anita asked.

"Yes, he does. Actually, if you come back to Kauai with me you'll get to meet him. His name is Damian. Right now he goes to school at Harvard because he is getting a degree in law. I think he'll be your type," Leilani said.

"I'm interested already," said Anita.

They got home and sat outside for a while. They discussed going to Hawaii, and where they would go once they got there.

"Maybe we can rent a boat and go around the island today!" suggested Anita. "There's a nice secluded beach on the west side of the island. We can have it all to ourselves!"

"That sounds like fun, but it is getting a little late. Maybe another day when we have more time," Leilani said.

"Okay. Well then, how about we go up the side of the mountain? There's a farmer's market up there, and a really nice restaurant." Anita suggested.

"Sure, that's a great idea!"

They walk to Nico's bar, get into their Jeep, and drive up the mountainside, into the little village. They walked up and down the village roads and looked at what the merchants were selling. Anita bought quite a few spices and some jewelry to take home to her parents.

They then made their way up to the little restaurant.

"What a cute little place!" said Leilani. They walked up to the front patio and sat down at a little table with a checkered tablecloth on it.

"Hello there," said the waiter. "What can I get for you?"

"What do you recommend to drink?" Anita asked.

"Beer is perfect for a hot day like this," he said.

They ordered a beer each and tzatziki with pita bread and fish. Everything was so tasty with lots of good spices and flavours.

"Have I seen you in town before?" the waiter asked Leilani.

"No, you're thinking of my twin sister. I just found out about her."

"Oh, my goodness. You two really do look alike. What's your name?" he asked.

"Leilani. It means 'heavenly lei' in Hawaiian. Like a garland with flowers," she explained.

"What a beautiful name."

"Thank you. This is my friend Anita. We go to school together in Austria."

"Nice to meet you!" he said to Anita. "What are you taking in school?"

"Music. I play the piano, I've played for the past six years. I also study a few languages."

"Wow, very impressive!" he said.

"Thank you," she said, blushing.

Surprising them both, he took a seat with them. They didn't mind at all, because he had been so nice.

"Can I give you some advice about your twin sister?" he asked.

"Sure," Leilani said, "but first, can we buy you a beer?"

"Oh, I'd love one, but I'm still technically working."

"You're sitting with us, though!" Anita said.

"Okay, but just one."

They asked another waiter to bring him over a beer and to put it on their tab.

After he took his first sip he began. "If I were you I would stay out of her way. She causes a lot of trouble for everyone on the island. I don't know her personally, but I know she is bad news. If she has it in for you, she will go after you. She might be watching, you so be careful. She has her ways. So stay close to your place and don't venture out anywhere alone."

"Wow," Leilani said. "It sounds like my sister has hurt a lot of people on this island. It's sad, really. But yes, we will be careful."

"Yes," Anita said. "We've been sticking together at all times."

After a while Leilani said, "Okay, we'd better let you get back to work. We should get going. Thank you for everything, especially the advice."

"Okay. It was nice meeting you girls. Have a good evening!"

They paid their bill and left. "What a nice man and what a cute place!" Anita said.

"It is cute," Leilani agreed. They got into the Jeep, and Leilani started driving them back to their bungalow. As they were nearing it, they noticed the silver sports car.

"Uh-oh, here comes trouble," Anita said.

The sports car came closer to them. Leilani continued to drive calmly, until she noticed it was following them.

"What is she doing? She is getting so close to us!" Anita panicked.

"Let's hurry it up then!" Leilani said as she stepped on the gas.

But the Jeep didn't have as much power, so the sports car caught up and started honking at them. Leilani kept driving and tried to throw her off.

"Be careful!" Anita cried as she clung to the door when Leilani turned a sharp corner.

As the sports car approached, Leilani tried to throw it off by moving into the opposite lane and speeding up. As she did this, all of a sudden, another car came around the corner, coming directly towards them. Their only way out was to pull onto the beach, directly over the curb.

Leilani did this, and Maya pulled up near them.

She got out of the car and started to scream at them. "How dare you disrespect me on my island!"

"You lay one hand on me or Anita and I'll flatten you on the street!" Leilani yelled back.

"You wouldn't dare, you little bitch," Maya spat back.

Maya started running towards them, and as she got closer, Leilani didn't even flinch. She stood tall and grabbed Maya by the legs and flipped her onto her back. Maya landed with a thud on the ground.

Maya stood up with hatred in her eyes. "You'll pay for this, you bitch."

Leilani said, "I didn't do anything, you started this."

Maya just glared at her and then turned on her heels. She walked back to her car, got in and drove off.

Anita said, "Look at everyone!"

Leilani looked around and, sure enough, everyone around them on the streets was standing and watching, smiling or laughing in awe. They all gave Leilani a cheer of support or a thumbs-up.

"I just showed her who's boss. Thank God I took self-defence!" Leilani laughed.

"Yeah, you definitely did! You go, girl!" Anita said.

"Thanks, I feel so much better now that I know she is afraid of us," said Leilani.

"Now no one will bother us on the beach. The locals will protect us." Anita said. "Except I'm sure Maya has some friends on her side, so we will need to stay clear of them."

"I wish we had gone to a different island," Leilani said.

"Me too. You know, we should write a book about this!" Anita said.

"Adventures on the island of Kos'! they laughed.

They stayed at the beach in a cabana the rest of the afternoon. Then they had dinner and a swim in the ocean. Then they went to Bar 52 and had a nice coffee with Niko. By the time they got there, he already knew what had happened because word spread so quickly on the island.

"Good for you," Niko said. "You showed her who's boss."

"She really didn't have any other choice. Maya looked so vicious!" said Anita.

"When does your mom come in?" Niko asked.

"Tonight! Actually, I'd like to meet them at the airport if that's okay with you, Anita? They will be renting their own car but it'll be nice to greet them there," Leilani said.

"Not a problem!" said Anita.

The girls finished up their drinks, and then Leilani said to Niko, "Niko, thank you so much for all your help these past few days, since we've arrived here. We owe you dinner."

"Yes, thank you," Anita said.

"Not a problem!" he said, "but I will kindly accept your offer."

"Okay, let's get going," Leilani said.

Chapter 27

THE THREE OF THEM FOUND A NICE spot for dinner, and they all sat down and ate together. They enjoyed fresh Greek food while they looked out at the water. It was a sunny day, and the girls asked Niko where else they should go sightseeing.

After finishing their meals, they went out back to where the Jeep was parked. There they found that all four tires had been slashed.

"Oh, my God…" Niko said. "Guess who did this?"

"Yes," said Leilani, "It's not too difficult to guess. What do we do now?"

"We'll have to go report this, but as for getting to the airport…" Niko thought for a moment. "Well, I could take you on my motorbike, Leilani, and I can ask my friend to get you, Anita."

"I guess that could work," Leilani said. "Or I can call Grandpa Greggo."

"That's not a bad idea," he said.

Leilani dialed his number, and she began explaining the situation to him.

"Are you sure Maya did this?" he asked.

"Well, I don't think anyone else on this island hates me as much as she does," Leilani said.

"You're right," he said. "Okay, well, I have a driver and I'll send him over to meet you, and he can drive you to the airport."

"Perfect. Thanks, Grandpa," Leilani said and hung up.

Not much later, the car arrived, and the girls said goodbye to Niko and made their way to the airport. They arrived shortly after, and thanked the driver. They knew that Tashi and Josh were renting a car, so they had a ride back.

About half an hour later, Tashi and Josh finally arrived at the airport. It was a great reunion, and Leilani threw herself into Tashi's and Josh's arms. She introduced Anita to them, and they all shook hands.

Leilani picked up Tashi's bag and they all started walking out of the airport.

"Wow, you have beautiful friends, Leilani," Tashi said.

"Yeah, she is beautiful, but wait till you meet my twin sister."

Tashi stopped dead in her tracks. "Your sister?"

"Well, it just so happens that I have a twin sister, and she lives on this island," Leilani said.

"Oh dear," Josh said. "It sounds like we have a lot to talk about."

The topic was dropped until they rented the car and had arrived at the bungalow that Tashi and Josh would be staying in.

"So," Josh said, "tell us everything, Leilani."

Leilani told them the story of how she met Maya and her Grandpa Greggo.

"Wow," Tashi said. "I should've told you earlier."

"You knew?!" Leilani said.

"I knew you had a twin sister somewhere in the world, because your mom told me long ago, but I didn't know where she was. I knew she had been in Greece at some point, but I didn't think she would be on this island," Tashi explained. "What a strange coincidence."

"I'll say," Leilani said.

Leilani continued the story and explained the fights she had with Maya, and how her tires were slashed that morning.

"Oh, my gosh, this is dangerous," Tashi said.

"Don't say that, sweetie. I'm a lawyer, we'll sue them all!" Josh laughed.

"Josh, we have to be serious! This is not a funny situation," Tashi said.

"Don't worry, there's four of us, and one Maya," Josh said. "We'll be okay."

"Maybe you two should stay with us?" Tashi asked Leilani and Anita.

"No way!" Leilani said. "You two are on your honeymoon! I don't want to stay with you."

"Yeah, the girls should have their own place," Josh said. "They'll be okay."

"Alright, if you say so," Tashi said. "I think I need to meet your Grandpa Greggo."

"Yes, I think you should too. He wants to meet you as well," Leilani said.

Tashi stood up and walked back and forth, "I just wish I had told you earlier."

"Why didn't you?" Leilani asked.

"I don't know. Something just told me not to."

"Don't worry, Mom," Leilani said.

"You're right, I'll just go talk to her and straighten things out," Tashi said.

"Oh, no, that's not a good idea," Leilani said. "She is crazy, she won't listen." Leilani gave her Grandpa Greggo's phone number. "Here, why don't you call Grandpa now? It will make you feel better."

Tashi took the phone number and dialed it. She talked to him for some time, and then decided to meet with him the next day.

"Okay, until then, we need to have some fun," Anita said. "Let's all go somewhere for dinner."

They all agreed, so Tashi and Josh got changed out of their jeans, and into shorts. While they changed, Anita and Leilani waited outside by the pool.

Tashi put on a little cotton dress and her sandals, and then put on her shades, and carried her hat.

"Why don't you put your hat on, sweetie?" Josh asked.

"I just think it looks more fashionable this way," Tashi said. He laughed and kissed her.

The four of them went to Leilani and Anita's usual restaurant. They got a bottle of red wine, and had some tzatziki with white bread, and of course, a Greek salad.

"Now we all smell like garlic!" Anita said.

"At least we all do," Josh said, "otherwise, we wouldn't talk to one another."

Next, the four of them make their way to Leilani and Anita's bungalow, and the girls showed them around.

"It's cute!" Tashi said.

"But a little small," Josh added. "It's about the same size as your closet back home, Tashi!"

"It's big enough for us," Leilani said.

They walked back to Tashi and Josh's place and all sat by the pool.

"Are you sure you girls don't want to stay with us tonight?" Tashi asked.

Josh rolled his eyes, jokingly.

"No, Mom!" Leilani said, "I would be a honeymoon crasher!" They all laughed. "Just relax, Mom."

"Okay, but when it gets dark, I'd like Josh to drive you home." Tashi said.

"No way! We can walk," Leilani said.

"Are you sure?"

"Yes. We'll start walking now," Leilani said.

She and Anita both gave them hugs and left for the evening.

"My goodness," Tashi said. "What a beginning to our honeymoon."

"Yes it is. But please stop worrying. Those girls can take of themselves," Josh said. "Now come here and give your husband a kiss."

Tashi walked over to him and put her arms around his body, and they shared a nice, long passionate kiss.

"Oh, that was delicious!" she said.

"Was it?"

"I could taste every little piece of garlic," she said.

"Oh you're such a tease," he said and kissed her again.

Not much later they both fell into bed and fell asleep right away.

Meanwhile, Anita and Leilani were still up talking in their bungalow.

"Wow, your stepdad is one hunk of a man," Anita said.

"I thought you might like him," Leilani said. "Just wait until you see his son!"

"If his son looks anything like Josh does, I'm in love with him already! Those green eyes and lashes...mmm!"

"Damian looks almost the same, just younger!"

"Wow, do you think he would be interested in me?" Anita asked.

"Of course! I'll introduce you two one day," Leilani said.

"Come on, let's go in to Bar 52 and visit Niko," Anita suggested.

So the two girls walked there and sat at their usual table and had a couple of drinks. They talked to Niko about what to do with the Jeep, and decided to just walk and get rides from Tashi and Josh.

They spent the evening there, and time passed by quickly. They finally went back to their bungalow and talked in bed before they fell asleep.

"Wow, this vacation is more exciting than I thought it would be," Anita said. "It'll be nice to go see that huge house again tomorrow when we visit your Grandpa Greggo."

"Yes, that house is magnificent."

"Who do you think he'll give it to when he passes away?" Anita asked.

"Oh, I'm sure he'll give it to Maya, since he has lived with her since she was a little girl," Leilani said.

"Maybe he'll give it to you!" Anita said.

"I wouldn't want it! I don't want to live here," Leilani said.

"Why not?" Anita asked.

"My home is Kauai. I don't want to live all the way out here."

"Well, what would you do if he did give it to you?" Anita asked.

Leilani thought for a moment. "I would make it into an orphanage, probably. But a really nice one, where kids feel loved and spoiled, like they should be."

"That's actually a really good idea, Leilani," Anita said.

"Yeah, I don't need that big home. It's way too big for me, and would make me always think of my biological parents, and I barely remember them. It would haunt me a little," Leilani said. "But anyways, he will probably give it to Maya."

"Hmmm, I guess so," Anita said and she yawned.

"Should we call it a night?" Leilani asked.

"I think so."

They fell asleep quickly.

Chapter 28

THE NEXT MORNING, THE GIRLS HAD BREAKFAST and then called Tashi and Josh.

"How about we come down and see you? Unless you want to be alone." Leilani giggled.

"Don't be silly!" Tashi said. "Come on over."

Leilani and Anita gathered their things and walked over to their place. They knocked on the door and Josh opened it.

"Sorry, I already gave at the office, come back later," he said and closed the door.

Leilani and Anita looked at each other with puzzled looks on their faces. They knocked again.

"Didn't I already tell you I gave at the office? Josh said when he opened the door again. "But you might as well come in!"

"You silly old man!" Tashi said from behind him. "Let those two girls in and stop fooling around."

"Old man?' he asked. "Your mom always tells me I look old. Now tell me, girls, do I really?"

"Oh, no," Anita answered right away, "you don't at all."

"Well, let me see," Leilani said and inspected his face, "my mom might have a point."

"Oh, you crazy girl!" Josh said. "Come on in you two."

Anita and Leilani stepped inside. "Leilani, you are too much like your mother. Anita, thank you for being on my side. Unless you're just trying to be polite?" Josh asked.

"No, I mean it!" Anita said.

"Of course she does," Leilani said. "This girl is in love with you!"

Anita turned beet red. "I am not!"

"It's okay, I'm already taken, though," Josh consoled her.

They all joked some more and then decided to go swimming.

"Skinny dipping?" Leilani asked.

"Oh, no." Josh said. "Not a chance."

"Oh, yes."

"We do it all the time. You know the custom in Greece — all the ladies take their tops off," Anita said.

"Do you actually?" Tashi asked.

"No, I'm kidding. We don't. But the other women here do," Anita said.

"Well, in that case, I'm going for a walk on the beach," Josh joked.

"You're a nutcase." Tashi laughed.

"You should see it, though," said Anita. "Tourists come here by the busload, and all the big, old ladies drop their tops, and you can see everything."

"Oh, no!" said Josh "I don't think I want to go to the beach anymore."

"They do it at a lot of places," Anita said. "All over Europe."

"I know," Tashi said, "but thankfully back home in Kauai that is not a custom."

"Okay, well, anyways, let's get into the pool, with our tops on," Leilani said.

They all hopped into the pool and swam around for a while, and the girls tanned on the lounge chairs.

Finally they all dried off and changed because it was time to visit Grandpa Greggo. Leilani directed them to the house while Josh drove. Tashi and Josh were amazed with the beautiful white house when they pulled up in front of it.

They knocked on the door and the maid let them in and directed them down the hall to the living room. Grandpa Greggo was sitting on the couch, waiting for them with some tea and desserts.

"Hi, Grandpa," Leilani said. 'You remember Anita, and this is my mom, Tashi, and her husband, Josh."

"Hello, nice to meet you. Come on in." He shook all their hands.

"Is your other granddaughter here too?" Tashi asked.

"Yes, she's upstairs. Although I don't know if she will join us. You never know what that girl is up to. Please, sit down," he said.

Tashi sat down, and Josh sat beside her, putting his arm protectively around his wife. Anita and Leilani sat opposite them on the other couch.

They began discussing Greece, and the strange coincidence of Leilani travelling to the same island where he lived. It was very pleasant, and they enjoyed each other's company.

Just as Grandpa began talking about his son, Nick, Maya walked into the room. She was dressed up in high heels.

"Maya, come over here and meet Leilani's parents," Grandpa said.

Maya came in the room but there was only one person she wanted to look at — Josh. She walked straight up to him. "Nice to meet you," she said.

He shook her hand but saw it in her eyes, that she was up to no good.

Meanwhile, Maya was thinking of how to get him into bed. She looked at Tashi, but didn't say anything.

"Well, it's nice to meet you, we sure heard a lot about you," Tashi said.

"I'm sure you did, after everything that happened since Leilani arrived on the island and pretended to be me," Maya said.

"People thought I was you, but they liked me better because I wasn't so mean all the time," Leilani said.

"Hey, don't say that," said Josh.

"Okay, sorry," Leilani said.

"Well, what are you all doing here anyways?" Maya asked.

"Maya, you don't have any right to ask such a rude question. You can either sit down and join us, or leave," Grandpa Greggo said.

"It's my house," Maya said.

"No, it's not. It's my house," said Grandpa Greggo, "and if you don't watch it, I will kick you out."

At that, Maya turned around and went back to her room upstairs.

"Sorry about that," Grandpa Greggo said. "I am so happy you are all here and that I get to meet you. How long are you staying?"

"Two weeks," Tashi said, "but that's two weeks too long by the looked of it. I wish I was back in Kauai."

"I wish I could make it better, but she has a mind of her own. She is impossible to deal with," he said. "But then again," he continued, "my son, her father, was like that too."

"Yes, it was so wrong for him to do what he did," Tashi said.

"Yes it was. I never even knew about you, Leilani," Grandpa said. "Otherwise, I would've looked for you."

"Well, fortunately for me, I was able to raise Leilani, thanks to that," Tashi said.

"Yes, you raised a very good girl," he said.

At that, they decided that they should get going.

"It was nice meeting you!" Tashi said, and she gave Grandpa Greggo a hug.

"You too. I hope to see you all again soon," he said as they left.

CHAPTER 29

LEILANI AND ANITA WENT BACK TO THEIR place. Anita asked Leilani if she wanted to see Niko. They decided to go in to see Niko and find out what was new in town. On the way, they stopped and admired the beautiful ocean.

"Do you want to stay out here and watch the sunset?"

"Let's go inside and see Niko, maybe grab a cup of coffee also."

So they stepped inside despite the loud music playing.

"I wonder if they're celebrating something. Who knows?"

Some guys were dancing in a circle. Leilani said to Anita, "Don't you dare get into that circle. You will get us into trouble."

Anita replied, "I'll get us into trouble? Look where you got us into. You got us into a lot of trouble pretending to be Maya."

Niko called over from the bar, "Hi girls, come over here. There is some space for you by the bar." They went over and sat beside Niko. He asked how their day was.

"It was nice. We visited my parents and Grandpa."

Niko said, "Oh, boy, I hope it was nice. What would you like to drink?"

Leilani said, "I don't really feel like a coffee, maybe a nice cold beer."

Then Niko asked Anita, while admiring her beauty.

"Niko, I'd also love a cold beer," she answered.

Niko grabbed them two cold beers. The girls simultaneously drank their beers, enjoying the cold drinks after the hot weather they'd experienced during the day.

Somebody called for Niko from the other corner of the bar, so he had to leave. The two girls stood up and watched the dancing guys. One of them asked Leilani if she would like to dance.

"I would love to," replied Leilani, and she went over to the circle. The guy changed the music on the jukebox, interrupting his friends during their groove. He changed to faster music and danced with Leilani.

Niko stood beside Anita and remarked, "Look at those two, they could be professionals."

"Oh, Leilani is quite a dancer, much like her mother."

"Yeah? I would love to meet her mother."

"I'm sure you will. Leilani will drag her into the bar one day."

Once the music stopped, the other guys joined Leilani to dance.

"I think have I lost her for tonight," Anita said to Niko.

"You should go over there and dance too. If I wasn't so busy with the bar, I would dance with you," said Niko.

"Do you need any help?" asked Anita.

"I sure could use a couple of hands" replied Niko.

"What would you like me to do?"

"Ask the people over there what they would like."

So Anita went over to some tables and began to collect orders. As Leilani danced the evening away, Anita made quite a large amount of money in tips.

Once Leilani had had enough, she came back to Anita and asked, "What are you doing? Niko gave you a job?"

"Yeah, I'm hired full-time now. Look at all the tips I am receiving."

"Oh, wow, are we ever rich. What are you going to do with all that money?"

"Well, we can always spend it, can't we?"

At the end of the night, Niko offered both of them a drink on the house. "What would you like?"

"Well," Leilani said, "I don't want anything hot. I must've sweat off a whole pound of water after all that dancing. It was fun and I got my exercise for today. Do you have any mineral water?"

Niko found her a bottle of mineral water with some lemon.

While Leilani enjoyed her water, Anita said to Niko, "Well, I quit my job now. Look at all the tips I got."

"Holy smokes, I've never seen so many tips. How come they never tip me?" Niko asked.

She said, "Well, you're not exactly a good-looking woman, are you?"

The three of them cracked up laughing. Anita offered to share the tip money but Niko declined her offer.

"I've never seen this place so busy. It must be because you two girls are here, bringing all of the guys to the bar," Niko said.

"Well, maybe you owe us money?" Anita replied.

"Now don't get carried away," retorted Niko.

Afterwards they exchanged goodbyes and went home, and easily fell asleep.

CHAPTER 30

THE SUN WOKE THEM EARLY THE NEXT day. They went for a walk on the beach before grabbing breakfast.

Leilani asked if they should go get breakfast with her parents, but Anita insisted that they would probably like to be left alone.

"Well, if my mom needs me, I do have my cellphone," replied Leilani. Shortly thereafter, her cellphone rang.

"Hi, mom, we're just going for breakfast. Enjoy breakfast with Josh and we will come to see you right after we finish. See you in a short while. Bye," said Leilani on the phone. She clicked off her phone and she and Anita went over to the restaurant to their usual table and had some coffee.

Anita asked, "What do you think your parents would like to do? Do they want to see the island? We could show them a little bit."

Leilani said, "Mom's been here before, she knows the island."

"Well, since your mom knows her way around the island, maybe we can grab lunch somewhere?"

"That would be interesting. Let's do it."

They finished their breakfast and headed back to their house to make themselves presentable for later on. Tashi was already waiting for them when they arrived. She opened the door and welcomed them into the garden.

They discussed their plans for the day. Tashi told them not to worry about their car; they could go in Josh's car. Tashi left to get herself ready.

Once she was ready, they got in the car and drove along the beach before getting onto the highway. They entered a city and contemplated whether or not they wanted to park and check out the stores. They decided to park the car and walk around the city. Leilani headed over to the bank to find out scheduled hours for Josh.

"It looks like the bank isn't going to be open while we are here. They seem to close around lunchtime, like a lot of the restaurants and shops around here in Greece," Leilani said.

"What?" Josh asked. "That's very odd."

"The bank has very short hours and we can't wait for it to open later on in the day," said Leilani. "But Anita made lots of tips last night."

"What do you mean, Anita made lots of tips last night?" asked Josh.

"Well, we went to Bar 52 last night and while I was dancing the night away, Anita offered to help Niko with the tables and she collected a lot of tips."

"You guys did what?"

"We know the bar owner. Niko is our friend, and we go there every night."

"You do?"

"Yes, he wants to meet both of you also. We can go there tonight if you want."

"Sure. But anyways, what is this with Anita and tips?"

"Well, we went in there to get some cool drinks, I started to dance with a handsome guy and then Anita helped Niko because he was really busy last night. She took some orders and received money in her pocket for tips."

"Josh, if I can help you out with money, I can give you some of my tips," said Anita.

"No, no, I can manage for now, but thanks," said Josh.

"You guys like to have a good time in the bar, then?" said Tashi.

Josh replied, "They're old enough now they can have fun in the bar. I am getting a bit tired in this weather. How about we grab a cold drink right now?'

Tashi replied, "Sure why not, the girls will probably enjoy this too." So they sat outside, opposite the harbour, right where Leilani had sat when people thought she was Maya.

Another waiter mistook her for Maya again. Leilani corrected him and the waiter looked dumbfounded when he found out they were twins. "I thought you looked different. Your hair is a little longer than Maya's," said the waiter.

"Yes, that's right, my hair is longer," said Leilani.

"Well, that is some surprise. Anyways, what can I get for you guys to drink?" asked the waiter. "I was wondering why Maya was acting so nice." He took their order and brought back their drinks.

Tashi said, "I can see why you get in trouble."

"Yeah, especially when Marco came around and kissed you, huh?" said Josh.

"Yes, that was kind of cute. I didn't realize what was going on," said Leilani.

"I just stood there and watched the whole thing," said Anita. "I wondered, why is that not happening to me?"

So they all laughed again. When they had finished their drinks, they decided to get back in the car and go somewhere else. They ended up on a side road near some shops, where once again Leilani was mistaken for Maya.

Leilani saw Marco coming from the end of the road. "Goodness, there's Marco again," she said to Anita.

"I wonder what's going to happen," Anita said.

Tashi asked, "Do you need any help, Leilani?"

"Oh, no, Mom, I can handle this," replied Leilani as Marco neared.

Marco was not so sure which twin he was staring it. He exchanged pleasantries and began to ask which twin he was looking at. He grabbed her to give her another kiss but she pushed him away.

"Well, do you know which one I am now?" Leilani asked.

"Yes, I know it's Leilani now. Oh, my goodness, am I ever in trouble now."

"You are already in trouble, Marco."

"I'd better leave." He turned around and left the other way, shaking his head.

"Leilani, what are you doing?" asked Josh.

"I wanted to see if he knew who was who, don't worry he is not my type," said Leilani.

"I'd hope not," said Tashi. "I think it's time we take you off this island."

Josh took Tashi's hand and said, "It's time we get going."

People continued to stare at Leilani as they walked through the side roads. They decided not to grab lunch and went to get ice cream instead. They enjoyed their ice cream while people continued to mistake Leilani for Maya.

"This is starting to annoy me," said Tashi.

"I think it's kind of cute," said Leilani.

"I think it's going a bit too far," Tashi said.

They all walked back to the car while everyone looked at them and waved to Leilani every once in a while.

"Wow, this has got to stop. This is getting on my nerves," Tashi said.

"I don't mind it. I feel like I'm famous!" Leilani joked.

"Well, you can become famous back home in Hawaii. I need to get you back there," Tashi said.

"Alright, Mom, but let us enjoy the rest of the day without you worrying too much," Leilani suggested. "Anita, would you like to go to the beach?"

"Sure! Let's go," Anita said.

"Okay, well, maybe Josh and I will go shopping then. What do you think about that, Josh?" Tashi asked.

"I like that idea. We need to have some sweets in the house," he decided.

They all agreed to meet later in the evening.

After they dropped Leilani and Anita off at the beach, Josh and Tashi drove a little further up the road to where there were some little stores. They hopped out and walked past them. There were some clothing stores and souvenir stores, and finally, they came across a store filled with lingerie.

"Let's go in here." Josh pulled Tashi in without waiting for her answer.

They had everything in the store — bras, bodysuits and cute silk pajamas.

"Can I buy something for my bride?" he asked.

"Of course. Whatever you select, I will wear for you."

"Oh, good. I'm really pleased to hear that." He looked around and finally picked out a few things. Tashi watched as he picked out one piece of lingerie after another.

"Isn't that enough?" she finally asked.

"Oh, no, that's just the beginning!" he said. He then asked the sales lady if there was anything else in the store that she recommended. The lady showed him a few things, one of them being a one-piece lace body suit, all in black.

He had been hoping to find something like it. "This is perfect. What other colours do you have?" he asked.

"Well, we have red, beige, black, silver, and blue."

"Wow, okay, maybe I'll hang on to the black." He took everything up to the counter and paid for all of it. They left the store carrying multiple bags. They headed outside, grabbed some ice cream on the way to the car and then headed back to the bungalow.

Once they had put all their shopping away, they met Leilani and Anita at the beach. They had a fantastic time in the sun, and everyone went swimming except for Tashi, who liked her pools only.

After a few hours, Josh got a call. Tashi could hear him.

"What? Oh, no. How bad is it, Dad?" He paused, "Is Damian home yet? Okay. Well, I will make the arrangements for tomorrow. Is that soon enough?" he asked. "Well, hang in there, Dad. Love you too. Bye." He hung up.

"Josh, what's going on?" Tashi asked. She came over to him as he put his head in his hands.

"Mom is at ICU at Vancouver General Hospital. She passed out and now she's in a coma. They don't know what's wrong with her. Dad called and asked if we could come home. And we need to, Tashi. Damian is already on his way and will be there tomorrow."

"Oh, my gosh. I'm so sorry, Josh. I'm so sorry, darling."

"Me too, Tashi." He pulled her into his arms and held her to his chest.

The two girls stood behind them after hearing everything and were quiet like church mice, not knowing what to say.

"Okay, well, do you want to book the flight for tomorrow and I'll talk to the girls?" Tashi said.

"Yes, let's do that." Josh walked back to the bungalow while the three girls stayed on the beach.

"Look, girls," Tashi began. "We have to go back home tomorrow. I think you heard everything."

They nodded.

"I would like for you two to come along. I don't want you alone on this island with everything going on with Maya. It's not safe. Anita, I'd love you to come with us too. Would you like to?"

"I'd love to. I just have to call my parents," Anita said.

"Yes, of course. Let's head back to the bungalow and we'll let you call from there," Tashi said.

So the three of them packed up their beach things and walked back to the bungalow. Once they were inside Anita called her parents. She talked to them for quite some time, but finally she got off the phone with a smile on her face.

"I can come with you," she said.

"That's so great. It'll be nice to have someone with me," said Leilani. "I don't want my grandma to pass away." And tears started falling from her eyes.

"Oh, Leilani, don't worry, she'll be okay," Tashi consoled her as Anita gave her friend a hug.

"Sweetheart, no one says Grandma is dying. She is in a coma. And we need to go there because they always say that talking to someone in a coma will help to get them out of it. Who can do that better than you?" Tashi said to Leilani.

"You're right, Mom. I will try to help her rather than just sitting here and crying," Leilani said. "Okay, Anita, let's go back to our place and start packing."

The two girls said their goodbyes to Josh and Tashi and went back to their own bungalow.

When they stepped inside, they were in shock. All their clothes were lying all over the floor and on the bed, and they were shredded into bits and pieces. All the drawers were open, and not a single clothing item was left untouched.

"Maya" was all Anita could say.

"Yeah, it was her alright," Leilani said. "Let's grab the rest of our things and then head back to Josh and Tashi's place. I don't feel comfortable sleeping here knowing she can break in."

They went back over and told Tashi and Josh what had happened.

"Well, thankfully you two had your hand bags with your passports and documents!" Tashi said. "But it's such a shame. I can't believe someone would do that."

"Not just someone, it's my sister!" Leilani said.

Anita agreed. "It is crazy."

Josh then let them know that the flights were booked for them to fly back to Vancouver, so they all went to sleep, sleeping restlessly thinking of Maya.

The next day they took the flight through Munich and back to Vancouver. They arrived at around one o'clock in the afternoon and hopped into a limo that took them down to their penthouse. They made their way up and dropped their bags in the foyer.

Anita just stood in the foyer, a look of shock on her face. "Wow, is this an apartment?"

"It's a penthouse. My mom inherited it from her dad," Leilani explained. "You'll be nice and comfy here."

While the girls were talking, Josh headed straight for the phone and gave Damian a call. Damian was in the hospital with Grandpa, and they were sitting with Grandma Rosa. Josh decided to meet them at the hospital and asked that the three girls come along.

They all piled into his Ferrari and headed to the hospital. They found the room that Grandma Rosa was in and met Grandpa Ted in the lobby outside her room.

"Dad, I'm so sorry," Josh said as he embraced his dad.

"I know. There is hope, though, you know. She always pulls through, so I believe that she will this time too," he said.

Damian, Tashi and Leilani all joined in the hug.

Josh looked over at Anita, who was standing by herself.

"Come over here, Anita."

She walked over to them and Damian looked at Anita and pulled her into the circle. "Welcome to Canada, Anita. I have heard a lot about you. Sorry these aren't the best circumstances."

Everyone nodded in agreement.

"Don't be sorry, I'm glad I could be here with you."

Just then, the nurse came out and invited Josh and Tashi to go into Grandma Rosa's room. They made their way inside and sat down beside her.

"Mom, wake up! This is Tashi," she said as she picked up Grandma Rosa's hand. "I have so much to tell you! Please, Mom, wake up, we all love you."

Rosa didn't move, and her hand felt limp in Tashi's. Tashi turned around and started crying.

"Don't worry, sweetheart," Josh said. He took his mother's other hand and kissed her on the cheek.

"Listen, Mom, we're all here, and we all love you. We need you to wake up. We love you to bits and pieces, so please, please come back." They stayed in the room a little longer, and then Leilani and Damian came in to see their Grandma Rosa.

"Grandma, Leilani is here, and she loves her Grandma so, so much. I have a lot to tell you, so you have to wake up. You have to be around when I get married and when I have children, so you need to wake up. We love, we all love you, and Damian is here too and also needs you to wake up."

Leilani began crying again while she talked. Both she and Damian gave their grandmother a kiss on the cheek. Finally after some time they left the room as well.

"Oh, Leilani, don't cry. We will get her through this, I know we will."

They all decided to go home and get a good sleep. There was no use sitting through the evening because they would all fall asleep anyways. They all went to their cars.

As Damian stepped into his, he said,

"Anita, would you like to come with me? I know the Ferrari gets squishy sometimes."

"Sure," she said and got into the passenger seat.

Leilani looked over at Tashi. "Mom, I have a feeling that there will soon be a new romance between these two."

"Don't be so sure yet," Tashi said.

"Oh, I can see it. Didn't you see how he admired her?"

"I noticed," said Josh. "She would be a good daughter-in-law to have."

"That's true," Tashi said.

In no time, they were all back at the penthouse.

IV: THE MORNING HOUR HAS GOLD IN ITS MOUTH

CHAPTER 31

OVER THE NEXT FEW DAYS, THEY EACH took turns visiting Grandma Rosa. Also, Leilani and Damian showed Anita around Vancouver. In no time, just as Leilani had predicted, Anita had fallen head over heels for Damian. Leilani suspected that Damian also felt the same way, but she wasn't sure.

One day, while Damian was out, Leilani went shopping with Anita and decided she would bring up the topic that day.

They went shopping on Robson Street, where there was every type of store you could want, and a few malls nearby as well. In a couple of hours, Anita had a bunch of bags to carry home.

"Leilani, you didn't buy anything!"

"No, I don't need anything. I have a closet full of clothes." They continued to walk. "Do you want to go for some coffee somewhere?"

"Sure, I'd love that."

"I think my mom and Josh might need some time for themselves anyways. They've been with us since we arrived here!"

They continue to walk down Robson, past all the stores and towards one of Tashi's favourite coffee shops that she had recommended to Leilani.

"So how long can you stay? Did you ask your parents yet?" Leilani asked Anita.

"I can stay as long as I like! There are some online courses I can take if I need to. I'm sure we'll both be fine, especially you, since you passed all those language courses with flying colours!"

"Thanks! You'll be completely fine too. You're a little brainiac also," Leilani said.

Anita smiled and thanked her for the compliment. "You know, since we both play the piano, we could play music together, and go on tours around the world."

"Oh, no, that's not for me," Leilani answered quickly.

"Why not?"

"I want to meet the man of my dreams, and raise a family with a lot of kids."

"Hmmm… So where do we find this dream man for you?"

"Well, we can start by walking up and down Robson until I find him!"

Anita laughed. "I'm sure that you'll find him one day, and then you'll just know it's meant to be."

Leilani nodded her head in agreement. "I think you're right. What about you, Anita?"

"Oh, me? I think I already found the man of my dreams."

"Damian, huh? He's not finished with all his studies yet, though."

"I know, but I can wait."

"I'm happy for you, Anita." Leilani thought for a second and then continued. "So would you like to come to Kauai with us when you go back?"

"I'd love to, actually! I mean, as long as your parents don't mind."

"I'm sure they'll love it! And so will I. You can be my wing woman to help me search for my man."

"Girl, you don't need a wing woman. I saw that in Greece. You were perfectly capable by yourself!" Anita joked. "But honestly, I'd love to come with you. I'd just like to see Vancouver some more."

"Oh, I don't think we'll leave for a little while. We want to make sure Grandma and Grandpa will be okay."

"Yes, I understand that."

"We can do so many things here in the meantime! I can take you to Gastown and Stanley Park, and we can go to the aquarium. It'll be so much fun."

"I'd love that, Leilani!"

"And maybe when Grandma gets better, we can go up to Whistler. You'll love it there. There's so many people our age working up there. It'll be great."

"Oh, that sounds great! Maybe we'll find your dream man up there," Anita said.

"We can borrow my dad's Ferrari and drive up there together!" Leilani said excitedly.

"Is it a long drive?"

"It's quite a way to go."

"Maybe we'll take a bus. I don't know if I trust you to drive us there in one piece. I saw you driving in Greece. You were crazy!"

Leilani just laughed, not disagreeing.

"And anyways," Anita continued, "I'd like to get married to Damian one day, and how can I do that if I end up dead on the way to Whistler with you!"

"Oh, you want to get married? Does he know about this?"

"Not yet, but he'll find out eventually."

"Wow, your relationship is moving quickly!"

"When I first saw Josh, I wanted him, but I knew he was too old for me."

"Anita! Yes, he definitely is!"

Anita laughed. "Well, the great thing is that Damian looks exactly like him! He's so great in so many ways. I love him, Leilani."

"You love him already?"

"Well, I fell in love with Josh first, technically."

"Well, now I have something to hold over your head. If you're ever annoying me, I will just threaten to tell Josh!" Leilani joked.

The two girls continued walking down the street, and then picked up a coffee on the way back home. Anita noticed a beautiful jewelry store on their way.

"Do you mind if we go in?" she asked.

"Not at all."

So the two girls went inside, with all their shopping bags in tow.

"Hi, ladies, how can I help you?" a tall man asked when they stepped inside.

"I just wanted to look around," began Anita.

"Well, I have some beautiful pieces to show you." He showed them a few bracelets and necklaces, and then finally he said, "I also have this white-gold locket. It is one of my favourite items in the store." He pulled it out. It was heart-shaped. "You can put a picture of your loved one inside and carry it around, everywhere you go."

"Wow, I love it." Anita held it up. "What do you think, Leilani?"

"I think it's beautiful. I think my mom actually has the same one. Josh must have bought it here too."

"You can also put an inscription on the back," said the salesman.

"Yes, that would be great!"

Leilani asked, surprised, "You want to put an inscription on the back?"

"Yes," said Anita, "I'll write, 'from Damian, with all my love, forever and ever.'"

"What?! Are you serious!" Leilani and the salesman both looked at Anita, dumbfounded.

"Yes. And then I'll give it to him, and he can give it back to me!"

"Is this what young ladies do nowadays?" the salesman asked.

"No, but I will." Anita looked at Leilani. "Do you have a picture of Damian in your wallet?"

"Yeah, why?"

"Can we cut it up?"

Leilani shook her head in disbelief but nevertheless took out the picture. It had been taken the year before and he looked as handsome as ever.

"Can we cut the head off?" Anita asked, laughing.

"I guess so!" Leilani said.

Anita passed the picture to the salesman and said, "I'll take the locket, and if you could put this inside, that would be great."

So as they waited, they walked around the store. At first nothing stood out to Leilani, but then she saw something that caught her eye. It was a pair of beautiful earrings.

"I'll buy these for my mom." They had little teardrop hearts with diamonds on the inside. She bought the earrings, and shortly after, Anita's necklace was ready. They paid and said their goodbyes.

CHAPTER 32

EVENTUALLY THEY MADE IT HOME AND UP to the 52nd floor. Tashi was sitting by the piano, playing a sad song.

"Mom, why are you playing such a sad song?" Leilani asked.

"I'm just thinking of your grandma."

"She wouldn't want you to play a sad song!"

"You're right," Tashi said. "So what did you girls buy?" She looked at all their bags. "It looks like you found a few things."

"Oh, Mom, you should see what Anita bought." Leilani looked over at Anita, who was trying to motion to her to not say anything. "Anita, we're going to let my mom in on this secret."

"Yes, tell me!" Tashi said excitedly.

So Anita reluctantly passed Tashi the wrapped box from the jewelry store.

"Oh, wow, Anita, this is beautiful! It looks exactly like the one I have from Josh." She opened it. "Wait… Is that Josh?"

Anita and Leilani both giggled. "No, Mom, of course not. That's Damian!"

"Wow, they look exactly alike!" Tashi turned it around and read the engraving. "So, does Damian know you bought this?"

"Not yet," Anita said. "But he will. I think I'll slip it into his jacket pocket and then he'll find it."

"You are very clever," Tashi said to Anita.

"I only have clever friends, Mom." Leilani said in jest. She then pulled out a little box from her shoulder bag. "Mom, this is for you."

"For me? It's not my birthday."

"I know, but you've been so busy recently and you haven't had time for a honeymoon, and now you have to deal with Grandma being sick. You deserve this." So Tashi took the small box and unwrapped it.

"These are beautiful!" She held up the dangly earrings. "Oh, Leilani, I love them, thank you. They are so gorgeous. You are such a great daughter, and I'm so lucky to have you."

She got up and hugged Leilani, gave her a kiss and didn't let go until Leilani said,

"Mom, you're smothering me!"

Josh then walked into the living room and said, "What's with all this smooching when I'm not here?" He looked at Tashi who had tears in her eyes. "Tashi, what's wrong?"

"Nothing is wrong. Look at the beautiful earrings Leilani bought for me." She held them up for him to see.

"Oh, wow, those are beautiful." He turned to Leilani. "You are a sweet girl."

They all admired the earrings until finally Leilani said, "Would you like to see what Anita bought?"

Tashi looked at her. "Leilani, don't push it."

"What is it Anita?" Josh asked.

"Oh no, I can't show it to you." Anita said.

"Why not?'

"Because you'll tell your son!"

"No, I won't!" Josh promised.

"See, Leilani, you should have kept your mouth shut," Tashi said.

"Well, Dad is part of this family so I think he should know too," Leilani defended herself.

So again, Anita reluctantly pulled out the box with the locket, and handed it to Josh.

He opened it up, and pulled out the locket. "Oh, is this Tashi's locket?"

"No, no," Tashi said. "I have my locket. This is one Anita bought on Robson today."

"Oh, who's it for?" he asked.

"For myself," Anita said without further explanation.

He opens it up and looked inside. He was a little shocked and looked up with his green eyes at Anita. "Who is this man in here?"

"That happens to be your son," she said.

"And how did he get in there?"

"Well, I asked Leilani for a picture, and then I put it in there."

He flipped it around and looked at the inscription on the back. "Oh Anita, you're in love with Damian?"

"I couldn't help it," she said shyly.

"Well, I'd love to have you in my family, and I wouldn't wish for any more than that. But you know, we have to leave this up to Damian."

"Yes I know. I'm not pushing, I just really liked the locket," she said.

"Well, what happens when he asks who's in the locket?" Josh asked.

"I'll let him look."

"Oh, you are a wise girl, and a clever one too," he said. "You and Leilani both. You are one-of-a-kind."

Just in that moment, Damian walked into the apartment. "Hey, what are you all doing?"

"Oh, nothing," Leilani quickly answered. "Anita and I just got home from our shopping trip and now we're not sure what to do."

"Are you hungry, son?" Josh asked.

"Yeah, I am. I'd love a drink."

"Okay, I'll get out some wine." Josh suggested. As he brought out the wine glasses, everyone took a seat in the living room. Meanwhile, Anita was unsure where to put the locket, so she quickly put it around her neck.

Josh brought over a glass of wine for each of them, and they all chatted for a bit. Finally after some time, Damian, who happened to be sitting across from Anita, asked, "Anita, I love that locket. Did someone get it for you?"

"No," she said. "I bought it myself. I found it today on Robson Street."

"Oh, it's beautiful. I think I've seen it before though," he said.

"Yes, I bought one for Tashi when we were in Vancouver," Josh said.

Damian continued to look at it. "Tashi has your picture inside, right, Dad?"

"She does," Josh answered.

"Well, what do you have inside, Anita?"

"I can't tell you right now." Anita turned beet red.

"Why not?"

"I'll tell you later, but just not right now." Everyone else in the room struggled to hold in their laughter.

Damian stood up and walked over to Anita. He took her hand and said, "Can you come with me? I need to talk to you for a minute."

Anita stood up and walked with him down the hall, towards the roof garden.

"Why did you turn beet red in there when I questioned you?" he asked her.

"I can't really tell you."

"Can you show me?" he asked.

"If I have to."

"Well, I would like to know who you keep on your heart," Damian explained. He reached over to the heart around her neck, and opened up the locket. With disbelief, he stared at the image of himself.

He looked at her with his green eyes and said, "Does this mean…?"

"Yes, that's what it means," Anita spoke as she looked directly into his beautiful eyes.

"Do you really mean that?"

"Do you think I would wear your picture for no good reason?"

He took a deep breath. "Anita, I have fallen in love with you too." He continued to look at her and then said, "Can I turn the locket around?"

"Sure."

He read the back. "Oh, my goodness, and you did this all before you knew I was in love with you?"

"Well, to be honest, I sensed it all along. I knew there was something between us."

"I did too but, I didn't know it would all happen so fast. I didn't know you would buy this." He took a deep breath. "But it shows me how much you love me."

"I really do." She paused. "Although I did fall in love with your dad first."

"You did what?!"

"I thought he was so handsome when I first saw him. But of course, he's too old for me, and married. So I was so thankful when I met you, because you are perfect for me."

"And you are perfect for me." He took her hand again. "Can I take you in my arms, Anita?"

"I've been waiting for that." He put his hands on her face and looked into her beautiful dark blue eyes.

"You know you have the most unusual eyes."

"If anyone has unusual eyes, it's you."

He continued to look into her eyes, eyes that sparkled with all the love she had for him in that moment, and he felt like he was falling into them. He bent down very slowly, and touched her lips with his own, very tenderly. He then opened her mouth with his tongue and tasted the inside of her. She felt weak, and almost felt like collapsing.

When they finally came up for air she said, "Wow, I have never been kissed like that before in my life."

"I haven't kissed a woman like that. You're the first one." Anita looked at him and was about to say something, but he continued, "And I'd like to keep it that way."

She put her hands around his neck and then kissed him, and suckled on his lower lip, "Mmm, you taste good."

"I hope you don't eat me."

"I just might."

They started kissing deeply, and soon lost track of time. After a while Damian pulled back and said, "Maybe we should go back to the others, because if we continue this, I'm going to have to take you to bed. But I'd like to wait a little for that."

Anita blushed and gave him a quick peck. "Okay, if you say so. Maybe I'll go back first to not make it too obvious, and then you can follow behind after."

"Good idea," he said. She walked away and Damian leaned up against a wall. *Oh, my God*, he said to himself, *What a woman. I have to have her for myself.* After some time, Damian walked back into the living room to find everyone sitting together, still drinking the wine and talking. He took a seat beside Anita.

"Well," Josh said, "it's getting late but before we all go to bed, who would like to play the piano?"

"Leilani should play!" Tashi suggested.

"Mom, how about the two of us?" Leilani asked.

"No, I think I want to stay here snuggled up to my husband."

"Alright, I'll do it myself then." Leilani sat in front of the piano. "Actually, since I'm going to be working hard, I think I deserve another glass of wine."

"Alright, it's a deal," Josh said and poured her some more.

Leilani then started playing and it was so beautiful. Her fingers moved so quickly and easily, and she flowed from one song to the next. Tashi was cuddled up next to Josh, and he had his arm draped around her, and Damian did the same to Anita. They all listened as she played Mozart and Beethoven. It was flawless and perfect.

After an hour, Leilani took a sip of wine and said, "Well, I can give you all my CDs if you want to keep listening, but I'm going so bed, I am so tired!"

"That was beautiful, sweetheart. I think we should all go to bed," Tashi said. So slowly, everyone stood up and put their wine glasses away. Before he went to bed, Josh called the hospital to check to see how his mom was doing. He updated the family that nothing had changed.

Tashi and Josh went into their bedroom and Josh said, "Well, I guess you and I won't be doing anything special tonight. We will just shower, and spoon in bed."

"That actually sounds great for tonight, I'm so exhausted," Tashi agreed. In no time, they were in each other's arms and in la la land.

Chapter 33

THE NEXT MORNING, JOSH WAS THE FIRST one up and he was already making breakfast in the kitchen.

"Good morning," Tashi said as she walked into the kitchen.

"Good morning, beautiful." He gave her a peck on the lips. "How did you sleep last night?"

"So great," she said. "Let's hope today is a good day and we hear some good news about your mom."

"Yes, I hope so." He stirred something in a bowl as he talked.

"What are you making there?" She looked over his shoulder.

"I'm making pancakes for my lovely wife — just how she likes them, with blueberries and a lot of butter."

Tashi gave him a kiss on the cheek. "Well, aren't I lucky?" She sat by the island and waited as he finished cooking.

Then they sat and ate together. While they were eating, Josh tickled her and she tickled him back.

"So, would you like to go back to bed and fool around together?" he whispered in her ear.

"Now? With everyone in the house?"

"Why not?" he asked.

"One of them might hear us!"

"Fine, you're right. I was just testing you."

"Testing me? So what if I said yes?"

"Well, then I would be obliged to agree," he said.

"I see... Well, a lady can always change her mind, can't she?" A smile crept across her lips. "Let me take a shower first."

So Tashi went to take a shower, while Josh walked over to the roof garden and began to water the plants and clean up a bit. He was still outside when Tashi came out, dressed in shorts and a cute top.

"So, what did my lady decide?" he asked.

"I'm sorry, Josh," she kissed him, "but we'll have to wait for another time because the girls are up already."

"Alright, I guess I will wait." He fakes a sigh.

They finished watering the plants and then sat outside together, enjoying the early morning air. Josh brought them both some coffee and they drank it slowly. After Josh finished his coffee, he left to do some work in the office, but Tashi stayed sitting outside, basking in the sunshine. Eventually Leilani, Anita and Damian also joined her. They start talking among each other, and Tashi just laid her head back to listen. She thought about how wonderful it was to have all these young people in her life. It was such a pleasure to be around them. They were always full of life, and excited for the future ahead of them.

Damian interrupted her thoughts when he asked, "Mom, I heard that you and Dad bought a property in Kauai?"

"Yes, I would like to build a new house there," she said excitedly. "I already made a rough design of what I want it to look like. I just need to hire an architect."

"Yeah, Dad told me all about it. He says he loves it." He took a sip of coffee, "Especially the master bedroom."

"Oh, what's in the master bedroom?" Leilani asked.

"Dad told me that there is bar attached and a TV, and huge closets. Basically everything your heart desires."

"Wow, Tashi. That sounds amazing," Anita said.

"Thanks. But this is still just a dream. I don't know if it will come true."

"Why shouldn't it?"

"There's just still a lot of work to do," she explained. "But I hope it works out."

"Mom, so if you put all this stuff in the bedroom, where will you have closet space, or an ensuite?"

"Well the entire upper floor is our master bedroom," Tashi said. "So I think there will be room."

"Oh, wow," Leilani exclaimed.

"Yeah, and all around will be a wraparound patio," Tashi continued.

"That sounds like a gorgeous house," Leilani said.

"Well, you'll be able to visit, but we will give the other house to you. And Damian, it will be up to you where you'd like to live," Tashi explained.

They continued to talk about the house and fantasize about future plans.

Finally Damian looked at his watch. "Hey, Mom, is it okay if I go to visit Grandma now? And then I'll have the rest of the afternoon off, so I can show Anita around Vancouver?"

"That's perfectly fine with me," Tashi agreed. "Leilani, would you like to go with him?"

"No, I think Anita and I will get ready together now and go for a walk, and I'll go later this evening."

"That's a great idea," Tashi said.

Damian got up and Anita followed him to the kitchen to clean up and talk about their plans for later that evening.

Tashi and Leilani were alone outside, and when she was sure that Damian and Anita were out of earshot, Tashi asked, "So what do you think of those two?"

"Oh, I think it's great! I couldn't ask for a better sister-in-law to-be!" Leilani assured her.

"Do you think that maybe everything is happening a little too quickly?"

"Well, the same thing happened with you and Dad, right?"

"Yes, it did. But we had some bad times too," Tashi explained.

"Right, that was unfortunate, but I feel like these two will be okay. They both have great parents."

"Oh, thanks, sweetheart." Tashi took another sip of her now cold coffee. "So do you have anyone in your life? You never tell me."

"No, I don't, Mom, I would have told you."

"Do you like anybody?" Tashi probed further.

"No, not really. I mean, I've seen men I like, but no one that I have fallen in love with yet," Leilani explained.

"Well, I'm sure you'll find the right one soon," Tashi assured her.

Chapter 34

THE NEXT FEW HOURS OF THE AFTERNOON went by quickly after Damian left. Anita and Leilani went to Stanley Park while Josh worked in the office and Tashi cleaned up around the house.

After some time, Tashi and Josh decided that it was time to visit Rosa in the hospital. After putting away all the cleaning supplies, Tashi went into her bedroom to get ready for the day. She put on her jeans, a blouse and the silver necklace with a locket that she got from Josh, and finally the lovely earrings her daughter had given her. She then put her shoulder bag on and make sure she has had everything in there. Finally she sprayed Donna Karan perfume on herself - — Josh's favourite.

Josh was in the kitchen and looked up when Tashi walked in.

"Look at my beautiful woman!"

"Mom, those earrings look great on you!" Leilani said.

"Thanks, honey, I love them."

Josh said, "And I love the locket on you! Can I see who's in there?"

"Of course." She smiled.

Josh looked inside and saw a picture of himself staring back at him. "Oh, good, it's not Damian. I just wanted to make sure."

Tashi laughed. "Oh, don't worry. I know my man."

"So I phoned the hospital and Mom is still there and in about the same condition. If you want, we can go there and release Damian so he can take Anita out. Leilani, will you stay here?"

"Yes. I'll go over there later and maybe read something to her. I was also considering taking a CD player and playing some of my own music for her."

"Leilani, that's a great idea!" Tashi said. "Okay, we'll be off then. We'll see you later." She gave her daughter a swift kiss and hug.

Josh took Tashi's hand and they went downstairs and headed off to the hospital in his Ferrari.

Once they arrived they went up to the ICU and saw Ted standing by the front desk.

Tashi ran over to him and gave him a kiss on the cheek.

"How are you, Dad?"

"Oh, I'm fine. I had a good night sleep so I'm feeling much better. But Mom is still the same. They still don't know what's wrong with her."

"Oh, she's just having a long rest," Tashi consoled him. "She'll wake up, though, don't worry."

"Well, I sure hope so. That's what the doctors also say. They figure they'll get to the bottom of it soon."

"So can we go down and see her?" Josh asked.

"Yeah, of course. But Josh, I'd like to talk to you before you leave."

"Sure, Dad, not a problem."

Josh and Tashi walked down to the hall to see his mom. Damian was sitting there, so they sent him off to take Anita out and have a break.

Both Tashi and Josh leaned over to his mom and gave her a kiss on the cheek. Then they sat down and Josh held her hand in his. Tears started running down Tashi's face.

"Don't cry sweetheart, please, don't cry."

"When I see Mom like this, I just can't help but cry. She was just so vibrant and lively, and now she is like this," Tashi explained.

"Well, don't worry, she will wake up, and everything will be okay." He looked over at his mom, "Do you hear that, Mom? You have to get up soon. Because if you don't we will move you and get you up ourselves!"

A smile crept across Tashi's face. "Oh Josh, you're so funny."

"See, you have to be serious with her, otherwise she won't listen," Josh said.

So they sat together in silence and waited.

After about ten minutes or so, a nurse came in and asked them to leave while they cleaned her up and ran some more tests.

Josh took Tashi's hand and they walked out and back down the hall.

"Let's go see what Dad wants," He said.

"Dad, what's up?"

"I'm so worried about your mom."

"I know. We are too. She's healthy though, so she'll come out of this with flying colours. She'll get better and then laugh at us for worrying so much, just wait and see."

"Well I sure hope so," Ted said.

"Yes, don't worry," Tashi assured him.

"Is there anything we can do for you, Dad? Can I go in to work for you?" Josh asked.

"No, thanks, though. I need to get my mind off things and focus on something different. Otherwise I'll just sit here and brood."

"What about in the house?" Tashi persisted.

"No, that's okay. I have a lady who took care of all that."

"Okay, well, if you change your mind, please let us know," Tashi said.

"So did you drive yourself over? Or do you need a ride?"

"No, I have my car in the parking lot. I'm not a cripple, you know!" Josh's dad began to laugh. "Anyways I should probably get going to the office."

"Alright, we're going to get going too." Josh walked in between Tashi and his dad, and took each of their arms.

"Josh, I'm also not blind, you know!" his dad said.

"I'm sorry! I forgot!"

All three of them laughed and headed down the elevator together. They walked out to the parking lot together and said their goodbyes.

"Well, it's just the two of us now. Nobody wants us! Do you realize that?" Josh asked Tashi.

"Well, I want you," she said.

"I want you too." He kissed the top of her head. "Would you like to do something tonight, just the two of us?" he asked.

"I'd love that. Maybe we'll go home and I'll make a nice dinner. Then Leilani can take the Porsche out tonight and do something with her friends?"

"Oh, I see what you're saying. We'll have the house to ourselves then. Good thinking, my wife!" Josh said.

They got into the car and drove home. Leilani was sitting outside on the roof garden so they went up to tell her about her grandmother.

"You know what, I'm going to go there now. I'll take my music and sit there with her for hours if I need to," Leilani said determinedly. "I'll take a book with me and play her my music. She's always loved that."

"Yes, that's a great idea, sweetie. You know you don't have to do this on a beautiful day like today, right?" Tashi commented.

"Yes, I know, but I love my grandma and I want to do this for her," Leilani said.

"You're an amazing woman," Tashi said, and gave her daughter a kiss on the forehead.

"Thanks, mom." Leilani started packing up her things. "I don't know when I will see you. I may go to Granville Island after and meet some of my friends."

"Oh, if you go, could I ask you to pick something up for me?" Josh asked.

"Yes, of course. What do you need?"

"Some of my favourite sausage and that specialty cheese they have too."

"Not a problem!" She gave them both a hug and then headed off towards the garage. They heard her as she drove off in the Porsche.

"Oh, finally, we are alone," Josh says.

Tashi agrees. "You know when you have kids around, you never have a moment alone!"

"Yes and I've been dying to take my wife in my arms and smother her with kisses and tell her how much I love her." He takes her hand and leads her to their bedroom. "Now do I want to undress you, or do I just go for it?"

"It's up to you." She smiles.

He decides to undress her completely. He started with her earrings, and then takes off her locket, explaining, "We don't want this to get ruined while we're being wild."

"Oh, it's going to be that kind of night?" Tashi asks.

"It's always that kind of night with my tigress," he says. He then takes off her watch and puts it on the dresser. He starts opening up her buttoned blouse and then takes it off and lays it over the chair.

"Mmm, you're wearing one of those cute bras we bought in Greece! I'll wait until I take that off." He takes off her sandals and then her pants. "Oh my, my, my. You look so sexy, Tashi."

Tashi does a little twirl.

"Wow. I just want to bite right into you! You're ripe to be eaten!"

She laughs. "I've never heard that before!"

"Well, now you have!" He looks into her eyes and says, "You know, Tashi, I can never get enough of you. I could look at you forever. Come here in my arms." Josh took her in his arms and held her for some time, and then they start kissing, first softly and then passionately.

"I think we need to get you out of this bra finally," he says and he swiftly undoes the back, letting it fall to the ground. He then slips off her panties and throws them off to the side.

"Well, what about me? Should I undress you?" Tashi asks.

"If you want," he says slyly.

"Of course I do." Tashi takes his shirt off slowly and lays it over the chair. She stands back and looks at him, walking around him.

"What are you doing?" he asks.

"I'm just looking at the perfect upper torso of my man. Everything looks like it's in perfect condition," she says.

He laughs. "I'm not a car, you know."

"Well, I just wanted to make sure that you're in perfect condition, and you are. Okay, now I will continue." She unbuckles his belt and unzips his pants, letting them fall to the floor. He stands there in his sexy underwear. Tashi walks around and checks out his butt. "Wow, so ripe he's ready to be eaten." They both laugh.

"So now what? Are you just going to spend all day walking around me?" Josh asks.

"Are you kidding? I definitely want to do more to you than that."

Josh finally has had enough of waiting so he picks her up in his arms and asks her, "Where would you like to be? In the bathtub or on the bed?"

"Oh, the bed for sure."

Josh drops her on the bed and she bounces a little.

"You know what? I'd better lock this door just in case somebody comes home." He quickly walks over to the door and locks it. On the way back to the bed he slips off his underwear and then crawls on top of her. He starts kissing her from the top down, beginning with her neck and her shoulders, and then moving over to her breasts. He always gets stuck there for some reason. He suckles them and then comes back up to her mouth and runs his hand through her hair while she does the same to him. He then kisses her all the way down to her belly button and her side. By now he knows exactly what she likes, and she begins squirming around on the bed.

"Do we have to do this?" she asks.

"Well, why not?"

"It's been a long time."

"A long time since what?"

"Since we had sex," she explains.

"What? Has it been?"

"Yeah and I don't think I can wait too much longer," she says.

"Well then, I won't make you wait. You surprise me all the time, Tashi, I want to give you a good time but you're so impatient!"

"We can have a good time after," she says.

"Sure, if I can do it again."

"Sure you can, you're a young man."

He takes this as his cue, and the next moment they are pressed against each other, having a beautiful love session.

When they are finished, he says, "Wow, that was beautiful."

"Yes, every time we do it, it's great. You and I make beautiful music together."

"We sure do. I could do this all day every day with you, Tashi."

"I could too, but if we did that we would have a whole closet full of babies!"

"Probably, and I wouldn't want that." They laugh together. "Do you want a few minutes to rest or do you want me to start all over?"

"Please, Josh just give me a minute."

"Give you a minute? I thought you wanted me to keep going!"

"I do, but I just want to rethink this new game I want to play with you," she says.

He lies beside her and just as he does she jumps on top of him and straddles him.

"Holy smokes! You told me you need to think this over!"

"I did. I thought and now I'm ready to go again."

"This woman is unbelievable. God, please help me."

"God won't help you. As long as I'm around you, he will leave us alone. He only listens to me when we're together."

"Well, that's good because this way I'll have you forever." Josh kisses her.

"Now, let me do my thing." She bends down and started kissing him on his earlobes. This drives him wild; she knows that.

"Oh, my, you know exactly what you're doing, don't you?"

"I know exactly how to drive you crazy," she says and then sticks her tongue in his ear.

"I can't take much of this," he says.

"I know." She goes to the other one and does the same. Then she goes to his mouth and started sucking on his lips, which she loves to do.

"It's amazing I still have a lip with you around."

"I'm just addicted to it." She then makes her way down to his chest and his nipples, and that drives him wild too.

Then he says," You know what, sweetheart? I think you have tortured me long enough." He flips her on her back and they again have wonderful sex together.

When they are done, they lie beside each other. Tashi puts her head on his chest and plays with his nipple, while he plays with her hair. They look so good together, just like a picture.

"You know, I have a painting at home for your mom, and I was going to surprise her with it. It's the two of us together." She looks over at him. "I didn't show it to you yet because I was going to surprise you too. Your mom always wanted a painting of me to put on the wall with the rest of the family, but I figured a painting of both of us would be better."

"That would make her so happy."

"I'm almost finished, but it needs a few final touches. When you go back to Kauai, I will finish it. When she's out of the hospital I'd love to have them over for a while, and then I could give it to her."

"That's a great idea," Josh says. "But first we need to make sure she gets the treatment she needs."

"I know," Tashi agrees.

After a few minutes of holding each other, Josh finally says, "Okay, did you have a long enough rest? Would you like to get up and get dressed?"

"Sure, but maybe let's hop in the shower first?" Tashi suggests. "I think we made ourselves pretty sweaty from all our exercise."

They go in the shower and when they are all finished, and have stepped out of the shower, Tashi wraps him in a towel. Josh does the same to her and then starts rubbing her down.

"Let's stop that or we'll end up on the bed again," she says.

"Alright, then. Put your clothes on, woman. Otherwise, I'll give you a spanking," he says.

"Okay, I will, because I have your fingerprints all over me again."

"I can give you more!" he says.

"Not right now." She starts getting dressed and so does he.

He has begun to put his pants on when she says, "You know, those are too dressy. I'd rather see you in a pair of jeans."

"Okay, well, you can get me a pair if you like."

So Tashi goes into his closet and pulls out a pair and brings them over. "There you go. That's better."

He puts them on and turns in a circle. "Is that good enough for you?"

"Mmm," she says approvingly.

After they are both fully dressed, Tashi brings out the hair dryer and lets the hot air blow through her wet hair. "Come here, Josh, and I'll dry yours a bit too."

He goes to her and lets his hair be blown up and all over the place. "What are you doing?!" He laughs as he looks in the mirror.

"Well, hold on a second, I just need to comb it." So she does and his hair falls perfectly into place as usual. She gives him a quick kiss on the lips. "Now get out of here so I can do my own hair."

She finishes drying her hair and put a little lipstick on and then she's ready.

When she walks out of the bathroom, she says, "Now we look good again and innocent as if nothing happened."

Chapter 35

JOSH AND TASHI WENT TO THE KITCHEN and looked through the fridge to make something to eat.

"I know Leilani is going to Granville Island after she visits Mom, but I'd sure love some of that sausage right now," he said.

"Well, would you like to go to Granville Island right now?" Tashi asked.

"Sure! We can eat something there."

Tashi got her bag and then they went down the elevator together and got into their Ferrari.

"You're going to have a tough time finding a parking spot."

"I know, but I'll just cruise around until I find one." Eventually they did, and then they started walking towards the market.

"Let's go look at the sausage and cheese first," he said.

"Wow, you are really hungry, aren't you? If you weren't a man I'd think you were pregnant," she joked.

They went into the market and Josh headed towards the sausage counter right away.

"Oh, Tashi, look at all these sausages…and these buns and breadsticks! Holy smokes. I wish we could get all of this in Hawaii."

"Well, we have most of it now." Tashi walked over to the cheese counter. "Oh, look. All these look great. I have to buy some to take home. All my favourite cheeses are here."

"Don't buy it yet, because cheese smells!" Josh pulled her towards the fish. "Look, they have ahi ahi! We could have that for lunch if you like?"

"No, we have that in Hawaii." They moved along and looked at all the flowers. They walked all the way to the end of the building, to a stand where you could have a nice barbecued salmon burger.

"There we go. This would be perfect for lunch," Josh said.

"Yeah, this smells great," Tashi agreed. "I'll go sit down and you can get us our food." Soon enough Josh came back with a tray full of food.

"We need a lot of napkins for these because they're so juicy and they always drip a lot of liquid."

"I know. Try not to get it on your shirt because the stain will never come out!" she warned. She took a big bite out of her kaiser bun and tasted the juicy salmon.

They devoured their burgers in no time. "What a mess!" Tashi looked around once they were finished eating. They cleaned up and then decided that to wash the burger down they should have some beers. They walked over to the Granville Island Brewery, where they each had a beer.

It was beautiful out that day, so they went for a walk around the island and looked at all the nice boats, each of them painted differently. They walked until their legs became tired.

Finally they bought some groceries from the market. They picked up a lot of sausages, and then decided to have a nice steak dinner the next evening.

"How about we invite Dad over for dinner tomorrow also?" Josh suggested.

"That's a great idea," Tashi said. "How many steaks do we need?"

"Eight?"

"Eight! How many of us are there?" she asked.

"Three girls, and three of us men."

"That's six."

"Well us hungry men might want an extra one."

"Alright."

So they bought eight steaks along with all the sausage, and then of course they picked up some cheese and bread as well.

They carried all their groceries back to the Ferrari, and on the way home Tashi gave Leilani a call.

"Hi, sweetie. I just wanted to let you know that we ended up going to Granville Island, so you don't need to pick anything up for us anymore."

"Alright, mom, thanks for letting me know," Leilani said on the other end.

"How's Grandma doing?"

"The same." Leilani sounded discouraged. "She hasn't moved a muscle."

"Oh, Leilani, don't worry. She will wake up," Tashi reassured her.

"I hope so. I'm going to stay a while longer, though. I haven't given up yet."

"Okay, Leilani, but when you get tired, just come home."

"I still might go to Granville Island later. Don't worry about me," Leilani said.

"Alright, honey, just text me later. I love you."

"I love you too, Mom."

By the time Tashi was off the phone they had arrived back home. Josh carried all the bags of groceries as they made their way up the elevator.

They unloaded everything and fill the fridge top to bottom. As they were doing so, Josh noticed that there was a message waiting for them on the answering machine.

"Tashi, this is in Greek, you'll have to translate it."

Tashi listened to it. "It's Niko."

"Well, what is he saying?"

"He says something happened on the island since we left."

"What happened?" Josh asked.

"I'm not sure, but he says we should give him a call."

"Oh, boy," he said. "Do you really want to call?"

"I don't." Tashi thought for a minute. "Maybe I'll wait until Leilani arrives home and she can give him a call."

"That's a good idea. Whatever it is, we can't help because we're not there anymore," Josh said.

Tashi nodded in agreement but continued to look at the phone. "Maybe I should phone. I'm anxious to know what happened." She looked at the clock. "And he is up right now, working at his bar. But I shouldn't disturb him. I'll just wait until Leilani comes home."

Josh walked over to her. "Don't worry about it, Tashi. Whatever it is, I'm sure it's okay. Let's just wait until Leilani arrives. In the meantime, don't think about it." He kissed the top of her head. "Do you mind if I go to the office for a little?"

"No, not at all," Tashi assured him. "I should go down to my studio too."

"Don't get too busy and start on a new painting, because we don't know how long we'll be here."

"I know." So off they went to do their separate work.

After some time, Tashi felt exhausted and went to find Josh. He was still sitting at his computer.

"Hey, Josh, how's work going? Would you like to have a glass of wine?"

"Yes, I'd love one. Work is okay, but there's a lot I have to do, especially since Dad is busy with Mom right now."

Tashi went to the kitchen and poured herself a glass of white, and a glass of red for Josh. He met her in the kitchen and then they brought out some of their groceries from earlier to snack on.

"I just love the smell of these sausages!" He cut it down the middle, just the way he liked it. He ate one, then two and then a couple more.

"Oh, my, I'm going to have a big fat man if you keep this up!" she joked.

"Oh, no you won't, you keep me too busy in bed. I'll never get fat." That made Tashi laugh. Tashi began to eat her cheese.

"Yuck, Tashi, that cheese smells disgusting!"

"But it sure tastes good!" she said and handed him a piece.

"No, thanks, I'll stick to my sausage."

They sat there and devoured the sausage and cheese for some time. Finally Josh asked, "Do you have more of that red stuff?"

"What red stuff? You mean the wine?"

"Yes, it's delicious!"

"You're finding everything delicious today," joked Tashi.

"Yeah, including my wife." They both laughed. "Boy, I had a good day today."

"So did I, except for visiting Mom. That still makes me so sad."

"Yes, except for that. Well, hopefully they will know what's wrong with her soon, and then they'll be able to wake her up," said Josh.

"Hopefully. I'm so proud of Leilani for going there and spending all that time with her grandma. I really think listening to her music can help her too."

"I agree."

"Did you know that Leilani meditates? She believes in the subconscious power of the mind. I think that is the power she is trying to apply to your mom."

"That girl definitely has something about her," agreed Josh.

"So are you full yet?" Tashi asked.

"Oh, no, I'm going to keep working on these sausages. What about you?"

"If you're not done, then I'm not either."

"Uh-oh, does that mean I'm going to have a fat wife pretty soon?"

"Don't worry about me! I don't eat all the fat sausages like you do."

"No, but you eat so much cheese!"

Tashi laughed and they both had some more wine and food.

Finally they were both full, so they packed up what was left over and put it back in the fridge. They then walked over to the living room, and Josh brought over the two bottles of wine.

They sat down holding their glasses of wine, and Tashi rested her head back onto his chest.

"I'm going to close my eyes now, and dream about you and me."

"Don't fall asleep, Tashi."

"I won't, but the wine does make me sleepy."

"We are still a little jet-lagged."

"Well, do you want to play a game to keep ourselves awake?" she asked.

"What kind of game? Like husband and wife?"

"No." She laughed. "Not that kind of game. Hmmm, what to do…"

"I know," Josh suggested. "How about you play the piano?"

"Oh, so I have to work while you just get to sit and relax?" she joked.

"Pretty much."

She laughed. "Well, I could, but I'm not sure my fingers will work because I think I've had too much wine."

"Try then."

"Do I have to?"

"No, but I would love for you to play the piano."

"Okay." She got up. "The things I have to do for my man are unbelievable."

"Thank you, now I can lie down on the couch." He stretched out.

"Oh, you little devil."

"Don't call me that or I'll have to put you over my knee and spank you."

"You wouldn't dare." She started tickling him.

"Don't tempt me…" he said as he squirmed to get away from her.

"Well first you'll have to catch me."

"I can run faster than you, little lady," he said.

"I don't think so!" She threw a pillow onto him and then started tumbling her fingers in his hair. He grimaced, and then she pretended to pull the hair from his legs.

"Okay, that's it. I've had enough!" he said jokingly as he stood up. "Now you're going to get it!"

Tashi started running down the hallway and ran out the door to the roof garden.

Chapter 36

SHE TRIED TO GO INSIDE THROUGH THE other door, but it was locked, so she had only one way to get back — though the door she came through. She opened it very slowly. She looked around and the room was quiet. All of a sudden, a hand reached up and grabbed her. She screamed.

"Gotcha, girl!" They both started laughing. "Now it's time to give you a spanking."

Josh picked her up and she was screaming with laughter over his shoulder. He carried her to their bedroom, put her down and wiggled her jeans off and she let him, but pretended to resist.

"What a cute butt you have, but it's going to be all red when I'm finished with you." She screamed and tried to wiggle away, but not before he bit her butt.

"Josh!"

"Well, I told you that you were ripe enough to be eaten!"

"That kind of hurt! You need to kiss it better."

"Alright, fine." So he bent down and kissed the spot.

"I'm going to get you back for this."

"Oh, no, you won't." He started tickling her.

"And I will tell everyone what you did. Just try me!" she gasped as she again tried to squirm free. Finally she got loose and said, "You watch out because I will come after you."

"Alright, alright, I'll stop." He laughed. "Come over here and give me hug."

Cautiously, she made her way over to him. Slowly she stepped into his arms and allowed them to embrace her. He kissed the top of her head. "I have so much fun with you, Tashi."

"Yes, but I got eaten up by my man! Do you think I'm a snack or something?"

"No, but you taste as good as any steak."

"Uh-oh, I better watch out now."

"Well, you started it. You didn't let me lie on the couch in peace and quiet!" Josh said.

She started kissing him but then stopped and looked up as they both heard something. "Someone's home," she whispered.

"Well, put your jeans back on."

So she slipped her jeans on quickly and then there was a knock on the door.

"Mom, can I come in?" It was Leilani.

"One second, honey!" Tashi checked herself out in the mirror quickly, to make sure she looked decent, and then opened the door.

"What's going on in here?" Leilani asked.

"I just bit your mom in the butt," Josh said casually.

"You did what?!"

"Well she was torturing me so I had to get her back," he explained.

"So, what's up, honey?" Tashi asked.

"Well, I just wanted to let you know that Grandma is the same, and I will go back to see her tomorrow. I promised myself I will do everything I can to get her out of this."

"You're a good girl, Leilani," Josh said and gave her a hug. "You know we all love you, don't you?"

"You do tell me every day, so I think so!" she joked.

"Are you hungry, sweetie?" Tashi asked.

"No, I ate on the island."

"Okay, good. Tomorrow we will have a nice steak dinner, and invite Grandpa over too," Tashi explained.

"That sounds nice!"

"Oh, and by the way, Niko called and left a message. He wants someone to call him, because something happened on the island," Tashi told her.

"Oh dear." Leilani looked at her watch. "I guess I can't call him right now, though. I'll have to call him in the morning."

"Yes, you're right. For now, though, don't worry about it," Tashi assured her.

"Well, I'm going to go take a shower and freshen up." Leilani started walking away.

"Okay, and then maybe you can play the piano for us?" Josh suggested. He loved when his two girls played.

"Oh, no, I'm not playing tonight," Leilani said.

"You won't play for me; your mom won't play for me. What am I supposed to do?" he asked.

"Dad, didn't you learn how to play?" Leilani asked.

"Sure but I need a lot of practice. All the plants in this house will die if I play for them."

"Leilani, would you like a drink at least?" Tashi asked.

"Sure, a glass of white wine would actually be great," Leilani answered. "I'll just go shower first and then I'll meet you in the kitchen."

Once Leilani left, Tashi said to Josh, "That girl must be so exhausted. You know that she's not only playing music, but also doing some meditating for Grandma. She's trying to wake her with her mind."

"Oh, I see," Josh said. "She sure is a good girl."

"Yeah, she is. As soon as you brought her here to the apartment on the first day, I loved her. I knew I would do everything in my power to keep her safe," Tashi said.

"And I will too, and I will keep you safe as well," Josh said. "Now, I will go get us some wine, and you can go lie on the couch and enjoy it while you have it to yourself."

"Okay, that sounds nice." Tashi lay down on the couch in the living room, while Josh went to the kitchen and brought out the wine and glasses. He opened the fridge door and quietly said to himself,

"I'd better not get any sausage, or the girls will make fun of me."

Tashi heard Josh murmuring to himself and asked, "What was that?"

"I said I'd better not get any sausage out of the fridge, because you'll make fun of me!" he said louder.

"Oh, my, are you saying you're hungry again?"

"Not quite."

"Oh, boy."

He came by and passed her a glass of wine and kissed her.

"You had a piece of sausage, didn't you?" Tashi asked.

"How'd you know?"

"I can smell it on your breath," she said.

They continued to talk about Leilani, and her use of meditation. "You know, I wouldn't be surprised if she pulled Grandma out tomorrow," Tashi said. "I've seen how much help it can be for other people."

"That would be amazing," Josh said. "Actually, I should give Dad a call now."

He dialed the number and waited as the phone rang.

"Hey, Dad, where are you?"

"Just in the hospital, about to go see your mom."

"Well, I just wanted to tell you that Leilani was there all afternoon, and I think she may have made some progress," Josh began.

"Oh, really?"

Josh explained to his dad how Leilani used her mind to strengthen her grandma.

"What a girl you've got. I hope that works," his dad said.

"Oh, by the way, you're invited over for steak tomorrow at our place. Can you come by at five?"

"That should work! Thanks, son."

"No problem, Dad, I'll talk to you later."

"Love you, son."

"Love you too, Dad." Josh hung up the phone. "Now, where is Damian? He's really hitting it off with Anita."

"Yeah, he is. They remind me of another couple and how they met a long time ago," Tashi said, smirking.

"It wasn't that long ago! How old is Leilani now?"

"Well, she's eighteen," Tashi said. "So that was about twenty-two years ago."

"That is a while ago. I'm in love with you as much as ever, though."

"I am too, Josh." Tashi gave him a quick peck on the lips just as Leilani walked out into the living room, looking fresh and glowing after her shower.

"I decided that tomorrow I will get Grandma out of her coma!" she announced. "I am determined."

"I truly believe you can, sweetheart," Tashi said.

"I do too," said Josh. "In fact, if you do, I will let you use the Ferrari for a whole week."

"A whole week? Really?! Thanks."

"Well, you will deserve it," he said. "Your mom and I will have to squeeze into that little Porsche."

Tashi started laughing her head off. "You mean I have to fit into that little sardine can of mine?"

"Yes, you will. We'll survive for a week though," he assured her. "Or we'll have to walk everywhere."

"Or I can drive you in the Ferrari if you like!" Leilani offered.

"That's true. When you were younger, we drove you everywhere, so now you'll have to take us around," Tashi said.

"Alright, you have yourself a deal." Leilani poured herself some wine. "So where are Damian and Anita?"

"I'm not sure, they're still out," Tashi said. "Honestly, we might have to get prepared for a wedding sooner than I thought!'

"I like that girl," Josh said.

"Me too," Tashi agreed. "I'm happy for them."

"She's not bad," Leilani chirped in sarcastically. "Honestly, I'm happy for myself too. It'll be great to have her as part of the family."

CHAPTER 37

BY THE TIME LEILANI HAD GONE TO bed, Damian and Anita were still not back home.

"Do you think they're okay?" Tashi asked Josh.

"Oh, I'm sure they're fine. Let's get to bed. Damian has a key and knows where the food is."

"You're right. Okay, let's get to bed."

Tashi and Josh walked to their bedroom.

"My butt is sore thanks to you," she said as she started getting undressed.

"Your butt is sore? I'll have to take a look at it."

"Oh, no, I don't trust you anymore."

"You don't trust me? There's nothing to worry about," he said.

She walked towards the shower and as she did he took a look at her butt. "Holy smokes! Did I ever take a bite out of you!"

"You're a nutcase," she said and stepped into the shower, Josh following her shortly after.

They kissed in the shower, but were both too tired to do anything more. They hopped into bed, and shortly after were asleep.

The next morning, Josh was up earlier than Tashi and already having some cereal when she walked out into the kitchen.

"Good morning, beautiful."

"Good morning! You're up early."

"Yes, I have some work to do. Would you like some cereal?"

"Sure. Thanks, sweetie," she said as he passed her a bowl. She poured some raisin bran into her bowl and covered it with almond milk. They sat across from each other and chewed quietly. Tashi looked up and studied Josh's face, and began to grin.

He looked up and noticed. "Why are you grinning?"

"With your hair all tousled, you look like a little boy."

"Hey, I'm no little boy! Maybe the top of me, but not the rest of me."

"Oh, I know that. So many women would be happy to have your hair, Josh."

"Well, it's mine! So they can't have it."

"It's mine too," she said, and continued to eat her cereal. After a few moments she looked up at him and started grinning again.

"Now what?" he asked when he noticed.

"Your green eyes just drive me absolutely crazy."

"What's wrong with them?"

"There's nothing wrong with them. They're just so sexy and so alluring. I can't stop looking at them. They are like cat eyes."

"You're my cat, though, my tigress."

"Well, you are my tiger."

"They are just so beautiful," she continued.

"Well, so are yours," he said. "They are so deep, they make me drown inside of them."

"Here we are sitting at breakfast, and we can't stop staring at each other's bodies," Tashi said. "Let's talk about your mom. What's on the agenda for today?"

"Well, I have to go to the office to do some work today."

"Okay. Maybe when Leilani gets up I'll go to the hospital with her," Tashi suggested.

"Sure, and maybe I'll meet you there with Dad," Josh added. "More coffee?"

"Please!"

So he topped up her cup.

They drank their coffee together until they were both finished. Then Josh went to do some work, and Tashi decided to play the piano.

She sat down and played Beethoven, hitting the keys strong and forceful. She then moved on to lighter songs, starting with her favourite, "When a Man Loves a Woman."

Damian came into the living room and sat down beside Tashi.

"Mom, move over, I'll join you." So they played the next few songs together, in perfect harmony.

Josh eventually came around the corner and said, "Is there a party going on over here?" He looked at Damian. "Oh, Damian, how nice of you to come home!"

"Well, of course I came home! Dad I'm old enough to come home when I want."

"I guess you're right," Josh said. "So what's your plan today, Damian?"

"Well, should I come to the hospital with you?"

"No, it's okay," Tashi said. "We are going, and Leilani will be going too. She wants to pull Grandma out of her coma, and will continue to play her music."

"And if she succeeds, I told her she can have the Ferrari for a week," Josh added.

"What? A week?!" Damian said. "Maybe I should try that out first. I can play some music for Grandma too."

"No, this is different," Josh said, "Leilani knows what she's doing. She is using meditation."

"She is good at that," Damian said. "She probably will succeed too."

"So Damian, do you want some breakfast?" Tashi asked.

"Sure, but I'll make it," he said.

"There's some sausage and cheese in the fridge," Josh offered.

"Nope, I ate it all yesterday," Damian said.

"You did what?!" Josh ran over to the fridge to check. He let out a sigh. "Good thing you were lying, boy."

Damian looked over at Tashi. "Honestly, what is it with him and sausage?"

Tashi laughed. "Well, he's just a sausage man."

Damian got himself some breakfast, and Josh got back to work. Damian sat down just with Tashi.

"So, did you two have a good time last night?" she asked.

"Yeah, I really did," he said. "Actually, can I talk to you about something?'

"Sure, do you want to go out onto the roof garden?"

"Sure."

"So, what's on your mind?"

"Well, is it really possible for you to fall in love with a person as soon as you meet them?"

"Well your dad and I did."

"I know, it's just so ironic that it's happening to Anita and me too."

"I think it's wonderful. Does she feel the same way?"

"Does she ever! You saw her locket."

"That's true. I think you two would make a wonderful couple. And we're all so happy for you. She will be a wonderful wife and mother for your ten or fifteen kids," Tashi said.

"Oh, no, no more than three!"

"So you talked it over, you two? That you want to get married in the future?" Tashi asked.

'Yes, we're making plans already," he said.

"You're making plans?"

"Yup, I'm going to get her an engagement ring. I want this girl to be my wife. I don't want anyone to snatch her away!"

"Good boy. You're working faster than your father did!"

"Well, I saw what happened to him and I don't want to make the same mistake."

"Good for you, Damian. I admire you," Tashi said. "So, when are you going to get a ring?"

"Actually, I think I may go today," he said.

"Will you bring her with you?"

"No, I will surprise her."

"That's a great idea. You're very romantic, just like your father. You realize he's quite romantic, don't you?" she asked.

"Well, I see how he acts with you, but I did not see it with my mom."

"Well, that's a different story."

"I never want to have a relationship like that," he said.

"Don't worry, you won't," she said. "Will you show me the ring first? Before you give it to her?"

"Yes, I definitely will."

He paused. "I also think I should meet her parents sometime soon."

"Yes," Tashi said. "You definitely should. It would be a good idea for the two of you to plan a trip to her hometown after you propose." Tashi thought for a minute, "By the way, when are you thinking of proposing?"

"Well, I'm not sure yet. I was thinking of doing it tonight when everyone is over for dinner, but it wouldn't feel right while Grandma is in the hospital."

"Well, maybe Leilani will get her out of her coma, and Grandma will be over sometime this week."

"That would be great," Damian said.

"In that case, you'll have to go to Germany pretty soon," Tashi said, "probably in the next couple of weeks. Will that work for you? When do you go back to school?"

"Well, actually, I was going to talk to you about that also," Damian said.

"What is it, Damian?"

"Well, I was thinking that instead of going back to the U.S. to finish school, I could transfer to UBC, and finish my degree here. That way I could also work in the meantime," Damian suggested.

"Actually, that's a great idea, Damian," she said. "Just remember not to get too overworked, and to focus on finishing your degree."

"I know. I will be okay," he said. "So, Mom, you'll keep this all a secret, right?"

"Yes, of course I will. You have nothing to worry about."

"Do you think I should tell Dad?"

"It's up to you! I won't tell him, but if you feel like you should, then you can. He won't mind being surprised though."

"Okay, maybe I'll let him be surprised then," he said. "So where are the girls? Still sleeping?"

"They should be up soon," Tashi said. "Leilani has to call Greece."

"What for?"

"Something happened over on the island, and Niko wants her to call."

"Oh, boy, I hope it's nothing bad," Damian said.

"Well, it really doesn't concern us anymore," Tashi said calmly.

"You're right." He started getting up. "Thanks for listening, Mom."

"No problem, I always will."

"I'm going to take a shower, do you need help cleaning up?"

"No, I'll do it, don't worry."

"Okay, thanks."

Damian walked inside and shortly after Tashi also went inside. She found the two girls sitting at the island eating breakfast.

"Good morning, girls. Anita, how was last night? Did Damian show you around?"

"It was great! He showed me so much that it was difficult to take it all in!" she said.

"Well, you can always go back and do it all over!" Tashi joked. She then looked at Leilani. "You should probably call Niko."

"Yeah, you're right."

"Niko called?" Anita asked.

"Yes, I think something happened on the island," Tashi said.

"Uh-oh. It's probably something Maya did," Anita said. "I'm glad we're not there."

"Me too. But I guess I still need to call back." Leilani picked up the phone and dialed Niko.

She began speaking to him in Greek and, of course, Anita and Tashi both understood.

"Are you kidding me? They don't know where she is? And how is he? I wish I could see him, but I don't want to come back to that island." She talked a while longer and then finally hung up.

"You will not believe what happened." Leilani let out a sigh and sat back down on the chair. "Maya and Grandpa Greggo had a fight. She ended up shoving him down the stairs. The housekeeper found him and called 911 right away, and the ambulance came to pick him up. He has a broken hip and arm, and a concussion."

"Oh, my God," said Tashi. "How can she do this to her grandfather?"

"I honestly have no idea," Leilani said, shocked.

"What else?" Tashi said.

"Well, she is missing now," Leilani explained. "She's nowhere to be found." She took a deep breath, "and Marco is gone."

"Marco is gone?" Anita said. "You mean she took him along?"

"No, I mean… They found his car with the doors open, and his body was lying over the steering wheel. She must have shot him." Leilani started crying.

"Oh, my God." Anita put her cup down and went over to hug her friend, while tears started pouring down her face.

"And the sailboat is gone," Leilani said between sobs. "They found it way out in the ocean upside down. They don't know where she is, though."

Tashi started crying too. "You know what? We left right at the right time."

"Yes we did," Leilani said. "I can't believe this."

They all sat in silence, letting the tears stream down their faces.

"I'm just worried about Grandpa Greggo," Leilani said.

"Yeah, we'll have to check in with Niko again later today," Tashi said. "I'm going to go tell Josh." So she walked down the hall. Leilani and Anita stayed, hugging and comforting each other.

Josh and Tashi walked back out to the kitchen together.

"Girls, don't worry about this," Josh said. "I know this is sad, but it sounds like Grandpa Greggo is okay, and we are far, far from Maya.

We have nothing to worry about." He gave them each a hug. They all sat together for a little while, thinking of Leilani's faraway grandfather, and ways in which they could help him.

Finally, once the tears had stopped falling from Leilani's face, she said, "We need to stop thinking about this and focus on Grandma Rosa."

"You're right, sweetie," Tashi said. "I'll come with you. We can go to the hospital together now."

"Yes, let's go. I'll just get ready and then we can leave. I need to work for this Ferrari!" Leilani joked, and they all laughed.

She got up and went to go get ready, and Tashi did the same.

When Leilani was all set to go, she came back out, but Tashi wasn't quite ready yet. Leilani went outside to the roof garden to get some fresh air, and found Damian outside.

"So Damian, where are you going to take Anita today?" she asked.

"I think we'll go to Whistler today," he said.

"I was going to go with her! And Dad says he is cooking steak tonight."

"Hmmm... The steaks are a valid point," he said. "Maybe I'll take her to White Rock then."

"Or Grouse Mountain!" Leilani suggested.

"Oh, good idea! Thanks, kid."

"Kid? I'm the same age as Anita."

"I know, but to me you will always be my baby sister."

"You really like her, don't you?" Leilani said about Anita.

"Yes, I want to be with her forever, Leilani."

"Well, I'm happy for the two of you," she said.

"Thanks."

Leilani looked at her watch, "Well, I'd better get going to see Grandma. I'll check if Anita is ready for you."

"Okay, thanks. And good luck today!"

Leilani walked in and found Anita in her room packing the last few things into her bag.

"Wow, you look gorgeous today, Anita. Damian will fall in love all over with you." Anita was wearing white shorts and a nice blue top to go with them, and her hair was loose and long, falling to one side.

"Did you put makeup on today?" Normally, Anita didn't wear too much makeup, as she always liked to look natural.

"Yeah, I did," she confessed.

"Well, I'll let you in on a secret, "Leilani said. "Damian is taking you up to Grouse Mountain today, so just be aware that your makeup may start sweating off. It gets pretty hot up there. And anyways, you look great without makeup."

"I like the look of it, though!" Anita said.

"It's nice for the evening, but I like you better without makeup. You look more beautiful," Leilani said.

"Okay, well, tomorrow I won't put it on," Anita decided. "But if I try washing it off now I'll have raccoon eyes."

"Fair enough," Leilani said. "Here, I'll get you some sunscreen, and I'll let you borrow a hat. The sun gets so strong up there."

As she started walking out, Leilani added, "Also, do you have a sweater?"

"What for? I thought you just said it would get pretty hot!"

"I know, but in the evening it'll get pretty cool, and who knows how long you two will be up there. Do you want to borrow one?" Leilani asked.

"Sure." Anita followed Leilani down the hall to her bedroom. Leilani picked out a navy blue sweater with embroidery on the front to go with Anita's outfit. "Perfect!"

"Thanks, Leilani." She put the sweater into her bag, and then Leilani passed her some sunscreen and a hat, which she also placed in her bag. "Well, I'll see you later. Good luck with your grandma today!"

"Thanks, have fun!"

Anita walked out to the foyer, where Damian was already waiting for her by the elevator with Tashi.

"Wow," he said. "You look great!"

"Thanks. Leilani warned me that we're going to a mountain, so I had to pack some extra things. Sorry for making you wait."

"No, that's fine! I'm glad you're prepared."

"Okay, you two, have a wonderful day!" Tashi said.

As they are leaving, Leilani said, "Damian, when you get home, you will see your grandma tonight. I promise you I'll get her up!"

"If you do, you can have my car too!" he said.

"Oh, no, I won't need it if I have the Ferrari," she said.

Anita and Damian left, and Tashi closed the door behind them.

"What will I do when that boy leaves?" Tashi asked.

"Back to Harvard? Mom, it's only two years," Leilani consoled her.

"Yes, that's true. He is actually also thinking of staying in Vancouver and going to UBC," Tashi explained.

"Well, that would be nice, and it's only six hours away."

"That's true," Tashi said. "What about you, when do you go back to school?"

"Actually, I was thinking of doing the same. I can finish my degree online, or I can finish it in Honolulu because they have a sister school."

"That would be great. You don't have that much left anyways," Tashi said.

"No, but I was thinking of taking something else, though."

"Like what?" Tashi asked.

"Well I'm not sure yet," Leilani confessed. "But I always thought I just wanted to raise a family, but now the more time I spend away from school, the more I miss it, and the more I think that I should pursue a career."

"Well, you'll figure it out between now and the time you finish your studies. You'll know when your calling comes," Tashi reassured her.

"I hope so," Leilani said. She hesitated for a little bit and then continued, "I was also thinking that if Anita goes back home to see her parents, I might go with her."

"Well sweetie, that may be sooner than you think," Tashi began.

"What do you mean? I thought Anita wasn't sure when she was going home yet." Leilani studied Tashi's face. "Mom…do you know something I don't know?"

"No!" Tashi quickly answered.

"Yes, you do. You're keeping something from me," Leilani said.

"No, there's nothing." Tashi said. Just then, Josh came around the corner.

"What's going on here?" he asked.

Leilani said, "Tashi knows something I don't, and she won't tell me."

"What is it, Tashi?" Josh asked.

"I can't tell. I promised I wouldn't."

"Oh," Leilani said understandingly. "I think I might know what it is."

"Just shut your mouth," Tashi said, "and pretend you didn't figure it out thanks to me."

Josh said, "I don't get it, what's going on?"

"We can't tell you!" Leilani and Tashi said simultaneously.

"Oh, so now you're both keeping it from me! I'm part of this family too. I should know as well," Josh said.

"Well, can you keep a secret?" Leilani asked.

Tashi laughed. "Leilani, I wasn't supposed to tell you, so you can't tell your dad!"

"Sure she can tell me, I deserve to know as well! Spill the beans, Leilani."

"I think I should let mom tell you," Leilani said.

"No, I won't," Tashi said. "I promised I wouldn't."

"Well, do you want me to take you in the bedroom and bite you in the other cheek?"

"You wouldn't dare! You saw how red it was the other night!" Tashi said.

"I don't want to hear about all this!" Leilani said quickly. "I'll just tell you. I have this feeling that Damian has fallen madly in love with

Anita, and we're going to see a proposal in the very near future." She looked at Tashi. "Right, mom?"

"I didn't say a word!" Tashi said.

"You don't have to. I can see your nose wrinkling."

"Oh, jeez."

"Is she right, Tashi?" Josh said.

"I didn't say anything, she just guessed!" Tashi said. She shook her head and walked away.

"Where are you going?" Josh asked.

"I'm leaving this conversation. Remember, I didn't say a word!" Tashi said.

Leilani and Josh laughed together. "She's going to get in big trouble," Josh said to Leilani.

Leilani brushed it off. "As long as we don't make any hints that we know, it'll be fine."

"So my son is going to propose to Anita?"

"Yes, and then they will probably go to Germany together shortly after, to speak with her parents," Leilani explained.

"I had a feeling this would happen," Josh said. "And I am so happy about it."

"Me too. The romance they have reminds me of the romance between you and mom," Leilani said.

"I trained that boy well," Josh joked. "Alright, well I should get back to the office." He gave Leilani a quick kiss on the forehead and then headed down the hall.

Leilani collected the last few things she needed to go to the hospital, and then looked for her mom.

"Mom, I'm ready to go. Are you coming with me?"

Tashi's voice travelled to her from down the hall. "I'm coming!" A few moments later she was in the foyer. "Okay, let's get going."

CHAPTER 38

THEY WENT DOWNSTAIRS AND INTO THE CAR. Tashi drove, and once she got out onto the street she said, "I feel really bad about telling Damian's secret."

"Don't feel bad. You didn't tell anyone; I guessed. He will never know anyways."

"I'm not so sure. Josh might say something."

"He won't because otherwise I'll scratch up his Ferrari to get even with him."

"Oh, Leilani, you are something."

Once they arrived at the hospital, they walked up to the front desk to make sure that they could go in and visit.

"Before you go," the nurse said, "the doctor would like to speak to you." She called him down, and asked them to wait.

The doctor came around the corner and asked them to follow him to his office. Tashi and Leilani both felt worried, unsure of what he was going to tell them.

"Well," he started, "I have some good news."

Both Tashi and Leilani let out a sigh of relief.

He continued, "Your grandma shows all the signs that she will wake up soon."

"Really?" asked Tashi.

"All the vital signs are okay, and her fever is gone. She moved a few times throughout the night and this morning, and I have a feeling that she may fully wake sometime today."

Tashi and Leilani both had big smiles on their faces and looked at each other.

"We're just not really sure what happened," he said. "We don't know how she improved." He then looked specifically at Leilani. "I heard that you may have helped her, though," he said. "I heard you used meditation and your music to try to wake her mind."

Leilani nodded.

"Right now, there is no other explanation, and I think that may have been what helped her."

Leilani's smile grew.

"So, I suggest that you go back in today, and use the same method as yesterday, and she might fully wake thanks to you."

"Oh, thank you, Doctor," Leilani said.

"Don't thank me," the doctor said. "You're the one who did all the work."

"You did it, Leilani. You are wonderful," Tashi said as she squeezed her daughter's hand.

"You are," the doctor said. "Have you ever thought about pursuing a career in medicine?"

"I haven't." Leilani sat and thought for a moment. "But, now that you mention it, I may be very interested in that. I have always played the piano, and I learned to speak many languages, but I know that I don't want to become a performing pianist, or to have a travel-related career. Becoming a doctor though, may be perfect for me." She looked over at Tashi. "I need fulfillment in my life, and this could be perfect."

"It would be," he said. "You would make a wonderful doctor."

"It looks like I'm figuring out what I want to do with my future sooner than I expected," Leilani said to Tashi.

"Oh, I love this idea!" Tashi said.

"You can come talk to me after you are done visiting your grandma," the doctor said.

"Alright," Leilani said. "Thank you so much."

After some more discussion, Leilani and Tashi left the doctor's office, and walked down the hall to Grandma's room. They sat down beside her and immediately noticed that her head was in a different position than it had been the day before.

Tashi took Grandma's hand in hers and said, "Hi, Mom. Tashi is here. How are you today?"

Grandma's fingers moved in Tashi's hand.

"Grandma, it's Leilani. I am here to play you more music again today. We are getting you up today! Give me a sign if you hear me."

Tashi was still holding onto Rosa's hand, and she felt a little squeeze in her hand.

"I felt something, Leilani!" Tashi looked over to her mother-in-law. "Mom, give me another squeeze."

Again, Tashi felt a gentle squeeze. "Leilani, I think you did it! She's waking up slowly!"

"I can't believe this!" Leilani said.

"You did this! This is incredible! I'm so happy." Tashi said.

"Me too!"

Leilani set up her music, while Tashi talked to her mother-in-law. She filled her in on the happenings of the world outside, like how they were planning a barbecue, and that of course she was invited if she got better by then. She talked about Josh's work and their home. She also talked about Anita, and mentioned that Damian might propose to her very soon.

Leilani looked up at Tashi.

"What? Don't give me that look!" Tashi defended herself, "I'm just telling Mom. She deserves to know, and won't tell anyone." Tashi then got up and started massaging her mother-in-law's legs and feet.

"Her legs are warm," Tashi said, and then tickled the bottom of Rosa's foot. The foot moved a little. "Did you see that, Leilani?" Tashi asked excitedly.

"I did! Mom, I can't believe we're so close! Okay, I'm going to turn the music on, that means you have to be quiet now," Leilani said to her mom.

"Would you like me to leave?" Tashi asked.

"Well, I don't, but it may work better, because my mind needs to concentrate on Grandma's mind. Our minds need to be unified."

"Okay, no worries. I'm going to go out and speak to that doctor a bit more."

"Thanks, Mom."

"I think I may take a taxi home, and then I'll let you drive the car back when you're done."

"Are you sure?"

"Yes, my sweet girl. I trust you, and need to give you your space to work on this."

"Thank you."

"I love you so much, Leilani, you don't even know."

"I know, Mom, you show me every day and I'm slowly starting to believe it."

"Slowly starting to believe it?! You'll believe it when you're driving our Ferrari, though, won't you?"

Leilani laughed. "I love you too, Mom."

So Tashi left Leilani alone with Grandma, and went to find the doctor.

"I can't believe this," she said to him. "Thank you for all your help."

"No problem. But really your daughter has done most of the work," he said. "The music she was playing is beautiful. Where did she buy it?"

"Oh, she didn't buy it! That's hers."

"That is absolutely amazing," he said. "She really has a gift."

"Oh, yeah, she is a gifted person," Tashi said. "I'm so happy that you suggested she become a doctor. I think she would be great at it. She couldn't decide what she wanted to do. She knew she didn't want to be a concert pianist like her biological mother was…"

"Oh, you're not her biological mother?" he interrupted.

"No, I adopted her when she was five," Tashi explained.

"Oh, I would've guessed you were related!" he said.

"No, her mom was my best friend, and she died in a car crash with her husband."

"Oh, I'm sorry to hear that," he said. "Well, she would've made her mother proud. She will become a great doctor."

"Thank you," Tashi said. "So the reason I came in to talk to you was to ask, what was actually wrong with my mother-in-law?"

"We still don't know," he said. "All of her signs were normal, except of course that she was in a coma. She must have fallen and hit the back of her head. Other than that, all of her vital signs are fine. Maybe she just needed a nice long nap!" he joked. "Sometimes, things like this just happen with older people."

"Okay, I understand," Tashi said. "Well, I should get going. I know you're a busy man. Thank you again for your help, and for inspiring my daughter to think about becoming a doctor."

"My pleasure," he said.

Tashi walked out of his office and down the hallway, out into the fresh air. She waved down a cab and took it home. She walked upstairs and found Josh still in his office. She gave him a kiss on the cheek.

"Hey, honey, where's Leilani?" Josh asked.

"Oh she's still at the hospital, I took a cab home and let her have some alone time with Grandma."

"Why didn't you call me to pick you up?"

"Well, I know you're busy, and I don't mind taking a cab every once in a while," she said.

"How's Grandma?"

"Do you have a few minutes so I can tell you about everything?"

"Sure, let's go to the kitchen. I need a break and a cold drink anyways."

So she took his hand and pulled him along to the kitchen. "What would you like to drink, my hard-working husband?"

Josh sat by the island and looked at his watch. "Well it's only eleven-thirty, so a little too early to have a beer."

"Well, in Europe it is past five o'clock, so why not?" Tashi poured him a beer.

"What about you?" he asked, motioning to the beer.

"I'll just have a sip of yours." She took a quick sip and then began her storytelling. She explained everything that had happened. First she described his mother's condition — that Rosa was getting better quickly, and that she might come out of the coma soon. She then told him about what the doctor had said to Leilani, and her plans to pursue a career in medicine.

"Wow, that's incredible," Josh said. "So she's spending all day there?"

"Yes, and hopefully by the time she gets home, your mom will be awake."

They both took a sip of the beer and then Tashi asked, "Hey Josh, before you get back to work, can I ask for your advice on some of my paintings?"

"Of course."

They got up off the couch and she led him into her studio. There were a bunch of paintings everywhere, and Tashi began looking through them.

"Ah, here they are!" She pulled out two big blue paintings, and hung them up on the wall, side by side.

"What do you think of these?" she asked. "I think I want to throw them away."

"Throw them away?!" he said. "Tashi, these are beautiful."

"I think they have too much blue."

"Well they are very blue, but I think that shows how connected the sky and water are," he said as he interpreted them. "I think they are different from your usual artwork, but that's why I like them."

"I'm not sure, these are some of the first paintings I did and I just wasn't very good yet."

"Well you can't just throw away your art! Especially if these are some of your first paintings. You worked so hard on these." He continued to think. "We can put them in my dad's office, or hang them up somewhere in this house!"

"Well, alright, maybe I'll ask the rest of the family what they think when they come home."

"I'm sure they'll agree with me." He placed his arms around her shoulders and crossed them over her chest. "I think you did a wonderful job with them. I think they are worth keeping." He kissed the top of her head. "So what else were you thinking of throwing away?"

"Well, I have a few more over there in that stash. I'm going to go through them again see what I think."

"Put them up on the wall, and I'll help you decide."

She put two of the paintings on the wall in place of the others.

"Tashi, you are ridiculous. These are all great! You shouldn't throw away any of these! You know people love your paintings." He kissed her again. "Leave these all out and I'll ask Dad and the kids what they think."

"Okay, Josh, we'll see what they decide."

"So what time are the kids coming home anyway?" he asked.

"Leilani should be home around three, I think."

"And Damian and his bride-to-be?"

"Oh, Josh, don't say that!"

"I'm only teasing you." Josh walked through the studio. "Okay, well, I should get back to work. I still have some things to finish before I go meet Dad at the hospital."

"Okay, thanks for your help."

"No problem. Don't throw anything else out before you ask me!"

"I won't," she said.

Josh went to his office and back to work. Tashi looked through the paintings again, and then decided to do some cleaning. She set up the table for dinner later, and polished some glasses. She set out cutlery and placemats. By the time she was finished, she was exhausted. She sat down on the couch and opened up a book, but reading it made her so sleepy. She decided to take a little cat nap.

Chapter 39

TASHI AWOKE TO SOMEONE TICKLING HER FEET.

"Hey, what are you doing?!" She squirmed as Josh continued to tickle them.

"I was just watching you sleep, and then I started to miss you, so I decided to wake you up!"

"I was so comfy though!" she said.

"I can make you feel better than comfy," he said. "You just look so delicious in your cute little shorts, with your beautiful hair draping over your body."

"Oh, Josh."

"I considered rolling you over and biting you on the other cheek," he said as he sat on the couch.

"Well, good thing you didn't." She sat up and straddled him, pressing her body against his.

"Oh, don't do that. You know what I'm going to do with you now that you've started this."

"And what's wrong with that?" she asked.

"Well, we don't have that much time until someone comes home," he said as he wrapped his arms around her.

"We can always go in your walk-in closet and close the door," Tashi suggested.

"Oh, Tashi, you are really tempting me," he said.

"Then stop holding yourself back." She kissed him on the ear.

At that, he picked her up and carried her to the bedroom. "We don't have a lot of time, so this will have to be a bit quick." He started taking her clothes off after he dropped her on the bed, and then he stripped his off. They decided to hop in the shower together, and they had sex in there.

They both stepped out smiling.

"That was the best shower I've had in a long time," he said.

"Me too. Now let's quickly put everything back on in case someone comes home."

They got dressed and then Josh said,

"I should get back in my office so that no one knows what we were up to."

"Okay, I'm going to do some more cleaning," Tashi said.

As she was walking out of their bedroom in front of him he turned around and said, "Thank you."

"For what?"

"For the lovely shower!'

"Oh, no problem. We can have another one tonight if you want."

She smiled and continued to walk. She thought about how wonderful her life was with him. And as Josh sat down at his computer, he thought the same about life with her.

Three o'clock came and Josh was off to meet his Dad at the hospital. Tashi did some more cleaning around the house, as she was expecting Leilani to come home shortly after Josh left.

Finally, she heard the front door opening and Leilani was running in. "Mom!" she said.

"What's going on?" Tashi said to her daughter.

"I have great news! I'm getting the Ferrari for a whole week!"

"Grandma's awake!" Tashi gave her daughter a hug. "Oh, I knew you could do it!"

"Yeah! She woke up to all the nurses standing around her bed and she just said, 'What the heck! Why am I not at home?' And then she wouldn't shut up after that," Leilani said excitedly. "She says she didn't remember passing out, which is good."

"Oh, that's great!" Tashi said.

"She knew I helped her out of her coma, Mom. She knew all along!"

"Of course she did!" Tashi said.

"She has to stay in the hospital two more nights. They will monitor her to make sure she is fully recovered," Leilani explained. "So unfortunately she can't come to dinner tonight. But she knows we will all be together and thinking of her."

"Yes, that's too bad, but I understand," said Tashi.

"Yeah, and Dad and Grandpa came in shortly after she woke up, so they're talking to her now."

"That's good to hear. They both must be thrilled," Tashi said.

"I think so. I filled her in about everything too."

"Oh, like what?" Tashi asked.

"Well you know, I told her that Damian is home and that he has a girl. I think I will tell him to visit Grandma with Anita tomorrow."

"That is a good idea!" Tashi said. "I hope you didn't tell her that he's going to propose?"

"No, I didn't tell Grandma that, because I knew she would say something, especially since she wasn't able to talk for so long! She wouldn't be able to hold herself back!" Leilani joked.

"Good thinking, girl. I am so proud of you. You have no idea." Tashi gave her a hug. "Here, take these and go out for a spin —" she handed Leilani the keys to the Ferrari "— and then you can come back and help me prepare dinner before Grandpa Ted and Dad come home."

"Okay, thanks, Mom!" Leilani said as she ran towards the door.

Tashi was left in the kitchen alone, feeling happy about the good news. She had known deep down that her daughter could do it, especially after today's meeting with the doctor, but she couldn't help but be a little nervous.

She began preparing dinner, cut up some vegetables and started cooking the potatoes. By the time Leilani got back from her first drive in the Ferrari, Tashi had almost everything prepared. Leilani helped her set out the wine glasses, choose a wine to serve, and decide what music they would play in the background. Just as they finished perfecting the last touches, they heard the front door open, and in walked in Josh with his dad.

Tashi went to greet them at the door.

"How are you doing, Dad?"

"So much better now that Rosa is awake."

"Oh, I bet. Isn't Leilani wonderful?"

"She truly is," he said. "So do you need any help with dinner?"

"No, thanks, everything is ready! Josh will fire up the barbecue as soon as the rest of the kids come home." She walked over to Josh and gave him a quick kiss.

"Hi," he said.

"Hi." Tashi smiled. "So what would the two of you like to drink?" she asked.

"I would love a nice cool, glass of beer," Grandpa said.

"I would like one too," Josh agreed.

"Okay, two beers coming up!" Tashi handed them their beer, then the three of them sat outside, and then Leilani came outside to join them with a glass of wine.

"So where is Damian?" Grandpa asked.

"Oh, he's out with Anita!" Leilani informed him.

"I like that girl!" Grandpa said.

"We all do. And between us, Dad, she may become a part of the family!" Tashi said.

"Well, wouldn't that be something!" he said.

"So, Dad," Tashi began, "I was thinking. And I think it might be nice to take Mom home with us to Kauai once she is out of the hospital. I think the warm weather will do her good, and it's very peaceful in Kauai. I could really look after her."

"Well," he said, "that maybe something to think about. I don't know if she'll go without me, though, because she always worries about me and if I'm eating enough and all that."

"Well, we have to convince her then!" Josh said.

"Yes, that's not a bad idea."

Just then, Damian and Anita came in. They had huge smiles on their sunburnt faces.

"Oh, wow! You two got some sun!" Tashi said as she looked at them. "You'd better put some lotion on!"

"Yeah, we'd better!" Anita said. "Do I have time to take a quick shower?"

"Of course, sweetie, we'll start barbecuing steaks now," Tashi said.

Anita motioned for Leilani to follow her down the hall, and two girls began giggling as Anita told Leilani about her day.

Damian and Josh started preparing the steaks together, while Tashi and Grandpa stayed on the roof garden.

"So, did you two have a nice time?" Josh asked Damian.

"It was great," he said. "I couldn't have wished for a better day. I love this girl."

"Yes, you remind me of Tashi and I when we were young. Does she love you too?"

"Yes, she told me," Damian said. "Dad, what would you think if I proposed to her?"

"Are you losing your senses?!" Josh said.

"No. I don't want her to go back to Europe without a ring. She might get snatched up by someone else."

"That makes sense. You'll have to go to Europe with her at some point though, to meet her parents."

"I had that in mind anyways, but I want to give her a ring beforehand."

"Well, your happiness is my happiness. So whatever you decide, son, I will support you. She is a great girl. I think you've found a good one," Josh said.

"What are you two up to out there?" Tashi poked her head around the corner to where the barbecue was. "Are you heating up the barbecue, or are you slacking?"

"No slacking going on over here!" Damian said. "We'll let you know when it's ready.

"Alright." She laughed and then went to sit back down.

Soon the two girls come back out, looking fresh. They sat down with Tashi and Grandpa, and Anita told them about her day with Damian.

After a few minutes of nice chatting and enjoying the warm Vancouver sun, they all moved inside. Josh and Damian brought the steaks in, and a new bottle of wine was opened. They each poured themselves a little and made a toast to each other, to their wonderful family and the health of Grandma.

Then they dug in. The steak was juicy and so easy to cut through. The mashed potatoes were perfect, and there was a boat of gravy to pour all over them. They also had garlic bread and a nice salad to go with their meal.

"So, Leilani," Damian said, "I hear you want to be a doctor?"

"Yeah," she said. "Grandma's doctor suggested that I become one after he saw me using meditation to wake Grandma up."

"That's great! I'm so proud of you, little sis," he said.

"She is very talented," Grandpa said about Leilani. "I will never forget what you did, Leilani. You made me so, so happy."

"Great job, Leilani," Anita said to her. "You figured out what you'd like to do for a career after all."

"I did!"

They all chewed in silence.

"Everything is delicious!" Anita said.

"So great!" They all agree.

"So," Josh looked at Tashi, "don't you think it's time we tell them the news?"

"Let's finish eating first," she said, holding back a smile.

"What news?" Leilani asked. "Mom, are you pregnant?"

"No, sweetheart, I'm not."

"Oh, I'm disappointed. I was hoping to have a little sister or brother. Wouldn't that be nice, Grandpa?"

"Well, I think they may be getting a little too old for that now," he said.

"Excuse me!" Josh said. "No one is old here. We are just making a decision not to."

Grandpa laughed. "Alright, whatever you say."

"So what's going on then?" Damian asked.

"Well —" first Tashi filled up her wine glass and then Josh's "— do you want to start?" She looked at Josh.

"No, the beginning is yours, so go ahead."

So Tashi began by telling them the story of how she and Josh met on the beach. She talked about Josh running after Hero, and how she stood frozen in the sand.

"Sorry to interrupt," Damian said, "but whatever happened to Hero? "

"He passed away from old age," Josh said sadly.

"Oh, that's too bad. We should get another dog," Damian suggested.

"We can talk about that later," Josh said.

"Anyways, sorry, Mom. Continue."

So Tashi continued her story of how they fell in love, and how their love led to a baby girl. She told them about how Josh didn't know, because he couldn't contact her, even though he tried.

"Why didn't you tell us?" Grandpa asked Josh.

"Well, I didn't think I could find her. I thought she was gone, either with another man, or that she had moved for good. I didn't know what else to do," he explained.

They were all shocked to hear that Tashi and Josh had had a baby together, and then they became even more shocked when Tashi explained what had happened to separate them.

"Really, Mom? Your dad did this to you?"

"You never met him, Leilani. So although I tell you about good stories of him, he also had a very, very dark side about him."

Leilani started tearing up. "Mom, I'm so sorry for you. So you never met her?"

"No, I didn't." Tashi started crying too. Josh took her hand and squeezed it.

Tashi carried on with her story. She explained how she went to Europe and then came back home, and after a few years her father passed away. She then talked about how she adopted Leilani, which they all knew already, but then she also explained how she saw Josh again during the adoption process.

"I've seen you looking off into the distance, with a blank look on your face many times, Mom, especially when you played the piano. You were thinking of her, weren't you?" Leilani asked.

"You saw that?" Tashi asked.

"Yes, and I couldn't figure out why you were so sad."

"Why didn't you ask?"

"I didn't dare," Leilani explained. "I thought I may have done something to upset you."

"Oh, sweetheart," Tashi said, "you never upset me."

"Mom and Dad, I'm so sorry to hear about all this," Damian said.

"Don't you start crying now too," Josh said, "or I will have to start as well."

Then Josh took over telling the story, He spoke about his divorce and how he moved his office to Hawaii to be with Tashi. He looked over at Damian. "Tashi and I never fell out of love. And Damian, when you met her, you fell in love with her too."

"Yes," Damian said, "That was the best decision you ever made, Dad."

"You don't have to tell me this son, I know," Josh said. "Every morning when I wake up, and every night before I go to bed, I am thankful for my wife."

"That is so sweet," Anita said. "I am getting tears in my eyes."

"Well, why don't we all have a good cry then," Leilani said.

"You guys, stop that. Good thing your Grandma isn't here, because she would be sobbing! You'll have to tell her this when she's out of the hospital."

"We will," Tashi said.

Josh finished his story, and said, "And here we are, and we've had some wonderful memories since then, haven't we, Tashi?"

"Yes, we have, honey bear."

"Honey bear?" Damian said. "Dad, I like that name for you."

Grandpa looked over at his son. "Me too."

"Thanks, Dad, I appreciate your support." He laughed. "Tashi used to give me animal names all the time— I was a fish, a bear, a swallow. The list is never ending."

They all laughed.

"Oh, you two are hilarious," Anita said. "I'd love to write a book about you two."

"I wouldn't put it past you." Tashi smiled.

"So, have you ever thought about finding your daughter?" Grandpa asked.

"Oh, yes," Josh said. "I contacted some orphanages in Europe, but it's very difficult to track any one down that way."

"Do have any leads?"

"Not yet," Josh said.

They all talked some more about Tashi and Josh, and their beautiful love story, and about the sadness of losing their little girl. They brought out dessert, and after they were all so full that they couldn't eat any more, Josh invited them to Tashi's studio to give their opinions about the paintings she made when she was younger.

They looked at the paintings that Tashi had wanted to throw away.

"Wow, Mom, these are beautiful! They're so different!" Leilani said. "Why on earth would you consider throwing them away?"

"I just didn't care for them. But now that you all say you like them, maybe I will hang on to them," she said.

"Tashi, I told you!" Josh said.

"I still don't know what you see in them."

"Well it's all the beautiful details. You brought them to life!" Josh explained.

"I don't think there's enough colour, but if you all like them, then I will hang on to them."

Damian turned around and looked at the other wall, "Mom, were you going to throw these away too?"

"I was."

"They are so great, though!" he said. "When I have an office, can I have one?"

"And when I'm a doctor, can I put one in my office too?" Leilani asked.

"Of course, you can all get one!" Tashi said.

"Well," Grandpa looked at his watch, "I am so exhausted from this week, and I want to stop by the hospital quickly before I go to bed, so I should get going." He opened his arms to Leilani. "Leilani, come here and give me a big hug. You made me so happy!'

"No problem, Grandpa," she said.

"I hear you will be getting the Ferrari for a week?" Grandpa asks.

"That's right.'

"Be careful and don't press the pedal too hard or you'll bang it all up!" he warned.

"I'm a great driver!" Leilani said.

Anita started coughing to cover her laugh.

"Okay, Anita, what's the truth?" Damian asked.

"I can't say," Anita quickly said as she saw Leilani's piercing gaze aimed towards her.

"Oh, just tell us!" Tashi said.

Anita laughed. "She'll kill me!"

"We'll protect you," Damian said.

"Well, if you must know, Leilani may have driven on the wrong side of the road multiple times in Greece, and just evaded an oncoming car."

Tashi turned white in the face. "Maybe we should rethink this deal…"

"Oh, no, don't worry Mom. I will never do it again. I was just trying to stay away from Maya."

"If you say so," Tashi said, hesitating.

Leilani looked at Anita. "I am going to get you back, you tattle tale!" she joked.

"Oh, no, you won't lay a finger on my girl," said Damian.

"On that note, I'm going to head out," said Grandpa. He said his goodbyes and headed out the door. Anita and Leilani helped with cleaning up, and put everything the way it was before.

"Well, I am so tired," Tashi said. "I think I will head to bed."

"Me too," Josh said. "Feel free to stay up, kids."

"I think we will watch a movie while you two old people go to bed," Damian joked.

"Like I said earlier. We are not old, we just make decisions that make us look old sometimes." Josh said. "So what are you plans for tomorrow?"

Damian, Anita and Leilani discussed their plans and then decided to go to Whistler the next day.

"That's a great idea," Josh said. He placed his hand on Tashi's back, and walked with her to their bedroom.

CHAPTER 40

"WOW, WHAT AN EVENING THAT WAS!' JOSH said. "Poor Dad, he has a lot to digest."

"Yes, we told him a lot of shocking news," Tashi agreed.

They got ready for bed and then lay down in each other's arms.

"I think we should just spoon tonight," he said. "I'm beat."

"I think so too," Tashi said. She gave him a goodnight kiss and then, as he laid his head down, she gave him a kiss on the ear.

"Hey, what are you doing?" he asked.

"Just kissing you goodnight," she said, and continued to kiss his ears, one and then the other.

"You know that this will lead to more than spooning," he said.

"Will it?" she asked coyly, and continued kissing him, all over his chest now. She went back up and stuck her tongue in his ear.

"Oh, woman, why are you torturing me?" he asked.

"I'm not torturing you. Just lie back and enjoy it." She went down to his nipples and kissed him there, and then ran her nails up his chest.

"Okay, that's enough. Now I'm going to torture you." He flipped her over so that she was underneath him. He started with her, and soon enough they were having sex.

After they were done, they lay spooning together.

"So much for just spooning," he said.

"Well, I think what we did was the better option."

He kissed her on the cheek and they fall asleep just like that, side by side.

CHAPTER 41

THE NEXT MORNING, SHE WOKE UP AND kissed him. He looked at her, into her blue eyes, with his green eyes.

"Good morning, Mrs. Steel. How are you feeling? Any ribs broken? Bruises? Anything broken?"

"No, I feel great. What about you, Mr. Steel?"

"Oh, I feel great too. I had this wonderful dream that there was a tigress in my bed and she did some crazy things to me."

"Oh, I had a dream that a honey bear did the same to me," she said.

"Aren't we lucky? We both had good dreams. Gee, what would we do without them?"

"I just don't know."

He kissed her mouth. "Don't you think we are a naughty couple?"

"No, I just think our life is full of spice, and I love that."

"Me too."

Tashi stretched from here to there, like a cat.

"Look at you, just like a cat."

"Do you want me to meow too?"

"No, you'll wake up the whole house." He laughed.

"Would you like some coffee? I can make some and bring it back in here?" Tashi offered.

"That would be great." He pecked her softly.

"Alright, hot coffee coming up!" She went into the kitchen and started making it. Once it was ready, she put it on a small tray and brought it back to their bedroom.

"Here you are, my old boy."

"Old boy? Didn't I just prove to you last night that I'm not an old boy?" he asked.

"That is true, honey bear," Tashi said.

They sipped their coffee and then Josh said, "So it's Mom's last day in the hospital."

"Yes it is, but I wouldn't be surprised if she got out sooner," Tashi said.

He laughed. "Oh, you're probably right."

"I think I will give her a call at some point today. Other than that I will do some more painting."

"That is a great idea," he said.

"And I know your plans. You will be working today, I presume?"

"Yes, that is right. I still have quite a bit of work to do for Dad."

"I know my honeeey bear's plaaans." Tashi began to sing and bob her head around.

"You are such a silly woman, sometimes." Josh laughed.

"A silly woman!? I think the honey bear has to sleep by himself tonight. Under my bed!"

"Under your bed?!'

"Yup."

"You'll have a tough time doing that," he teased.

"We'll see tonight!" She kissed him on the cheek.

"Okay, let's be serious for one second," he said. "Mom and Dad are coming over for dinner tomorrow, right?"

"Yes, my honey bear."

"Maybe we should call them and ask what they would like for dinner. It will be Mom's first big meal out of the hospital."

"That's a great idea!" Tashi said.

"I just hope she chooses what I like."

"I just hope it's not a pot roast!" They both laughed.

They then hopped into the shower, and as they are stepping in Josh said, "Okay, no fooling around in the shower today, Madame of the house!"

"Alright, Monsieur of the house."

Josh turned the water on and Tashi screamed when it hit her in the leg.

"Why are you screaming?!"

"It's cold! You should walk into the shower first next time!"

They finished shampooing their hair and then stepped out and dried off.

"So we should go shopping today, maybe to Granville Island again?" she asked.

"Oh, that's a great idea. I can buy some more sausage!" Josh said.

"No, you're not buying any more, the fridge is still full with that!"

"Fine, but maybe we can buy some fresh bread. Would that be allowed?"

"I guess so." She smirked.

They then both got dressed and head out into the living room.

All the kids were sitting by the island, already dressed and fed.

"Oh wow, you're all ready!" Tashi said.

"Well, we should get going soon. Whistler is quite a ways away!" Leilani said.

"What time will you be back?" Tashi asked.

"I'm not sure," Damian said.

"Well, if we're not on the couch, you'll know we're asleep," Josh said.

"I figured that." Damian smiled.

"Okay, have fun! Take some pictures!" Tashi said.

"We will, thank you!" And they headed out the door.

"My dear wife, I am going to have to work now," Josh said and gave her a kiss.

"I know, I know. I will get to work too."

"Maybe I'll get a nice lunch with sausage and bread?" Josh asked.

"Maybe, if you behave," Tashi said, and she gave him another kiss before heading down to her studio.

She gets into her smock and dips her paintbrush into some white paint. She then stands in front of the canvas, not moving.

"I can't think of anything," she says out loud. "This has never happened to me before, my mind is blank." She is unsure what to do, so she stands for a few more minutes before she decides to go out on the roof garden and think.

She takes off her smock and rests the paintbrush. She goes outside and sits down and closes her eyes.

She thinks about Leilani and Damian, and how happy they are. Then her mind wanders to her other daughter, the one who grew inside of her, but who she never had the chance to meet. She wonders what she would look like now that she is grown up.

All of a sudden she sits up and says, "I got it."

She walks back to her studio, puts her smock back on and closes the door. She works quickly, moving from the top of the head down to the shoulders. She works and works. She strokes the brush back and forth until she can make out a girl on the canvas. She continues to work until she is almost satisfied.

"Something is missing." She thinks and thinks, and then she realizes. "The eyes! They need more life in them." So she works on the eyes for a while, and then decides to work on the mouth too. She tries to paint exactly the picture she saw in her mind's eye.

"By golly, girl, you got it." But there is one thing she needs to add — the locket. So she paints the locket on, the one she received from Josh so many years ago, and then steps back. "That's it. That's her. This is exactly how our daughter will look now. Now I will be able to find her for sure."

She opened the door and said, "Josh, come quickly!"

He came running around the corner. "What happened?"

"Oh, nothing. I just have something to show you!"

"You scared me."

"Close your eyes," she said.

He did, and she led him into the studio, stopping him in front of her painting. "You may open your eyes now."

He looked at her painting and said, "My God, Tashi, is this our daughter?"

"Yes, Josh. I came in here earlier and my mind was blank. So I went to sit outside and think about what to paint. I thought of her, and this image came into my head. So I came back here, and painted it."

"Wow." He was speechless.

"This is what she will look like, Josh. We will find her," she said.

"You're right. Actually, I will take a picture of your painting and post it on the internet as a means to find her."

"Yes! What a smart lawyer I have!" she said.

"You are the smart one," he said. "How did you do this?"

"I just saw it in my mind's eye, and that's how I painted her," she explained.

"She is beautiful."

"She is."

"Just like her mom." Josh took a step towards the painting. "What colour are her eyes?"

"If you look closely, you can see they are a blue, but not as blue as mine. They are a blue-green, a mix between ours."

"Do you really think she has this colour of eyes?"

"I do."

"Wow, we make beautiful kids. If I knew this, I would've wanted to make a dozen more!" Josh said. He stepped back again to get a full look at the painting.

"You are unbelievable, Tashi, you really amaze me."

"Well, I guess we all have our little talents. You have yours, and this is mine."

"Mine are mostly in the bedroom, don't you think?" he asked.

"Well, a lot of them," she said, "but not all of them. You have many talents, Josh."

"Well that's very sweet, but I was hoping you would say yes!" he teased. "Okay I'm going to take a photograph of this, and I'll put it online as soon as possible." He went to get his camera and took a snapshot. "Wow, Mom and Dad will be so surprised."

"Well, Dad knows, but Mom doesn't," Tashi reminded him.

"Hopefully he doesn't tell her!" he said.

"No, he won't. He says he would let us tell her ourselves," Tashi said.

"Well, maybe we'll show Mom the painting first, and then tell her it's her granddaughter."

"Are you kidding me?"

"No, if that's the way you see her, then I believe you," Josh said.

"Thanks, Josh."

"What do you think her name is?"

"I'm not sure, it's hard to say. There are so many names, and depending on who adopted her, it could be anything."

"You're right," Josh agreed. "Well, I think after this we need a nice drink."

"I would love one," Tashi said, and she followed him out of the studio and into the kitchen.

"What time is it? Isn't it lunch time, so I can have some sausage?" Josh asked.

Tashi laughed. "You can have sausage whatever time of day you like, Josh."

"Good point." He pulled out all the sausage, and then poured Tashi some red wine and got himself a beer.

They both enjoyed the food and drink, looking at each other while they ate, then grinned at each other at the same time.

"What's so funny?" Tashi asked.

"I don't know. I was going to ask you the same thing!" he said.

"I just can't help but grin when I look at you."

"Same with me, Tashi. You are perfect for me," he said.

"And you for me. Your eyes, I just can't get enough of them. They follow me in my sleep."

"Well, that just sounds creepy," he said.

"No, it's wonderful," Tashi said. "I always know I'm safe."

"You are, Tashi. I will always keep you safe," he said.

Tashi reached over and grabbed a piece of sausage.

"Hey, that's mine!" Josh said.

"Can I just have one bite?" she asked.

"I guess one bite," he teased, "but no more than that."

"Don't be greedy or I'll take the rest of it and put it down the garbage disposal."

"You wouldn't dare!"

"Well, you know me. You said I was unpredictable."

"Oh, yes, you've proved that many times over and over."

She got up and looked in the fridge, closed it and then walked over to Josh. She kissed him on the ear.

"Are you hungry?"

"Not really." She kissed him on the ear again.

"So what is this with my ear?"

"I'm just tasting."

"And?" he asked.

"You taste absolutely delicious." She kissed him on the neck and then ran her fingers up his back and through his hair.

"Oh, woman, you make me crazy. How am I supposed to concentrate and eat my sausage when you are working on my body?"

"Well, take your mind off your body and focus on your sausage," she said.

"Which one?"

She laughed and then said, "Just see how long you can stand it."

"Oh, you want to play a torture game with me?"

She didn't answer but just kissed him on the other ear and then stuck her tongue inside.

"Oh, you." He dropped his sausage onto his plate and said, "You are a bad girl." He took her onto his lap. "We may have to do something about this, won't we?"

"Just eat your sausage and be quiet." She kissed his neck again and then lifted his shirt and kissed him on his lower back, running her kisses up underneath his shirt. "Mmm, you just smell so delicious, and are so much more enticing than my lunch." She then put a big smack on his lips, held his head between her hands and said, "Look at me."

He looked up at her with his big green eyes.

"Josh, I love you and, all fun and games aside, I want to find our daughter."

"I love you too, Tashi, and we will. Especially now with your painting."

"Do you think she is happy? And that she is a good person?"

"Oh, Tashi, if you look at the two of us, how could we not create a good person? You don't harm anybody, I don't harm anybody, so why wouldn't our daughter be just as good?"

"Yes, you have a good point. But we don't know what sort of circumstances she grew up in. It could've been bad. Maybe she will blame us for it."

"Well, I think it is worth the chance to look and find out anyways. We both want to meet her, at least once. And if she is mad at us it will be difficult to deal with, but," Josh consoled her, "you have to know that we couldn't have done anything differently at that time,"

"You're right."

He continued, "If she accepts us, then that's great, and if not, we can try to convince her."

"I know."

"Will you stop worrying then, sweetie pie?"

"Yes." She put her hand down on his lap. "Uh-oh," she said, playful all of a sudden. "It's gone." She touched the place on his pants that used to be hard.

"Yes it is! After this serious talk, it went away!"

Tashi gave him a kiss on the cheek, and then she went back to her studio and he went back to his office. Once in her studio, Tashi picked up the camera he used to take a photo of the painting, and took a look at it.

This is perfect, she said to herself. She walked over to her computer, uploaded the photo onto the computer and then sent it to Josh.

For the next couple of hours, she worked on another painting, this one of a landscape. She painted more slowly this time, as she was not as anxious to finish it. The minutes flew by and she didn't even notice, as she was doing what she loved to do. She was focused on painting, so she didn't see when Josh snuck up behind her.

"Ah!" She jumped a little.

"It's just me, baby, don't worry."

"You scared me, Josh!"

"I know. I'm sorry. I just wanted to check to see how you were doing." He kissed her neck. "And to pay your back for the way you tortured me with your kisses earlier." He continued to kiss her.

"My God, you drive me crazy!" She started moaning.

"Well now you know what it feels like, don't you?" He kissed one ear, and then the other. He then wiggled his fingers, motioning her to follow him.

"Nuh-uh, I'm not going to follow you."

"Why?"

"I'm just proving a point that I'm strong and resistant."

"Oh, really? I'll count to five and walk towards the bedroom, I bet you will be there." So he walked down the hall, "One, two, three...."

By that time she was already standing in the bedroom.

"I didn't even make it to four!" he said. "You're a fast mover!"

"I know."

"So what are you doing in here? What do you want?"

"Nothing, I just came in here to straighten out the bet," Tashi said.

"Oh, it's already straightened out."

"Okay, well, in that case…" She walked over to the door to lock it, and then walked up to Josh.

Without waiting, he started undressing her. "Wow, what a delicious package under your clothes." He undressed her to her bra and panties, and then she started to undress him. She then took off her bra, threw it beside the bed and slipped off her panties.

"Come here, Mrs. Steel. I need you close to me right now."

So she slid underneath him, and then he started kissing her and nibbling her everywhere, knowing this drove her absolutely wild.

"Josh, stop!"

"Okay, I'll get to the point now," he said, and then they had long, passionate sex.

"Oh, that was absolutely wonderful," Tashi said when they were all done.

"It was excellent," he said, and then kissed her.

"I couldn't have a better lover than you."

"Well, have you ever had another one?"

"No."

"Well then, how do you know?"

"I just think that there's no one else like you."

"I think the same about you, Tashi." He pulled her into his arms and hugged and kissed her.

"Okay, well either we get out of bed, or we carry on where we left off," Tashi said.

"You know I would love to carry on, but I should really get up and do some more work," he said.

So off to the shower they went. They rinsed themselves off, and got dressed. Tashi made the bed, Josh helping her, and then he gave her a quick peck and went back to work in his office.

CHAPTER 42

LATER THAT DAY, TASHI AND JOSH WENT to visit his mom.

They took the Porsche, since Leilani still had the keys to the Ferrari and had taken it up to Whistler. Josh squeezed into the front seat, and Tashi had to laugh as she watched. They drove off to the hospital and went up to Rosa's room in the ICU.

She was sitting on her chair, reading a book.

"Oh, you look like you're ready to go home."

"Oh, I am, but I can't leave yet, according to the doctors," she said.

"I was hoping to take you home anyways," Josh told her.

"Oh, could you? That would be great!'

Tashi said, "Josh, don't do this to your mom. You know she isn't supposed to leave yet."

"She looks perfectly fine to me!'

"That's what I say too!" his mom said.

"Well, I guess you could always go talk to the doctor but…I'm not sure," Tashi suggested.

Josh went to get the doctor and came back with him shortly after.

"So Mrs. Steel," the doctor said, "you want to go home? Well, all your vital signs are perfect, and you seem to be in great shape. I can let you go home if you promise me that you won't do any housework, and that you'll take it easy."

"I promise!" she said anxiously.

"I have two witnesses here, and if you don't behave, they will bring you back."

Josh and Tashi nodded at him in agreement.

"Okay then, I will sign you out."

"Well, I'd better call Dad to tell him the good news!"

Josh phoned his father to let him know Rosa could leave. Ted told Josh that he would be there in a few minutes.

They say their goodbyes to the doctor, and started helping Rosa out of bed.

"Mom, where are your clothes?" Tashi asked.

"Actually, I don't think I came with any extra clothes," she said. "And the ones I had on the day I fell are nowhere to be found."

Tashi looked around. "Well, there is a coat in the closet."

"A coat? What kind of coat?"

"A housecoat," Tashi answered.

"I have to walk out of the hospital in a housecoat?!"

"Well, I don't see anything else," Tashi said.

"What about the hospital gowns?"

"They have an opening in the back, so that may not be the best outfit for you," Tashi said. "Here, I'll call Dad back and let him know to bring you some clothes."

"Oh, no, that's alright. I'm just going home so I'll get changed there. Who knows what clothes that man will bring me."

Tashi laughed. "Mom, by the way, we're having you over for supper tonight with Dad. What would you like to eat?"

"I'd like a small juicy steak. I haven't had that in a while."

"Good," Josh said. "I thought you were going to ask for a pot roast."

"Oh, no, I'd like a steak with peppercorn sauce."

Tashi chimed in, "And I'll make mashed potatoes and asparagus to go with that."

"That sounds fantastic," Rosa said.

"We also have a big surprise for you tomorrow evening," Josh said.

"Oh, I can hardly wait! I'm looking forward to tomorrow evening."

Just then, Ted came rushing through the door and took his wife in his arms and gave her a kiss.

"Look at those two lovebirds," Tashi said.

Josh agreed. "They are cute."

Josh and Tashi left to go to Granville Island, while his mom and dad went home.

At Granville Island, they picked out some vegetables, bread, meat and, of course, dessert. Then they walked over to the flower stand.

"Who do you want to get flowers for?" Tashi asked.

"For my two beautiful women."

"Oh, for two? That's good." she said.

He said to the flower salesman, "I'd like to have some nice red roses for my mom. She's coming home from the hospital today and we want to surprise her with them."

"Okay" he said. "I have some real nice red roses with the smaller buds still closed and we have a few of them in the fridge. Would you like those?"

"Perfect, perfect" said Josh. "Then I'd like to have some for my beautiful wife here! And they'll have to last today and tomorrow for our dining-room table centrepiece, our bedroom, bathroom and living room."

"Holy smokes," said Tashi.

The salesman looked at him and said, "Okay, how many dozen do you want?"

"Well what do you think? A few dozen, right?"

"Exactly."

"So just give me the nice ones too, the ones that are still nicely closed."

"Will do," he said, as he started getting everything in order behind the counter.

Tashi looked at Josh and said, "Boy, you are a romantic."

The salesman looked up and said, "You sure are a romantic man. I wish all my customers were like you."

"Well, this won't be the last time I show up."

"Well, I hope not."

"You will see me again soon!"

Tashi laughed as Josh paid for the order. "Alright now, may we go home and put all our food away and the flowers in the fridge and in some water?"

"Yes, of course!"

And the salesman came out and helped them load them in to the car, saying, "Just be careful — you can't be in here too long with them."

Tashi said, "We know, we're going home right away."

So they drove home, less than ten minutes to their place. They carried everything over to the elevator and went up to their penthouse.

Josh said, "Are you going look after the roses or would you like me to do that?"

"Really, you want to do that?"

"Yes, I would love to do that."

He took the roses for his mom and placed them in the fridge. Then he took the roses for his beautiful wife and got them ready on the dining-room table. The air inside was not too hot because of the air conditioning. Then he got a rose and put it on Tashi's night table. He took some outside to put on the back deck, and the rest he put in the living room.

Then he said to Tashi,

"I am all done. How about you?"

"I've put all the stuff away too! The meat and the dessert!"

"Okay great!"

They began making dinner and shortly after, the elevator doors opened up, and Grandma Rosa and Grandpa Ted had arrived.

"Hello, you two wonderful people!" said Grandma Rosa.

They all hugged and kissed each other, and then Josh poured everyone some wine.

"So we have some surprises for you, Mom, but we will wait to tell you when the kids come home," Josh explained.

"I can hardly wait," she said.

"Are you two hungry? Did you eat anything at home? We might have something really good for you," Josh said as he jumped off the couch, "I've got the perfect thing for you."

"Oh, you do?"

"I know what you like, Mom. And I bought some today. Would you like to sit in the dining room or at the island?" he asked.

"Oh, no, no. I can climb up on those stools and I'd love to sit at the island." So all four of them took a seat.

"So," Tashi began, "I think when Josh and I go back to Kauai that you two should come with us and have a real great holiday, and I will look after you. Dad, you'll be able to get your work done without having to worry about Mom."

"Oh, yes," said Rosa, looking at Ted. "I would love you to come along if your work permits it."

"Yes, I will Rosa. I think this is a great idea too," he said. "We will both get great tans!"

"Oh, we have to get Mom a bikini," said Josh.

"Well, you could! She still has a beautiful figure," Ted said.

"Well, they still have one-piece bathing suits. We'll get you one of those and they have lots of them in Kauai," Tashi said.

"We can go skinny dipping," said Josh.

"No way! Not me!"

"We didn't expect you to go skinny dipping with us."

"Well then, why did you mention it!?" Rosa asked.

"Well, Leilani always goes in," Tashi explained.

"When you're around?" Grandma Rosa asked.

"Well we don't just stand there. We usually go somewhere else like the beach. While the girls go out in the dark," Josh explained.

"So should we fill Mom in now before the kids come home? The kids heard it yesterday and so did Dad," Tashi asked.

"Okay, what is going on?" Grandma Rosa asked.

"Well, we have a big surprise. First I am going to bring out a painting for you. You stay where you are and just look at it and you tell me who this is," Tashi said.

She brought out the easel with the painting of their daughter, and Grandma Rosa studied it, as well as Grandpa Ted.

"So this girl has bluish green eyes?" she asked.

"Bluish green eyes," they answer.

She looked at both of them and said, "He has green eyes, you have blue eyes. This girl has bluish green eyes. Are you meaning to tell me you two have a kid together?"

"We do."

"And where is she?"

"Well, we don't know." Josh explained the whole story.

Grandma Rosa said, "Oh, my gosh. You poor thing, Tashi. You had to go through all those years without telling us."

"I didn't know how to tell you," Tashi said.

They told Grandma Rosa the rest of the story, and continued talking through dinner.

CHAPTER 43

THE NEXT FEW DAYS PASSED BY SLOWLY. Tashi and Josh checked every day for emails after they posted the painting of their daughter. They got emails, but the stories didn't match up, and they knew that they had not found their real daughter yet.

One Monday morning, Tashi went on the computer as usual and read through the emails. After reading the eleventh email, she stopped on the next one.

I believe you must be my mom. I have a picture of myself that looks exactly like the one you posted. I will send it over. My name is Iris.

Iris? Tashi thought. *What a beautiful name. I wonder if that's her.* She continued to read.

I saw your painting online, and read the description under it. I am adopted, and have been looking for my real parents for some time. I was told my mother gave birth to me in a home for unwed mothers, but that is all I know.

I live in Landshut, Germany, and am a painter. I was adopted but then my parents split up, and now I live with my very loving aunt, above an art gallery. I have just always wanted to know where I came from. I think that I may be your daughter.

Sincerely,

Iris.

Tashi looked at the photograph that was attached. Iris was wearing jeans and a blouse, the same outfit she had on in Tashi's painting. Tashi looked at it closely and then said to the screen,

"Hi, Iris, I think I'm your mom."

"Who are you talking to?" Josh came up behind her.

Tashi showed Josh the picture.

"Wow, this could be her," Josh said. He got excited and read the full email from her. "Well," he said, "should we ask some more questions?"

"Sure! Introduce yourself. Maybe we should send a picture of us," Tashi suggested.

"Great idea. I'll get Damian to take a photo of us," Josh said. He left and shortly after came back with Damian following him.

"What's going on?" Damian asked.

"We may have found your sister," Tashi said.

Damian looked at the photo of Iris. "Holy smokes, how did this happen so fast?"

"Well, I am a lawyer, remember?"

They filled Damian in on everything, and then he took a photo of them, which they then uploaded. Josh sat down and did everything he needed to do. He read, and reread the emails. Finally after about an hour he noticed another email in his inbox.

I have beautiful parents if you are them. Sorry I didn't answer for a little bit. I was crying so much. I really hope that I can meet you one day.

"Wow," Tashi said. "Do you think we should take the risk and go to Germany?"

"I do. I really think this might be her. I just have to try to get some time off work," Josh said.

"Well if you can't, then I will go by myself."

"No, I want to be there with you." Josh called Damian back into the room. "Son, could you take care of some things at the office for me so that we can go away?"

"Sure, I'd love that!" Damian said.

"And then when we get back you can plan your trip to Germany with Anita," Josh continued.

"Not a problem," Damian said.

They then replied to Iris, asking some more questions and suggesting to her that they could come and visit.

Iris quickly answered that she would love to have them visit her, and that anytime worked.

"Let's leave next week, Tashi," Josh said.

"That's short notice." She thought about it. "But okay, we should go now. I can't wait to meet her, Josh."

"Me too, sweetheart." Josh kissed her and then he started looking for flights while she went to go pack.

For the next couple of days, they corresponded back and forth. They spoke to Anita, who was from Dingolfing, a town near Landshut, and she arranged a hotel for them.

They were both ecstatic that they would finally be meeting their daughter.

Chapter 44

IN THE WEEK BEFORE THEY FLEW TO Germany, Josh and Tashi had visitors.

One afternoon as Tashi was working on her paintings, Donna called.

"Hi, Tashi, is it alright if I come by to your place? We're in Vancouver."

"Of course, but who is 'we'?"

"Christopher and I," Donna said.

"Oh! Sure. Does tonight work?" Tashi asked.

"That's perfect. See you then!"

Tashi hung up and told Josh the news.

"Oh, that's strange. I wonder what they are doing here."

A few hours later, Tashi and Josh were preparing dinner. They were almost done when Donna and Christopher arrived.

"Tashi, it's so good to see you!" Donna said. "I have some good news!"

"Yes, we have a little surprise," said Christopher.

Donna, Christopher, Tashi and Josh all exchanged hugs. Then they all sat down.

"So, what's the surprise?" Tashi asked.

"We got married!" Donna said.

"What?! Oh, wow! Christopher, you old devil!" Josh exclaimed.

"Congratulations, you two! I'm so happy for you!" Tashi flung herself on the two and Josh embraced them as well.

"Let's get some champagne ready!" Josh said. He took out champagne glasses. "So when did you get married?"

"We couldn't wait to get married, so we got married on our vacation, and then decided to come here and surprise you."

"Wow, I can't believe you didn't tell me!" Tashi teased Donna.

"I know, I just... I guess we surprised ourselves as well," Donna explained.

"Well, well, well," Tashi said. "I'm so, so happy for the two of you! Will you have kids? Five? Ten?" she teased.

"Don't say anything yet!" Christopher laughed. "Give us some time!"

"Donna, do you want kids?" Tashi asked.

"First we want to enjoy ourselves before we even think about kids. All those little toes crawling over everything, dirty diapers and all that fun!" Donna laughed.

"So what are your plans, Christopher? Will you move to Kauai?"

"Well, not quite, because I can't, boss." He looked at Josh.

"Well, I think we can work something out for you," Josh said. "We definitely need to celebrate tonight though!"

"Did you have a wedding?" Tashi asked.

"We had a very simple wedding. No one else knows we got married yet," Donna explained.

"Who were your witnesses?" Tashi asked.

"We found strangers off the street! We just didn't want to tell anyone. And we were so excited and just wanted to do it," Donna explained.

"Wow, that's great!" Josh said.

"Well, listen, since we're celebrating tonight, you guys are free to stay the night if you want. You know we have an extra bedroom," Tashi offered.

"Oh no, we're going to go home! You might listen outside our doors!" Donna said.

"No, we'll be too busy ourselves!" said Josh.

"Oh, we wouldn't listen," Tashi said. "We would just open the door!"

"Tashi! You wouldn't dare!" Donna said.

"Oh, yes I would!" She laughed.

Tashi and Josh finished preparing dinner and since it was a warm and sunny day, they sat outside to eat.

Tashi said to Donna, "What would you two like for a wedding present?"

"We don't need anything. We have each other!" said Donna.

"Okay, well let me know if you think of anything," Tashi said.

"What you guys did is just so unbelievable. And so exciting!" said Josh.

They drank their wine and shared some laughs, and talked about future plans. The world looked beautiful to all of them on this happy evening.

"So, Tashi, you mentioned that you two might be going to Germany?" Donna asked.

"Yes, we are going next week to meet our daughter finally."

"Oh wow, you must be so excited," Christopher said.

"We really are; we just can't believe we found her!" said Josh.

"That is fantastic. And how is your house hunting going?" Donna asked.

"Well, we bought a property in Kauai, and we will build our own home," Tashi explained. "And when Leilani comes back from school, we will give her our old house. She loves that house and I never did, because of my dad. So if she is happy, I would love her to have her own place. It will be close to us. Maybe Damian will also want to come and stay every once in a while. Whatever she decides, though, I want to support her, because I know her childhood was slightly tough. I think her best friend might stay with her too, and I think that will be good for her."

"I am so pleased that you have this plan, and I truly hope everything works out for you. And I'm happy for your parents, Josh," Donna said.

"Yes, I am too. And they love Tashi. Just like me, just a little bit," Josh joked.

Tashi rolled her eyes. "Just a little bit?"

"I can't give it to you all the time. She is a man-eater, Christopher."

"Don't get near her!" Donna joked.

"Oh, you guys, shut up," Tashi said.

They continued talking and having wine together, until Christopher looked down at his watch and noticed it was past ten.

"Well, anytime you want to go, I'm ready," Donna said.

"Alright, I think maybe we should call it a night then," Chris said.

"Well, thank you for spending the evening with us. We really are so happy for you," Josh said.

"We understand you need a honeymoon. We never had one either!" said Tashi.

Donna and Chris walked off to the car, said their thanks and drove away.

Josh put his arm around Tashi. "That was great to see. I am so happy things worked out for them."

Tashi agreed. They walked back inside together and cleaned everything up.

Tashi looked at Josh and said," How about I finish this and you can go in the bedroom and make a romantic bed for us."

"A romantic bed?" Josh asked.

"Just use your imagination!" Tashi said. He kissed her on the lips and pressed against her from behind.

"Oh, there's something rotten going on in Denmark!" Tashi laughed.

"It's not rotten!" he said.

"Should I take a look?" she asked.

"In the bedroom." He smiled as he walked away. Tashi finished cleaning and then walked down to the bedroom.

Music is playing softly, and he has placed a piece of chocolate that he found in her secret chocolate stash on her pillow. He is in the bathroom, already waiting for her to go in the shower with him.

"It looks real romantic, sweetie," Tashi says.

"You told me to!" Josh says. "Are you ready for the shower?"

"Just a shower okay?" Tashi says. They shower and then towel themselves off. She brushes his hair with her fingers and then messes it all up.

"Hey, what was the point in that?" he asks.

"I love to see it messy! You look like a young boy!"

"Do young boys look like me when I stand up in the nude and show you something?" he says.

"No."

"What am I, then?"

"You are my god."

"That's better, Mrs. Goddess." They laugh at their silliness. They head into the bedroom.

"So what is with this chocolate?"

"I wanted you to have some instead of having honey tonight."

"Do I get honey every night?" Tashi asks.

"Yes, my honey." He winks at her.

"So I don't get honey tonight?" she asks.

"I guess you can have both," Josh says. "Let's see what I can do for my goddess." He kisses her neck and her mouth.

She puts her hand in his hair and tousles it around.

"You look so innocent." She says to him.

"Really?" he asks.

"Yes, you always looked innocent to me. When I met you, wasn't it me who seduced you?" Tashi says.

He laughs. "I think it was the two of us who seduced each other."

"That was so wonderful," Tashi says. "Young, innocent..."

"Well, we weren't that innocent."

"Yeah, that's true. You saw what happened." She got a sad voice. "I'm sorry, that's not what I meant."

He kisses her again, and kisses her everywhere this time. He plays with her breasts, and goes around her nipple with his tongue in circles, driving her crazy. He then goes to the other breast and does the same. He works his way down, until he gets to the apex between her thighs.

He looks up at her and says, "Now tell me what you want. Do you want me to keep going? Or to stop?"

"I want you to stop, and I'll take over," Tashi says.

Josh comes back up and lies down on his back.

She puts her hand in his hair and gets really rough with him and kisses him.

"Wow, aren't you a tigress?" he says.

"I just want to ravish you tonight."

"Well, you do every night!"

"Not like this, I want to show you my wild side," Tashi says. "Close your eyes."

He closes his eyes.

She goes down and kisses his eyelids, then kisses around his face and gently bites his lower lip and then lets go. Then she sticks her tongue in his ear and he moans. She suckles on his bottom lip and slips her tongue in his mouth, and he answers her with his. She pulls free and starts kissing down his body, lower and lower. She goes around and around and around. "Do you want me to?"

"Well, should I turn off all the lights?" He asks.

"Nope." She kisses down his leg, to his toes, and then comes up the other leg. She goes around his manhood with her tongue, and takes it in her hand and starts playing around.

"What are you doing to me?"

"Just having fun!"

"I will show you fun in a minute." In a minute he gets up into a sitting position and rolls her onto her back.

"It's my turn to tease you! Where's that cake?"

She laughs. "We don't have cake tonight, honey!"

He starts caressing her all over and kissing her everywhere.

"I can't take this any longer, I'm going to explode!" Tashi says.

"I don't want the house to explode, so I should do something!"

"Yeah, you better!"

So he goes inside of her and they make passionate love. They stop once they are so tired that they can't even get into a different position.

Tashi wakes up in the middle of the night and pulls the covers up. *Wow, what a wonderful life I am having with this man,* she thinks. Josh wakes up, "What's going on?"

"Nothing honey, just covering you up because it's chilly tonight," she explains. They cuddle together and fall back asleep.

CHAPTER 45

THE NIGHT BEFORE THEY WERE TO LEAVE, Josh and Tashi had dinner with the kids.

Josh got the barbecue prepared with his son and Tashi got the table ready with the girls. The girls arrange the seating plan with Tashi and Josh sitting beside each other. Tashi suggested that she and her husband sit across from each other.

"Come on girls, the food is ready," said Josh.

Nobody responded until Josh discovered that they were all already sitting at the dining table. Josh started pouring wine in everyone's glasses. "You know, you're too young to be drinking this wine," he said.

"Yes, I do know that. Maybe I will think about quitting soon," said Leilani.

"Don't worry, Josh, you won't find a bottle of wine in our house," said Damian.

"Oh, I will have to hide it, then," said Leilani.

"Good for you. Never let him control you like that," said Josh and Tashi while laughing.

They finished dinner and the girls began to clean up the table. Someone offered to make coffee but everyone said no.

"I'm so full I don't even feel like eating sausages today," said Josh.

"Oh, don't worry there will be lots of sausage for you to eat in Germany," said Anita.

"Oh? I can't wait to go then. Well, it may be time to go to sleep. We have to get up early in the morning. As for the Ferrari, I will lock it up in the garage, or maybe at the airport."

"Well, I wouldn't leave the Ferrari at the airport," said Damian.

"Why not? They have a watchman at the guard desk."

"Oh, but it will be left in the open for the public. I don't think that's very safe."

Damian handed the keys back to Josh. "I promise I won't take the car out while you are gone."

"Maybe I will have to hide the keys," said Josh to Tashi. "The kids will look everywhere for them. Maybe I will take them with me to Germany."

The group laughed and headed over to the living room. They began to have fun with the piano and Josh and Damian decided to sing a duet.

"Why would we need to go to the theatre? We have such great entertainment here at home," said Tashi as she listened to the beautiful singing. "Well guys, I think it's time for everyone to hit the sack."

"Encore, encore," shouted Leilani and Anita.

"Why don't we go out on the roof and enjoy watching the stars?" said Damian to Anita.

"Why don't you go out with them also?" said Josh to Leilani.

"Oh, no, I have no fun when they're out together. I don't want to interrupt them," said Leilani.

"Well, if it seems like you have become a third wheel, then girl, maybe you should hang out with us?" said Josh.

"Oh, please no, I had to watch you guys so often as a kid, that would be even less fun than watching Damian and Anita," said Leilani, laughing.

"I think it may be time for you to find someone now, girl," said Josh to Leilani.

"Maybe," replied Leilani. "I think it's time we take you home now."

"Okay, maybe Damian will take us home. Can you do that for us Damian?" asked Josh.

"Yes, sure. Can I bring Anita along?" asked Damian.

"Sure, why not?"

As both couples prepared to leave Leilani said, "Wow, look, you guys are leaving me alone here."

"Aw, would you like me to give you a kiss to make you feel better?" asked Josh.

"Oh you are such a silly old man," said Leilani.

"Did you just call me an old man?" said Josh. "Did you hear that, Tashi? She called me an old man."

"I heard. What are you going to do about it Josh?" asked Tashi. "Give her a spanking?"

"I should, shouldn't I?" replied Josh.

"No, you wouldn't dare," said Leilani. "Besides it wouldn't work. I can run a lot farther than you and I'm trained in judo, karate and kickboxing."

"Well, in that case, I'd better not touch you," replied Josh. "Is everyone ready? So we'll see you all in the morning and if not we'll say goodnight now."

"You keep watch on those two," said Tashi to Leilani.

"Don't worry, Mom, I will."

"Okay, see you around, kids," said Josh and Tashi. They prepared everything for the next day and fell asleep as soon as they got into bed.

They woke up in the morning, and said goodbye to the kids.

"I'll drive you guys to the airport in the Ferrari," said Damian.

"Oh not in the Ferrari, maybe in your car," replied Josh. Damian drove them to the airport in his car.

"Well, this is where I say goodbye," said Damian to Tashi and Josh.

After goodbye hugs, Josh and Tashi headed into the airport, boarded their plane and settled into their first class seats.

Chapter 46

AFTER A LONG FLIGHT, THEY LANDED IN Germany.

"So should I call Iris now?" asked Josh.

"Oh no, it is late here. Remember, we are nine hours ahead," replied Tashi. "Would you like to go for a walk?"

"I'd rather go to sleep," said Josh. "I don't know this city and it is quite dark outside."

They woke up really early in the morning and decided to go for a walk. They asked the hotel attendant in the lobby for directions to a good breakfast spot. Tashi also pulled out Iris's address and showed it to the attendant.

"I think this is the address to the art gallery, It opens up at ten," said the attendant.

"Great, thank you," said Josh.

"Could we go down to the river until then?" asked Tashi.

"Oh, you smart woman," replied Josh.

"We can see an old church that looks like a castle and also grab breakfast close by," said Tashi.

"Oh, you have it all figured out, don't you?" said Josh.

"Of course, I love to plan ahead when we go out. Besides, I'm not a lawyer so I have lots of time to look into these things."

Josh pinched Tashi on the butt. "Well, you deserved that, didn't you?"

They went out and began walking. "It is so beautiful here, I wish we could live here instead of metropolitan Vancouver," said Tashi.

"There is a church here, but it doesn't open until later, so let's go have breakfast. They eat sausage for breakfast here, so I think you will enjoy that a lot."

"Do they? Wow, it feels just like home. I think I love this place too," replied Josh. They went to the restaurant and got some coffee.

The waitress prepared their coffee and directed them to the buffet, where there was an array of breakfast delicacies including sausages, omelettes and buns. Josh admired the variety of sausages staring back at him.

"You're going to eat all of those, aren't you? How can you possibly do that?" asked Tashi as she put some buns and cheese in her plate.

"Just watch me," said Josh as he piled sausage into his plate. "I'm glad you aren't grabbing a lot of food, Tashi. I wouldn't want you to get fat now."

"Oh, look who is talking. You have so much sausage on your plate, you will have to work out when we get home."

"Why? Do you see some fat on me?"

Josh finished devouring his sausage and asked Tashi if she would like to get more food. They spoke to the waitress before leaving and tipped her nicely.

"The way she was looking at me, I think she was falling in love with me," said Josh.

"Oh? All she had to do was direct you to the sausage to make you fall in love with her," said Tashi.

"Well, I remember you had to pull all of your tricks on me to make me fall in love with you. Didn't you practically ravish me on the beach?"

"I have to admit I did that, but I was so in love with you."

"I was still a virgin then."

"Oh, I know."

They laughed and went back to the hotel.

"How do we always end up in this discussion after eating? Maybe we should get some rest."

Tashi quickly fell asleep. Josh admired how beautiful she was with her hair all tossed on the pillow. He tried not to move so as to not wake her from her sleep. He tried to reach for the TV remote, but his slight movement caused Tashi to wake up.

"Did I fall asleep for too long? Look at my clothes. They seem wrinkled."

"No, no, we are still on a good schedule. Here, let me fix your pants." Josh reached around and helped smooth out the wrinkles on her backside.

They freshened up in the washroom and prepared to leave. Tashi had memorized the directions to the art gallery. They walked down the hotel's beautiful, white, spiral steps lined with a majestic carpet. They admired the art hanging along the walls.

"I'm getting really nervous," said Josh.

"So am I. Please hold my hand."

"Don't have a panic attack on me, Tashi."

"I can't promise anything."

"Well, I put a box of Kleenex in your purse just in case."

"Did you take this from the hotel? Well, it might come in handy."

They walked to the art gallery. They stopped before going inside to gather themselves while watching the people walk into the gallery.

"Do you have enough courage now? Can we go in?"

"Yes, let's go in."

They walked into the art gallery through the massive doors and were met by an elderly lady.

"Can I help you?" she said.

"We came to see Iris. Is she here?" said Tashi.

"Yes, do you have an order for her?" said the lady.

"No, we have an appointment."

"Okay, I will get her, please wait here."

A few minutes later a trembling Iris walks through the door. Both she and Tashi start crying as they hugged each other.

"Why are they crying? What's wrong?" The lady asked Josh.

"We are Iris's parents. We haven't met her before, so Tashi is very emotional."

"Oh yes, Iris told me you would be coming soon. It was so nice to meet you. Have a fun time."

Josh moved towards Iris.

"Well, can I get a hug too? I am your father after all."

"Oh of course," said Iris as she hugged Josh.

"Look, you are making that elderly lady cry by the front desk."

"That's my mom. Aunty. I live with her." Iris walked over. "Oh, Aunty, please don't cry, this is such a happy moment," Iris said in German.

"Even though I never saw you before I imagined in my mind what you looked like and painted this picture of you," said Tashi.

"Wow, she looks just like how you painted her, with her beautiful blue-green eyes," said Josh.

"I like to paint also. Come over here and I will show you some of my paintings," said Iris.

Josh and Tashi admired their daughter's work.

"Oh, you are your mother's child after all. Look at all of your beautiful work," said Josh.

He and Tashi thanked the old lady for taking care of their daughter. They offered to take Iris out with them.

"I would love to. But unfortunately I have to stay here and help Aunty until the shop closes," Iris said. "How about you enjoy your day, get to know Landshut and then we can meet up tonight?"

"That sounds great, sweetie," Tashi said.

"How about we take you and Aunty out for dinner? There is a beautiful restaurant in our hotel," Josh said.

"That sounds fabulous," Iris said.

The three of them talked some more, about how great it was to finally meet each other, and how Iris had found them online.

But Iris had to get back to work, so they decided to meet at six at Tashi and Josh's hotel and said their goodbyes.

CHAPTER 47

"SO," JOSH ASKED, "WHAT SHOULD WE DO now?"

"Well, why don't we do some shopping?" Tashi said.

"That's a great idea."

They walked towards the cathedrals in town and stopped to look inside because Josh really admired them. They walked across the road and Josh said,

"Oh, look, Tashi. I see a sweet shop!"

"Oh, not again!"

Instead of a sweet shop, it was a store that sold ladies underwear. They walked inside.

"Well, well, well. Look at this," Josh said. "My favourite store. Maybe I will find something in here for my honey bear."

"And maybe I will find something in here for you," Tashi said.

"Well, how about this? I want to surprise you, Tashi. How about we split up for the next hour, and then meet back outside this store after we both shop?"

"Okay. Deal. I will buy something for you, and you will buy something for me," Tashi said.

"Exactly." They kissed each other, and off they went their separate ways. Josh found a saleslady to help him, while Tashi was on the other side of the shop with another saleslady.

She shopped for Leilani and Anita, and then buys Damian some underwear as well as black muscle shirts. She also buys underwear for Josh.

An hour later, they met in front of the store, and made their way back to their hotel.

But first they walked up to a majestic castle on top of the hill. They walked for about twenty minutes to get there, and once they arrived, they went to the Wirts Haus, where they sat down to have a beer each.

"You know, I could eat something," Josh said.

"You just ate breakfast!" Tashi said.

"I know but I could have a snack right now."

Tashi sighed, waved the waiter over and asked the waiter to bring her husband a giant pretzel with lots of butter, extra cheese, and a beer.

Finally the pretzel arrived.

"Oh, boy," Josh said.

"Can you eat all this?" she asked. "You can give me a little corner, right?" She took a bite. Soon after, Josh has finished his pretzel.

"I could eat another," Josh said.

"Another?" Tashi asked. "I think you should not. But I would suggest you go pee-pee before we leave because it's a long way down and those beers will go right through you."

"I'm a big man. It goes all through me before it comes out," he said. But nevertheless, he went to the bathroom.

When he came back he said,

"Gee, there's an old lady who's sitting with a wooden basket in the front of the bathroom. I dumped all my change in there for her."

"Well, that's very nice of you, but just wait and she'll go home now," Tashi said.

She was barely done talking when they saw the old lady get up to go home.

They walked hand in hand down the hill and back to the hotel.

Once they got into their room, they sat on the bed, and laid out all their boxes and bags from shopping.

"Can I take a peek in one of those boxes?" Tashi asked.

He said, "No you may not."

"Why not?" she asked.

"Not until later on, when it's nighttime and I have time to ravish you as much as I want. Then I'll let you open the box," Josh said.

"Oh, you little devil," she said. "You want to ravish me, then you will let me open the box? I'll have to seriously think about that before I go along with this plan."

"Oh you will go along with it, I know you will."

"We'll see about that," she said.

He said, "Well, you know what? Let me see what you got."

"Oh, no. I can show you what I've got for the girls, though." Tashi went and took out the things she bought for the two girls.

"Oh," he said. "Those are sweet little things."

"They are for two sweet little things," she said.

"They will love you, Tashi, they will love you forever when you buy them all this beautiful stuff. What's in the other boxes?" Josh asked.

"Well that's for your son."

"Oh, for my son? You bought him sweet little things?"

"I did."

She opened the bag with Damian's things and Josh said,

"Holy smokes! You picked those undies for my son?"

"Well, I can just imagine those on his father, can't I?'

"Well you could, but you didn't buy any for his father, did you?" Josh counters.

"Nope, his father didn't deserve anything!" she said.

"He didn't? Was he a bad boy?"

"He's always a bad boy. Don't you know that?"

"Well, let me see what else you've got," Josh asked.

Tashi pulled out a white T-shirt.

"A white T-shirt? Oh, how sexy!" he said.

"Yeah, that's what I figured. It'll look good on you with your nice jeans."

Tashi brought out a few more bags and showed Josh the other shirts she had bought for him. Then, she pulls out a very, very sexy pair of black underwear for him.

"Wow, these will look great on me!" he said.

"I know, why don't you try them on?" she said.

"Oh, no, because then you will ravish me, and we don't have time because we have to meet Iris and Aunty soon."

"Alright." Finally she said, "So what did you buy for me?"

Josh handed her a box, and she opened it up. Her eyes widened as she looked at a white, one-piece Lycra bodysuit.

"Oh. My. God. Josh, you expect me to wear this?"

"Well, yes! Not in public of course, just for me! The lady at the store told me it has little doors." He winked at her.

"So it opens on the bottom?!"

"Yes, but that's the whole point isn't it?"

"Well I don't know if I like that part!"

"You won't know until you wear it, right?"

"That is true. I guess I'll have to give this a try," she said, slightly skeptically.

Josh passed her another box. Tashi opened it and out came another outfit, similar to the white one, but it was a nice green colour, almost the colour of his eyes.

"Wow!" she said, "I like the colour on this one! And all you need is a few feathers on these and I could go out on stage!" she said, laughing.

He said, "Yes, we could do that. We could get you on stage with this thing and some feathers."

He handed her another box, and she took out a pair of red panties. They were really beautiful, she had to admit.

"Wow these are gorgeous, I love these."

He said, "I knew you would, I fell in love with them the moment I looked at them!"

"And the lady showed you all of this?" Tashi asked.

"Yeah, but she knew it was all for you!"

"How embarrassing!" she said.

"What's to be embarrassed about?" He handed her another few boxes. "Here."

"More, Josh?" She opened the first one. Inside was a bra and matching panties, in blue. "These are gorgeous! But when do you expect me to wear it all?

"Well every day you can wear a different one! This way I can see a different outfit when I undress you each night," he said.

"Are you serious?"

"Yes, I am serious! I would like to see my sexy wife in these outfits."

"Okay, well you can pick out which one I should wear tonight," she said.

"I'd like that. How about we put all the boxes aside for now. Did we come to Germany just to buy everyone underwear?"

"Well, it looks that way!"

"And of course to eat pretzels and drink beer." Josh looked at his watch, "We should get ourselves ready to be downstairs. The two ladies will arrive soon."

"Should I change?" Tashi asked.

"If you want to."

"I brought along a dress and some high heels."

"Oh, would you please put that on, and put one of those sexy outfits underneath?" Josh begged.

"Alright, I will do that," she said. In no time, she had all her clothes off and was in one of those cute outfits.

Josh said, "Hold it! Before you put that dress on, I want to admire you!" So he looked at her and said, "Wow, I really have good taste, don't I, Tashi?"

"You sure do, Josh. I love it!"

"I do too," he said. "Now put your dress on before I ravish you!"

Tashi put on a nice blue dress and matching black heels.

"Now what about you?" she asked.

"Should I put on my cargo pants?"

"If you want to, it's up to you. But in the evening German people usually wear longer pants when they go out for dinner," Tashi explained.

"Well, good thing you told me. I brought a pair of dress pants along." Josh put them on and he looked great.

Tashi said, "Just come here and let me fix your hair for you!"

"Oh dear," he said. "My woman always has to fix my hair for me."

Tashi fixed it and said, "Now you look good." She gave him a kiss on the lips and said, "I love you, my little honey bunch."

He said, "I love you too, my little honey bear."

"Let's get out of here." She looked around the room. "Look at this place! It looks like a tornado went through here!"

Chapter 48

TASHI AND JOSH WALKED DOWN THE GRAND stairs in their hotel. There were already people waiting in the lobby for the dining room to open up, and they all watched as Tashi and Josh walked down the stairs. They were a breathtaking couple.

Tashi said, "Oh, Josh, don't let me fall."

He said, "Of course not! I have your hand."

"Good" she said. "I am getting kind of wobbly in my legs with all those people watching us."

"Well, they probably think we're movie stars, you know?"

"Yeah, I have this feeling you're right," she said.

When they got to the bottom of the stairs, the young man behind the desk said, "Mr. Steel, I have a message for you." He handed Josh the message and Josh opened the envelope. It was from Leilani.

Hi Dad and Mom, I miss you, I love you to bits and pieces. Wish you well. I'm having a grand time. We found the key for the Ferrari and Damian bashed the car up in all four corners, but don't worry! We're having a good time. Enjoy yourselves in Europe! Love, Leilani!"

"Oh, that girl! I'll kill her when I get home!" Josh said.

Tashi had to laugh so hard. "She sure knows how to get under your skin, doesn't she, Josh?"

"Oh yeah! But who knows, maybe they did find the keys and bash up my car!"

"No, they didn't, they're just pulling your leg, and you always fall for it!"

"Okay, then," he said.

Josh took her hand and thanked the man behind the counter for the message.

The hotel clerk watched them because they were laughing while they walk away to the front door, and other people continued to stare at them.

Tashi said, "You know, I feel uneasy. Everybody is looking at us. What's wrong with us?"

"Nothing is wrong with us. We're just two beautiful people! Don't you understand that, Tashi?"

"I do, I do. I just don't like it when people look at us like that."

"Do you want me to kiss you in front of them? Then they really would stare!" Josh teased.

"You wouldn't dare!"

"I wouldn't dare, you say?" Then he just grabbed her and gave her a hard kiss right in front of all those people. "So there you go," he said. "Now what? Now people will just turn around and look the other way."

"Josh!" She couldn't help but laugh.

Just at that moment, Iris and Aunty walked in. They all greeted each other with hugs and kisses. The dining room doors opened, and since there was a long line, Iris suggested going to get a table.

Josh said, "Don't worry, I ordered us a table way before those other people even thought about that." He turned to Iris and Aunty. "How are you two feeling? I hope you're hungry because I am so hungry, I could eat a bear!"

"A bear?" the aunt said.

"Yeah, a bear!" Josh looked and noticed that the crowd was gone. He took Iris's hand and said, "Come on, girl, I'll take you for supper." Tashi and Aunty followed behind.

Once they sat down at their table, the waiter came by and Josh ordered a bottle of red wine. Then he opened up a menu.

"It's all written in Spanish!"

All three girls answered, "No that's German!"

Tashi offered to read the menu for Josh. "Okay, there in the knodle..."

"Kanoodle! My favourite!" Josh said.

"Not 'kanoodle,' *knodle!*" Tashi emphasized.

Iris started to laugh and said, "You two are so funny!"

Tashi continued to read the menu for him and he decided he would like to try everything, because it all sounded so good. Tashi decides on wiener schnitzel.

"What is that?" Josh asked.

"Well it's a wiener, with a schnitzel!" She laughed, and so did Iris.

Iris said, "Oh, you two are so cute, and you're my parents, my real parents!"

"So you see what you have to look forward to? What would you like to order, Iris?"

"I think I'll have the Sauerbraten."

"Okay, I will too!" said Josh. Aunty agreed to have the same.

The waiter came by and they all ordered. Then Josh asked him, "Do you make really good Canoodles here?"

The waiter looked at him and said, "Canoodles?"

Tashi said, "He means Knoedle."

And the waiter said, "Yes, we make really good Knodles here."

"Okay," said Josh, "I would like some of those."

So the waiter took the order and left.

Iris said, "I don't know if we can eat in peace and quiet with you, Dad. You make me laugh too much."

Aunty absorbed all this and said to Iris, "You know, Iris, I think you're going to be a lucky young lady from now on with those two as your parents!"

Iris said, "Oh, I think so too, Aunty! I can't even take it all in yet, it's all so new for me. You see how beautiful my mom looks?"

She looked at Tashi and Tashi turned and said,

"Look how beautiful my daughter looks. That picture you saw, on the internet, is the one I painted of you. We took a picture and put it on the internet."

"Really? That was a painting before?" Iris asked.

"Yes, I painted you!"

"How can you paint me like this when you've never seen me?"

"Well, that's the secret I don't understand. I've seen you in my mind's eye and I've put you on canvas and now that's what's come out of it."

"Wow, that is amazing," Iris said. "So what are you two doing tomorrow? Aunty and I were talking and we want you to come over to our place tomorrow, and have dinner with us in our apartment above the store. We can sit down and talk, and I'll get to know you better without being in public."

"That sounds like a good idea," said Tashi, "I like that already!"

"Good, how about you come by for lunch, between eleven and twelve, so we can have all afternoon together?" Iris suggested.

"Okay, we can do that," said Tashi.

The waiter came by and dropped off their food. Josh looked at his plate and said, "That's a canoodle?"

"A Knoedle!" said Tashi. "Not a canoodle!"

"Oh, I like what you have on your plate, sweetie. What is that?" Josh asked.

"It's the Wiener-Schnitzel. I told you that!"

"Okay, can I taste it before I taste my meal?"

"Oh, I knew that was coming, I just knew it! Okay, you can have one bite!" Tashi laughed and rolled her eyes.

"Mmm, that's delicious! Can I have another piece?" Josh asked.

"No, you may not."

"What about those potatoes? Can I try some of those?"

"See this, Iris. Now I have to feed him." Tashi laughed.

She picked up some of the potatoes from her plate and put them in his mouth and he said,

"Oh, I love those too! Are you sure you don't want give me another piece of that schnitzel before I eat my meal?"

"How about you go and eat your meal now?"

Josh started digging in to his meat and said, "Oh, boy, is this delicious. Tashi, you have to taste this."

"I know sauerbraten. I have had that lots of times before. I know what it tastes like!"

Josh continued to eat his sauerbraten and then dug into his Knoedle. "Oh, these canoodles they are just so delicious."

"Knoedles!" Tashi said, "Can't you at least learn one word of German? Just say Knoedle."

"Cannadle, canoodle," Josh joked.

"Oh, whatever. Just eat!"

So they all sat there, eating. Iris was sitting beside Josh and laughing, while Aunty was very quiet and just absorbing everything.

After a while Josh said to Tashi, "Can I have another bite of your Wiener-Schnitzel?"

"Here we go again," she said while she cut him another big bite.

He said, "Mmm, that was delicious! I have a feeling you won't be able to finish your meal."

Iris just shook her head and said, "Unbelievable, this is unbelievable!"

"Oh believe it, just believe it," Tashi said. "The longer you see it, the more you get to know it."

"Oh, please give me another bite!" said Josh. So she cut him another bite and fed it to him. "Oh that is very good you know," said Josh.

"I know, that's why I ordered it for myself," said Tashi.

"But don't you think it's too much for you?"

"Oh, for heaven's sake," she said, and she cut the schnitzel in half and put it on his plate.

"Oh, that is very nice," he said. "How about some of those potatoes?"

She put some potatoes on his plate and asked, "Are you happy now?"

He gave her a giant smile and said, "Oh, honey, that makes me so happy."

"Oh, how can anybody resist you?" Iris then said, laughing. "You are hilarious."

Tashi then said, "I'd better eat my Schnitzel quickly, otherwise he will take the last piece from me!"

"No, I wouldn't do that, I'll order you another one if you want?" Josh offered.

"Me? You should've ordered yourself one and left mine alone!" Tashi said.

When they were finished eating, the waiter came over and offered them dessert

"Do you have any Tiramisu?" Josh asked.

"Yes, we do," the waiter answered.

"Oh, no, not Tiramisu!" said Tashi.

"Why not?" asked Josh, "I love Tiramisu!"

"I like Tiramisu," said Iris.

"Me too," said Aunty.

"Well, I guess I am outnumbered. Tiramisu it is!" said Tashi.

So they ordered tiramisu, some coffees and a tea for Iris.

The dessert arrived shortly after, and Josh looked at it curiously.

"Tashi, are you sure these are Tiramisu?"

"They sure are. These are pieces of real Italian Tiramisu."

"They look so different from the ones at home, the ones at home look more like a cake but from here they're different. I hope they taste as good as the one at home. I love the ones you buy," Josh said.

"Oh, I know," Tashi said, blushing.

"So," Tashi continued, "tomorrow, where would you like to go for lunch?"

"No, no, I would like to cook for you two," said Iris.

"Oh? Did you hear this, Tashi? Our girl will cook for us! What are you making for us, Knoedle?"

"No, not Knodle. You'll see when you get there."

"That's my girl. Don't tell him everything, he's very nosy," said Tashi.

"Well, he is a lawyer," said Iris, laughing.

"She picks up quickly, doesn't she, Tashi?" Josh said.

"She does," Tashi said.

"Are you sure you don't want to be a lawyer too?" asked Josh.

"No, I love painting. I know that is what I would like to do for the rest of my life," Iris said.

"Well you're a great artist, just like your mom," Josh said. He looked at her closely, "You know, your mother was right when she painted your eyes blue-green. They are exactly that colour. You have beautiful, unusual eyes."

"And so do you, Dad!' Iris said. "You have the greenest eyes I've seen on a man!"

"How many men's eyes have you looked at?" Josh asked.

"Well, I can look at men, I am old enough," Iris said.

"Sure you are, as long as you just look at their eyes."

Iris laughed. " and you believe this, mom?"

"I believe it, I believe it. I live through this every day with this man," said Tashi.

Aunty was just shaking her head the whole time; she didn't understand much because of the language barrier.

When they were finally all done their dessert and were full and happy, Iris said,

"I had better take Aunty home. She gets very tired being in the front of the store all day."

"Okay, we understand," Josh said. "How about your mother and I walk you two home?"

"That sounds nice. I'd like that," Iris said.

"Okay then, let's help Aunty out of the chair and we'll walk you home," Josh said. He asked the waiter for the bill, paid, and then all four of them slowly made their way back to Iris and Aunty's building. "Will she need help getting up the stairs?" Josh asked.

"No, it's okay," Iris said. "She uses a cane to help her up."

"Smart woman."

"Okay, well, we will see you tomorrow?" Iris asked.

"That sounds great, honey. We will see you between eleven and twelve," said Tashi.

Iris and Aunty went into their place, while Tashi and Josh walked home. Josh put his arm around Tashi's shoulder and said, "What a great day."

"It really was," Tashi said. "I can't believe we are in Germany, meeting our daughter." She pecked him on the cheek. "And now I get to spend the rest of the evening trying on my new outfits."

They made their way up to their hotel.

While Josh is in the bathroom brushing his teeth, Tashi puts the white bodysuit on, and puts her hair up high, then slips on some high heels. She plucks two roses from the vase in their hotel room and puts one in her hair and the other between her teeth. Josh walks out and stops in his tracks.

"Holy smokes. Just stand there, I need to get my camera!" He takes a few pictures. "Face me with your head with the rose in your mouth. Wow, Tashi you need to paint this to put in my office."

"No way! Everyone will see it!"

"You have a bodysuit on, no one can see anything." He puts the camera down and takes the rose out of her mouth.

"Was that a good rose?"

"Oh, yes."

"Oh, Tashi you look sensational in this outfit. And the high heels. Wow, and you smell like roses! You are a good girl. Now I really have to eat you up."

"If you want to, I'm all yours!"

"What a treat I'm in for." He takes the other rose out of her hair and pulls her hair back. "My beautiful, beautiful, beautiful wife, you have no idea what you're doing to me."

"I know, I can see it in your pants!" Tashi laughs. She touches it.

"You keep that up, and I'll explode."

"Please don't do that so soon."

"I'll try not to, but you better take your hand away!"

Tashi moves her hand away and then struts up and down for him and shakes her butt around.

Josh just stands still, gawking at her beautiful body. He finally moves towards her, puts his arms around her and says, "And now, it's time to ravish you."

"Let me just get some water, you know we always get thirsty. Would you like anything else?"

"No, I've had enough of it with those drinks! Thanks, though. My stomach is pinching here and there. I'm just a little bit too full."

"I knew this would happen!" Tashi laughs. "Would you like something for your stomach?"

"No, thanks, it'll go away."

Tashi goes out into their living room, and brings a few waters back into the bedroom.

"What are you doing in there?" she asks.

"You'll see when I come out." He is in the bathroom, combing his hair and putting his aftershave on. Then Josh walks out into the bedroom, wearing the underwear that Tashi bought him.

"Wow, I really like your bikini pants. They look great on you, Josh," she says. She pulls them down in the back a little bit. "Oh, you have a sore there!"

"Where do I have a sore?"

She bites him in the butt.

"Hey! What was that for?"

"I said I would bite you one day! Now we have matching tattoos!"

"Well you better watch out now, Tashi!" he says. "Come, lie beside me on the bed." They are both still dressed in their outfits.

"Well, now I have to find out how to get into this thing," Josh says as he feels her body.

"Well, it has secret doors, and I won't show you where they are. You'll have to find them. Maybe you will, maybe you won't!" Tashi teases.

"Are they that hard to find?"

"You'll have to find out!"

He touches her breasts first and feels around that area. "There are no secret doors here. Where are they?"

"I'm not showing!"

He goes further down, doesn't find anything, and looks at the back, doesn't find anything again.

"Well let me examine your little bikini pants first and then I'll tell you where they are."

"There's nothing to examine on my bikini pants."

"What's inside is what's important." She starts kissing his belly button, and then his ears, and then suckles on his bottom lip.

"Wow, my woman is hot and I love it, love it, love it," Josh says.

And she whispers in his ear, "My man is hot and I love it, love it, love it." He squirms as she does this.

She comes back to his mouth and kisses it. "Close your eyes, my wonderful man." She kisses his eyelids.

"What's that for?"

"I want to get close to your eyes!"

"Can I open them again?"

"Sure, but I'm not finished with you!" she goes down to his chest and suckles as much as she can on his little titties.

"I'm almost ready to explode because this outfit is doing something to me too!"

"Well, you better wait! You still have to find my secret doors." Tashi whispers.

She sticks her tongue in his belly button, and then keeps going down, and lifts up his little bikini bottom. "He just looked at me."

"Well, did you look back?"

"What did he say?"

"You can have an ice cream cone."

The both laugh.

With her nails she goes around the bottom of his underwear and reaches in and comes up from the bottom. "Oh, my God, you'd better stop. Don't go any further," Josh manages to say.

"You're that close already?"

"Yeah."

"I never get to play with you, I always have to stop!" Tashi whines.

"I have the same problem with you too! I always have to stop."

"Are you ready to show me the secret doors now?" Josh asks.

"You can't figure it out on your own? I'll stand up."

He turns her around, looks and looks but doesn't see them. "I don't know, I don't see anything."

"I guess I have to show you then." She pulls the straps over her shoulders and her breasts pop out. "It's stretchy, remember!"

"How could I forget that! You were pulling my leg!" he says.

"Of course I was! And you fell for it."

"You mean that entire suit comes down like this?"

"Well that's how I got in!" Tashi says.

"Well that's not very practical for a man!"

"Depends what you want to do with it. If you want to take her out in the evening, then it's better that it doesn't have any doors!" she jokes.

"Should we take it off then?" Josh asks.

"Well, I'll lie on the bed and you can struggle with it."

He pulls it off the arms and starts playing with her.

"I found the doors!" he says triumphantly.

He kisses her ears and mouth and everything.

"Honey bear can't wait much longer."

"And his tigress is right on the edge too!" she says.

"Are you really?"

"Uh huh." He starts folding down the entire body suit. He has it over her hips and kisses her. Then he throws it on the floor.

He starts kissing her everywhere and she begins to moan and groan.

"Wow, I think, I think…" she says in between breaths.

"Wait!" he slips into her and they have the best sex they have had in a while.

He lies down beside her and then she says, "Flip over, I want to take a look at your butt." She looks at the bite mark she gave him. "Oh my, it's swollen! Maybe I'll put some antiseptic on it!"

"Ah, it's nothing!" he says.

"Well, should I do it again?"

"No, no, no!"

"Well, maybe we should get real tattoos on our butts! On opposite cheeks! And we can go nude on the beach!"

"Oh dear…really?"

"Yeah! It doesn't have to be on the butt but I would like to get a tattoo."

"I don't know if I want this."

"Well, will you chicken out?" she asks.

"No!"

"Okay, so do we do it or not?"

"Maybe we'll think about it when we get home?"

"Fine, you chicken," she says.

She rolls over into his arm, and he begins to stroke her hair. "I will sing you a lullaby." He starts singing "When a Man Loves a Woman." He knows all the lyrics, but he can't quite hit all the notes.

"Wow, Josh, you are a good singer, I didn't know you had such a beautiful voice."

"Oh, you be quiet."

He continues to sing, though, getting louder and louder. Finally Tashi tells him to shush up. They lie snuggled up together.

"Goodnight, Mrs. Steel."

"Goodnight, Mr. Steel."

Chapter 49

THE NEXT DAY WAS SUNDAY, AND JOSH and Tashi woke up early, excited to meet Iris and her Aunty for lunch. They decided to buy some flowers on their way there, but noticed everything was closed. They went back to their hotel and asked to speak with the manager.

The young lady at the front desk led them to the manager's office.

"Please come in and sit down," he said. "My name is Hans Schmidt."

"Thank you. We are Mr. and Mrs. Steel."

"Is everything okay?" he asked.

"Oh, yes, we didn't come in to complain, we just have a favour to ask you," Josh explained.

"And what would that be?" he asked.

"Well, we are visiting our daughter and we found her here in Germany. We were looking for her all over the place. And she lives with her Aunty here and we're going there for lunch and the stores are closed. We would like to buy them a whole bunch of flowers and some chocolates if we could. Is there any possibility we could get something like this with the stores being closed?" Josh explained.

The manager said, "No problem, I will arrange it all for you"

"Oh," Josh said. "That would be so wonderful!"

"What time do you need it for?" he asked.

"Well, we're supposed to be there between eleven and twelve and it's just a couple of blocks down from here. It's actually right near the art gallery."

"Oh? Is your daughter Iris?" Hans Schmidt asked.

"Yes, that's our daughter."

"For heaven's sake!" he said.

"Yes, she was taken away as a baby and adopted here. We just found her," Tashi explained.

"I am so pleased to hear that you are reunited," he said.

"So are you able to do this for us?" Tashi asked again.

"Yes, no problem! If you come back within a half an hour. It's almost eleven so I had better hurry up. Be here by twelve o' clock."

"Sure!" they said and went outside for a walk.

"See?" Josh said to Tashi, "All we have to do is ask. Money will buy everything. Anything that you want!"

"Yes, I noticed that even though the stores are closed."

So they went window shopping a little bit. But truly everything was closed so after a while Josh checked his wristwatch and said, "I think we should turn around and go back to the hotel, he must have everything by now." When they got back, the manager was by the front desk and he had a big gift basket with chocolates and wine, champagne, cheese and everything your heart could desire. It was all in a basket, surrounded by a beautiful flower arrangement.

"It's so beautiful. We really appreciate it. Could you please put it on our bill?" Tashi asked.

"Yes, I will do that. Not a problem," said Hans Schmidt.

Josh and Tashi walked to the address Iris had given them. They rang the doorbell.

Iris opened the door, She was wearing a cute little blue dress and sandals on her feet. Her hair was in a ponytail because she was cooking. She took a look at the basket and said, "Oh, what did you buy?"

"It's for you and Aunty!"

"Oh, is it ever beautiful!" Iris said.

They followed her upstairs and Josh unloaded the basket on the kitchen counter while Tashi put the flowers on the living room table.

Aunty admired all of it. "For goodness sakes, that's so nice!"

"It's the least we could do," Tashi said.

Josh sniffed the air and said, "Boy, it smells good in the kitchen! Can I go take a whiff from the pot?"

"No," Tashi said. "You have no business in the kitchen. You stay right out here."

"I am getting hungry!"

"You just ate breakfast for heaven's sake!" she said to him.

"But it smells so delicious!" Iris laughed as she puts her apron around her dress again.

Josh and Tashi accompanied Aunty into the living room, as Iris insisted on finishing cooking. Josh got up and looked at all the paintings on the wall — all Iris's paintings — and he said,

"Look, Tashi! Don't these look a lot like the ones you have hanging in your studio in Vancouver?"

"For sure!" she said. "Isn't that amazing how she paints the same way that I did when I started out painting?"

"Yes, there has to be some sort of unexplainable connection between you two, because this is incredible," Josh said.

Aunty said, "She sells quite a bit of her paintings, you know."

"Yes, I can see that," said Tashi. "Great talent!"

"Lunch is ready in the dining room!" called Iris.

The three of them made their way into the dining room where Iris had set a beautiful table with a pristine white tablecloth. On top of it were placemats and blue and white dishes with tiny little yellow flowers designed on the plates. She had the wine glasses out and the flowers she just received were in the centre of the table.

"What is all this?" Josh asked.

"It's a German potato salad with endives and it's very delicious if you've never tasted it."

Tashi said, "Oh, I know it's delicious but Josh has never tried it."

"Well, it's his first then, right? I made Wiener-Schnitzel as well."

"Oh, Wiener-Schnitzel? I heard that word!" Josh said.

"Oh now you've got him interested!" Tashi laughed.

"And I made Bratwurst," Iris continued.

"Bratwurst!" said Josh. "What is a Bratwurst?"

"Well, you will see. Just be quiet now," said Tashi.

Josh said, "Oh boy, does that ever look good. What kind of mashed potatoes are those?"

"Those aren't mashed potatoes, it's a potato salad!" Tashi said.

"What's the green stuff in it?" he asked.

"It's endive, it's a salad."

"Will that be tasty?" he asked.

"Well of course it will be tasty, your daughter made it!"

So Josh picked up the bowl and gave it to Aunty first to help herself, and then she passed it to Tashi and Tashi to Iris and Iris pretended like she was ready to put the bowl back down on the table.

With his green eyes, Josh gave her a look that communicated 'Don't you dare!' so Iris passed on the potatoes to him while Tashi laughed. He helped himself, but didn't take too much because he wasn't too sure how it would taste. She passed the wiener schnitzel around and Josh chose the biggest one on the plate.

He looked at the Bratwurst, and Tashi said to him,

"You know, if I were you I would eat the Wiener-Schnitzel first before I devour a Bratwurst."

"Yeah," he said. "Maybe that's a good idea."

They decided to bring out some white wine for the meal and they toasted each other, saying,

"Let's make this a nice afternoon because we'd like to get to know you."

"Yes," Iris said. "I would love to get to know you better too, Mom and Dad."

Josh devoured the first schnitzel and grabbed himself a second and he took more potatoes and said,

"You know what, Tashi? This is a great potato salad. Maybe you could make this at home too!"

She said, "Sure, but we can wait until Iris comes to Hawaii and she can make it for you too!"

"Okay, sweetie," he said.

While devouring his second schnitzel he said "I need a Bratwurst!"

"I feel ashamed of my husband," Tashi said. "I have never seen him eat so much!"

"Neither have I! I don't know what's wrong with me!"

"He's a growing boy, Mom. Look at him!" Iris said, smirking.

He said, "Hear that, Tashi? She called me boy."

"Oh yeah, I heard that. And you'll take that, Josh?"

"I have to," he said, "I have to, she's my daughter."

"Why?" Iris said.

"Well, he doesn't want to be called a boy. He's a man, don't you know that, Iris? Men don't like to be called boys." Tashi laughed.

"Oh, for heaven's sake," Iris said.

He finally reached over and got himself a Bratwurst with mustard. Tashi looked over at Iris and Aunty and they all chuckled.

Tashi said, "I can't even watch him eat that, I'll be sick."

He said, "Why should you be sick when I am the one eating all that stuff?"

"Oh, dear," she said, "I give up!"

He asked, "So do you still have dessert?"

"Oh gosh!" said Tashi. "Now please, Josh, you couldn't possibly eat dessert now?"

"Oh yes I could," he said, "but I could wait a while."

"Well," Tashi said, "I am so grateful that you said that, I would hate to see you get sick."

"I wouldn't get sick," he said. "That was just a small meal!"

And they all burst out in laughter.

"Why don't you go out in the living room and pour yourself a whisky? I have a bottle there and you can help yourself and wait until we're ready," Iris suggested to Josh. "I've just got to put everything in the dishwasher and put the food away and then I'll come out and sit down."

The three women went to the kitchen and Iris said, "Aunty, please go and sit down too. You do enough during the week."

"You don't mind?" she said.

"Of course not!" So Aunty left to go to her own room because she needed the rest.

The two women finished what needed to be done in the kitchen and came out to the living room to see Josh sleeping. "Would you believe this? He fell asleep on your couch because he over ate! I knew this would happen," Tashi said.

"Why don't we let him rest? I know he enjoyed his meal," Iris said. "Why don't we go out on the balcony and wait there until he wakes up?"

The two women went out on the balcony. "Why don't we sit here and get to know each other better," Tashi said.

They looked below to watch the people scurrying like ants on the bridges of the quaint little Bavarian city.

"Do you like it here, Iris?"

"Well this is all I know. When Aunty took me away, this is where we lived because that's where she used to live. So she rented the little house, put the art gallery below and we now live above it, so that was perfect."

Tashi said, "So what are your future plans, Iris? Because you could come over to Canada. You don't have to stay here. We have lots of money and you won't have to save anything anymore. We will help you in any way because you are our daughter. We couldn't do things for you before and now we can finally do something for you."

"Well, that is a very gracious offer. I'll have to think about it. I've always wanted to go somewhere else, and always thought about meeting you. But it's scary," Iris said. "I would have to leave behind everything I know, including Aunty."

"Yes, I understand. Think about it and let us know." Tashi said. "You could have a beautiful art studio in Hawaii or in Waikiki." Tash

"I've always wanted to go there!"

"Well, here's your chance! We have a big house there and Vancouver is a metropolitan city, you must have seen it on television when it had the Expo and the Olympics."

"Yes," she said. "It is beautiful!"

"Your Grandma and Grandpa are there too, you could meet them. You have a half-brother, from Josh's first wife, and then you have Leilani, the girl we adopted, and she would be your sister then. And you would love her and she would love you too. You two could have so much fun," Tashi explained.

So they talked about all the possibilities in the near future. Tashi also told her that Leilani, Damian and Anita would all be going to Germany soon too.

"Oh," said Iris. "Maybe I'll get to see them while they're over here."

"Yes, they'll come over here to visit you for sure!" Tashi said.

"That's wonderful!" said Iris.

"Is there anything, before we go home tomorrow, that we can do for you?"

Iris shook her head and said, "No, Mom. The best thing you've done already is finding me and so at least I know I have real parents."

"Well sweetheart, you know how long we've been without you. I suffered with it over the years not knowing where you were. Then I did the painting and posted it on the Internet and, just like that, we found you," Tashi said.

"I know Aunty always said if I get married and want to stay here, she would move back with her sister. Her sister has a small house and is all alone and she would love to live with her sister," Iris said.

"Well that would be perfect, wouldn't it?" Tashi said.

"Yes it would help Aunty. She wouldn't have to sit all day long in the art gallery by herself."

"Yes, that is true. Where does her sister live?"

"She lives in Darmstadt."

"Darmstadt? Where's that?" Tashi asked.

"It's close to Frankfurt."

"So is that where Aunty is from?" Tashi asked.

"Yes, that's where she's from."

"Okay, so that would make her happy?"

"Yes, that would make her happy."

"So if we help Aunty with that, and get her a good start, that would make her happy?"

"Yes, that would make her happy because all they have is their little pension, which really isn't enough," Iris explained.

"Then we'll take care of that," Tashi promised.

"Great!" Iris said. "That would be nice."

"What about this building here?" Tashi asked.

"Well, it doesn't belong to us. We just rented it."

"So that makes it easy then to move on? So you could move on?"

"Yes, we could," Iris said.

"Do you have a boyfriend?" Tashi asked, smiling.

"Well, sort of," Iris said slowly.

"Sort of? What does that mean?"

"Well, I have a boyfriend, but we're nothing serious, we go to movies and dance at the occasional bars, but we haven't talked about a future or anything like that," Iris explained.

"So leaving him behind, would that hurt you?"

"Well, maybe, maybe not. I can't really say," Iris said.

"I suppose that is something for you to figure out then," Tashi said, squeezing Iris's hand.

"Yeah," she said. "But I am so excited that I have a chance to go someplace!"

"Yes, you have that now. So how long would it take you to get rid of the art gallery and move Aunty to Darmstadt?" Tashi asked gently.

"I think it could all be done within a month."

"Well, that would be nice. Then you could come over to Vancouver and Josh and I could meet you there first and you could meet your grandparents. God, would they be happy to see you! Should we kind of work around that time period?"

"Yes," said Iris. "I am really getting excited for that too."

"And you already speak English, so you won't have to learn that," Tashi said.

"I always wanted to learn it, so I took it!"

"Well, good for you!"

Suddenly they heard a noise in the living room.

"I think your father woke up. Now watch out what he's asking for, probably where the dessert is." Tashi laughed.

"Girls, where are you?" Josh asked.

"Why don't you find us?" Tashi said back.

He came out on to the balcony and said, "Wow I must have slept for five minutes!"

"More like six hours!" said Tashi.

He looked at her with morning eyes. "Five or six hours?"

"Five minutes turns into hours," she said.

Iris looks at Josh and he gave her a big grin as if to say, *What is your mother talking about?*

"Well, may I come and join you?" he asked.

"Sure," said Iris, "there's a chair."

All of a sudden, Josh said, I thought I smelled coffee!"

"Josh!" Tashi said, "Is food the only thing you think about?"

"Should I give you something cold to drink?" Iris asked.

"Depends on what time dessert is," Josh joked.

"Well, if you want some dessert I can give it to you. But Dad, don't you want to wait until everyone has dessert?"

He said, "Well, I guess I should. You two must have discussed quite a bit while I slept for six hours."

Tashi said, "Yes we already discussed everything."

"Good," he said, "Now I can go back to sleep!"

Tashi said, "Iris can either repeat what we discussed or I can tell you later, it's up to you."

"Well let me see…" He pretended to think. "If I don't get up I will fall asleep again."

"Well," Iris said, "if you'd like, we can go for a walk. We can take Aunty along, she's not too good on her feet but we can take her along. She is up in her room probably taking a rest."

"Yes" Josh said, "probably like I did, just having a five-minute rest." Josh sat down with them. "Iris, do you know a dog breeder here who raises German shepherds?"

"Oh there are all kinds around. Why, would you like to buy a German shepherd puppy?"

"Yes," he said. "I had one when I first met your mother on the beach." He told her the story about Hero.

"Well, what happened to Hero?" Iris asked.

"He got old and died. They can't live forever. So I would like to get two of those German shepherds and have them nicely trained."

"I know a good trainer here. We could go right now if you like?" Iris suggested.

"Really? Can we walk there?" Josh asked excitedly.

"No. I'll have to take my car."

"You have a car?" Tashi asked.

"Yeah, a Volkswagen."

"Well, perfect! Let's get going!" Josh said.

"I'll just go tell Aunty!" A few minutes later Iris came back and said, "Aunty is asleep and so I left her a note and put it on her night table."

They went around the building to the other side where Iris kept her car.

"Dad, do you want to drive?" Iris asked. "I think you'll be more comfortable in the front seat."

He said, "Oh boy, I've never driven one of these before,"

Tashi said, "Well, there's always a first right?"

"Yeah, there's always a first!"

Iris squeezed into the back seat, Tashi sat in the passenger seat and Josh squeezed into the driver's seat. He didn't know where to put his long legs.

"Holy smokes! How do I shift gears with all my limbs?"

"Well," Iris said, "you'll just have to learn!"

He tried to start up the car but *pup pup pup* it didn't start.

"Oh, have you never driven a standard?" Iris asked.

He said, "Well, yes, but not a little kraut can!"

"Okay, give it a try again."

He gave it too much clutch and it stopped again.

"How about you sit in the back and I'll drive?" Iris suggested.

Josh said, "Give me one more try."

And he tried again and the same thing happened.

He said, "Well, I give up, I'll probably get a ticket driving here."

Iris and Tashi got out, and Tashi said, "Well, I guess I'll get in the back now and you can have the passenger seat and Iris will drive."

Finally they got going. Tashi said to Josh, "See how simple that is when you know how to drive?"

He looked at her with those telling green eyes. They were saying, *You better wait till we get back to the hotel and you're gonna get it.*

Iris drove for about twenty minutes. Then they got to a secluded house with a big wired fence around it, Josh could already hear a German shepherd barking. Iris and Josh got out and they helped Tashi get out of the back seat. People came out because Iris had called ahead and they greeted Iris and her folks. They stayed outside behind the fence and spoke with the owners. The owner showed them the dogs' papers.

Josh said to Tashi,

"Well, what do you think of the parents?"

She said, "They look just like Hero, don't you think?"

Josh made a deal with the couple that he would take two of the pups. He wanted a female and a male.

"For breeding?" they asked.

He said, "Oh, no, not for breeding." He wanted them to be a little bit house-trained before they came out to Hawaii. The breeders said that it could all be arranged and Josh let them know he'd give them a down payment.

"Okay, so you'll pick the best ones then, Iris?" Josh asked.

"Of course!" she said.

Tashi then turned to Josh and gave him a big squeeze, saying, "Thank you for letting us have the two dogs!"

"Well, you will still have to wait till they're really here," he said.

Iris asked, "Do you two want to go anywhere else?"

Josh replied, "Oh, no, it's too hot in that little car. I'd rather go back to your apartment, if that's okay?"

They had to get Tashi back into the car, so they all squeezed into the little Volkswagen.

CHAPTER 50

WHEN THEY GOT BACK, IRIS PARKED RIGHT behind the house. While they were out, meanwhile, Aunty had gotten up and prepared coffee.

"Oh," Josh said. "What a wonderful smell!"

Aunty laughed. She knew he wanted coffee and she had the table set.

"Iris has made us a Black Forest cake," Aunty said.

"Oh, wow!" said Josh. "I've never had anything like this before!"

"Well," Tashi said, "don't you get any ideas from that cake either."

He gave her one of those looks and said, "Pshh! Don't talk so much, Tashi!"

She said, "If someone should be quiet, it should be you!"

When they sat down, Tashi said, "Josh, you pour the coffee now. The ladies have done enough for one day."

He poured the coffee and said,

"May I give the ladies a piece of cake, which has been pre-cut in to pieces?"

He handed them out and said, "I can't wait to taste that!" With his first bite he said, "Wow! Iris, you outdid yourself. I like the booze in that cake, what is it?"

"Kierschwater," she said.

"Kierschwater?" he said. "You can buy that? Is it real booze?"

"Oh yeah," she said.

"Oh wow," he said. "So you mean if I ate the entire cake I'd be drunk?"

"Well, you could be, and you could be sick too!" Iris said, as Tashi just shook her head.

After they had cakes and coffee, their tummies were full again.

When Iris asked if anybody would like an after-dessert drink, they all declined.

Tashi said to Iris, "I would love to go down to your gallery to take a look at all your paintings, and maybe you'll be able to show me what you're working on now."

"I'd like that, but first I will help clean up," Iris said.

When she was done cleaning, they all went downstairs. Tashi looked at all the art and asked if she had had a chance to sell it.

"Well, I can try, if not I'll put it in to other art galleries to see if they could sell it for me," Iris explained.

"Yeah, you could do that, or we could take off the frames, roll them up, put them into tubes and ship them over to Vancouver," Tashi suggested.

"That's not a bad idea," Iris said.

"Yeah," Josh said. "I don't think we should sell everything. We should bring some home with you."

Iris agreed. "Yes, I know I want to keep some!"

"Should I select some for you?" he asked.

Iris said, "Yes, show me what you would select, Dad!"

"Well, I love that one..." Tashi agreed and he kept moving and pointing them out. "I love all of them but if you can't take all of them with you, then that's the one I'd like to put into my house." He pointed to one hanging right in the centre of the wall.

"Okay," she said. "Dad, it's yours!"

"Great!"

"And you, Mom?"

"Honey, I want you to choose the one you like. I think it's important that you are happy with the choices," Tashi said. "And you can continue painting if you come with us. Maybe we could paint together in my art studio, I have everything in Hawaii! You would love to sit there and paint."

"Yes," Josh said. "Especially when we have our new house."

"Oh, it sounds so exciting," Iris said.

"Yes, it is exciting. It will be exciting for all of us," Josh said.

Soon it was time for them to say their goodbyes.

Iris asked, "Should I walk you down to your hotel?"

"No, it's okay, sweetheart, we'll be okay," Tashi said.

They both gave her a hug, and then Josh took something out of his wallet. He pulled out a cheque and gave it to Iris. She looked at it and said, "Dad, this is fifty thousand dollars, what am I going to do with it?"

He said, "You need the money, you need to dispose of all of your stuff, try to sell your paintings, start being a painter, you need money now, you can't be working anymore, you have a lot of things to do. You will have some money for yourself, which you can put in the bank or do whatever you want, it's yours. Maybe help Aunty a little bit, if you decide to do so. The choice is yours. Once you live with us, once you come over to Vancouver or to Kawaii, you don't have to worry anymore. Is that understood, Iris?"

"Well, Dad, I don't know about this. I can look after myself."

"Yes, I know you can, but that's not the point. The point is we finally found you and you're happy. We can help you and that is the whole idea. We will finally be able to help you. So please accept that and don't argue with your young dad here. Otherwise you will really upset him. Right, Tashi?"

Tashi said, "Yup. Iris you don't want to upset your dad. Otherwise he will eat twice as much as he did today." They cracked up laughing again.

Josh rolled his eyes and said, "Oh, my God."

He said, "We will say goodbye now and we will stay in contact through a phone or computer. We can talk to each other every day. I don't want to see any tears from either one of you."

Tashi had begun to cry already.

"Tashi, what did I just say? Tashi, you don't understand. This is a happy moment. We have found out that our daughter will come over to move with us. You should be so happy."

"I am but we have to leave her behind."

"It won't be for much longer."

Tashi went over to Iris and hugged her. "Don't listen to him. I'm so happy we found you."

"What do you mean? I am happy we found her too, but I do not like the tears." He handed Iris a Kleenex to wipe her tears and said, "Goodbye, my dear, I will see you at home." He took Tashi's hand and pulled her out through the doorway and waved back to Iris.

They went down by the river and he said, "Come on, Tashi. We will go for a walk."

"Oh no, no bowl of ice cream." So they walked on along the river, watching the ducks and the birds and the people. They walked through all kinds of small roads and found a secluded area where there was a restaurant. They sat down and ordered a beer and talked about how nice it would be for Iris to come home.

"You know, Josh, we have to change that house now."

"Why? Why do we have to change the house?" asked Josh.

"Well, Iris is a painter and it's not good to have two painters in the same studio. It doesn't work that way, sweetie. You interact with one another and you lose your momentum. You have to be all by yourself when you paint."

"Oh I see. What I think we do, we put a separate house on the property for Iris. We have a big enough property. How does that sound?"

"Yes, I think that sounds nice. I think she would prefer the distance than living in our house. She's used to being her own boss."

"I can just see it, it's so beautiful the way I design it in my mind. She will have her own garage and her own connecting way to get to the pool to use when she wants."

"You mean we can't go skinny dipping?"

"We will let her know what hours are reserved just for us."

The light was starting to dim so they got lost a couple times trying to find their way back to the hotel. They began to prepare for their flight the next day. Josh asked, "So what would you like to do? Would you like to go down to the restaurant and eat? Or do you want to sit on the bed and talk? What would you like to do?"

She said, "Well, how about you strip down to your underwear, and I will strip down to mine and then we can talk." So he complied and they did that. They talked about their plans for Iris's house. Then they got in the shower and got things ready for their morning before getting back into bed.

He asked, "Would you like the lights off or on?"

She said, "Off, I can't wait to get home tomorrow."

He said, "Oh you're always in such a hurry, I just can't wait to get home. I am so tired."

"I'm not surprised, especially after you ate all of that food today. It's time for us to go back to Kauai and slow down," she said.

"With all of that food you will clog your arteries."

"Oh don't worry. I work out when I'm home."

"We'll get you into the yoga room and get you all limbered up before working out."

"Oh don't worry, that'll be so easy. I'm so easy."

"Oh, I know."

"Why don't you come over here and kiss me and we spoon then?" They spooned and the next thing, they were asleep.

In the middle of the night Tashi wakes up, looks at a clock and realizes it's only three in the morning. She turns around and wakes up Josh.

"What is up, sweetie?"

"I can't sleep anymore."

"So you woke me up because you can't sleep?"

She begins to kiss him behind his ear, and does a few of her tricks.

He says, "Oh, my God, this woman is just unbelievable. I'm a man who was peaceful in his sleep and then this tigress wakes me up because she can't sleep."

"Any more complaints?" she asks.

"No more complaints," he says. "I was just stating a fact."

She kisses him on the lips before rolling him on his back and kissing his ears again. She circles her tongue around his nipples as her hands move further down.

He says, "Uh-oh, you're going to be in trouble soon, if you don't leave that alone you're going to be in trouble very soon."

She brings her hands up and puts them on the sides of his face and says, "Oh, how are my green eyes doing this morning?"

"They're doing wonderful when they're looking in those blue eyes."

"So what are you waiting for?"

Her hand starts moving down again before he says,

"That's it woman, you're going to get it now."

She says, "I hope so."

So they make passionate love again. After, they spoon again and go to sleep until the morning.

CHAPTER 51

IN THE MORNING THEY WOKE UP AND showered before heading to the lobby for breakfast. Josh couldn't resist the sausage and piled it on in his plate again as he said, "This is my last chance." Finally, it was time for them to leave so they brought their suitcases down and checked everything out. A waiting taxi took them to the airport. They checked through and caught their first class seats back to Vancouver.

They landed at the international terminal in Vancouver. Damian was there to pick them up in Grandpa's Ted's car. Damian said, "Oh, Dad, wait to see what those girls did to your car, they really smashed it up this time."

Josh said, "Oh, Damian, that trick doesn't work on me anymore."

Damian said, "Well, I'm telling you the truth."

Josh didn't believe him.

Damian said, "You'll see it when you get there."

They got home and Damian left to return Grandpa's car. Leilani would be picking him up at their Grandpa's office. Josh and Tashi got their luggage before entering their house. Tashi stopped Josh from looking in the garage and reminded him that Damian liked to trick him. Josh went to look in his shoe closet for the key he hid in a shoebox.

He said, "Tashi, the key isn't there anymore."

She said, "Of course not, I moved it."

He said, "What? Why would you move it?"

Tashi said, "I knew the kids would look in shoeboxes. I used to do it myself. Come here, I'll show you where I put it."

They went back to the bedroom and she looked in an old cleaning material can and pulled out the key.

He said, "Oh, you smart cookie. I would've never figured it out. Why don't we find out if the kids looked through the shoeboxes? I will say my key is gone."

She replied, "No, no, you can't say that. They won't admit they looked in your shoeboxes. Just put on your newest shoes and ask them if they admired them and then we will know for sure."

He complimented her on the plan. "Oh, you're tricky, Tashi."

"Well, that's how Leilani tricked me the other day with Damian's engagement."

In no time the kids were back and Tashi began to direct Josh. The excited kids came in and hugged and kissed their parents.

They looked down at Josh's shoes and Leilani said,

"Oh, those are nice shoes, Dad." Anita agreed.

Damian said,

"Yeah, I like those shoes."

Josh said, "Really? I wore them before and you guys never said anything."

Damian said, "No you didn't, they were still in the box brand new."

Tashi proclaimed, "What were you doing in your dad's shoebox?"

Anita looked anxious.

Josh asked, "What were you doing in my closet, in my shoebox?"

Damian answered, "Well, if you really want to know, Leilani wanted the key for the Ferrari."

Josh looked at Leilani. Leilani replied, "Well, I could've had the Ferrari for a week, right?"

Josh responded, "Only when I'm here, girl. Otherwise, no. Your mom is smarter than you guys are. She knew you would look in the box so she moved the key."

Tashi reminded the kids that she was once young and mischievous. Josh agreed and reminded them that she was also a lawyer's wife and that she still learned every day.

Afterwards, they sat down and talked about Iris and everything else that went on in Landshut. The kids got excited after hearing about the German pups.

Anita said, "We should get a little wiener dog too. They make such nice house pets."

Josh asked, "A wiener dog? What's that?"

Tashi agreed with Anita. "It's a dachshund. I always wanted one. How can I explain to you what it is? Maybe we have a picture that we can show him? No? Well, he'll find out anyways when we get it. Could you bring me one the next time you come, Anita?"

Anita agreed and asked, "Would you like a black one?"

Tashi replied, "All black, just black with longer hair. Soft but long hair."

"They have long ears too," Anita replied. "They look really cute."

Tashi said, "I already have picked out a name. I'll call it Kiwi."

Josh said, "Kiwi? That's a fruit."

Tashi replied,

"Well, my doggie will be named Kiwi, I love that name for a little dachsie. I think it will be really cute on her. So we have Kiwi, and then we will have Hero and Shady."

"You can't call a female Hero," Josh retorted. "We will call one Sadie and one Shady."

"Well, that sounds good, Sadie and Shady please come over for dinner, I like it, said Tashi. "That's it. We l have Sadie and Shady, as well as Kiwi. Holy smokes, the family is getting bigger. Who knows? Maybe Iris will bring a dog for herself also. I wouldn't be surprised. That should be fun."

"Well, you wanted the key to the Ferrari, Leilani? You wanted to test it out?" Josh asked his daughter.

"No, I would never touch it, especially after you asked me not to," she replied.

"Okay, I believe you, but why were you looking for the key?" asked Josh.

The kids revealed that they were going to hide the key from their father.

They all laughed and Josh commented, "Tashi was smart, she hid it from me and from you. Smart woman I've got there."

"So how are Grandma and Grandpa doing?"

"Oh they're doing fine," said Leilani. "They're doing really well. I go almost over every day and spend time with them. They're so happy; they want me to play the piano. You wouldn't believe how happy they are."

"So you haven't been going out with Anita and Damian?"

"Oh gosh, no, they wouldn't want me to."

"Well that's what happens. Leilani. You should get yourself a boyfriend soon."

"When the time comes. I have lots of time."

"Oh, yes you do."

Damian interjected, "You don't know what you're missing, girly."

Leilani replied, "Yes I do, but I'm in no hurry. I have a lot of things on my mind right now in regards to what I would like to study."

"So have you thought it over yet?"

"Yes I was talking to the doctor and the professor and they were testing me. One said I should be a psychologist for sure. I told them I would love to work with children. So he mentioned becoming a pediatrician. I thought about it, but I'd also want to become a neurosurgeon."

"Oh my God, a neurosurgeon?" asked Tashi.

"I could treat Grandma. We never knew what was wrong with her. That's another reason why I would love to be a neurosurgeon."

"You really have quite the plan in your mind, don't you, Leilani? Where would you study all this?"

"Well, I would go to Honolulu if they have it there."

They talked some more, and then Leilani headed out to go do a couple of errands, while Anita and Damian went out for a walk.

"Would you mind if I went to the office to check out what's happening at work?" Josh asked Tashi.

"Not at all, I'm going to be in the kitchen cooking," she said.

When Josh was done looking at his work emails he started to look at the news.

"Why are you looking at that? The news is always terrible," she said as she began to dance and cook at the same time.

Josh went into the dining room. "Girl, you smell like garlic. Did you eat a whole clove?"

She said, "No, it's on my hands. I am cooking with it, you silly man."

Josh got the table ready and waited for his wife. When she arrived he acted like a gentleman and pulled her chair out before she sat down. Tashi notices of all the things that he does for her and really loves him for it.

"It's too bad I can't act like this with the kids anymore," said Josh.

"We parents have to realize they're not kids anymore. They are beginning to become adults," said Tashi.

"That's true, they have a lot of fun. It's nice that Leilani is willing to teach us some of her new tricks now, though."

"Yes, maybe you should take her up on that."

"Well, I'll have to think about it. Isn't it just great that she wants to be a pediatrician, psychologist or neurosurgeon?"

"Quite ambitious goals that our daughter has, quite a tough thing to do."

"I wouldn't want to do that. It's too much work."

"She is a quick learner, so I think she will do fine."

"She's such a fantastic and wonderful young lady, she will be great at whatever she chooses."

"Leilani has become brighter and brighter as she has gotten older. She is so humble and doesn't even realize how beautiful she is."

"Well, she is beautiful much like our other children."

"She's taken from her mother but has her father's long legs and arrogant walk."

They both laughed.

"What a great conversation we have had. I wonder when the kids will be over for dinner or if we will have any food for them," said Tashi as she helped Josh clean up the table.

They washed the dishes and then moved to the living room, where they snuggled up together on the couch.

"Will you stay with me in Honolulu for three days? I will need to be there for at least three days. Christopher is drowned with work and I will have to help him."

"Of course, I hate travelling alone, plus I will have no one to come home to."

"But you used to travel alone all the time when weren't together."

"They were very lonely trips without you, my love. Anyways, while you're working I will be able to check out some of my favourite art galleries there."

"I have lots of friends in Honolulu and Waikiki you haven't met yet who you will really love."

"I'm sure they'll be nice to meet, but I love spending time with you alone the most."

"There will be lots of time for us to do that there also. I promise."

CHAPTER 52

THE NEXT FEW DAYS PASS BY. JOSH and Tashi decide that it is time to go home for good, to Hawaii. They want to bring their dogs to their real home, and they both need to get back to work, especially Josh, who needs to make that trip to Honolulu. Leilani, Damian and Anita will be joining them.

They arrive in Kauai in the evening, and the next morning, Josh and Tashi have a flight to Honolulu.

"Maybe it's time we go to sleep. We have a flight tomorrow."

"I used to love planes, now I don't like flying at all."

"We will be fine but I hate flying also."

"I guess we're getting old."

"What time is it anyway? Is it really only eight?"

"Yes, I guess it's going to be a really long sleep for you then."

"Maybe if it's too long I will get up and do some work."

"The kids will be disturbed by the noise you will make."

"Oh, that's okay, I think they will be disturbed enough when they come home and find out that we're already sleeping."

"Maybe we should leave a note for them so they don't get worried about where we are."

"Oh, they're smart, they'll know we will be sleeping."

They head off to bed. Josh massages Tashi a bit so that she can fall asleep.

"I hope you give me this treatment one day."

"Oh, is that why are you doing this? You are a tricky, tricky man."

"Well, I am a lawyer, after all."

"You're a sneaky little devil lawyer."

Josh begins to snore as she gives him a massage. She stops when she hears him fall asleep.

"Oh, is that all? I didn't really fall asleep. I was just tricking you to see what you would do."

"Wow, you are so sneaky. I am tired now. I think we should go to sleep."

They snuggle together and fall asleep.

Chapter 53

IN THE MORNING, JOSH HEADED TO THE backyard and thought about what he had to do once he got back home from Honolulu. He decided to check his email to see if Iris had sent him an email. She has said that she had begun to sell her paintings, and the rest she would give to Aunty to sell so she can take care of herself. She said that she can't wait to meet everybody.

Josh wrote her back and let her know about his plans in Kauai and to stay in touch. He checked and replied to the rest of his urgent emails. He went to the kitchen and put on a cup of coffee. At seven o' clock he went to check on Tashi. She was still sleeping so he decided to leave her alone.

He decided to read a magazine in the backyard. Somebody surprised him and covered his eyes. As she moved her hands away, he saw her beautiful blue eyes.

Tashi was looking at him with a cup of coffee in her hand. Josh told her about the email he had received from Iris.

"Oh, I'm so drowsy but I really wanted to surprise you."

"Why don't you go catch some more sleep?"

"Oh, I'd rather not. I don't want to start the day so late. Do you want another cup of coffee?"

"No, I've already had two cups. I talked to Christopher and told him about our plans."

"That's great."

"Yeah, maybe we will have dinner with Chris and Donna."

"Oh, that will be fantastic! I am looking forward to it."

"Anyways, for breakfast would you like some bacon and eggs?"

"No, I'd rather have some sausages," Josh said.

"Well, at least you're becoming normal again."

"Don't start knocking on wood, I am just being myself."

"Well, there's all that cheese and sausage in the fridge after all."

"Oh please stop teasing me," Josh said.

"I am going to make you an omelette. Would you like to eat inside or outside?"

"I think we should eat inside."

Tashi prepared the omelette and invited Josh inside. Josh brought his coffee inside and sat at the table with Tashi.

"Would you like orange juice with that? I didn't pour you any because I wasn't sure whether you liked it with omelettes or not."

"Oh, no, I am okay."

"Would you like some fruit?" Tashi asked.

"I think this omelette will be enough for me."

After breakfast they left for the airport to catch their flight to Kauai.

That evening, Christopher and Donna met them and all four sat down to have dinner together and catch up.

Josh and Tashi explained everything that had recently happened in their lives, and about how Iris was coming over in three or four months. They talked about Leilani's career choices. They talked about Iris's own little house on the property. They talked about how Damian would stay in Vancouver now that he had gotten into UBC Law. They talked about how he was almost engaged and would likely get married after he finished law school. They talked about how Maya had taken off with someone on a sailboat and how they didn't know who he was or where he had taken her or how they would find her. They talked about how Maya was cut out of her grandfather's will.

"And also, we now have three puppies!"

"Three puppies?!" Donna said.

"Yes, a dachshund, and two German shepherds," Tashi answered.

"Oh I love dachshunds! What's his name?" Donna asked.

"Kiwi." Tashi smiles.

"So is it a fruit or a dog?" Chris joked.

"I really like that name," Donna said.

"Oh, you women always stick together," said Josh as Christopher laughed.

"So what's next?"

"We will hire a contractor to build a new house for Iris," Josh explained.

"Why are you building her a new house?"

"So she can have her own privacy."

They laughed.

"So what is going on with the Greek grandfather?"

"Leilani called him. Niko helped their grandfather get a phone in the hospital. He talked about how they had found out that Maya may have faked the sailboat accident. She was seen with another man and they don't know where she is or if she is even alive. She has money, so she may have tricked all of us."

"So what about Leilani?" Donna asked.

"Oh, this girl, she wants to be a pediatrician, neurosurgeon or psychiatrist."

"Wow, she has a lot of work left to do. How is Damian?"

"He is getting prepared for law school at UBC and has fallen madly in love and will most likely get engaged soon."

"Oh, he has a girlfriend?"

"Yes, Anita is her name. She is one of Leilani's friends from Germany. They fell in love right away when they met. Anita had a locket made for Damian and she kept for herself."

"Boy, times sure have changed, haven't they? The girls are way more open and forward with their feelings," Chris said.

"Oh yes, they're almost proposing themselves. But I can't judge, I almost did the same with Josh," Tashi said.

"Yeah, she ravished me on the beach to get my affection," said Josh.

"Oh, I don't believe that," said Christopher.

"Just ask her, she will tell you."

"Tashi, is that true?" Chris asked.

"Pretty well, but you can't ravish a man if he doesn't want it. But I was pretty aggressive for sure."

"Well, you're a lucky man, Josh."

"What do you mean he's a lucky man? You don't think you're a lucky man?" asked Donna.

"I'm just saying that because Josh is my friend."

"What else is Damian up to?"

"Damian is about to start his lawyer career since his Dad is going to need help with his work soon."

"It's so nice to see when the parents are in a happy marriage and the kids are helping them out," said Donna.

"I hope we have the same," said Christopher.

"Any kids soon?" asked Josh.

"I won't say anything about that," answered Donna.

"Any signs?" asked Tashi.

"Maybe, I won't say though," said Donna as they all began to wonder.

"Well, Christopher, are you ready to become a father?"

"I think so, I'll take some time off from work but it'll be easy because I know you'll be great babysitters if we want to go out at some point."

"So how's this grandfather in Greece doing?" Donna asked.

"Well, he is in bad shape, health wise, and he is quite unhappy with Maya. He has taken her out of his will so she will not be entitled to any of his assets later on."

"Oh, dear."

"He said he might sell the house and move somewhere else."

"Maya could always look for him, though, if she has a lot of friends."

"I hope she never comes to this island. That would be troublesome," Tashi said.

"At least Iris will be here in three or four months," Donna said.

"That should be great."

"Did you see the designs for our new home? I might change it, as I saw these grand stairs in our hotel in Germany and I'd love to have that in our house."

"Our house will not be big enough for those, Tashi."

"That's true. However, we want to build the entire upper floor for ourselves. We'll come up with something with our architect and move on from there."

"She always figures something out. We'll probably get those stairs in there somehow," Josh said.

"Josh has already designed our bed."

"What's to design about a bed?" Chris asked.

"Well, he absolutely fell in love with this massive bed in the hotel in Germany. It's so wonderful."

"So what are your plans for the future, Christopher?"

"Well, I'll do it as we had planned, but I might be making more trips and working off of a computer more often."

"But I wanted to know about your plans for your home."

"Well, I asked Donna if she wanted to move, but this is her island. So we decided to stay on this island and will start looking for properties on the island soon. Probably somewhere close to a public school if we want to have kids."

"That's great. I can't wait to see where you guys move. Is there anything else new on the island?"

"We have a Costco now, and some people that you don't know died."

"Well, at least there's a Costco."

They laughed. Finally they all got in the pool and went for a swim. Josh watched as Tashi swam quickly and gracefully from one end of the pool to the other. They had a good swim and a great time. Josh offered to grab Christopher a beer but he declined. They discussed how they would start looking for matches for Leilani and Iris and laughed about how the daughters would react when they heard.

Eventually, Donna and Christopher headed out, and Josh and Tashi were left alone. They sat outside, Tashi resting her head on Josh's shoulder as they watched the sun go down.

"It took 1825 sunsets before I found you again, Josh," Tashi said.

"Don't worry, sweetheart, you will never have to watch another one without me," Josh said, and kissed the top of her forehead.

They watched the sun until they could no longer see it. Then Josh took Tashi's hand and pulled her up. "Come on inside, sweetheart, I'm craving some tiramisu."

Preface: Will the dynasty crumble?

What will happen to the Steels next? Will Leilani become a doctor? Will Iris come over to live permanently in Kauai? Where will Anita and Damian live? And where is Maya? All these questions will be answered in the sequel.